The Lady Rogue

Also by Jenn Bennett

Alex, Approximately

Starry Eyes

Serious Moonlight

Chasing Lucky

The Lady Rogue

JENN BENNETT

SIMON PULSE
NEW YORK LONDON TORONTO SYDNEY NEW DELHI

SIMON PULSE
An imprint of Simon & Schuster Children's Publishing Division
1230 Avenue of the Americas, New York, New York 10020
This Simon Pulse paperback edition August 2020

Also available in a Simon Pulse hardcover edition.

Cover designed by Heather Palisi
Interior designed by Tom Daly
The text of this book was set in Adobe Garamond Pro.
Manufactured in the United States of America
2 4 6 8 10 9 7 5 3 1
The Library of Congress has cataloged the hardcover edition as follows:
Names: Bennett, Jenn.
Title: The lady rogue / Jenn Bennett.
Description: New York : Simon Pulse, 2019. |
Summary: In 1937, teenaged Theodora Fox and her crush, Huck, set out through the Carpathian
Mountains seeking her missing father and the cursed ring of Vlad the Impaler, which he was seeking.
Identifiers: LCCN 2019003220 | ISBN 9781534431997 (hardcover)
Subjects: CYAC: Adventure and adventurers—Fiction. | Missing persons—Fiction. | Magic—Fiction. |
Rings—Fiction. | Blessing and cursing—Fiction. | Vlad III, Prince of Wallachia, 1430 or 1431–1476 or
1477—Fiction. | Carpathian Mountains—Fiction. | Transylvania (Romania)—History—1918–1940—Fiction.
Classification: LCC PZ7.1.B4538 Lad 2019 | DDC [Fic]—dc23
LC record available at https://lccn.loc.gov/2019003220
ISBN 9781534432000 (paperback)
ISBN 9781534432017 (eBook)

To meddlesome girls

The Lady Rogue

N
TO BUDAPEST
KINGDOM of HUNGARY
HOIA FOREST
CLUJ
ORIENT EXPRESS
SIGHIŞOARA
TRANSYLVANIA
ROMÂNIA
YUGOSLAVIA

CARPATHIANS
SOVIET
UKRAINE
MOLDOVA
BRAŞOV
SNAGOV
WALLACHIA
BUCHAREST
BLACK SEA
DANUBE RIVER
RUSE
TO ISTANBUL
BULGARIA

JOURNAL OF RICHARD FOX

June 18, 1937

Budapest, Kingdom of Hungary

Jean-Bernard and I left Munich early this morning to sunshine and outstanding views of the mountains. Was so full of fine drink and finer oysters at lunch that I slept through Vienna stop. Orient Express never fails to impress.

Arrived in Budapest just in time to make my meeting with Mr. George Rothwild, a Hungarian aristocrat who commanded troops for the wrong side during the war. Odd fellow. No sense of humor. Lots of money, though. Enough to hoard a collection of items once owned by the object of his obsession: Vlad III. Better known as Vlad Dracula ("son of the Dragon") or Vlad Țepeș ("the Impaler"), the brutal medieval tyrant who impaled his enemies alive. Hell of a guy to obsess over.

Obsessed he is though. Rothwild's home looks like a medieval torture chamber. Weapons. Iron spikes. Racks. Just being there made me feel queasy. (Or perhaps that was all the oysters I ate earlier?) As for the job . . . it's a strange one. Rothwild wants me to verify the authenticity of a grotesque item in his collection: a ring of bone that once belonged to Vlad Dracula. Rothwild claims he acquired the ring in a private sale—some collector in Bucharest parted with it the day before he died, conveniently enough. Here's the mystery of it: Rothwild believes the ring to be a fake. A reproduction. He wants me to compare it to two other rings rumored to be in Romania and let him know if his is, indeed, genuine—and if not, acquire the real ring "by any means necessary."

The sum he's dangling is not insignificant.

Jean-Bernard and I intended to take the Arlberg Orient Express down to Athens on Friday, but he's willing to indulge me in a detour to Romania for a week or so. I have mixed feelings about all of this, mainly because I haven't stepped foot in Transylvania since Elena's death. Maybe it's time. She had a soft spot for Vlad Dracula and would say, along with many of her fellow countrymen, that he was a national hero, not a monster. Or maybe a national hero AND a monster. No one is wholly bad or good, are they?

Romania is a strange, haunting place. Better to investigate this now, while Theodora is safely home in New York for the summer. If she were here, she'd be driving me up a wall, hunting for any and all manner of superstitious folklore.

Girl's imagination is too damn big as it is.

November 24, 1937—Istanbul, Turkey

I STOOD IN STOCKINGED FEET WITH MY HANDS UP IN THE air, like Napoléon surrendering after the Battle of Waterloo. Outside the narrow stockroom—the scene of my current humiliation—the bustle of afternoon shoppers in Istanbul's Grand Bazaar echoed down arched stone corridors perfumed with wisps of fragrant smoke and spices. A crowd was gathering near the jewelry stall. One would think they'd never seen an American girl strip-searched by the merchant's wife.

Better to be remembered than forgotten, I supposed.

If you'd asked me two weeks ago how I imagined I'd be spending my time in Istanbul, being arrested for shoplifting wouldn't have been at the top of the list. Yet here I was, accused of stealing a gold ring and close to having a stroke at the tender age of seventeen. A crying shame. I had so much to give this world.

The dark-haired woman kneeling in front of me didn't care about my impending death in a Turkish prison. She was too busy aggressively patting down every inch of my body, from the neck of my striped top to the hem of my black gored skirt, with the gusto of an angry lover. She'd already looked inside my shoes, emptied my handbag, manhandled my prized Leica camera inside my camera case, and turned out the pockets of my coat.

"I think you missed a spot," I joked when she brusquely lifted my calf to inspect the bottom of my foot while I hopped on one leg.

Unsatisfied, the merchant's wife sighed and stood up, giving me another critical once-over as she wiped her hands on the long folds of her billowing red dress. Her eyes fell on the silver charm that hung around my neck: a nearly fifteen-hundred-year-old coin stamped on one side with a crowned, haloed woman: Byzantine Empress Theodora. Daughter of a bear trainer. Renegade. Prostitute. Spy. Queen. Heretic. Saint. All-around-fascinating female. The coin came from a hoard my parents discovered near the Black Sea on the day my mother found out she was pregnant with me, hence the namesake . . . maybe one I subconsciously tried to live up to. It's good to have goals.

"Not on your life!" I said, covering the coin with my hand. "I told you already, my late mother gave me this. You'll have to kill me to get it. And I mean that quite seriously."

The merchant's wife rolled her eyes at me but lost interest in my coin charm. Hopefully now that she'd found nothing in her humiliating pat-down of my entire body, she also understood that I was not the pickpocket she'd thought I was.

"*Bulmaca yüzük?*" she said for millionth time, which I believed meant "harem ring" or "wedding ring." It was a Turkish novelty ring made of interconnected bands, and the story behind it was that if the wife took it off to have a tryst, she wouldn't be able to reassemble the bands and would be caught by her husband. A flawed concept, if you asked me. One, it assumed the wife couldn't reassemble the puzzle rings, and two, she needn't even take the ring off to bed a lover in the first place. Why does the entire world think the female species possesses brains made of cotton candy?

Insulting is what it was. Much like this farcical strip search . . .

"Like I told you a hundred times, I'm not a thief," I said. She muttered something under her breath that I couldn't interpret and exited the tiny stockroom, slamming the door shut behind her. A loud clicking noise caused my pulse to rocket.

I jiggled the locked handle vigorously and pounded on the door. "Hey! You can't lock me in here. I've never stolen anything in my life. I was only taking a photograph. You *do* realize what you're doing to me now is kidnapping, right? Can someone please call my hotel, as I requested? The woman I'm traveling with—my tutor, Madame Leroux—she speaks Turkish. Is anyone listening? Hello . . . ?"

In frustration, I kicked the door and stubbed my big toe, shouting an unladylike expletive, which briefly halted the muffled squabbling on the other side of the door.

Good profanity is never lost in translation.

But, sadly, it wasn't getting me out of this stockroom. I quickly slipped my black Mary Janes onto my feet and buckled the thin straps, miserably wishing I'd taken the time to learn more Turkish before this trip. If I had, then I wouldn't have needed stupid Madame Leroux and could have fully understood what was being said outside. Had they summoned the market's guards? Or were they going straight to the police? I told them the hotel staff would vouch for me. Hopefully? The concierge wasn't overly fond of me. Neither was my tutor, frankly. The more I thought about it, the more I worried that there was no one in Istanbul who'd stand up for me. . . .

Things hadn't always been this miserable. My first week in Istanbul was delightful: palm trees, the Hagia Sophia, the blue water of the Golden Horn. Minarets for days. Endless *kepaps* and strong Turkish coffee. I'd been having such a good time, I'd almost forgiven my father for leaving me behind with a hired tutor—"for your safety," his standard tired excuse—while he trekked across Turkey hunting treasure. But as often happened on our trips, things rapidly deteriorated. . . .

First of all, Father was supposed to return from Tokat and collect me three days ago; we were to head to Paris together to see a friend of the family. Not only had Father failed to arrive, but he hadn't telegrammed to say why he was delayed. And while I worried myself to death, waiting to hear from him, I managed to get food poisoning. Then the rains came—apparently there's a rainy season here. Who knew. And now, when I was only trying to make the best of things, when I dared escape my stick-in-the-mud tutor and the hotel room in which I'd been cooped up for days, I ended up . . . well, in these dire straits.

I glanced around the tiny stockroom. *Too tiny.* My breaths quickened.

"Steel spine, chin high," I whispered to myself, a mantra my mother would repeat to fortify and hearten me when I was upset. If she were here—Elena Vaduva, a woman who'd never been afraid of anything—she wouldn't be panicking. I lifted the ancient coin around my neck that she'd given me and kissed it for good luck. Then I strapped my brown leather camera case across my body and swept my scattered possessions back into my handbag.

As I slipped into my coat, something changed in the chatter outside. I stilled and listened. After a few moments the lock clicked and the stockroom door flew open. My hired tutor blinked at me in the doorway.

"Thank the gods," I said, sagging in relief. The merchants must have telephoned my hotel after all.

"Foolish girl!" Madame Leroux scolded in French. Elegant hands trembled beneath the cuffs of her traveling coat. Her pin-straight blond hair was in disarray below her hat, as if she'd rushed here after being woken from a nap. "What did you do this time?"

"Nothing! I was only taking a photograph. I swear. The jewelry market is rumored to be haunted just around the corner of this stall, and there are some strange symbols painted on the wall—"

"Miss Theodora Fox," she said, voice thick with disappointment.

"I just wanted to photograph it, you know, so that I could study the symbols, and the next thing I knew, I was being accused of stealing a golden harem ring, which is ridiculous, of course, because I don't have a harem."

She didn't find this amusing. "*And* you broke a lamp?"

"Barely a crack, and that was an accident," I argued. "I was trying to get a good shot of the wall—that's where people say they've seen jinn. Or ghosts. Either way, it's supposed to be haunted, and I was only trying to photograph it to see if anything interesting would show up on film."

Madame Leroux squeezed her eyes shut and shook her head.

"Look, I know you don't believe in magic or anything supernatural, but I do—" I began to say, but she cut me off with the sharp flick of a hand that motioned for silence.

"They found the ring under one of the display cases," she said coolly.

Relief surged through my limbs. "Really?"

"Apparently, you knocked it to the floor when you were pretending to be a bull in a china shop, so they've agreed to let you go if we pay for the broken lamp."

That was it? After being treated like a common criminal?

No matter. I'd been proven innocent.

"Come," she commanded. "Before you embarrass yourself any further."

Not possible.

Feeling a thousand pounds lighter, I rushed to follow my tutor out of the horrible stockroom, through the cramped jewelry stall, and past the crowd of gawkers who'd gathered in the market corridor with uniformed guards. Madame Leroux said something in halting Turkish to the merchant couple and handed them a signed traveler's check from the booklet that my father had left in her charge. Satisfied, the merchants accepted the payment and made a shooing gesture in my direction.

Glorious, sweet freedom!

I let out a long breath as the guards dispersed the crowd. Nothing to see here. The humiliation of a teenage girl was now complete; thank you for coming. In mere seconds it was as if nothing had ever happened.

"Whew! What a day!" I said to my tutor. She didn't answer or acknowledge me. She merely marched away from the glinting gold of the jewelry section of the market. I trotted to keep up, and we merged into the fringes of pedestrians strolling under vaulted ceilings. On either side of us, merchants bargained with locals and tourists alike, selling stacks of patterned cloth, rugs, food, spices, and copperware—just about anything you could want. Unless you were a girl with a camera, apparently.

I tried a second time to break Madame Leroux's icy silence.

"I'm really, truly sorry you had to come down here," I told her. "I know you're probably pretty peeved at me right now—"

She stopped suddenly, swinging around to point a finger in my face. "No. I am *furious*. And tired of making apologies for you. I was hired to accompany a well-bred, studious lady through Europe. You, Miss Fox, are no lady! You're a she-demon who attracts anarchy and bedlam."

"Everyone has a talent?" I said sheepishly with a strained smile.

"You ruined a priceless rug in the middle of the hotel lobby—"

"But I had food poisoning!"

"—and you have the entire Pera Palace staff smuggling newspapers into the hotel for that insatiable habit of yours."

"Crossword puzzles, Madame Leroux. You're making me sound like a drug fiend. There's not a daily crossword in the *Cumhuriyet*." And if there were, I couldn't solve it, because the clues would all be in Turkish.

"You caused that poor maid to have a breakdown, reading those devilish books of yours."

"It was the Egyptian *Book of the Dead*—an ancient funerary text. I was practicing writing hieroglyphics." But to be perfectly honest, I'd also been reading a rare translation of *Hammer of the Witches*, which detailed a selection of medieval magical spells, a subject I found endlessly fascinating. Had I known the housekeeping staff at the hotel was a gaggle of fainting Victorian ladies in need of smelling salts, I would have been more discreet with my personal reading matter.

Madame Leroux, however, had no sympathy. Right now she was shaking her head, eyes squeezed shut, as if somehow in the few short weeks I'd known her, I'd managed to become the biggest disappointment in her life. Well, I had news for her: it takes *years* for me to properly disappoint someone. Just ask my father . . . whenever he decided to show up.

"I promise to stay in the hotel until Father returns," I told

Madame Leroux. "Cross my heart, fingers, and toes. Does that make you happy?"

"Do what you want. I cannot stop you. I quit."

"What?" I glanced around, aware that we were attracting attention.

"You heard me," she said, long fingers straightening the brim of her hat. "I am done. I quit."

"You can't quit. Father has the return train tickets to Europe."

She tugged down the hem of her jacket. "I've been invited to travel through the Middle East."

I paused, brow wrinkling. "With the hotel's lounge singer?"

They'd been secretly meeting up after I went to bed. He bragged constantly that he was touring regional hotels, making gobs of money crooning sentimental love songs to drunken tourists.

"Your father will return soon," she said.

"You're . . . leaving me? In the middle of a foreign city?"

She shrugged and waved a hand. "You are no little mouse. Have you not traveled the world with your scoundrel of a father?"

"Hey!" I said sharply. No one gets to besmirch my family but me. "He's a distinguished adventurer and historian. He's been hired around the world by dukes, sultans, and contessas."

"*Yes*, I *know*," she said, voice sodden with French sarcasm. "You boast of all the places you've been with him. Am I not your 'hundredth' tutor, useless and interchangeable, as you so often remind me?"

Yikes. "I don't think I've ever said that." I had. Yesterday. During our last argument. "And of course I need you. You speak the local language, and—"

She snorted. "Obviously you are comfortable storming through the city alone like a typhoon. And the hotel staff will cater to your every whim, so it's difficult for me to feel sympathy. Goodbye, Miss Fox. I hope our paths do not cross again. Ever."

She marched away, blending into throngs of pedestrians ambling down the market's corridor, while I stood rooted to the floor in shock. It took me several panicked heartbeats to realize that she carried the book of traveler's checks; all I had was a few bills in my handbag, enough for a taxi back to the hotel and little more. I called out to her, snaking my way through the crowd. "You have all the money!" I shouted.

"Consider it my severance fee," she shouted back before her head disappeared in a throng of shoppers, leaving me behind.

Alone.

In a foreign country.

With no money.

And no word from my wayward father as to when he'd return.

What in God's name was I going to do now?

I SPENT AN HOUR WILDLY SEARCHING THE MARKET'S labyrinthine corridors for Madame Leroux like some orphaned puppy in disbelief that its owner had truly gone. Then I came to my senses: she was probably back at the hotel. Maybe I could still convince her to stay.

When I found my way outside, the late-afternoon drizzle had turned to a steady rain, and there were no taxicabs in sight. Everything was muddy and ugly, and when a speeding car veered too close to the curb, splashing foul-smelling gutter water across the front of my skirt, I wanted to break down and cry.

Honestly, I blamed my father for all of this. Yesterday I sent a telegram to a hotel across the country in Tokat to ask why he was delayed. No response. This wasn't entirely unusual. Likely he was still up in the mountains on his treasure-hunting expedition—that is, if he hadn't fallen off the mountain and his body wasn't currently being torn apart by buzzards. Either way, I'd bet my last lira that when he found out about Madame Leroux's betrayal, it would somehow be my fault. Because she was right about one thing: disaster seemed to follow me wherever I went.

But I wasn't the only one. This was genetic. My father courted disaster as if it were the belle of the ball. Hiring a tutor who deserted me and stole all our money was just one in a long list of things my bullheaded father had botched. To the public, Richard "Damn" Fox was a decorated war veteran, a medieval historian, a wealthy antiquities collector, and a brash adventurer who never met a risk he wouldn't take. But what people didn't know was that he was also unbelievably selfish, would rather die than apologize or admit mistakes, and often was an all-around terrible father.

Mentally cursing his name, I shook out my leg in a feeble attempt to rid my shoe of mud as a car stopped in front me. A taxicab—finally! Breathless, I climbed into the back seat and gave the driver the name of my hotel. My body wilted with relief when he nodded, and the car pulled away from the historic covered market. Away from the scene of my misfortunate afternoon.

I peeled off a black beret—one that I always wore when traveling—and shook fat droplets out of the soft wool. I was soaked from head to foot. This really wasn't my day. As the old city rushed past my rain-spattered window, my thoughts turned over the incident in the market and everything Madame Leroux had said. On one hand, I wasn't surprised she'd want to quit. I traveled with my father several times a year, and each time he had to hire a new tutor for me. And to be honest, Madame Leroux and I had started off on a sour note because it wasn't until he'd hired her, until we'd traveled by train from Paris and arrived in Istanbul, that my father confessed the truth about the job that had brought him here. We'd had a terrible fight about it before he left. Screams. Threats. Tears. Begging.

I hadn't exactly made a good impression on my new tutor.

But in my defense, my father had blindsided me. Though he almost never allowed me to accompany him on his expeditions, he did allow me to research them. I spent several days before our trip across the Atlantic collecting information on a Byzantine treasure hoard rumored to be hidden in the mountains outside Tokat; however, when we arrived here, he revealed the real reason for his travels.

A client had asked him to find a ring that had once belonged to Vlad Țepeș.

As in Vlad the Impaler. Prince of Romania. House of Drăculești. Fierce warrior and enemy of the Ottoman Empire. Notoriously cruel and bloody. Possible inspiration for the famous fictional vampire Count Dracula.

My mother had told me countless wild stories about both the man and his myth. He'd become an antihero in my mind, someone who dared to rise up against tyranny. Someone who had his own moral compass. A folk hero like Robin Hood, William Tell, or Paul Revere. Just with a lot more blood.

There's a bit of lore that says when Vlad was killed in Wallachia, his enemies, the Ottomans, took his head back to Turkey, to prove he was dead. My father became convinced that Vlad's ring may have been buried with his head. And that's where my father was now. In northern Turkey—a place Vlad was imprisoned as a boy—searching for the Impaler's grave.

Some might think that the skull of Vlad would be the more important historic find than a ring. But it wasn't just a random piece of jewelry. Vlad's ring imbued the wearer with some kind of dark, magical power, if one believed there was any grain of truth in the stories that surrounded it.

Most of what I knew about the ring came from a brief entry in *Batterman's Field Guide to Legendary Objects*—my favorite book and an illustrated catalog of artifacts purported to be cursed, lucky, magical, mythical, and mysterious. Excalibur, the Book of Thoth, the Spear of Destiny, the philosopher's stone. And Vlad the Impaler's war ring was included there too, alongside a medieval woodcut of Prince Vlad. In it, he was depicted wearing the ring while sitting at a table dining in front of his impaled enemies. There wasn't a detailed description or firsthand account, only a brief caption: stories circulating in the late 1400s after his death said the ring was rumored to help Vlad in battle, a sort of occult talisman that may have been cursed.

And I know a thing or two about cursed objects.

One killed my mother.

Now my father was hunting down another. . . . To hell with my mother, and to hell with me. Maybe he wouldn't come back this time. Maybe our last conversation would be the nasty fight we'd had over Vlad's ring when he'd left me here, and I'd be orphaned in Istanbul for the rest of my life. In a way, that felt decidedly apropos, but I wasn't sure if it was better to feel sorry for myself or mad at my father. I supposed either was preferable to worry.

By the time the taxi finally reached my stop, I'd managed to drag myself out of those swampy emotions and instead focused my thoughts on catching up with Madame Leroux. She had to be here, and I had to convince her to stay in Istanbul for a little while longer. That's all there was to it. Clutching my handbag and the tattered remnants of my pride, I sprinted from the curb to the hotel's entrance under the doorman's offered umbrella. Then I stepped into my current home-away-from-home.

The Pera Palace Hotel.

Lauded as the grandest hotel in Turkey, its arabesque mosaics and Murano chandeliers were an impressive mix of Orient and Occident. The marble floors were Carrara; the service was white glove. A five-star experience, truly. Earlier today I couldn't bear to spend another moment inside these walls, but now it felt like what I needed most: a safe and familiar haven.

As I hurried past an enormous arrangement of hothouse flowers that smelled deceptively of springtime, the hotel's bearded concierge glanced up, spotted me, and waved me toward his desk. Embarrassed about my muddy dress, I attempted to ignore him, but he caught up with me halfway through the lobby, in front of the main salon.

"Miss Fox!" he shouted.

No ignoring him now. I slid my eyes in his direction and pasted on a weak smile. Behind me, scents of roasted pistachios and rose water drifted from the hotel's salon along with lively notes from a grand piano. After my lousy afternoon, I could use a cup of tea and something sweet. Might as well go out in a blaze of baklava.

"Good news! Everything is arranged," the concierge told me. "When your luggage is ready, please telephone me at the desk. Your departure tickets are being exchanged and will be held at the railway station. You'll be boarding a night train that leaves at ten o'clock tonight."

"Mr. Osman," I said, confused. It was hard to concentrate on what he was saying, because my eyes went to the bald notch that had been clipped out of the top of his hair; he told me yesterday that his wife was angry at him when she trimmed his hair. Emotions and hair clippers make terrible bedfellows. "I have no earthly idea what you're talking about."

"Your tickets."

"What tickets?"

"The train tickets to Europe?"

I was trying to make sense of what he was saying and was sure he had me confused with another guest. Yes, we'd booked train tickets to go home, but that was for next week, after my father returned. "What do you mean, you've exchanged them?"

"For tonight's train, as requested."

"Requested? By whom? Was it Madame Leroux?" Maybe she'd changed her mind. "Is she here?"

Mr. Osman's nose twitched. His gaze dropped to the muddy stain on my dress. "Miss," he said, scratching his beard. "Are you . . . ? Has there been . . . ?"

"Yes, there has," I said without explanation. "Can you please send someone up to my room to fetch my clothes for cleaning?"

"Right away."

"Is that where Madame Leroux is?" I asked.

"Madame Leroux left a half hour ago."

"With the lounge singer?"

"And her luggage."

I quickly surveyed the lobby, still unable to fully process that she was actually gone. I didn't see her blond head anywhere, but I did, however, notice a dark one: Behind me, a middle-aged man in a long black coat bent to pick something off the marble floor. When he stood back up, dark eyes stared at me from a pale, bearded face that was thin and angular, handsome in a dark-and-brooding Heathcliff of *Wuthering Heights* sort of way. "Pardon me, miss," he said in an Eastern European accent. "You dropped this."

He held out a folded Turkish banknote between his index and middle fingers. I accepted it automatically before I looked closer and realized it was an old bill. Very old. Not the same size as modern paper currency in circulation.

"Oh, this isn't mine, sir." I tried to hand it back, but he only shook his hand.

"I saw you drop it," he insisted, and made a motion that indicated it fell from my coat pocket. Something about the man was strange and off-putting. When I was trying to decide why exactly, the concierge interrupted.

"Regarding your brother," the concierge said.

"One moment please," I mumbled, holding up a finger to Mr. Osman, but when I turned back around, the man in the black coat was already exiting the hotel. I frowned at this for a moment, dazedly pocketing the old banknote, as Mr. Osman's words quite suddenly sank into my thick brain, making me forget all about the Eastern European man.

"Pardon?" I said to the concierge. "Did you just say . . . my *brother*?"

He nodded emphatically. "Indeed. Your brother said he'd prefer to wait in your room. He insisted."

I was an only child. I had no brother.

Suspicious and mildly alarmed, I stared at Mr. Osman. He stared at me. An awkward smile slowly lifted his cheeks. Was it possible my father had returned from Tokat while I was busy getting strip-searched in the market?

"Do you mean Richard Fox?" I asked. "My father? Is he the one who asked you to exchange the tickets?" He was the one who had them, after all. It had to be him.

Before hope could lift its head, Mr. Osman crushed it back down.

"No, miss," he said almost pityingly. Then he looked at me

strangely, mouth twitching, as if something was not being said. But before I could question him further, his manager beckoned, and he jogged back across the lobby, harried and apologetic. Just like that I was completely forgotten.

What in God's name was happening?

The only logical explanation was that Mr. Osman had confused me with another guest. It had happened once before—he'd brought me a message intended for the unmarried daughter of some British noble who was staying on the floor above mine. The more I thought about it, the more I was convinced: this was a mix-up, plain and simple. I'd just go upstairs and check to be sure.

Equal parts apprehensive and curious, I stepped into the hotel's ornate black birdcage lift, and the operator took me to the fourth floor, where I made my way down a long hallway. Hand-woven Oushak carpeting muffled the heels of my muddy Mary Janes until I came to my room.

I paused outside with my ear to the door. Silence.

The handle wouldn't budge. Locked, as it should be.

Cautious, I unlocked the door and peered inside to find . . . nothing. Empty. Just to be sure, I entered the room with my head, craning my neck, and when I spotted no initial danger, my feet followed.

Housekeeping had been here while I was out: the bed was made up. All my imported newspapers were stacked in two tidy piles, one with all the single crossword pages I'd removed. Across the room, the door leading to the balcony was standing wide open to the ancient city, the dark blue water of the Bosporus Strait snaking past stone buildings with clay roofs. A cool breeze carried drizzle into my room.

Hold on. That wasn't right. The maids never left the balcony door open.

Pulse picking up speed, I peered outside, scanning for an intruder, but stopped short when a muffled noise floated from the room's en suite bathroom.

Uh-oh.

My thoughts flipped back to the strange man in the lobby. But he hadn't had time to get up here, had he? I supposed it was possible. Whoever it was, they were in my bathroom, and that couldn't be good. Dipping into my handbag, I retrieved the only weapon in reach: a small, clothbound travel guide—*Istanbul (Not Constantinople): Gateway to the Orient*. I wielded it in front of me, arm extended stiffly, then threw open the bathroom door.

I wished I hadn't.

A few feet away, near a claw-foot bathtub, stood a boy about my age, his handsome face marred by an old white scar that stretched over one cheekbone. Dark hair, a shade lighter than my own raven-black, was clipped short at the sides and neck; the top was a mass of overlong mazy curls.

Every inch of his rangy build was covered in lean muscle, quite a bit of which was brazenly on display: he wore nothing but a towel, slung low around his hips. Water puddled beneath his feet on the tiled floor.

Eighteen-year-old Huxley Gallagher, better known simply as Huck.

My former best friend.

My former more-than-a-friend.

My former more-than-a-friend, who left last year without a single goodbye.

Something tremored deep inside my chest. It quickly grew into an earthquake that shook my entire body. I just stared at him, tongue-tied and dumb as a box of rocks, forgetting everything that had happened that afternoon—the Grand Bazaar, Madame Leroux, the dark-and-brooding man who'd given me the old banknote in the lobby. All of it vanished from my thoughts.

"Hello, banshee," Huck said, using the pet name he'd called me since we were kids. His deep Northern Irish lilt bounced around the tiled bathroom like a rubber ball. "Miss me much?"

I STOOD IN THE BATHROOM DOORWAY, STARING AT Huck, utterly astonished. Neither of us said a word for several heartbeats.

After being orphaned, Huck moved in with Father and me—just after my mother died, when I was ten and he was eleven. He became an unofficial member of the broken and grieving Fox household . . . until an unfortunate incident on my sixteenth birthday, summer before last. The best night of my life. Before it turned into the worst.

I hadn't seen Huck since.

Yet here he stood, still and wary, his body a collection of sharp lines and tensed muscle. A tentative smile revealed a tiny, strangely attractive gap between his front teeth. But that smile was a lie; he was nervous. I knew him too well.

At least, I used to.

The fog around my brain cleared, and I blinked lashes damp with unshed tears. The little earthquake inside my chest had leveled small villages and toppled trees, and I now stood in the clearing dust, waiting to assess the damage.

"Been a while," he said, sounding perfectly breezy. Lie.

"More than a year." *Since you left us. Since you broke my heart.*

"One year, four months, nine days."

A small noise escaped my mouth. He'd been keeping count?

His shrug was barely perceptible. "It was your birthday. Easy enough day to remember, isn't it?"

"Right. Yes. Easy to remember," I said dumbly, unable to look at him directly in the eyes. "How . . . ? What are you even doing here?"

As if a switch had been flicked, all the tightness suddenly left his limbs, and he was casual and loose. Transformed. His old devil-may-care self. Maybe he wasn't as anxious as I'd thought; maybe that was only me.

Nonchalant as could be, he tilted his head to the side and shook his earlobe to clear out water, one eye squeezed shut. "Well, I *thought* I knew, but the way you're scowling and threatening physical violence upon me with that book of yours makes me think I've committed a crime."

I floundered, lost for words. It was as though it was the most natural thing in the world for him to show up in my hotel room halfway across the globe. Maybe I'd somehow hit my head, and all of this was some kind of brain-injury fantasy. If I blinked enough, maybe he'd disappear.

But he didn't.

"Huck?" I finally managed.

"Yes, banshee?"

I wanted to tell him not to call me that anymore. It felt too intimate, too painful, like my heart was being pierced with tiny needles. *Breathe*, I told myself. *Steel spine, chin high. Steel spine, chin high . . .*

"You're in Northern Ireland," I said.

"Am I?" He pretended to look around the room. "Funny. Thought this was Istanbul. Or Stamboul? What are they calling it these days? Used to be Constantinople, didn't it? I was never good at history, if your memory serves," he said, mouth quirking upward. "Cut your hair, I see."

I huffed out a soft laugh, frustrated by the absurdity of such a trivial thing while simultaneously being drawn into his overconfident charm. My Achilles' heel.

"You let yours go wild," I said.

"Should've seen me an hour ago. Reckon I looked like a cave troll. Took half an hour to shave my face," he said with good humor, stroking his jaw.

He looked impossibly older. The same . . . but different. A boy's smile. A man's body. The little earthquake in my chest rumbled again; it was a wonder I was still standing.

"More than your hair has changed," he said, eyes roaming over my hips. "Quite a lot."

"Watch it . . . ," I warned, feeling self-conscious but trying to sound irritated.

The corners of his eyes crinkled. "Not a straight and narrow lane anymore, are you?"

"I'll gladly punch that freshly shaven jaw of yours if you say another word about my hips, Huxley Gallagher!"

"Steady now . . . It was a compliment. They're very nice hips—hey, whoa!" he said, backing away with one hand up. "Guess that hot blood of yours is the one thing that hasn't changed. Let's start over again. What about a simple 'Hello, Huck; good to see you'?"

"Why am I seeing you at all?" I said, exasperated. "What are you doing in Istanbul, much less my room? How did you get here?"

"Well, let's see. I drove all day from Tokat."

Tokat? "You were . . . with Father?" A dozen emotions sprang up inside me like unwanted weeds in the middle of a perfect lawn. Anger. Hurt. Jealousy . . . If he'd been with Father, that meant Huck had been helping him with the Turkey expedition. Behind my back. Both of them lying to me.

"The two of you have been in contact? For how long? This entire time?" I mean, I knew that Father communicated with Huck occasionally at least. Enough to report to me that Huck was still alive and living with his aunt.

"Theo . . ." He said my name as if he pitied me and was trying to spare my feelings—which only made me angry. And paranoid.

"Have you been meeting up with Father at other expeditions?"

"Not necessarily . . . ?"

"What in the hell does that mean?"

"It's a bit of a long story," he said, eyes darting away.

"Oh-ho! I bet it is, and I've got plenty of time. And apparently so do you, since you're taking baths in my room and exchanging our train tickets—was that you?"

"Christ alive, this hotel is gossipy," he murmured. "Remind me to fill out a complaint card when we're checking out."

"And to top it all off, you told the concierge you were my brother?" I said, suddenly livid. "My *brother?* That's rich."

Worst part was, he nearly used to be.

Before the birthday incident last year—something I privately referred to in my head as Black Sunday—Father had treated Huck as if he were beloved heir and fortunate son. For the first few years of my teens, while I was continually left behind in hotels when we all traveled abroad together several times a year, Huck was climbing mountains and sailing the seas with my father, having glorious adventures. Huck knew how to fly a plane, pilot a boat, and pick a lock. If my father needed something done outside the law, Huck enthusiastically volunteered and was enthusiastically praised.

In Father's eyes, I was trouble, but Huck the Magnificent could do no wrong.

And as far as what *I* thought about Huck? That was complicated. When Huck first moved into our upstate New York Hudson Valley home, Foxwood, both us were children, grieving over the recent loss of parents. Huck's father was an Irish immigrant who'd served in my father's unit in the war; they were both awarded the Medal of Honor for swimming across a canal in France under fire to rescue a dozen imprisoned allies, an act that had created an unbreakable bond between our fathers.

After the war Sergeant Gallagher and his wife were killed unexpectedly in a terrible streetcar accident outside their Brooklyn apartment, one that Huck survived . . . the white scar on his cheek a continual reminder. Huck had no relatives in the States to take him in—and no money to return to Ireland. Father didn't even think about it. He just left Foxwood one afternoon and returned a few hours later with a scared eleven-year-old boy.

At the time I was struggling, grieving. Would wake up in the middle of horrible nightmares, wailing . . . which was when Huck dubbed me "banshee." Grief bonded us. We became inseparable friends. And the small, broken family of me and Father expanded to include Huck. We were more than family. We were a trio shackled by loss. A band of mourners, loyal to one another. Until I broke the rules with Huck . . . and broke my father's heart.

Black Sunday.

One minute Huck was in my life every single day, and then . . . he was gone. Poof! I woke up the next morning and he was on an ocean liner to Northern Ireland. No goodbye. No nothing. For months it felt as if I were in mourning all over again—as if he'd actually, physically died. Maybe sometimes I even wished he had, because that would have been better than knowing he was across the ocean, still very much alive . . . and very much unconcerned that he'd broken my heart into a million pieces.

But now here he was, standing in front of me. Brought back from the dead as if he were a cursed mummy, risen from an ancient burial tomb.

Like nothing had happened.

"You are *not* my brother," I remind him, poking his breastbone.

"Know that, don't I?"

"Why did you tell Mr. Osman you were?"

"Was the only thing I could think of on the spot that would get me inside your room," he argued, looking mildly sheepish. "It helped that the concierge was fairly easy to fool. By the way, is the man's hair cut like that on purpose? Looks as if he made an enemy of his barber."

"You could have waited in the lobby."

He shook his head. "Negative. I needed a bath like you wouldn't believe. Man was not meant to go without hot water and indoor plumbing for days while climbing mountains. It's a wonder I don't have lice."

It should've been *me* climbing those mountains and attracting lice—not him. I used to go in the field with my parents when I was a child—to ancient ruins, temples, and hidden gravesites. The three of us went everywhere together. But after Mom died and Huck moved in, Father became increasingly paranoid about my safety, claiming every expedition was "not a place for a young lady." And that's when I started getting left behind in hotels.

Huck ran a hand through his curls. "Let me just say, the shampoo here smells amazing. Like roses. Jesus, Mary, and Joseph, it feels good to be clean, I—" He stopped abruptly, glanced at my mud-soaked dress, and puffed up his cheeks. "*Woof!* Have you been rolling around in dog shite?"

"It was raining, and there was this harem ring . . ."

"Harem?" he said, one brow lifting slowly.

"I got falsely accused of shoplifting jewelry when I was only trying to take photographs of a haunted wall in the Grand Bazaar—"

"Wall?" he said, gaze dropping to my camera case. "Should I ask?"

"Probably not." Huck was superstitious and maintained a "best leave it alone" attitude toward anything ghostly or occult. "It's been a lousy day," I mumbled.

He nodded sympathetically. "That fellow downstairs mentioned your tutor quitting."

"She took all the traveler's checks, ran off with a lounge singer, and left me here alone!"

"I see . . ."

"No, I doubt you do, but let me explain. While you were running around Turkey behind my back with Father, I was being held hostage in the Grand Bazaar and then accused of being a she-demon, and now I don't have any money except this"—I pulled out the banknote that the stranger in the black coat had given me and waved it angrily in front of Huck's face—"which probably isn't real currency and definitely isn't mine, but apparently I'm a magnet for the uncanny today, and did I mention how long it took me to hail a taxicab that splashed me with excrement? But if it hadn't stopped, I was likely well on my way to being murdered in some back alley and being torn apart by wild dogs. So yes, that's been my day."

Wide hazel eyes blinked at me. Forget Helen of Troy: those eyes could launch a thousand ships. Sometimes golden, sometimes green, they peered out from a dark fan of overlong lashes.

"Well, then," Huck said evenly. "Good thing I showed up when I did, yeah?"

I started to lash out with a catty response; yet in that moment a glacier thawed inside my rib cage and flooded my chest, and I was just so thankful he was here. Not because I couldn't take care of myself. I could. Not because I'd mourned him as if he were dead and buried, sobbing my eyes out for months like some silly child.

It was . . . just such an enormous relief to see his face.

But I would've rather hacked off my own arm with a rusty butter knife than tell him that.

The light above the bathroom mirror cast deep shadows, and Huck's towel was thin and damp. Unexpectedly, my imagination filled in the blanks with gratuitous detail, and I felt my cheeks catch fire. I prayed he didn't notice. When our gazes connected, I knew that he had, and I wanted to fold myself up until I disappeared.

"Seriously, Huck. What is going on?" I said, flustered, making sure my gaze didn't slide downward again. "Where is my father?"

"Aye, Fox," he said. "I couldn't say exactly."

"What do you mean? Is he not with you? Why exchange our train tickets? Are we leaving Istanbul tonight?"

He blew out a long breath, and his cocky exuberance faded. "Your father is maybe, just possibly, a tiny bit missing in action."

"Missing? What do you mean? You lost him?"

"He lost *me*, if you want to be technical about it. On purpose."

I blinked. "He left you?"

"I think he has a plan, but I'm not entirely sure. Things got . . . complicated in Tokat. But not to worry. I've got instructions, and Fox will no doubt be fine. He has balls of iron, so there's no cause for worry."

I couldn't understand why he was being so blasé about my father's well-being. "He's in trouble? Is he trying to avoid arrest?" It wouldn't be the first time he'd been detained for violating international antiquities laws. "If he needs bail money, I can't—"

"No, it's not the police or the government. The people who are after us are unpleasant. I've seen strange things, banshee. . . ." He shuddered briefly and said quite seriously, "We never should've come to Turkey."

"I'm going to need more than that. Is Father in trouble or isn't he?"

"Aye, maybe. The short version of the story is that I flew out to Tokat to meet up with him, and we hiked up the mountains to search for . . . the thing he was searching for."

My jaw clicked as I flexed it. "Vlad the Impaler's ring."

"Right," he said, as if he would've been happier if he could have talked around it. "He mentioned that was a sore spot."

"Oh, is *that* what he told you?"

His eyes narrowed. "Do you want to hear this or not?"

I nodded curtly.

He continued. "As I was saying, we found an empty grave up there. No skull of Count Dracula, or Prince Vlad, or Mr. Impaler—whatever you want to call him . . . no ring, either. But we weren't the only ones looking. We were followed by a couple of men back to Tokat. Managed to lose them, though. Then Fox got a message from someone who claimed to have information on the ring. He sent me out to arrange transportation back to Istanbul, and when I returned to the hotel . . . Fox was gone."

"Gone?"

Still holding on to his towel with one hand, he gestured for me to move and ducked behind the door, where a canvas rucksack sat on the bathroom tile. Digging under a jumble of clothes, he pulled out a red leather journal bound with a matching strap.

I recognized it immediately. My father's travel journal.

He had dozens lined up inside a locked case in his home office, one for every year. I was never allowed to read them. No one was.

The Fox family crest was stamped into the cover with a Gaelic motto: *Mo teaghlach thar gach uile ní.* Family first. A sentiment I'd had chiseled into my brain since I was old enough to speak.

"He left this for me yesterday at the hotel desk with a note," Huck said, handing over the journal. "It's tucked there, on top."

I set down my travel guide on the edge of the sink and briefly ran my fingers over the soft leather before tugging a folded scrap of wrinkled paper from the taut straps. No mistaking my father's handwriting. I quickly read the scrawled note:

> **It's become far too dangerous. I need to finish this alone. Get to Istanbul as quickly and discreetly as you can and give my journal to Theodora for safekeeping. Take her to that royal hotel we talked about on the way here—remember the story I told you? That one. Don't delay. I'll meet up with you both as soon as I'm able. If I'm not there by Friday, don't stick around: take Theo back to Hudson Valley. Whatever you do, don't go to Paris.**
>
> **Beware of hounds on your tail: do not allow anyone**

suspicious near Theo. If you have a gut feeling about someone, trust it. If possible, try to keep the authorities out of this. We're beyond their help now anyway.

Tell Theo that if she loses the journal, I'll kill her.

And if you lose Theo? I'll kill you.

Family first,

Fox

Fear ballooned inside my chest as my father's words swam in my vision. The only part of his letter that I fully understood was the bit about not going to Paris. That was where Jean-Bernard Bisset lived. He was a wealthy Parisian antiquities dealer, a longtime family acquaintance, and my father's closest friend. We had plans to go to Paris after Father was finished in Turkey.

But apart from that, everything else he'd written was gibberish.

"Listen," I said forcefully. "If you don't start explaining everything that's going on here in the next five seconds, I will hurt the softest parts of you."

"Ah, see there. You *have* missed me," he said, one corner of his mouth twisting up.

I pointed the journal at his towel. "Something's going to be missing, all right."

"You know what they say. Violence makes the heart grow fonder."

"Five . . ." I began counting. "Four, three, two—"

"All right!" he said, shielding the front of his towel with one hand. "Jaysus, Theodora! Do you want to hear? If so, I'd ask that you lower the bludgeoning weapon, please and thank you."

"I'll lower it when you put some clothes on." My eyes wouldn't stop glancing at a dark line of hair that arrowed down his stomach and disappeared beneath the towel, and it was infuriatingly distracting. "I can't think straight. Please get dressed!"

"Afraid I cannot. Hotel is laundering my clothes. Been on a mountain for days, haven't I? Got nothing to wear that's clean."

"I swear to all things holy, if you don't—"

A noise outside the room drew our attention. We both froze in place and remained still as statues for several heartbeats. Then I heard Huck mumble a blasphemous curse.

"It's only—" I started, but he waved for me to lower my voice. "Room service."

"Room service doesn't pick the lock," he whispered back in a sober tone.

I listened harder to the soft, metallic clicks emanating from my door. The hair on both my arms lifted.

"The bastards followed me!" Huck whispered. Slinging his rucksack over one shoulder, he urged me out of the bathroom doorway. Then he swung around, desperately searching my room for something.

A place to hide.

My eyes followed his. To the bed. Closet. Drapes.

Balcony.

We quickly stepped outside into cold drizzle and closed the door behind us right before two large men entered my hotel room.

They were dressed in long black cassock robes, like Orthodox monks. If pressed to guess, I'd say they looked Eastern European. They searched my room like lions hunting prey.

Inside the rain-speckled panes of glass, a gauzy curtain covered the balcony door. Even so, I was afraid they'd see our silhouettes. Huck must've thought so too, because he dragged me out of view, and we huddled against the stone wall of the building. As traffic sped down slick streets below, I forced my overfast lungs to calm and dared a glance into the room. The curtain obstructed my sight, but I could tell that they were tearing my room to pieces. My clothes torn from hangers. Drawers pulled open. The mattress flipped over. My imported silk stockings twisted like wharf rope . . . and my imported newspapers with all the crossword puzzle pages removed and neatly finished, tossed aside like garbage.

Heathens!

One of the monkish men emerged from the bathroom and mumbled something to his cohort that I couldn't catch. Then he surveyed the room, and—

He spotted the balcony door.

I quickly moved out of sight.

"We can't stay here," Huck whispered urgently into my ear. "They'll kill us."

The look on Huck's face was grave. I didn't want to die. Particularly not in a foreign country with a nearly naked Huck.

There was barely room enough on the balcony for us and the small patio table that sat in the opposite corner. Nowhere to hide. We couldn't very well jump four stories to the street below.

My gaze flicked to our side. Each of the rooms on this floor shared one long balcony, broken up by waist-high iron railings. Terrible if you cherished your privacy, but at the moment it looked like a viable escape route.

"That's Madame Leroux's old balcony," I whispered.

Huck took a moment to think about it before quickly tossing his rucksack over the rail. With one hand grasping his towel, he swung his long legs and leapt over the iron divider, smoothly landing on the adjoining section of the balcony like a graceful cat. I, on the other hand, still clinging on to both my handbag and my father's journal, clambered over the rail like some sort of drugged sloth. He grasped my arm to stop me from slipping in a rain puddle, and we stumbled into the recessed shelter of the adjoining room's balcony door.

As Madame Leroux had only checked out within the last hour, I prayed this room was still currently empty and tried to make myself smaller to remove myself from the intruder's line of vision. Huck wrapped both arms around my back and pulled me closer. Too close. My breasts grazed his bare chest, and I could smell the rose shampoo in his hair. This was eight down in today's *Guardian* crossword: "To bait or ensnare." T-R-A-P.

On the other side of the dividing rail, my balcony door creaked on its hinges. And that's when I felt Huck's damp towel plop onto my shoes.

I didn't glance down.

I *tried* not to glance down.

Fine. I glanced down.

There was a blur of darkness and some . . . vague shapes in my peripheral southerly vision. It was hard to see in the rain, but I was more than aware that the fourth floor was not as high up as I'd prefer, because anyone walking on the street below need only look up to see us in a lurid state of disgrace. Just one more black mark on my stellar record.

A scream cut through the wind and drizzle. It was coming from my hotel room, and a commotion soon followed. Banging. Running. Shouting . . .

The robed intruder on my balcony disappeared, and a male voice—one that I recognized immediately—shouted for the police.

"Bless Mr. Osman and his awful haircut!" I whispered.

Huck, however, didn't share my enthusiasm. At that instant the glass-paned balcony door no longer withstood our combined weight. It flew inward, and we followed, hitting the floor together with a terrible *thump.*

The wind was knocked from my lungs, and it felt as if a horse had kicked me in my right breast. I seized in pain, unable to think straight. It took me several seconds to realize that my father's journal was painfully wedged between us.

Somewhere in the back of my mind, I was more than aware that I was sprawled atop a naked Huck. I'd been here before, and my body hadn't forgotten his, no matter how hard I'd tried to erase it from my memories. But that had been in kinder, gentler times.

In the hotel corridor, a guest yelled, "Here! They went this way!" Heavy footfalls gave chase, and a commanding voice ordered everyone to stay in their rooms.

That sounded promising. Were we out of danger now? Then I should move off Huck. Any second now I would. On the count of . . . something. Ten? Maybe on the count of twenty. He felt more pleasant beneath me than I cared to admit. Desperation does terrible things to a girl.

"Look at us," he purred beneath me. "Just like old times."

Only it wasn't. Because I remembered with a pang of disappointment that Father sent Huck here to fetch me instead of coming for me himself, that Huck had all but disappeared from my life, and now he showed back up, no apology or explanation—and only because he was instructed to come here. If Father *had* found Vlad Dracula's ring would I even have known Huck had been in Turkey?

Wrenching my father's journal from where it was jammed between us, I rolled away from Huck and stared at the hotel ceiling until I heard him groan. Then I shrugged out of my coat and blindly offered it in his direction. After a few moments I felt him tug it out of my hand to cover himself.

Neither of us got up right away. We just lay there together, listening to hallway noise.

"You all right?" Huck finally asked.

"Not really," I said. "It's been a very bad year."

He grunted an acknowledgment. "I'd raise a glass to that, but I think perhaps I need to put trousers on. Think the coast is clear? Sounds like those gobshites are gone, yeah?"

"Sounds like it. Huck?"

"Yes?"

"What were they looking for?"

"Probably the same thing they were looking for when I saw them in Tokat—something in that journal. Good thing they didn't get it, yeah?"

"Good thing," I repeated.

"Theo?"

"Yes?"

"We need to leave Istanbul tonight. It's not safe here anymore."

I was beginning to understand that now. "Where is that place my father was talking about in that letter—where he wants us to meet him?"

"Aye, that. It's where he stayed this summer. A hotel in Bucharest."

Bucharest? Romania—my mother's homeland! Wild. Enigmatic. Brimming with history, mystery, and dark superstitions.

I'd been to Romania only once, briefly, a few months after I was born, when my mother was attending her father's funeral. Never since. I'd been begging Father to travel there for years, but he would never take me. He had a thousand reasons why. *Nothing to see. I have other work. Too far. I don't have time.* What he never said was that he was avoiding Romania because it reminded him too much of my mother.

But my father never said a lot of things. Like that I'd ever see Huck again. Yet here we were, miracle of miracles.

I knew one thing. Whatever danger we were in, it was substantial enough to produce an even greater miraculous feat: it had convinced Richard Damn Fox to change his stubborn mind.

JOURNAL OF RICHARD FOX
June 19, 1937
Orient Express

We're soon headed out of Budapest and on toward Bucharest. Funny how similar those cities sound. Funny that I'm nervous to leave one and go to the next, as if I'll encounter Elena's ghost when we cross the Carpathians. I'm fortifying myself with dry martinis, and I suppose that's got me thinking sentimental thoughts, because my mind keeps returning to when I arrived in Europe, before I met with Rothwild about this Vlad-the-Impaler ring.

Three days ago I visited Huck on my way to meet Jean-Bernard in Paris. The first time I'd seen him since he left Foxwood. He was in good spirits. I wasn't. It was terrible leaving him. His aunt is a miserable woman, and I fear he'll rot there if he stays too much longer.

Truth is, Huck shouldn't be here at all. He should be home with us at Foxwood. What ever happened to "family first"? Because I feel as if my motley little family is utterly broken, and I don't know how to fix it. God do I wish Elena were still alive. She'd know what to do.

SEVERAL HOURS AFTER THE ROOM INVASION, HUCK AND I sat on opposites sides in the back of a car provided by the hotel, speeding through Istanbul in the brisk night air. We were headed toward the railway station to catch a train into Europe. Together. As if the last year or so of our lives had been erased.

Appearances could be deceiving though, couldn't they?

At night the ancient city was a maze of dark alleys and golden streetlights. I couldn't stop surveying the nearby traffic, making sure we'd not been followed. Every shadowy driver was a suspect, though we hadn't seen hide nor hair of the two intruders who'd trashed my hotel room.

"Relax. We're okay now," Huck told me in a low voice after I'd squinted too hard at a figure standing under a dull streetlamp. He adjusted a herringbone flat cap that was pulled down tight on his forehead, covering his mop of curls. He'd donned a long, charcoal wool coat that hung to his knees, one that I'd never seen him wear before. He looked calm, which was definitely the opposite of how I felt.

"*Are* we?" I asked, grumpy and anxious. "Are we really okay?"

"Probably," he said unconvincingly.

My thoughts circled around to the reason we were leaving Istanbul. I desperately craved more information from Huck about what had happened in Tokat. We'd barely had more than a few minutes alone, what with all the hubbub and annoying practical minutia—things like ensuring that nothing in my room was stolen and convincing the hotel manager not to summon the police after Huck reminded me of the warning in Father's letter. Then I had to sign a hundred pieces of paperwork to settle the hotel bill on credit, which required waiting for a cable authorization from Father's bank in New York.

And then there was Huck and what was between us. Or what *wasn't* between us. Whatever it was, it felt like we were sitting on opposite sides of a muddy wartime trench, and I wasn't sure if I could trust him ever again. Not like I did before he left.

I tried not to think about it. After all, we had bigger concerns, such as my father and where he was right now and the men who'd trailed Huck to my hotel room. All of it came back to Vlad the Impaler's ring, but I couldn't see how everything fit together. Not yet at least. Though I'd reread my father's letter to Huck several times, I hadn't yet had a chance to look through the red journal. It was currently burning a proverbial hole in my travel satchel, begging me to read it. I just needed to get settled on the train, where I could open it in private.

"I wish the driver would go faster," I mumbled.

"Patience," Huck said. "As the proverb says, bear and four bears."

"Forbear," I correct. "Bear and forbear."

"Mine's better. What requires more restraint than four bears?"

"If we make it onto this train, tonight I'm going to pray that four bears eat you while you're sleeping."

"It would definitely take four, on account of my Herculean strength and great manliness."

"Yes, I suppose it does take a massive amount of testosterone to leave your home like a dog with its tail tucked and retreat across an entire ocean to your aunt's house when the going gets tough."

"Ouch. I'm going to forgive that one. It's your free insult."

"Oh really? Going to make me pay for the next one? Feel free to take the only lira I still have out of my handbag, since my tutor stole the traveler's checks. That would be a fitting end to today."

He didn't answer, but I could tell by the way he folded his arms over his chest that he was upset. Good. That made two of us.

Thankfully, it wasn't long before we pulled up to Sirkeci Railway Station, which looked more like a Byzantine palace or a mosque than a train terminal, with its domed roof and stained-glass windows. We exited the car while the driver flagged down a railway porter and arranged for our luggage to be carried to the train. Huck helped, and I surveyed approaching passengers who marched past silhouettes of palm trees.

After everything was arranged, we entered the station and headed onto Platform No. 1. A friendly man behind the lone open ticket counter provided us with our exchanged tickets. We then passed under a series of moonlike clocks protruding from columns, dodging nimble porters who wheeled teetering stacks of luggage on long racks. To our left a handful of well-dressed passengers sat at café tables strewn with pistachio shells outside the station's restaurant, smoking cigarettes and drinking tea. And across the platform, under the soft glow of the station lights, were the peacock-blue cars of our night train.

The Orient Express.

Gold-crested cars sat along the track with the acclaimed Wagons-Lits company name above the windows. It was a short train tonight—only the engine and two sleepers sandwiched between a couple of baggage vans. There was no dining car for the evening leg of our trip; one would be added tomorrow morning, after we crossed the border into Europe, just in time for breakfast.

Clipboard in hand, a middle-aged conductor in a blue uniform stood near the steps of the second sleeper. Huck and I headed his way, and when he greeted us, Huck gave him our names: "Miss Theodora Fox and Mr. Huxley Gallagher."

"Ah, yes, from the hotel," the conductor said with a charmingly French accent, inspecting us over the silver rims of his eyeglasses. "Your destination is only to Bucharest?"

Many passengers would continue on to Hungary, at least, and many would ride all the way to Paris. The conductor reminded us that our journey would be broken up at the Bulgarian border, where we'd exit and take a ferry over the Danube before picking up a fresh train on the opposite riverbank in Romania to finish the final short leg of the trip to Bucharest.

"Your large trunk is stored in the baggage van, and the small valises have been placed in your compartment," the conductor informed us, reading from his clipboard. "You have been booked into the number two compartment in the first Pullman coach here. First class, two berths."

"And what about Mr. Gallagher's assignment?" I asked, adjusting the fur-trimmed coat on my arm. For train travel, I'd changed into a new skirt and top, leaving my gutter-water clothing behind in the hotel, as there was no time to launder it.

The conductor blinked at me. "Why, the same, *mademoiselle*. It is the only open compartment left until Bucharest, I'm afraid. There is a note here from the Pera Palace . . ." He ran a gloved finger along a penciled note before looking up at me, expectant. "You and the gentleman are siblings, *oui*?"

Not again. I briefly fantasized about snatching the clipboard from the conductor and smacking it against Huck's too-handsome face.

"Mademoiselle?" the conductor asked.

"Ah, yes," Huck said when I didn't answer right away, clearing his throat. "Good ol' sis of mine." He slapped me roughly on the back.

"A remarkable similarity," the conductor said dryly, gaze flicking between Huck's long body and the compact, sturdy build I'd inherited from my mother's side of the family tree.

"Different fathers?" I said, smiling weakly.

"And mothers," Huck murmured somewhere near the top of my head, a little too loudly. I poked his side until he made a muffled noise, pain mixed with laughter.

"Not my job to judge, *monsieur*." The conductor's biting tone was giving me the distinct impression he believed us to be unmarried lovers, trying to pull the wool over his eyes. If he only knew. Ugh.

"There's no chance you couldn't find another compartment for me?" I asked. I mean, surely I couldn't sleep in the same room as Huck. I'd rather have put my hand in a locked cage and watched rats feast on my fingers. "I'd prefer, uh . . . my privacy, you see? Maybe someone else in the train could be moved?"

The man exhaled slowly. "I cannot move passengers who've had reservations for weeks, especially when everyone is already settled and you are the last to board. If I may say so, you are quite lucky to get this compartment."

"But—"

"Everyone is already settled," he insisted sharply, making me feel like a spoiled child being reprimanded for demanding extra pudding. "I can make arrangements for separate compartments tomorrow night. One will become available after we change trains in Romania. Tonight, however, I must ask that you stay where you are put, if you please."

A silent scream filled my head. My heart grew legs and blindly raced around inside my chest, bumping into my rib cage and falling over, completely panicked.

Me. Huck. One compartment. Two bunks, sure. And we used to share rooms all the time when we were younger. But now . . . ?

Before I could protest further or drop onto my knees in front of the conductor and sob delicate lady tears on his well-shined shoes, the doleful sound of a train whistle cut through the steam that now billowed over the platform.

"That will be our signal to depart," the conductor said, motioning for us to board the train. "It is our pleasure to serve you through continental Europe. Please watch your step."

What could I do? Not a damn thing. The tickets were exchanged, and I certainly didn't want to sit around the station tonight, sleeping on a bench until the next express. The look Huck gave me was apologetic with a soupçon of panic as he murmured, "Family first?"

Touché.

The anxiety I was feeling manifested into a cold sweat that blossomed over the back of my neck as I climbed two metal steps and entered the train behind Huck. A moment later the conductor closed the door behind us, and the Orient Express trundled into motion. We made our way down the sleeper car's narrow corridor, past compartment doors on our right and windows to our left. Through the glass panes, the steam-wreathed platform shifted slowly, slowly, and then faster, until it fell away into the night. We cleared the station, leaving everything behind:

The Grand Bazaar.

The Pera Palace Hotel.

The strangely dressed intruders who wanted my father's journal.

And my father, wherever he was right now, may the devil take him.

All of these things disappeared from view but not from my thoughts, where they became tangled up with the conflicted feelings that I had about Huck and our current situation. On top of everything, like icing sugar sprinkled atop a cake, was the strange thrill that I always felt when traveling. My mother used to call it "travel fever"—a little fear of the unknown, a little excitement for adventure. Whatever it was, I embraced it like an old friend as I shuffled down the train corridor and wondered what she'd think if she could see me now, stealing away to Eastern Europe at night.

My mother had been no stranger to this sort of thing. Not to my father's fervor for adventuring or to the strange objects that lured him around the globe, because they lured her, too. To places like India and the discovery of a two-thousand-year-old copper crown, thought to be Greek in origin, perhaps from the time Alexander the Great tried, and failed, to invade the Indian subcontinent.

The markings on the box that housed the ancient crown spoke of curses and black magic. My father scoffed at that, saying it was silly, superstitious hogwash. He encouraged her to inspect it. And though he denied it now, I overheard him telling her that he had a buyer who'd pay far more than the government would for her expertise in authenticating it.

Anything for the thrill of the take. Even if it put your family at risk.

Because it did. The local workers warned my mother that the kiln worker who'd originally dug it up had died unexpectedly.

Three weeks later she was dead too.

To be fair, the official cause of her death was a particularly dangerous species of malaria, likely contracted days or even weeks before she touched the crown. There was absolutely no proof she was cursed or bedeviled. But she wasn't the last person to perish mysteriously after handing the crown; a government official from India's Ministry of Culture died too. After that the copper crown was reported stolen. No leads. No witnesses. It was there one day and gone the next, much like my mother.

My father said it was nothing more than dumb luck.

But I believed. In curses. And magic spells. The esoteric and supernatural. Things that couldn't be explained, things rarely seen and unproven. That's why I read everything I could get my hands on about magic. Why I photographed haunted walls in ancient markets and was desperate to find proof that ghosts were real. Because I firmly believed a cursed object took my mother. And if Father continued on his devil-may-care path, one of these days it was going to take him too.

If it hadn't already.

"Here we are. Number two. Guess this is us," Huck said, ducking through an open door, where our carry-on luggage sat on the floor, swaying rhythmically with the steady clack of the train as it rolled along the track.

The compartment was dim. Its only source of light emanated

from a small compact lamp on a foldaway table beneath the window. There was scarcely room for two people to stand without bumping into each other; otherwise, it was well-appointed: voluptuously polished wood paneling, a hidden washbasin with a gilded vanity mirror, a spray of lacy orchids thrust into a tiny vase. Two built-in berths had been lowered and outfitted with crisp white sheets and embroidered coverlets; a pull-down ladder led to the upper bed.

Behind me in the corridor, a young English attendant with ginger hair popped his head into our compartment. His cheeks were so ruddy, they made him look as if he'd been racing up and down the train. "Good evening. My name is Rex. I'll be your attendant," he informed us breathlessly. "You're Miss Fox and Mr. Gallagher?"

"Last time I checked," Huck said.

Rex smiled. "Anything you need, no matter the hour, just ring the call bell and a light will appear outside your door. Either myself or the conductor will appear promptly."

He then informed us that hot water was available in the brass samovars at the front of each sleeper and that the public lavatories contained full-size washbasins . . . and some other details that I couldn't focus on properly because I was acutely aware of the compartment's lack of personal space. "Is there anything at all you desire at the moment?" he finally asked.

"To sleep in my own compartment," I mumbled under my breath.

"Anything you need, just ring for me," Rex said.

I raised my hand. "I'll take every newspaper you have onboard."

"Still addicted to crosswords?" Huck said, sounding amused.

I slanted a glance at him. "Still picking locks for fun?"

"She's joking, brother," he quickly told the attendant.

"Um," Rex said, looking back and forth between us. "Newspapers will be on the dining car tomorrow morning."

"I'm sure she can live without it tonight," Huck assured him.

The attendant bade us a good night and bowed before closing the compartment door, muffling the intense *clack-clack* of the wheels gliding over the track. I took off my black beret and smoothed my wavy hair to cover my ears. Without the door open, the compact space shrank from tight to little more than a sardine can.

"Cozy," Huck remarked, touching the compartment's ceiling with his fingertips as if he were Atlas, holding up the world. "Remember being on that ship in the North Sea during that storm a few years ago? The berths were made for dolls, not people, and the walls were paper thin. We could all hear each other getting sick, like some kind of nightmarish echo chamber."

"Ugh," I complained, hanging my coat and camera case on a hook near the berths. "Don't bring it up. Just the thought of that night makes me queasy."

"Hey, at least this compartment is slightly bigger, and we aren't on choppy waters. *And* we weren't followed. We're on a winning streak, banshee."

I'd hardly describe today as anything remotely close to winning, but I could tell he was trying to put a sunny face on it, and maybe we both needed that right now. An unemotional truce between two old friends. Otherwise we'd both go bonkers. Or murder each other. Tomato, tomahto.

"Tell me more about those men who broke into my room," I said, proud that I could sound so professional and adult. See? I could do this.

"What do you want to know?" he asked.

"We have all night. Might as well spill it all," I said. "Start from the beginning."

ALL RIGHT," HUCK AGREED. "BUT THERE ISN'T MUCH to tell."

He raised a silky, tasseled pull-shade on the window to peer outside, but in the darkness the only thing to see was his own reflection. I studied his face briefly while he squinted stubbornly. His impossibly thick brows had a certain way of knitting together into a single dark slash over his eyes when he was worried. Did he not think we were safe now? He caught me watching him in the glass, so I quickly averted my gaze.

"The last telegram I received from Father was a week ago," I said, perching on the bottom berth. I set my travel satchel on the floor near my feet. "He said he was heading up the mountain." He just failed to mention that he wasn't climbing alone.

"Right, yes," Huck said, now looking for his own place to sit. When he eyed the empty space next to me on the bottom berth, I gestured instead toward the floor, but to no avail; invading my space, he propped up a pillow and settled back against it so that he could lounge on the railway bed with his legs stretched out behind me. "Fox and I spent three days in Tokat, which is no Istanbul, let me just say. While you were having fun, taking photographs of phantasms and cursed buildings—"

I flashed him a rude salute with one hand.

"Well, *that* hasn't changed," he mumbled as if he were offended. Which was absurd, because he was the one who taught me the gesture when we were kids, a week after he moved into Foxwood. We practiced on everyone who drove to the front door to visit one afternoon, hanging out of my bedroom window and giggling like idiots until we heard a bear stomping up the staircase. Father was *furious*.

Huck exhaled heavily. "As I was saying, Fox and I were in Tokat, visiting some boring historic mansion and talking to clerics in a mosque. Then we hired a local guide to take us out of town and up a mountain to the spot Fox was intent on finding. It was supposed to be a gravesite, but it turned out to be just a bunch of dusty rubble in the back of the cavern. It took us most of an afternoon to uncover it and another day to dig into the floor. Rocky, back-breaking work it was. The workers building the Great Pyramid of Giza never labored this hard."

He always exaggerated when he told me stories of where he and Father had been. *Always*. Once upon a time I had found it charming. "But you didn't find Vlad the Impaler's head?"

"Nor his crown. Only a small iron box about this big"—he showed me with his hands—"and inscribed in a mix of languages. Persian, Arabic, and Turkish. Our guide translated the Turkish bit."

"What did it say?"

"It was a warning. It said that the contents of the box were not to be disturbed and that death would follow those who ignored it, and there was a bit of dark poetry about rivers of blood—which was all I needed to hear. Even Pandora wouldn't have opened this thing. I wanted to leave it be and get out of there. But Fox had that sparkle in his eye. You know the one."

I did. My father's love of treasure and exploration was intense. He lived for the thrill of discovery. Loved it more than anything. More than me, I sometimes thought. "Naturally, he couldn't resist opening the box," I said, toeing off my Mary Janes and kicking them across the cabin floor.

"Naturally."

"What happened?" I asked.

"The lid fell apart when he pried at the rust. It was all for naught. Completely empty."

"Empty?" I said, frowning. "No rivers of blood?"

"Don't sound so disappointed that we didn't die on the spot."

"A girl can dream. . . ."

He snorted a soft laugh before sneaking a look at my face, as if he needed visual confirmation that I wasn't serious.

"Pandora's box was a bust," I said. "Then what happened?"

"We headed back down the mountain and returned to Tokat. Fox was in a black mood, due to not finding anything in the cave and to the fact that it seemed two men were following us and we didn't know why, but we had to take the long way around the town to shake them off our tail. And when we returned to the fleabag hotel we'd been staying at before the climb up the mountain, the hotel manager discreetly told us that someone had been inquiring as to our whereabouts."

"The plot thickens."

"On top of that two people had left Fox messages, urgently requesting to meet with him."

"Who were they?"

"The first one was a cleric at a mosque. We met him right before we left for the mountain. Nice enough fellow. Fox left after dark to meet up with him and didn't come back until midnight. By that time I was already half asleep and in no mood for a late-night chat, so he told me we'd talk in the morning about a new game plan for the ring."

"Did you?"

"No. When I woke up late the next morning, he was rushing out the door to meet with someone else. Didn't say who. Just told me to run into town and see if I could charter a small plane because we were leaving that afternoon to fetch you in Istanbul. Or he was. I was going back to Belfast."

"I see," I said coolly. So my suspicions were right: he'd had no intention of seeing me on this trip. I filed that in the back of my mind, curbing the hurt and resentment that threatened to rise, and prompted him to continue.

"Right, yes, so . . . I got dressed and left the hotel. At first nothing was wrong. I walked. Ate. Asked around, trying to find anyone with a plane—crop duster, whatever. Came up empty, so I tracked down the only car rental in town—which reminds me . . . Is Pooka still at Foxwood? Or did he sell it? He wouldn't tell me."

Pooka was Huck's car, a convertible with white-wall tires, which he'd Frankensteined together from several junked automobiles; Huck had built the engine himself. Lots of memories in that stupid old car. Our first kiss. Plenty of fights. Midnight rides to a secluded spot near the river.

The night after he left, I slept in the back seat, crying into the patched-up leather until Father found me.

"It's still in the garage," I said.

A small bolt of joy crossed his face. "Yeah?"

I nodded.

"Well, then, where was I?" he said, smiling briefly, as if that piece of information about Pooka was inconsequential. But was it?

"Right, well, as I was saying, I rented the car in Tokat, and that's when I started seeing people in the shadows. The same people from the mountain were following me."

"You don't mean the men who broke into my room, do you?"

He nodded. "Them and some other mate. He wasn't wearing black vestments like the rest of them, but that's about all I could tell you. Maybe he was their leader, or maybe he was someone else entirely. He kept his distance, so I barely got a look at him." Huck shook his head, dismissive, and crossed his arms. Shadows filled the deep hollows below proud, high cheekbones and accentuated the sharp line of his jaw. "This is going to sound daft, but I thought . . ."

"Yes?"

"I thought I saw a wolf following me."

"A wolf? Are there wolves in Turkey?"

He shook his head, blinking rapidly. "I was probably imagining it. Maybe it was just a stray mutt, salivating over my exquisite leg meats."

He chuckled to himself, but when our eyes met, I knew he was serious. He'd seen something. What that was exactly, I didn't know. But it had spooked him.

"I believe you," I said.

He exhaled forcefully, as if trying to rid himself of the memory, and absently scrubbed the top of his head with his fingers. "I swear to all the saints, banshee, I'd never felt so paranoid. I can't even explain it. I just knew in my gut something didn't feel right. And when I got back to the hotel with a rental car a few hours later . . . Fox was already gone."

"And you have no idea where he went? No clue at all?"

"None. Apparently he left the journal at the hotel desk about a half hour before I showed up. I searched the hotel lobby and restaurant. Our room. The street outside. Nothing. He just disappeared. All I know from the hotel manager is that a few minutes before I left to fetch a car, Fox left the hotel himself. An hour or so later, he strode through the lobby, went up to the room, and rushed back down with the journal. The hotel manager said he seemed distracted and unnerved. Like something had scared him."

I'd never seen my father scared. Not since Mom died.

The train rocked, clacking along the tracks. I didn't know what to think about everything Huck had just told me. My father's mystery meetings. The men following Huck. A wolf in the streets of Tokat . . . It all sounded like something straight out of one the pulp magazines that Huck liked to read—*Amazing Stories*, *The Black Mask*, *Weird Tales*. It was just that this story was missing half the pages. I pressed him for more information, but there was nothing more to give.

Maybe my father's journal would shed some light. I retrieved it from my satchel and unwrapped the leather straps that bound it; then I opened it up on my lap.

Thick pages were covered in my father's neat scrawl. A few things were stuck here and there—receipts, addresses, a flattened Tootsie Roll wrapper. Three photographs. The first was of Jean-Bernard, smiling in front of a fountain. He was an extraordinarily handsome man; I remembered my mother joking that he was unfairly prettier than her. I wondered where—and when—it had been taken.

The next two snapshots, however, were far more interesting.

"Is this . . . ?"

"Yeah," Huck confirmed. "That's the original ring, there. The one that the man who hired Fox has in his possession—his name is Rothwild. A Hungarian, I think. He's nuts for Vlad the Impaler. Knows everything about the man. And for some reason he thinks his ring is fake. A reproduction or something."

The black-and-white photographs showed a crooked band of bone with carved symbols on the side and some odd hatching along the top. Fascinating that this crude, strange ring could be the cause of so much chaos. My heartbeat increased, head spinning with what I knew about the ring from my *Batterman's Field Guide to Legendary Objects*. Shame that I didn't have access to an archive with more information about Vlad. If Father had only told me about the ring before we crossed the Atlantic on this trip, I could have helped him research, as I normally did. Maybe then we wouldn't be in this situation, hiding like mice while he put us all in danger.

I slipped the photographs into the back of the journal and thumbed through the pages, glancing at dates and places my father neatly logged at the top of each entry. It was so strange to have this in my hands, when it had always been off-limits. For him to just hand it over and trust me to keep it? Very odd.

Something caught my eye when I was flipping through the entries. A page had been torn out. "I wonder what this was," I murmured, feathering my fingertip over the ragged edge that remained. Then I noticed something on one of the pages that flanked the tear. It appeared that Father had written a word in cipher. Not just in this entry, but three pages later. And another.

A word or two here and there . . . a few longer phrases. Huh.

Puzzle pieces began rearranging themselves inside my head.

"Did you look through this already?" I asked Huck.

"What answer do you want to hear?"

"The honest one would be nice, but I know that's difficult for you."

His stare was hot lava pouring down a mountain. Absolute fury. "I *never* lied to you," he said in a low voice. "Not once. Not even about the weather."

I hated the way he affected me. "Apparently you've changed, because it seems to me you've been lying to me since you left home, running around with Father, God only knows where. Did you watch me check into hotels in Germany and France? Were you tailing us this spring when we sailed to Mexico, waiting for the moment that I was safely tucked away before joining Richard Damn Fox for an exciting no-girls-allowed expedition?"

"He visited me in Belfast this summer before he went to Jean-Bernard. That's it. He sent me a train ticket and asked me to join him in Tokat. I arrived there a day before him. I thought—"

"You thought what, Huck?"

He threw an arm up in frustration. "I thought you'd be there with him, okay? I made myself sick, sitting in that tiny hotel room, thinking you were going to walk into the lobby with him. When he came alone . . ." He shook his head, eyes darkening as he muttered, "It doesn't matter now. Fox tells you only what he thinks you need to know, nothing more. You should know that better than anyone."

He wasn't wrong. That's exactly how my father operated. Never admit mistakes. Never say you're sorry. Keep everything to yourself. Those were my father's personal mantras. He trusted no one but himself, and sometimes maybe not even that.

But what surprised me more was Huck's confession. He'd expected me to be with Father in Tokat? Had he made himself sick because he wanted to see me, or because he was dreading our reunion? I was too chickenhearted to ask.

After a tense moment Huck shook his head and exhaled loudly through his nose. "Yes, I breezed through the journal a little. I didn't have a lot of time, between the hiding and the driving and—"

"Bathing?"

One corner of his mouth tilted upward. "I smelled like a dead yak, banshee. You should be thankful. Anyway, what I did peep at in the journal was boring, and almost none of it was about me. Isn't that the only reason to read someone's private diary?"

"Well, when you were *not*-reading it, did you notice the code?"

"What code, now?"

"The cipher," I said. "He's used it in several places."

Huck sat up in the bed to look over my shoulder. "Like, espionage?"

"Like, he didn't want casual snoopers to read what he was documenting."

Father had always loved ciphers, and he was good at both writing and cracking them. He'd even helped decode enemy messages during the war. He'd taught me cryptography before Huck moved in with us, when I was a young child. . . . The Caesar Shift. The Cardan Grille. The Scytale Wraparound. He used to leave me coded messages in my room, mostly silly things. A lot of jokes and a few clues about where he'd hidden one of my books or a piece of chocolate.

But when my mother died, so did our ciphers; I guess we were too busy grieving to keep it up. I turned to crosswords for my word fix, and he turned to obscurer treasures that required more and more time out in the field.

Discovering that he'd been using ciphers privately made me feel a little marshmallowy. And now I couldn't help but wonder if he'd intended for me to decipher his journal. I mean, why else would he have instructed Huck to give it to me? Why not just let Huck keep it safe?

"Uh-oh. What's that?" Huck asked, waving his finger at my face. "That look right there—I recognize that. You're excited, aren't you?"

"Aren't *you*?"

"Should I be?"

"This is the most interesting thing Father's done in years," I insisted, feeling a rising sense of momentum for the first time that day. One that cut through the tension between us and made me temporarily forget our issues.

There were too many journals entries to skim at once; it would take hours to go through them all. Longer still to crack his code—I once spent an entire month diligently deciphering a message he wrote out for me, only to find that it said: STOP DECIPHERING CODES AND GO TO BED. Where to start with this cipher, though? Sometimes starting at the end has advantages, so I sneaked a look at the journal's final page:

JOURNAL OF RICHARD FOX
November 23, 1937
Tokat, Turkey

I'll never forgive myself. I should have never brought Huck and Theo here. This is my fault. What can I do? Theodora, if you're reading this, the Dragon—

Smeared across the paper, a line of ink trailed away from the last word, as if he were interrupted.

A sense of unease crept over me. "What is this?" I murmured. None of it sounded good. I reread it several times and pointed to the page. "What is he talking about here? 'Dragon'? Vlad the Impaler was sometimes called Vlad Dracula, *son* of the Dragon. It was his father who was the actual Dragon. I mean, so to speak. It was a byname, like . . . Alfred the Great. That sort of thing."

"Vlad the Dragon. Breathes fire. Not literally. Just don't piss him off."

"Like that," I confirmed. "And obviously both father Vlad and son Vlad have been dead for more than four hundred years—despite the loose connection to Bram Stoker's fictional Count Dracula, they weren't immortal vampires."

"You say 'vampire' as if it were a possibility. Have you run across something with sharp teeth and a hatred of garlic over the last year?"

"Sadly, my investigations have been vampire-free," I said.

"Good to know," he said, making the sign of the cross in the air for good measure. Then he pointed at the journal entry. "Look here at the date—yesterday. That's when I was arranging for transportation. He had to have written this before he slipped out of the hotel and left me in Tokat."

I thought for a moment. "So he took the second mystery meeting with an unknown person, returned to the hotel while you were out searching Tokat for a plane or a car, began writing this journal entry, and then . . . quickly left the hotel?"

"Seems to be so," Huck murmured.

Maybe the previous journal entry would shed more light. It had been written the day before the last entry:

JOURNAL OF RICHARD FOX
November 22, 1937
Tokat, Turkey

Returned from the cave empty-handed. The expedition was a failure. Now we're back at our hotel, which is barely better than sleeping in tents, as there is currently no running water here: the hotel's water main is being repaired. After a yelling match with the hotel manager, I left to meet with someone whom I wished I'd talked to before we went up the mountain. Would have saved me blood, sweat, and tears.

Vlad's Turkish enemies didn't behead him in Wallachia and take his legendary war ring across the Black Sea. It's not here. A retired Muslim cleric showed me a lockbox that had been taken from Topkapı Palace thirty years ago. Inside was a letter to the Ottoman sultan, dated 1891. It was written by a Romanian boyar, confirming receipt of a package that was sent from Turkey to Romania. And it was damn enlightening. . . .

Seems to me that there are three rings. Two fakes, one real.

I can't be sure, but I think the actual ring was duplicated in Turkey. Two reproductions were sent back to Romania along with the real ring, and all were distributed to three historic families there for safekeeping. ("The power is in one" is what was written in the boyar's letter, which I assume to be a reference to the war ring's supposed esoteric power or curse.)

Regardless, I think two duplicates were made to

confuse anyone who'd come looking for the real war ring. So maybe Rothwild was right: perhaps the ring in his possession is one of the reproductions.

That leaves two more—one real, one not. I need to retrace my steps back to my summer trip in Romania. Must talk to: XTTNMVGAFWVLWJQUIKLWLAUCJ. One of these three has the true ring, I'm certain.

The boyar's letter mentions what I believe to be a gruesome way to authenticate the ring, though I can scarcely believe it. No doubt Theo will say "I told you so!" and God knows I hate it when she's right. She gets this look in her eye exactly like Elena used to.

This was *definitely* more enlightening. I eagerly skimmed over the words again, absorbing them like sunlight, and asked Huck, "What did he mean when he said here that I was right? Why would I say 'I told you so'? I've never given him advice about this ring. What is he talking about?"

"Beats me," Huck said. "What about this gobbledygook here? And here? This is the cipher part?"

"Yes. Looks like he's trying to hide someone's identity—whoever showed him the boyar's letter in the lockbox, and then three people who may have the ring?"

"Can you decipher it?"

"Probably." I'd just need some time to study the patterns. Was it a Caesar cipher? That would be too easy. "Oh! I bet it's a Vigenére cipher. It's harder to crack. It's encoded with a passphrase—a random word that would determine how each letter of the message would be encrypted."

"How do you figure out the passphrase?"

"You normally wouldn't. That's the point. The person who encoded the message—in this case my father—would pick the passphrase and write the encoded message using it. He'd only share the passphrase with the message's recipient. You can't decode the message without it."

"Unless you could guess it?"

"Unless you could guess it," I confirmed.

"Well, count me out. Right now I'm so knackered, I couldn't guess how many feet I have." Huck settled back against the berth's pillow and rubbed a hand over his face. "I barely slept last night, and I drove all day, and now I need to sleep."

Not me. I was too wired to sleep. I stared at the open journal on my lap, mind spinning on both the words I could read and the ones that were encoded. How would I figure out Father's cipher passphrase? And who was the Dragon? And what did he learn in that second meeting that prompted him to leave and direct Huck to come fetch me in Istanbul? Whatever my father had gotten himself involved in, it must be bad.

But I did know several things: (a) that ring was more than just a piece of history, (b) someone besides this Mr. Rothwild fellow who'd hired Father to find the ring was interested in it—enough to send goons after us—and (c) Father's final journal entry was addressed to me, which meant he intended for me to read it.

And I would.

"Look," Huck said, stretching his neck from side to side. "There's no need to get worked up about cracking his code. We're going to meet Fox in Bucharest, just like his letter said. We'll be there tomorrow night. All we have to do is sit back, enjoy the first-class service, and have a little faith, and everything will be fine."

"That's nearly word for word what Father said when he dumped me at the Pera Palace Hotel and ran off to Tokat to meet up with you in secret. And look how that turned out."

Huck frowned at me. "You're going to stay up all night and decode his journal, aren't you?"

How could I not? This was my chance to do something besides sitting around hotel rooms for days at a time. "I'll require the bottom berth to work," I said. "The lamplight down here is brighter."

Huck sighed dramatically, pushed out of the berth, and headed across the compartment, mumbling something about finding our car's restroom.

"If you want to help," I called out, eyes on the journal pages, "ring that Rex fellow and order a pot of tea."

"What if I don't want to help? What if I just want to brush my teeth and go to sleep?"

"Even better. I'll work faster without your constant chattering."

"Comments like that could make a boy think you haven't missed him at all."

"Oh, really? Is that something like when a girl sends a boy a dozen letters across the ocean and he never replies?" I said.

Huck paused on the far side of the compartment and looked as if he might explain himself. Just for a moment. Then, without another word, he stepped into the corridor and pulled the door closed behind him, shutting me out. Making me feel as if he'd slammed the door on my heart, too.

I'd known sharing a compartment was a bad idea. He was going to sleep, and I was going to stay up all night wishing he'd talk to me. And then tomorrow we'd find my father in Bucharest, and he'd have some sort of explanation for all of this—one that was likely half as dangerous as I worried it could be—so Huck was probably right when he said cracking the journal's code was a fool's errand.

And I'd be an even bigger fool to try to suss out what had gone wrong after Black Sunday last year. Tomorrow I'd go back to New York with Father while Huck would return to Belfast. Who knows when I'd see him again.

Or even *if* I would.

A waste of time, all of it.

So why couldn't I let it go?

JOURNAL OF RICHARD FOX
June 20, 1937
Orient Express, somewhere in the Kingdom of Hungary

Rainy day. Should be hitting the Romanian border soon. Today I'm feeling less sentimental and more hungover, so I've put a temporary moratorium on martinis. Practically the picture of restraint, I am.

Sitting across from me in the restaurant car, Jean-Bernard is reading a history book on Transylvania and Wallachia, neighboring regions along the Carpathians. Fascinating history this area has. Everybody and their mother tried to claim those lands. But it all really went to hell in the Middle Ages, when the Carpathians sat between the Kingdom of Hungary and the Ottoman Empire.

And Prince Vlad wasn't interested in political tightrope. He wanted to stand his ground and keep his territory. He would not pay tribute to the sultan. Period.

Here's the thing: Vlad didn't have a big army or much of a coffer. Wallachia had little to trade. The only way he could keep his territory was through sheer tenacity and being a vicious monster. Rage was his weapon, and he was a damn angry man.

His war strategy was scorched earth. When the sultan came to fight him, he burned his own land. Poisoned wells. Dammed up the rivers. Left no animals for the invading armies to hunt. The Turks couldn't eat or drink, and they all got sick because Vlad sent people with the damn bubonic plague into the Turks' camp.

Rothwild thinks this bone ring I'm searching for somehow increased Vlad's rage. At least, that was the whispered gossip in Vlad's time. The bone ring was ensorcelled. Made with black magic. Created by an occultist. Maybe even given to Vlad by the devil himself. Sure: that and half the other so-called cursed medieval objects. I've yet to hold the devil's handiwork. Everything evil I've found was made by human hands.

I DIDN'T SLEEP THAT NIGHT. NOT MUCH ANYWAY.

Father's journal was mostly to blame. But even if I hadn't stayed up, skimming his words while trying (and failing) to guess his cipher's passphrase, I wouldn't have slept much. Extended post-midnight passport checks halted our train on the Balkan peninsula at the borders of both Turkey and, thirty minutes later, crossing into Eastern Europe, Bulgaria.

After the border checks, a dining car was added sometime in the morning, but I was too tired and cranky to roll out of the berth for breakfast, succumbing to that dull laziness brought on by train travel—something that turned Huck into the living dead, as I'd heard not a single snore from him last night. Nor a single word.

Noon came and went before I was motivated to leave our compartment, and that was mostly because my bladder was aching. I had to wait in line to use the public facilities. For the record, there is nothing more humbling than washing bits of yourself over a basin in a public lavatory on a moving train.

On the other hand, the glorious thing about rail travel is that the dining car is never officially closed. They may say it is, but I'd never been refused service. When I strode into our dining car in the early afternoon, Huck shuffling behind me, the main luncheon crowd had cleared out. Only a few stragglers sat at scattered tables, taking tea and reading or gazing out windows decorated with burgundy velvet curtains. There wasn't much to see; we were in Bulgaria now, and under gray skies, the scenery was flat as a pancake and never-ending.

In an hour we'd be debarking for the border at Ruse and taking a ferry across the Danube to Romania, where we'd pick up a simple train—no sleeping compartments—to Bucharest; we'd be in the Romanian capital city before nightfall. Even though I hadn't cracked the cipher in Father's journal, and perhaps because we were so close to our destination, I was feeling somewhat less anxious than I was when we stepped onto the train last night. There was even a copy of *Le Figaro*, a French newspaper, that someone had left on the table, and the *mots croisés* puzzle was still untouched—*c'est magnifique!* I could focus on that instead of having to make small talk with Huck.

A steward rushed down the narrow dining car aisle between tables set formally with china and silver to take our order. I couldn't decide, and hadn't eaten actual hot food since yesterday, so I requested one or five dishes and tried to avoid the steward's judgmental eyes.

"It's easily twenty degrees colder here than it was when we left Istanbul," Huck told me after the steward left our table. Several passengers in the dining car were dressed for chilly weather. Huck, too: over his long sleeves, he'd donned a soft gray cable-knit cardigan with tortoiseshell buttons. It looked nice on him, but I'd never say so in a hundred years. So I distracted myself with removing the crossword puzzle page from the French newspaper and folding into a small, neat rectangle, making sharp creases with the edge of my fingernail.

"Crack Fox's cipher yet?" he asked, oh so slowly rearranging his silverware, as if it were work that required a detailed eye and a surgeon's touch.

Okay, fine. I supposed I couldn't ignore him for the rest of the train ride. I would treat him like any other traveling companion, like he was paid by my father to talk to me.

"Not yet," I said, keeping my eyes on the rolling landscape. Father's journal was currently in my handbag, into which I now stuck my hand to search for a pencil. "But don't worry—I will."

"Naturally. Being pigheaded is one of your best qualities, if memory serves."

"It's called perseverance."

"Aye. That's what Fox calls it when he does it too. Like father, like daughter."

"I wouldn't know. You spend more time with him than I do these days."

"I spend more time getting cursed out by him. Besides, I would have much rather been in Istanbul."

"Is that so?" I said, frustrated to realize that my pencil was still in our compartment.

"You don't think I wouldn't rather be lounging on plush beds, having room service deliver jugs of wine, and scantily clad serving girls to feed me grapes?"

"It's a hotel, for the love of Pete, not Caligula's Palace."

"Shh. Don't spoil my daydream."

No worries there. I was too busy with my own daydream, which featured me as a black-hooded assassin, sneaking through hotels, eliminating ample-bosomed serving girls and poisoning all the grapes. "Do you have a pencil?" I asked in frustration.

"Afraid not." He squinted at me over the table. "Trying to ignore me for that crossword puzzle? You forget—I know you too well, Theodora Fox."

I forgot nothing. That was precisely the problem.

Luckily, I was saved by our steward, who soon rolled out a trolley laden with food, which he deposited on our table. Bottles of mineral water. Perfectly cut sandwich triangles. Blinis topped with caviar and crème fraîche. Some sort of potato terrine and tiny bowls of olives and shelled pistachios, to which I'd become addicted while staying in Turkey. And after lighting a flame beneath a silver spirit kettle, which steamed with freshly brewed tea, the steward wheeled the emptied cart away, leaving Huck and me on our own again.

"Jesus, Mary, and Joseph, I'm famished," Huck murmured, tucking into the finger sandwiches. He inhaled three before I could blink.

"I would have ordered more if I'd known you were practicing for a competitive eating contest."

He smiled. "You know what they say. Empty stomach, empty mind."

"No one says that."

"An uneaten sandwich never spoils."

"That doesn't even make sense."

"Hang on. I've got it now," he said brightly. "Six sandwiches a day keep the doctor away."

"You are still absolutely terrible at proverbs."

"*Pfft.* I'm a proverbial champion. A modern-day Confucius," he said, eyes twinkling as he dipped the end of his sandwich triangle into a cup of tea, pausing for effect before shoving it into his mouth. He loved to dunk. Bread in soup, cookies in milk, sandwiches in perfectly good tea. Sometimes I thought he did it just to annoy me; soggy food made me want to retch.

I flagged down the steward and ordered more sandwiches for Huck to ruin. We both ate heartily—some of us more than others—and after the plates began to empty, our forced conversation turned from our impending stop in Romania to my father and shared bits of what we both knew about Vlad the Impaler, me from books and my mother's stories and him from what little he'd gleaned on the trip to Tokat.

"Fox said Prince Vlad of many names . . . Vlad the third or Dracula or Tepid—"

"Țepeș," I corrected. "Vlad Țepeș. It means 'impaler' in Romanian."

"Huh. Did not know that. Anyway, Fox said he was either a national hero or a mass murderer, depending on who was telling the stories." He casually leaned back in his chair, long arms languid, a lazy king lounging on a throne. "I mean, sure, he skewered a few people on spikes to scare off invaders, but was it wrong if it was for the protection of his country?"

"Forty thousand people," I corrected. "He impaled forty thousand. He invaded Bulgaria"—I tapped the glass, pointing to the moving landscape—"somewhere out there and impaled twenty-three thousand Turkish forces stationed here when the Turkish sultan demanded taxes from him. Then, when the sultan marched north to Wallachia, he was greeted by the gruesome sight of another twenty thousand impaled Turks greeting him along a road for sixty miles."

Huck whistled. "That's a lot of skewered bodies. Imagine the stench."

"And the work. Impaling someone can't be easy. And supposedly Vlad preferred to do so while they were still alive. They'd die slowly for a day or two in utter agony."

"You'd have to really hate someone to go to all that trouble."

"Oh, he hated, all right. He hated the Turks. And his own half brother, Radu. Really, anyone who challenged his power. His own people, even."

"What you're saying is that Vlad was no candidate for the Noble Peace Prize."

"No*bel*. Not noble."

One side of his mouth curled like paper in flame. "I thought it was given to noble people."

"Guess they won't be giving it to you, then, huh?"

"Oof!" he said, clutching his chest. "One point awarded to Miss Theodora Fox."

I smiled to myself. Maybe this wasn't so bad after all. If I didn't think too hard about Black Sunday or why he hadn't written me back all these months, or how he'd turned me into an empty shell of a person with a giant Liberty Bell–size crack in my heart . . . Well, then, I supposed I could pretend none of it ever happened. We were simply friends, like we used to be when we were children. If he could ignore the elephant in the room, so could I. After all, we were always at our best when we were competing. This was just another sledding race down the hill in our backyard after Christmas dinner, or sneaking into Father's office to see how many priceless antiquities and medieval regalia we could rearrange before the housekeeper found us.

I tucked a loose strand of hair behind my ear, adjusted my black beret, and crossed my arms on the edge of the table. "Say, you know those photographs of Mr. Rothwild's bone ring that were stuck in Father's journal?"

"Sure. What about them?"

"I studied them last night when I was trying to crack Father's cipher. And I kept looking at his next-to-last journal entry, about how he found a 'gruesome' way to authenticate the real ring. Did he tell you what that was?"

Huck shook his head. "He kept most of the details to himself."

Not surprising. "Well, both the photographs and that 'gruesome' comment led me to wonder why Mr. Rothwild hired Father in the first place."

"Because Rothwild thinks his ring is fake."

"Right. And that's when I remembered the woodcut depiction of the ring in *Batterman's Field Guide to Legendary Objects.*"

"Your evil mythological object catalog."

"They're not all evil or mythological. They are—" I shook my head. "Never mind. I'm just saying that I pulled out my *Batterman's* last night to look at the woodcut. The illustration is crude, so it's hard to tell, but there seems to be a symbol on the top of that ring—a dragon with its tail wrapped around its neck, forming a circle. Almost like an ouroboros."

"A what-o-whatus?"

"A serpent eating its tail. I think it symbolizes eternal life, or cyclical time. Regardless, the bone ring in Father's photographs—Mr. Rothwild's ring—didn't have a dragon on top. It was just a single band with some strange carvings. Don't you think that's strange? That Rothwild's ring doesn't at all look like the one in the woodcut?"

"Maybe the person who did the woodcut took a lot of artistic license. I wouldn't believe everything in that book of yours."

He waved a dismissive hand through the air, and I had the sudden urge to pick up my fork and stab that hand, but became distracted when something tickled my foot. I lifted the tablecloth to peer underneath and was startled to find a large husky-like dog with fur the color of freshly fallen snow and pointed ears, straining against a leash.

My first thought: why was there a dog in the restaurant car?

My second thought, when my gaze traveled up the leash to the hand that held it: this wasn't the first time I'd seen this dog's owner.

The dark-and-brooding Heathcliff from the hotel lobby back in Istanbul. Before I found Huck in my room, the bearded man in the long black coat who handed me the banknote . . .

"Please forgive my Lupu," he said in a deep, rich Eastern European accent. "She is suspicious of strangers."

"I've seen you before," I said.

"Miss Fox, isn't it?" he said, and then he canted his head apologetically. "I don't mean to be rude. Please forgive me. I heard the concierge talking to you in the Pera Palace lobby when I . . ." He mimicked handing me money. "You remember."

Oh, I remembered, all right. Why was this man here? Was it a coincidence? Any other time, I might have thought so, but after what had transpired since I'd last seen him? No. Something was very, very wrong about his being here.

"I'm afraid you have me at a disadvantage," I said, schooling my features to appear bland while my heart thudded hard and fast beneath the cotton of my striped shirt. "You know my name, but I don't know yours."

"I am Mr. Sarkany," he said. "Small world, yes? I was in Turkey on business."

"With your dog?" I said, glancing at the animal.

He made a wry noise that wasn't quite a laugh. "I take her everywhere. She makes quite the impression, no?"

His big white dog sniffed my hand, which I immediately jerked away, and for the first time I realized that the hound was missing an eye. It had been sewn up at one time or another, I supposed, because there was only fur there now and nothing but the indication of an old scar.

"Do not worry," Mr. Sarkany said, his voice edged with dark humor as he reached down to scratch the dog behind the ear, where I noticed small, red designs had been stitched into the dog's collar. No, not designs: symbols. Strange ones that I couldn't identify, not without getting closer to the animal—something I certainly wasn't going to do. "She only bites when provoked or challenged. Lupu's mother was a Carpathian wolf. Give her a target's scent, and she'll run through hell itself to chase down her prey."

Wolf. Target. Prey. Nothing menacing about that. No, sir.

I flicked a look toward Huck. His face was positively frozen. It suddenly struck me why. . . .

I thought I saw a wolf following me.

A primitive part of my brain wanted to either bolt out of my chair or call someone for help. But another part of me, a part that was trying to manage the feeling of petrification that had taken hold of both my limbs and thoughts, told me to pretend that everything was normal. Just until it was safe to excuse myself. I didn't know if that was the right thing to do, but it was the *only* thing I could do.

"I assume that since you are on this train, your business in Turkey has also concluded," Mr. Sarkany noted, sparing a glance at Huck, who was sitting so straight and rigid in his chair, he looked as if Vlad Dracula himself had impaled him. "And I see you've picked up a traveling companion. Is this your protector?"

"Perhaps I am," Huck said in a voice that was as dry and flat as a burned field. Under the table, the toe of Huck's boot urgently prodded my Mary Janes. "I need to talk to you," he murmured as his serious gaze connected with mine. Then he added, "In private."

"Yes . . . ," I agreed, glancing from him to Mr. Sarkany to the wolf dog.

"Now," Huck said, voice stony and insistent. He pushed himself up from his seat and held his hand out to me, encouraging me to follow. Insisting.

The wolf dog let out a single bark—one that was so loud, I flinched. My heart pounded erratically inside my chest, as if it were a malfunctioning machine.

Mr. Sarkany said something low and indecipherable to the hound, and it quieted, retreating behind his master's legs. "I'm afraid Lupu sees you as a threat, boy," the man told Huck. "Why do you think that is?"

"Not sure, brother," Huck said in a low voice, giving the man a dark look. "Perhaps she knows I don't much like big dogs."

The man's mouth twisted. He ignored Huck and turned his attention back to me. "Forgive my rudeness, but I overheard some of your conversation just now. Vlad Țepeș. Quite a dark and complicated subject for two young travelers."

My blood ran cold. Huck and I shared a look, both of us alarmed.

At that moment, a crash diverted Mr. Sarkany's attention to the front of the restaurant car, where a solitary diner sat near the entrance to the kitchen and a server was apologizing for dropping a tray of dishes.

Seizing my chance, I grabbed my handbag and attempted to slip past the man and his dog. "If you could excuse us," I mumbled, but the aisle was narrow, and Mr. Sarkany made no effort to let me pass. For a confusing moment it felt as if he were blocking me. He said something I couldn't understand under his breath. It sounded like a command. Panicking, I twisted my body, held up my arms as armor, and forcefully pushed my way through.

"Pardon me, sir!" I said sharply, giving him the nastiest look I could muster.

"My apologies." The man acted as if nothing in the world were wrong. He only bowed his head briefly and added, "We will have plenty of time later to chat over the river crossing. We're all stuck together, aren't we?"

Then the man and his strange hound made their way down the aisle to the front of the dining car. Huck didn't wait to see him reach it. He just grabbed my hand and pulled me in the opposite direction. His legs were long, and I struggled to keep up, but we exited the car—the whoosh of wind and wheels clacking loudly as we slid open the connecting doors to pass through—and entered the connecting sleeper.

Green scenery flew past the Pullman's windows as Huck raced ahead to open our compartment. He practically shoved me inside and closed the door behind us, falling back against it when it was latched. For the first time since we'd boarded, the tiny space felt safe and welcoming, not prisonlike.

"Oh Christ," Huck moaned, his chest rising and falling with labored breath. "Sarkany? What kind of name is Sarkany? You saw that man in the hotel lobby in Istanbul?"

"He handed me a banknote," I said, patting my pockets. "He said I dropped it. Where did I put it?" Had I left it in the hotel back in Istanbul, or perhaps I put in my handbag . . . ?

"Are you listening to me?" Huck said, grabbing my shoulders to get my attention. "He's one of the men who were trailing me when I was hiring a car in Tokat—the scary one who stuck to the shadows."

"Are you certain?" I asked, my brain trying its best to rationalize something that was clearly not rational. "You said yourself that you didn't get a good look at him, right?"

"Banshee," he said, lowering his head to pin me with a somber look. "The bloody blackguard has a wolf."

Yes, there was that. . . .

"He just happened to 'overhear' our conversation about Vlad Dracula?" Huck said, using aggressive air quotes to enunciate. "*And* did you not hear what he said about his beast being a tracker? He's been following me—this is one of the people your father warned about in the letter."

My gut had known something was wrong when the man handed me that banknote. *Always listen to gut feelings*. My mother would be disappointed that I'd ignored my instincts.

"Okay, okay. Let's think about this," I said, pacing across the small space of our compartment. I felt a little sick. "If he trailed you from Tokat, does that mean that the intruders who broke into my room are with him? He's after the ring too? Or Father's journal? And why? Who are these people?"

"It's all connected somehow," Huck said. "I don't know how or why. I just know that your Mr. Sarkany and his bloody Carpathian wolf dog are not our friends. And if anything happens to you, your father is going to chop me into a hundred pieces and scatter them to the four winds. I had one duty, banshee. One single duty to get back into Fox's good graces. And now I've screwed it all up by leading this man right to you, and we're stuck here—don't you see how serious that is? We're in a rolling prison, stuck here with someone who may be dangerous. We're worse off here than if we'd stayed in Istanbul."

"All right, all right. Let me think."

"Why is this happening? I'm such a thick *eejit*," he mumbled, squeezing his eyes shut.

"If anyone's to blame, it's Father. Or me even—I saw the man in the lobby. I should have told you back in Istanbul. I just, I mean, with everything that happened . . . I forgot, I guess. But it's too late to worry about that now. We just need to stay calm and figure out what we can do." I pressed a palm against my stomach to steady my nerves. "We can't go back out there."

"Absolutely not," Huck agreed. "What if he plans to take the journal by force? Likely he could. That beast of his looks as if got in a fight with a lion and won. How did they even allow it on the train?"

"No idea."

"You still have the journal, right?"

I opened my handbag to check. "Still here."

He exhaled heavily, relieved.

A knock sounded on the adjoining compartment door, causing us both to jump. But it was only the attendant. His muffled voice carried through the wall, informing our neighbor that the train was approaching the Danube River crossing. Once we stopped, we'd have to get on the ferry and wait for all the train's luggage to be transferred. I glanced out our compartment's small window to confirm, and an old brick building came into view. And then another. The train would be stopping any minute now.

"How big is the steamboat they use for the crossing?" I asked Huck. "Are we going to be forced to sit near Mr. Sarkany? Is he going to follow us all the way into Bucharest? Maybe he wants to hurt Father."

"What if this man is the reason Fox left me instead of continuing on to Istanbul? What if he was trying to draw this Sarkany away from us?"

If so, it was a terrible failure of a plan. "I don't like this."

"You think I do?" Huck said.

I glanced around the room, frantic. I had no idea what to do. And then . . .

And then I did. "We need to escape the train," I said.

"You're damn right we do."

"No," I said. "I mean make a run for it. When it stops, we need to sneak out and leave. Run. Walk. Whatever. We take our chances out there," I said, gesturing to the rolling landscape. "Father told you to keep these people away, yes?"

"You know he did," Huck said miserably.

"Well, I don't know about you, but I damn sure don't want to lead enemies straight to Father once we get to Bucharest. Because they are our enemies. That much I know. Better to ditch the man and his white wolf now."

"You're *actually* suggesting that we run away from the train? With no plan? No destination? Just run off into the fields? This isn't the Pera Palace Hotel, banshee. That's wilderness out there."

"And a town—Ruse. Sure, it may be small, but we're stopping at the Danube, a massive river. People have used it as a trade route for centuries. There must be more than one way across. Look out the window—we're heading into civilization."

"A few lonely brick buildings are not what I'd call civilization, banshee."

"We'll find a way to the Romanian side," I assured him. "Then we'll catch a bus or another train—something. It will be an adventure."

He snorted a laugh. "Is that we're calling it?"

"Look," I said, frustrated. "All I know is that we'd be sitting ducks if we stayed here with that horrible man, and if we're going to lose him, we need to do it before we get to customs, while everyone is getting off the train. Agreed?"

To my surprise and great relief, Huck didn't need further convincing. He merely looked me in the eye, nodded firmly, and said, "Pack your things. Only what you can carry." He turned his back to me and dragged both his canvas rucksack and my overnight satchel down from the luggage rack. "Here," he said, tossing mine onto the bottom berth.

He opened the cabinet that hid our small sink and quickly dumped all the toiletries into his rucksack while I gathered necessities. A change of clothes. My *Batterman's Field Guide*. I shoved everything into my satchel. Atop all this, I crammed my handbag and passport—and all the crumpled notes I'd made trying to crack Father's code.

A loud noise rumbled from somewhere inside the train.

Then I felt it.

The train slowed considerably. My balance shifted, and a china cup on the foldout table near the berths clinked madly. Brakes squealed as we rolled up to a small, rural train platform. I couldn't read the Cyrillic script on the Bulgarian sign, but a few English words appeared:

RUSE BORDER CHECKPOINT

That was our cue to disappear. It was now or never.

High on adrenaline, I slung the strap of my camera case around my neck as Huck slipped into his long charcoal-colored coat. He hoisted his rucksack's straps over his shoulders to carry it on his back as a whistle blew, alerting the staff to open the doors. "We need to go, banshee. Try not to look guilty or conspicuous."

Holy night, we were actually abandoning the train!

How terrifying. And exciting.

With my satchel in hand and my coat on my arm, I stepped

into the corridor with Huck. We headed left, down the windowed corridor, past open compartments and passengers gathering their passports, skirting around attendants hauling luggage.

I took one last look behind us while the conductor unlatched the outer door. No sign of Mr. Sarkany or his white dog.

Yet as we descended the steps to the platform, I couldn't help but think about the extraordinary effort this man had taken to follow Huck all the way across Turkey—and now into continental Europe. Surely not for a ring with mere historical value. Why not just contact my father and offer a larger sum of money or try to strike some sort of bargain? Father was well known in Europe. The medieval collector's market was small and elite. Auction houses, estate agents, collectors, art appraisers . . . most of them knew my father's name and reputation. So why the goons, threats, and stalking?

This convinced me that the ring was more than a piece of history—that my *Batterman's Field Guide* was right and Vlad's war ring was truly bewitched or cursed. An actual, real-live magic ring! Could that be possible? I believed it could, and a little thrill went through me just thinking about it.

A little worry too . . .

Father was in more danger than I'd originally assumed.

We needed to catch up to him, and fast.

NO ONE WAS ATTENDING THE CUSTOMS WINDOW on the sleepy train platform. Two Bulgarian guards were smoking cigarettes and the customs worker was chatting with our engineer. Beyond the platform, a docked steamboat was visible through a break in the trees, waiting to ferry passengers across the Danube. We headed in the opposite direction.

It was simple enough to slip around a small outbuilding, which provided temporary cover while we picked our way over two additional sets of train tracks. However, to stay out of sight we were forced to skirt a small ravine. This seemed doable at first, considering that I was in a delirious state fueled by exhilaration, fear, and adrenaline. Half an hour later I realized several disappointing things: (a) the "small" ravine was several miles long; (b) the small Bulgarian town of Ruse was in the other direction; (c) there was nothing but damp woodland beyond the tracks; (d) the Danube was nowhere to be seen.

Oh, and to add insult to injury, my Mary Janes were positively ruined. I briefly considered digging a pair of boots out of my satchel, but there was no sense in muddying them, too.

"Um, Huck?"

A grunt was his reply.

"Do you know where we're going?" I asked.

"Away from the train."

Right. Excellent. "And do you happen to know where we are now?"

"I do not."

"All right, yes. I see."

"We should keep walking," he said. "We'll find something soon."

From one to ten, I'd rate my confidence in that happening a weak four. Possibly a three.

All I could tell about our current location was that we were most definitely in the Bulgarian countryside, which was all flat fields and jagged telephone lines. I wondered if this was some of the land that everyone's favorite impaler, Vlad, ruined during his Burn It All Down defensive military march. Certainly *seemed* like a good place for a haunting, which temporarily lifted my spirits and gave me something to focus on while we trekked.

Alas, I saw nothing that even hinted of the paranormal. There was, however, quite a bit of mud and more than a little dying, overgrown grass. It would be a laughable stretch to label this area picturesque—more like woeful—and it became downright depressing when we finally reached a road of sorts, a lane for horses. It wasn't long before we spotted two mares pulling a farmer's cart.

Huck suggested we wave the farmer down to ask for a ride.

"In the back of a wooden cart hauling manure?" I said, covering my mouth and nose.

He shifted his head to see it better. "You think that's what it is?"

"I don't think it, Huck. I *smell* it."

Huck made a face as the wind wafted it in his direction. "Oh good *God*—now I do too."

"Maybe we should wait for a car or a bus . . . something that doesn't involve dung?"

"Dung-free would be good," Huck agreed.

After a quarter hour passed, we spotted another cart in the near distance, this time pulled by a single horse, driven by a man in a dark hat. The cart itself was not only dung-free but laden with crates of clinking bottles.

"Smells like flowers," Huck said as we increased our pace and headed toward him.

It did. Roses. Perfume? Rose oil? Whichever, it was miles better than manure. "Maybe he's a trader."

One who took a suspicious look in our direction, guided his cart to a crossroad, and cracked a whip on his horse. We ran to try to catch him, waving frantically, but were only able to watch in disappointment as his clinking cart disappeared over a hill.

"Rose Valley," I said, breathless. "In the Balkan Mountains. Bulgaria is famous for its roses there."

"Is it?" Huck asked, incredulous.

"Bet you anything that man came from Rose Valley and is taking rose oil to market." And where there was a market, there was civilization. Maybe even other carts that would give us a ride. Or single horses. Cars? Cars would be nice! "We should follow him."

Yet, by the way the trader sped away from us—as if we were demons, freshly ascended from the netherworld—I privately wondered if finding *any* sort of ride might be a problem. We didn't speak Bulgarian. We were stranded in the middle of nowhere. And I had only a single Turkish lira to exchange for services.

Maybe we should have tried to flag down the dung cart, after all.

Best not think of it now. As Huck said, something would work out. It always did.

We followed the distant sound of the trader's clinking cart until we could hear it no longer. Then we rambled blindly in its direction. And rambled. And rambled. The initial excitement of escape had worn off, and I was no longer watching over my shoulder, expecting Mr. Sarkany's white dog to come barreling across the dreary landscape. Even hunting for the ghosts of Vlad's victims was getting dull.

An hour or more after we'd left the train, we gave up on ever finding the trader again. Or a market. Maybe not even civilization. Dispirited, I finally gave up the chase and set down my satchel in patch of non-muddy grass, forcing Huck to stop with me. "Do you have a compass?"

"No. Why?" he said.

"Because if we could figure out which direction we're going, maybe we could find the Danube. It runs across the southern border of Romania and is one of the longest waterways in Europe. How could we have lost an entire river?"

"Either we're extremely talented or complete morons," he said, stripping off his flat cap and surveying the landscape through squinting eyes. "Not sure which."

"Can you tell which way we're going from the sun's position?"

"What sun? All I see are clouds and gray sky. I can tell by my watch that we've got little more than an hour before sundown."

I whimpered. I *really* did not want to be stuck out here after dark.

"Hey, running from the train was your idea. I seem to recall you saying this would be an adventure."

"This isn't an adventure. It's a tribulation."

“Same difference.”

“Is it, now? You’re the expert, I suppose. And what exciting adventures have you been on for the last year and half in Belfast, pray tell?”

“I’ve been working at an airfield, if you really must know.”

“Doing what? Smuggling hooch over the border?”

He looked away and stared into the distance. “I’ve been doing engine maintenance.”

“Fixing engines and whatnot?”

“And whatnot.”

“What about flying?”

“I’m grounded,” he said. “They don’t let me fly.”

“Not ever?”

“Not ever,” he confirmed. “Administrator in the licensing office knows my family is Catholic, and he doesn’t like Catholics, see, so every time I go in to apply, he finds a new way to give me the run-around with the paperwork. And my boss at the airfield won’t let me fly with an American license, so . . . I’m grounded.”

This made me sad. Back when we were all still together, Father gave Huck a little yellow biplane named Trixie for his sixteenth birthday, along with flying lessons over the wide field near our house in the Hudson Valley. Huck *loved* Trixie. He used to take it up do aerobatics. Spins and stall turns . . . silly tricks to show off, until Father shouted at him over the radio, threatening to set fire to the yellow biplane.

Now it sat in a shed at the back of our property.

“You should be flying,” I said. “You’re a good pilot. You used to love it.”

“Know that, don’t I?”

“You must miss it.”

"Of course I do. You don't have something be a part of your life every day and then not miss it when it's taken away from you."

My heart squeezed. I struggled to keep my emotions in check as I stared at the back of his long wool coat. "No, you do not."

He gave me a quick glance over his shoulder. "Fox said you'd been volunteering at Vassar's collegiate library across the river."

"That was only during the summer. They received an extensive donation from a private book collection, and I was helping catalog it."

"And you got fired?"

He said this with a little amusement behind the lilt in his voice, and that made me think he and Father had been having a laugh about it when they were off on their little males-only jaunt in Tokat.

"I didn't get fired," I said as my cheeks heated. It was only that I'd gotten into a very small fight with another volunteer who didn't know Latin and was filing everything wrong. But the thing about that particular library is that your voice really carries, and maybe I used a few choice and mildly profane words that caused one of the less-sturdy librarians to have a fit . . . which in turn caused *me* to be politely but firmly dismissed. But I wasn't getting paid anyway, so technically you can't be fired.

"Not what I heard," he said as though he was trying to provoke me.

"Well, you heard wrong. It wasn't a real job."

"Was it not?"

"It was only temporary," I told Huck as frustration and embarrassment mounted. "Much like everything else in my life."

His shoulders tensed beneath the wool of his peacoat. He glanced over his shoulder but didn't look me in the eye. "What's that supposed to mean?"

"It means never count on people to be there when you need them. They only disappoint you."

Huck swung around. "What are you trying to say, Theo?"

Old anger and hurt welled up to the surface as if they'd been slinking in the dark corners of my broken heart, head down, tail swishing back and forth, waiting for a chance to pounce.

"You know damn well what I'm trying to say. You *left*, Huck. I woke up the next morning and you were gone. You didn't even say goodbye. You just dropped off the face of the planet!"

"I didn't leave by my own accord, banshee. I was thrown out of the damn house like a bum."

I stilled, caught between the old hurt I'd been eagerly unearthing and a shiny new doubt that stood in its way.

Huck had been thrown out of the house?

That was not what Father told me.

I blinked at Huck. "Father said . . . He told me you made the choice to go and live with your aunt. That *you* said it would be better for everyone."

"That's a bald-faced lie," Huck rumbled. His dark, bushy brows knitted together into a dark slash. "He gave me an ultimatum. He said if I didn't go back to Belfast and 'cool off,' I'd never see either one of you again."

My chest tightened. "What?"

"You know what he always says—family first. Well, according to him, I broke that rule. I violated his trust, committed a crime against God himself, and sullied his perfect angel of a daughter."

There was so much wrong with that, I didn't know where to start. "You didn't . . . sully me." Not any more than I'd sullied him. If anything, it was a mutual sullying.

"Apparently he saw enough to pass judgment," Huck mumbled.

My face heated even now. I remembered it all too well, what happened last year. My birthday. The impromptu party at Foxwood with some friends while Father was away in New York City. The glass of champagne. The fistfight between Huck and a boy who liked me. The broken china. Father's butler throwing everyone out. Huck sneaking into my room when it was all over, apologetic for ruining the party, his left eye red and swollen, already showing signs of a purplish bruise.

The champagne still swirling inside my head . . .

The next thing I knew, we were all over each other. His hands, my hands. His mouth, my mouth. Other parts of us . . . For the briefest of moments it was glorious. The world slipped away, and I didn't realize we were making so much noise. And that's when Father burst in.

After a rage-filled chaotic moment when Father was chasing Huck out of my room, threatening to kill him, I tried to confront him—which wasn't easy, because Father and I didn't talk about anything that made him uncomfortable.

And apparently figuring out that I had forbidden feelings for Huck was the absolute worst mistake I'd ever made. I went down to Father's study that night to apologize—even though I had nothing to apologize for. Even though he'd never in his life, not once, said the words "I'm sorry" to me for things he'd done—and he'd done a *lot*, believe me. Despite all this, I was humble and ready to do penance, and . . .

He gave me a look I'd never forget as long as I lived. It was something between horror, shame, and disappointment. I'd failed him. I was no longer his little girl. I was a shameful floozy.

And I thought I couldn't hate him more for making me feel that way. But now here I was, realizing that I had so much more bitterness to give.

But it wasn't all for Father.

"You just gave in to him without a fight?" I said.

One dark brow lifted. "What?"

"With Father. You didn't even try?"

"Of course I tried!" he said, throwing his arms into the air. "I begged and pleaded. I told him I was sorry, that I'd shovel horse shite and chop firewood. That I'd never even so much as look you in the eye again, and that it was all a huge, drunken mistake, but he didn't listen."

I didn't think it was possible for my chest to feel any tighter. My ribs were going to crack. "Well, I'm sorry that I was such a huge, drunken mistake!"

"I didn't mean it like—" He shook his head. "It doesn't matter now, because it *was* a mistake, Theo. Maybe not to you, because you're sitting pretty in your gilded tower, still the apple of Fox's eye. While me? I had to move to a strange country that I didn't even remember, because the last time I was there I was still in diapers. I didn't know any of my family there. I was a stranger in a strange land."

"But your mother's sister, your aunt—"

"Yes, I've been living with my aunt. I work nearly every day and, apparently, I'm a spoiled cur who's lived in a fancy house too long and should be reminded of his place. Not to mention that I give most of my earnings to her, because she has a bad leg and can't put food on the table—and hates me because I look like my mam!"

Oh. I hadn't realized . . . Father had made it sound like Huck had happily returned to the bosom of his Irish family. His real family, because we were only temporary. Silly me for thinking otherwise.

Father lied about all of it? Why?

"I'm barely living," Huck said. "I can't fly. I'm stuck in Belfast. And I lost everything—my life, my country, my family. Do you know how that feels?"

"I lost my mother!" I said angrily.

"So. Did. I," he said, thumping his chest with each word. "Right in front of my face. And my da. Every time I look in the mirror, I'm reminded, aren't I?"

As if magnetized, my eyes were drawn to the scar on his cheek, and I felt a prickle of shame for looking.

"You don't know what it's like to lose *everything*," he said. "You don't know what it's like to feel as if you're living on the edge of a knife, forever in debt to someone for pulling you out of the gutter. And how could you? You were born into privilege. No matter what trouble you get yourself into, you're still Empress Theodora in Fox's eyes, and I'm just a stray that he took in from the cold."

"You don't know what you're talking about!"

"Don't I? I know you fall into shite and come out smelling of roses and that you never think of consequences because you've never had to. Like now. We're lost in a foreign country at nightfall and everything's going wrong, but hey ho, it's an *adventure*," he said sarcastically.

That stung. Anger flared, hot and all-consuming, and I seriously considered slugging him in the stomach. "You're a jackass!"

"Maybe I am. But I'm a jackass who's responsible for getting you safely to your father, so I guess you're stuck with me right now, aren't you?"

"He always had your loyalty, didn't he?"

It was something my father demanded from everyone in his

purview. We didn't have to like each other, but we'd shed blood for each other. All for one and one for all. Even the Foxwood staff was devoted to the Fox cause.

I made a scornful noise. "Richard Damn Fox, god among men."

"He's the closest thing I have to a father anymore!" Huck shouted.

"Yeah, well, he's the farthest thing from a parent to me right now, so you two can have each other."

I snatched up my luggage and lengthened my strides across the rocky Bulgarian ground, leaving Huck several steps behind as I tried to cool down. He easily caught up to me. "Where are you going?"

"To find a boat. I'm going to Bucharest if it takes me all night. Then I'm going to strangle my father and go back home to New York. I don't care about this stupid Vlad Dracula ring anymore," I said, alarmed to feel angry tears brimming. "I was never intended to know about it anyway, and I'm just a mistake to you anyhow, so what do you care?"

"Banshee—"

"Don't call me that," I said, shoving him sideways. "Screw you, Huxley Gallagher. I wish I'd never seen your stupid face again."

After a loud, anguished bellow that echoed around the field, he didn't say another word to me, nor I to him. I could hear him marching behind me. For ten minutes. Twenty. Thirty. I wanted to turn around and confront him, but I was terrified I'd break down and sob my eyes out, and as my thickheaded father always said, Foxes don't cry.

Ugh. Why did Huck always get under my skin like this? No one hurt me like he did. No one! All the desperate, wounded feelings I'd experienced last year after Black Sunday came back at me like an ill wind, and my world fell apart all over again. Because it was just as I feared. That night meant nothing to him. A mistake. He was more concerned with losing Father's love than mine. And from the sounds of it, he blamed me for ruining his life.

Did I?

Was it my fault?

Were all the moments leading up to that night just in my mind? My heart used to race so fast when he stepped into the room. I lay awake in bed thinking about him, feeling as if butterflies danced on my skin when I pictured his face. His unruly curls. His smiling eyes.

Maybe what I felt for him was all one-sided. A mirage.

A drunken mistake.

After an hour or more passed, my brain grew tired of thinking and my heart was sick of hurting. I forced myself to push it all into the background and instead focused on basic survival worries. Because boy oh boy did I have them. My feet ached, and my shoes were caked with mud. My entire face was turning into an iceberg. We were still lost. What if we couldn't find a way across the river? Or even the river! Scanning the desolate grassland, I wasn't sure if we could find a house with indoor plumbing.

The sun began falling after another hour passed. We still weren't speaking. Huck just followed me in silence while we ran into little of anything resembling civilization. An abandoned farm. The occasional country home, with rounded roofs and clothes hanging out to dry, and several wide-faced peasants who retreated behind doors when I tried to beckon for assistance. But just when I was ready to wave a white flag and collapse into a muddy trench, I spotted something encouraging in the distance.

Just ahead, inside a dark forest, was a golden, flickering light. Enough light that I could see it, and we were easily a mile away.

"What's that?" Huck asked over my shoulder. The first words he'd spoken in a couple of hours. He sounded exhausted. And crabby.

"It's people," I said in a cool, even tone that I instinctually adopted after all our fights. And there had been *many* over the years. "Want to make a bet that the Danube is on the other side of that forest?"

He grunted. "Looks like a fire. A camp, maybe."

"People building a fire that close to the river are bound to either want to cross or know how it might be done."

"Or they're bandits who want to rob the coats off our backs," he mumbled.

"This isn't eighteenth-century France," I said. "Bandits are extinct."

"Oh, you'll believe in magic and myth, but you won't believe in bandits?"

"I believe in thieves, but I don't think they light campfires to lure unwary travelers. Anyway, if my guess is right, and if the Danube is on the other side of this wooded area, then once we find a way across, we'll be in Romania—and only a few hours' walk to Bucharest."

"Or we'll be stripped of our belongings and drowned in the river."

"Either way, it's better than trudging through mud."

Huck made a soft snorting sound. "You may be right about that."

The wind was getting colder and night was upon us, so we agreed to a compromise: to investigate the light in the forest from a safe distance. A good plan, I thought. And it was a relief to realize that even though things were still not okay between us, we could at least be civil.

We began trekking in the fire's direction and soon picked out a path made of wheel ruts leading straight to the light. Halfway there, we began to hear noise. A lot of it. Singing, cheering. Laughter.

"Is it a fair?" I asked. "A festival of some sort?"

"In the middle of Nowhere, Bulgaria?"

It did seem far-fetched. We concentrated on listening to all the sounds. In fact, we listened so intently that we failed to hear the approaching cart until it was too late.

JOURNAL OF RICHARD FOX
June 22, 1937
National Archives, București, Kingdom of România

Wasted a perfectly sunny day stuck inside the archives building, looking through proclamations, letters, maps, and anything else I could find relating to Vlad III and his bone ring. Only two things I reviewed are worth mentioning.

The first is a document related to the sale of a piece of Wallachian land. The steward here tells me it is the earliest written document that mentions Bucharest. Vlad wrote it in 1459 and signed it with a curse—basically, anyone who doesn't honor this agreement will be cursed by God and die a horrible death. For the people of Wallachia, who believed in spells, witchcraft, and curses, I'm certain this was an effective way to make sure both parties stuck to the deal.

The second document was only a fragment of a parchment letter, written in 1475 by a Catholic bishop to a Wallachian priest, presumably one who was ministering over Vlad's wedding to his wife, Jusztina Szilágyi. It was a warning of sorts, a for-your-eyes-only piece of information. The bishop claimed that Vlad had a previous wife, the illegitimate daughter of John Hunyadi, a famous military leader and prince of Transylvania, whose son would take the throne of the Kingdom of Hungary.

This isn't the first time I've come across Vlad's first wife, but that's neither here nor there. The important thing I learned today is that this woman was reputed to dabble in astrology and the occult. She died under scandalous circumstances, but exactly how we'll never know, because the letter was ripped in half, and only the top of it survived.

However, this reminded me that some of the symbols on the bone ring look remarkably similar to grimoires of that time period (*Hygromancy of Solomon*, etc.), which provided demonic seals, magical spells, and esoteric methods for conjuring both angels and devils.

Makes me more curious about exactly when (and why) the ring was made. . . .

HUCK PULLED ME OUT OF THE CART'S PATH JUST in time. The driver jerked on the reins, and his horse whinnied before coming to an abrupt halt. A single lantern swung at the front of his wagon, illuminating a young man's surprised face. He shouted something in a language weighted with Slavic tones—Bulgarian.

When we didn't respond, he switched to a Romance language, one I knew intimately. My mother's tongue: Romanian. "Are you lost?" he asked, holding his horse steady.

"Yes! We are very lost and very cold," I answered in Romanian, utterly relieved to be conversing with someone who spoke it. Relieved to be speaking to anyone at all!

The cart driver was perhaps a few years older than us, with a long, clean-shaven face. Dark, wavy hair spilled out of a floppy felt hat, and under a road-dusted coat, he wore a loose-sleeved tunic, a vest, and dark trousers.

"You are Romanian?" he asked.

"My mother was. She died seven years ago."

He placed a hand over his heart. "I am sorry. Is that why you are here? You are on your way to visit family in Romania?"

"Yes. We're here to . . . visit family in Bucharest." Well, it was partly true, wasn't it? "We're American," I said, gesturing toward Huck. "Irish American."

A handsome smile lifted the man's face. "Oh, I speak English!" he said eagerly. "I speak it very good. My name is Valentin Krastev."

"What a relief it is to run into you—well met, brother," Huck said, smiling back at him. "I'm Huck and this is Theo. We're lost travelers." He then quickly offered Valentin a bare-bones account of how we'd gotten here: We wandered away from the Orient Express and found ourselves lost, and then night fell.

"One of my fellow travelers saw you earlier and wondered why you were out here, trying to wave him down. We've been robbed before, so he's a little wary of strangers."

The rose oil cart. "I suppose we look a bit of a mess," I confessed. "We've been walking since this afternoon. But we're not bandits."

"We are very anti-bandit," Huck assured him.

He gave us a soft smile. "My wife told me to look for you, in case you needed help."

"We do. Can you tell us if the Danube River is close by?" I asked Valentin. "We need to find passage across. We're headed to Bucharest."

"Ah, *București*. Like you, Romania is my mother's birthplace, and I travel there several times a year," Valentin said. "The river is just beyond this forest, but you will not cross tonight. No boats. Not until morning."

My heart sank.

"Do not worry. You can stay with us tonight," Valentin said generously, gesturing toward the campfire in the distance. "I'm traveling with several traders and merchants. We're taking goods into Romania tomorrow—our last trip before winter—and have made a camp for the night."

"In the woods?" I said, skeptical.

"It's very safe," he promised me, then scratched his neck and added, "Usually."

"What about a hotel?" I asked. "You could maybe . . . take us to a telephone or a hotel?"

Valentin laughed, but not unkindly. "Miles and miles away. We are in the countryside. There are no hotels here. I just rode for two hours to fetch bread from a farmer, and he doesn't own a telephone."

Huck's eyes flicked to mine, questioning.

I hesitated. This was ridiculous, wasn't it? Heading off into the woods with a complete stranger?

"My wife would be angry with me if I left you alone out here. There is safety in numbers, and we have food, fire, and a place to lie down, yes?"

I thought of my mother and wondered what she'd do in this situation. She always said to trust my intuition. And my intuition thought Valentin had an honest face. Besides, it was cold and muddy, and what else were we going to do?

I nodded. "Okay. Thank you."

"Good! Come with me." Valentin patted the wagon behind him, which was half filled with crates of supplies and what smelled like fresh bread.

Huck seemed relieved. He took my satchel and chucked it onto the back of the wagon along with his pack. "You know what they say. Beggars can't be chosen."

I ignored his offered hand and hoisted myself onto the back of the cart. "That sounds about right."

Valentin guided his horse forward toward the camp in the woods. The ride was slowgoing and bumpy, and halfway there I considered suggesting that we get out and walk to spare his poor nag the disservice of having to haul all of us. But the chatter ahead was getting louder, and the night darker, and it wasn't long before our destination came into view: the traders' camp.

Just inside the forest, several canvas tents circled a large clearing where a dozen or so people were talking and drinking out of tin cups. Carts filled with crates and wooden barrels were lined up near horses that had been hitched to a line of rope tied between trees. And in the middle of all this, a brightly blazing bonfire sent a thick column of smoke up into the tops of the trees.

Valentin stopped the cart near the line of horses and hopped off. A couple of older men were draping blankets over the horses' backs, their breath visible in the chilly night air. I smelled fresh hay and the scent we'd caught an hour or so ago: rose oil. There was the little cart of clinking bottles beside us.

"Come!" Valentin said. "Be welcome. We do not bite." He gestured for us to follow him toward the center of camp, and we did, winding around people sitting on blankets spread over the ground, picnic-style. Curious faces, both pale and dark, looked up at us with blinking eyes. Mostly men of various ages, but a couple of women also, and at least two children. Valentin said something to one of the men in Bulgarian, and he relayed it to others around him as Huck and I lifted our hands in greeting.

Woodsmoke and the scents of both alcohol and garlicky meat filled my nostrils as we walked around the bonfire. Near a couple of tents on our right, I noticed a barrel-shaped vardo wagon. It had a window with shutters on the side, decoratively carved eaves under the roof, and a door with pull-down steps at one end.

"Are you travelers?" Huck asked, looking at the wagon.

"Romany, he means," I explained to Valentin.

He shook his head. "This place here, in the woods, is an old Romany campsite. We trade with them sometimes. I come from a town called Razgrad, where my father is a Bulgarian carpenter. He made this wagon for a Romany couple who are getting married. I'm delivering it to their families before the wedding."

"It's beautiful," I said.

He nodded. "It sleeps good too. Very solid," he said, knocking on the wood. "My father makes several of these caravan wagons every year. The Romany have a tradition to give a new wagon to young couples, and also to burn the wagon with all belongings when someone dies so that a *mullo* does not return to claim them. So we are always busy making new caravans."

"What is a . . . *mullo*?" I asked.

"Not dead. Not alive. When the spirit is angry or restless, or doesn't receive proper burial rites, like burning the possessions, then it can come back. The Romanians call them—"

"*Strigoi*," I said in chorus with him. "A revenant, returned from the dead."

"You know about this," he said with a smile.

I nodded. "I'm fascinated with folklore and legends. I've never heard the Romany term though."

"Wait, are you talking about . . . a vampire?" Huck asked, doing an admirable Bela Lugosi impression with his face and hands.

Valentin chuckled but shook his head. "That is fiction from your people, yes? Bram Stoker? Count Dracula? Your vampire is fiction, my friend, but many people in these lands believe that creatures like *mullo* and *strigoi* are very real, indeed."

"I certainly hope not," Huck said.

"Do not worry. There is safety in numbers. If they come for us, we will fight them, yes?" he said, elbowing Huck on his arm cheerfully. Then he looked up and spotted someone approaching and said, "Ah, here is my wife, Ana."

A plump, red-cheeked girl nearly as tall as Huck stepped to Valentin's side. She wore a long skirt that fell around her ankles and black, laced boots. Dark waves peeked from beneath a knitted hat. Valentin said something to her in Bulgarian, a long explanation during which I was able to pick out a few words like "Orient Express" and "*Amerikanski*" and then our names. She smiled and nodded.

"Ana says you are welcome and that she was right to make me look for you, which she is now gloating about," he reported with a grin. "She understands a little Romanian but doesn't speak English."

"Thank you for helping us," I told her in Romanian.

She smiled and nodded, and Huck and I smiled and nodded in return, and after a brisk back-and-forth between husband and wife—presumably about where we would sleep, as she gestured to the wagon and tents—Ana motioned for us to follow her toward a folding table near the bonfire. A makeshift outdoor kitchen had been set up there with a large pot.

"I must help with a few chores," Valentin told us. "But please eat and sit by the fire. Take a rest."

Before leaving, he helped Ana fill our hands with tin cups of plum brandy and bowls of hot polenta topped with a thick stew.

The metal dishes were dinged and beaten, and I wasn't entirely sure what kind of meat bits were in the stew. But when Ana guided us to an abandoned blanket to sit upon, and we were able to put down our luggage and warm ourselves near the fire, Huck and I both found the food to be satisfyingly good.

Mostly, anyway. The plum brandy . . . took some getting used to. The first taste burned the back of my throat, and Huck laughed at me—which only made me more determined to drink it. After the second sip, it was more bracing than harsh, and the warmth it provided was pleasant. Much nicer than the Irish whiskey Father sipped after dinner.

Several campers looked us over as we ate, and one friendly elderly man who spoke Romanian briefly stopped by our blanket—to opine that we'd gotten lost and reassure me that they'd take us over the Danube tomorrow. But mostly the campers just returned to their own conversations, unconcerned that we were there. We finished eating and watched as the two children I'd spotted earlier raced past the bonfire. A dark-haired girl and boy, maybe eight years old. They spotted us and stared, but their initial hesitant shyness fell away when Ana bent down to tell them about us and Huck held up a hand in greeting. Before long we were caught up in a tangle of arms and giggles.

"Whoa!" Huck said, chuckling, as he held them at bay. The boy snatched Huck's flat cap, and the girl laughed when Huck's wild curls sprang to life. They were like ants on sugar, climbing on Huck until he tipped over backward, causing a duet of delighted screams—until a Bulgarian mother came to collect them and lead them away.

"You're smiling," Huck said after the children were gone, retrieving his hat from the dirt to brush it off.

"Am I?"

"For the first time since we . . . left the train."

Since our fight, he meant but didn't say.

"That's because I'm not shivering from the cold and miserable," I said. Even the caked-on mud clinging to my shoes had dried in front of the fire—enough, at least, that I was able to kick and scrape quite a bit of it away.

"You were right about following the rose oil cart," he said. "This is turning out okay, yeah? Food. Kind people. It was the right thing to leave the train. Better here than with that man and his wolf dog."

For now at least.

We sat in silence for a while, watching the people around us. Things felt unfinished and awkward between us. Or maybe I was just self-conscious about being a stranger in a strange camp. So I drank more of my plum brandy, and it not only warmed my stomach but also loosened my tongue. "Interesting what Valentin said about the vampiric folklore, don't you think? *Mullos* and *strigoi*."

"That's right up your alley, isn't it?" he said. "People rising from the dead."

I flicked my eyes toward his, prepared to say something catty in response, but the look on his face wasn't combative.

"Plenty of folk in Northern Ireland believe superstitions like that too," he said. "My mam always threatened 'I will haunt you' when I was a terror as a child." He almost never spoke of his mother. I wondered if he still missed her like I missed mine. I wished she'd haunt me. I used to dream about her ghost visiting me in my bed. When I'd wake up alone in my room to find no ghost or spirit, not even a rustling curtain, it was the worst kind of disappointment.

Huck rubbed his hands together for warmth. "My aunt says the dead must be buried at home, because if not their spirits will rise and haunt the family. But I think this is more an inconvenience than something to be feared. I mean, who wanted to hear poor, dead Cousin Eileen wailing outside the window because you were too cheap to ship her body home when she died abroad?"

"If we die in Bulgaria, I hope someone ships our bodies home," I said, smiling a little. "I'll be most annoyed if I'm forced to spend eternity roaming the barren countryside like we did today."

"Aye. That makes two of us. But hopefully that won't be an issue. Tomorrow is Thursday, and Bucharest isn't all that far, right? We still have plenty of time to make it to the hotel by Fox's deadline." Huck rested his arms on bent knees. "And today was tough. Perhaps we both said some things we regret . . ."

"Did we?" I mumbled, sneaking a glance at his face.

He cleared his throat. "The important thing, though, is that we got away from that devil and his big white wolf."

"Yes. No more Carpathian wolf dog is a very good thing," I agreed, tipping my cup to swallow the dregs of my brandy. And, as if by magic, Valentin appeared with more.

"Hello, friends," he said cheerfully, sitting in front of us on the ground cross-legged and insisting on refilling our cups. "Did I hear you talking about a white wolf?"

"A wolf dog," Huck said. "But yes."

"White wolves are very good luck," he told us, gesturing for us to drink up. "They are said to be the spirits of the ancient people of the Carpathians and the Black Sea—the Dacians. Do you know about them?"

"Oh, yes! The Kingdom of Dacia," I said, excited. "They ruled Transylvania before they were conquered by the Romans."

Valentin nodded. "Do you know the stories about their wolves?"

I knew a few things. "When I was a girl my mother told me

that the Carpathians were once called 'the land of the wolves.'"

"And the Dacians were the wolf people," he said, animated. "There is an old story of a mountain priest who could talk to animals and gave sermons to the Carpathian wolves, who began to think of him as their master. A Dacian god named Zamolxis saw this, and he turned the priest into a white wolf. Do you know this story?"

"Is this the origin of werewolves?"

"Now you've done it, brother," Huck murmured to Valentin while smirking at me with slanted eyes.

"No werewolf," Valentin said, shaking his head. "Not a cheap story about the full moon. Imagine a man's soul inhabiting the body of a great beast—one who could lead the mountain wolves to help the people of Transylvania in battle. If anyone was in danger, they could trust a Carpathian wolf to appear and save them. They were not beasts to be feared. They were friends. Helpful friends."

"Lucky wolves," I said. "They shared a bond."

He nodded. "For years the Dacians trusted the great white wolf and his pack. Until the Romans came to conquer them. And because the Romans were tricky, they put doubt in the Dacians' hearts, and they said the white wolf was evil, a monster to be feared. They promised the Dacians a land deal if they would get rid of the white wolf's pack—kill the wolves, keep their land."

"Did they take the deal?" I asked, unfamiliar with this part of the story.

Valentin lifted his cup, nodding. "Unfortunately so. The Dacians turned on the Carpathian wolves, slaughtering them with their swords, until they were no longer a threat to the Romans. The giant white wolf priest was forced to flee. He took shelter inside a holy mountain, where he stood with the god Zamolxis and watched with sadness as the Dacians were defeated by the tricky Romans, who never honored the deal."

"That's a sad story," I said.

"Sadder that the wolves no longer listen to us. Back in those times, there were many stories of people of the old ways . . . people who could perform miracles and talk to animals. Now? Only a few," Valentin said quite seriously.

Huck lifted an eyebrow. "People who talk to animals?"

"You don't believe me. That is fine. I have no proof to give you, only faith," Valentin said before finishing his drink and pouring another. "But I do know one who follows the old ways. She knows the tongue of the beasts, a wisewoman in a village near București. Her name is Mama Lovena. The Romanian locals call her 'mother of the forest.' They also call her a *vrăjitoare*—a witch."

"Muma Pădurii," I murmured.

"You know her?" Valentin asked, brows raised.

"I know the legend," I said, feeling light-headed from both the drink and the conversation. "In stories she's said to be an ugly old hag who kidnaps children and eats them. To the Germans, she is the witch in *Hansel and Gretel*. In Russia she is Baba Yaga."

"And in the Balkans she is *Gorska Maĭka*," he said. "But Mama Lovena isn't a legend. She is a real person."

"Who speaks to animals?" Huck said, incredulous.

"Many say she does," Valentin assured him. "She is descended from old blood. Old money. Her sister is titled—a baroness—and Lovena herself is well educated. But she left her inheritance to live alone in a small house in the woods outside a village north of Bucharest. A famous church is there too, one that tourists like to see. But to the locals Mama Lovena is more famous," he said with a smile.

A witch in a cottage in the woods. How captivating!

I wanted to hear more, but before long Ana had joined our little group, and Valentin was leaving wolves and witches behind and telling us other stories—about how he and Ana met and how this trading group came to be, farmers and craftsmen who crossed the Danube to sell their wares. He also asked us a million and one questions about where we lived in New York and all the places we'd traveled. And maybe because the brandy was bringing out Huck's gregarious nature, he was eager to trade tales of life on the road.

The life I lived with Father wasn't all that different from what these traders did, crossing the country to take their goods to market. Father and I spent half the year traveling from place to place. He said the beauty of travel was that if you never came home for long, you never had to face your problems. There was always another town, another country, another treasure to distract. I used to think that Father was trying to outrun his grief and forget about Mother. But now that I'd read pieces of his journal, I wondered if being on the road so much made him feel closer to her. She'd left home when she was my age, went to university, then never stopped traveling. By the time she'd met my father, she'd already camped with Bedouin desert nomads outside of Morocco and spent several months at a Tibetan monastery, studying temple ruins in the Himalayas.

If she were here now, she'd love Valentin's stories. I rubbed the Byzantine coin around my neck and smiled to myself, glad I'd trusted my intuition to take up Valentin's offer of hospitality.

The night wore on. Father's last journal entry slid into my thoughts, and I wanted to ask Valentin if he knew any stories about Romanian dragons, but he was caught up in other stories. After a brief trek outside the camp to relieve my bladder from the strain of plum brandy, I returned to find most of the camp was retreating to their tents. A few wide-awake campers migrated to our side of the dying bonfire, and Valentin translated pieces of the conversation in both directions—stories from the road. Stories of the dead. And of the *mullo* and *strigoi*, who purportedly could shape-shift into animal forms, not unlike the fictional Count Dracula. Enraptured, I listened and found myself sitting closer to Huck. Close enough that, occasionally, our legs and arms would touch, and my heart would pitter-patter beneath my coat as if the last year were just a bad dream and our afternoon argument never happened. It wasn't forgotten, but it shifted into the background as we listened to the campfire stories.

And drank.

And laughed.

And drank . . .

In fact, it wasn't until the fourth or possibly fifth cup of plum brandy that my mind stopped listening to all the campfire stories and wandered back to all the things Huck had said during our walk from the train. *A stupid, drunken mistake. Empress Theodora.*

His words stewed and bubbled and hissed inside me . . . until I boiled over.

"I am not a mistake!" I said. Or shouted. Same difference.

In my hazy anger I was vaguely aware that I'd interrupted Valentin and that several pairs of dark eyes were blinking at me as if I had just insulted their mothers. Everyone except Huck, whose neck and ears were turning a dark shade of red.

"Theo—" he said, but I cut him off.

"I'm not a mistake," I repeated, trying to keep my voice down. "Or some spoiled brat born with a silver fork in my mouth."

"Spoon," Huck corrected.

"Whatever! I can do things. I'm smart. I know five languages and can swear in two more. I know history and archaeology and how to do cryto . . . cr-*crypt-o-grams*," I said, unsure why that was so hard to pronounce. "You don't know how, but I do! And you . . ." I pointed a finger at Huck's face. "You, buddy-boy, should be so lucky to even call yourself my *friend*, jerkface."

"Um . . . ," Huck said, eyes darting around the camp.

"I'm not spoiled, and I'm not a coward. I'm not." I shrugged to underscore my point. "Did I fall apart when I was falsely accused of shoplifting a stupid puzzle ring in the Grand Bazaar? Or when Miss Frenchy Tutor robbed me and left me for dead?"

"No one left you for dead," Huck mumbled, glancing around nervously.

"How would you know? Were you there? No, you weren't. I was alone, just like I always am. And I don't sit around crying over you and your stupid face. I don't even think about you at all." I tried to make a rude gesture while still holding my tin cup of booze, and it didn't work so well. Huck rushed to grab the cup out of my hand.

"Don't touch me! Am I embarrassing you? Well, I'm *soooooo* sorry." I pushed myself up from the ground with no small amount of effort. Gravity was not my friend, and it took the oomph out of my argument. And that's when I realized that for the first time in my life, maybe, just possibly, I was a little bit drunk. Maybe even a lot drunk.

"Uh, I think we need to call it a night," Huck said to Valentin, giving him a look that I interpreted to mean that the two of them were judging me.

"She is a lively one," Valentin said. "Wildcat."

"*Cat?* I'll have you know, I'm not an animal," I said, insulted, and then sloppily took out my coin pendant from where it was tucked inside my coat. "See this? I was named after a great empress. I'm royalty—nay, I'm an independent young lady! You may call me Lady Rogue."

Woo! Was I ever so proud of that speech! I held my hands up in victory while Huck mouthed something to Valentin and Ana. I had the distinct feeling he was apologizing for my outburst, which only made me want to give another angry speech. But when I started to do just that, Huck interrupted by handing me my satchel, and surprisingly, it was difficult to be mad and hold luggage at the same time. I wasn't sure, but I thought some of the campers were laughing at me, and like the sun dawning, regret crept over me. Then anger. Then more anger. Then I stopped caring about everything, and that felt much better.

Next thing I knew, Valentin had found a lantern and was leading us away from the dying bonfire, past several tents, to the steps of the vardo wagon.

"You can sleep here," he said, gesturing up the wooden fold-down steps.

"But this is a wedding gift," I argued. "And so small. Look at the tiny pixie door, Huck."

"I see it," he said before speaking to Valentin. "She's right, brother. We can't kick you out of the wagon."

Valentin insisted. "Ana and I have been sleeping it in for two nights. We brought a tent along for the ride back after we deliver it. We will sleep in that tonight." Then he said in a lower voice, "Honestly, there is more room in the tent. I am not doing you any favors."

Ana squinted into my eyes like a doctor giving an examination, and then she climbed a step to open the door, came back down, and gestured for us to go inside the wagon, "Up, up," she said in

Romanian before informing her husband something in Bulgarian.

"She says do not be sick inside or you will have to purchase the wagon. You break it, you take it," he translated with a small smile.

"I'm not going to be sick," I assured him. I tried to toss my satchel up the stairs and inside the wagon's small door, then kicked it when it fell back down and landed on my feet. And while Huck took it from me, I slowly climbed the stairs and ducked to enter the pixie door.

Miles away from the luxury of the Orient Express, the tiny space was half filled with supplies packed in crates and several pieces of wooden furniture—a table and chairs stacked and bound with rope. In front of this in the remaining space was a pallet of ragged, colorful blankets. Everything smelled of freshly sawed pine.

Valentin hung the lantern with its sputtering nub on a hook near the door. "It is humble, but it serves its purpose. There is a local expression—to make a whip out of shit. It means to do much with very little."

"It's perfectly fine," Huck told him.

I roughly fell back onto the pile of blankets, which was farther away than my backside expected. "Hey, Valentin? I'm sorry I snapped at you with my wildcat teeth."

He chuckled. "It is nothing. I admire the wildcat. They attack when you least expect."

"Hear that, Huxley Gallagher?" I said, grinning up at him. "Better watch your back."

"Good night, my friends. Tomorrow we will travel over the river." And with that, Valentin closed the wagon door, his merry whistling fading into the camp.

When he was gone, Huck looked down at me and asked, "You okay, banshee?"

"I'm peachy. Or maybe I should say plummy."

"I *think* you mean drunky."

"Don't judge me."

Huck chuckled and pinched out the lantern's candle, sending the small space into darkness. "Don't you worry, banshee. I won't tell Fox."

"And I won't tell him that you slept with me in a wedding wagon."

A string of mumbled obscenities filled the small space.

"It was just a joke. J-o-k-e," I spelled out. "Lighten up, Huxley Gallagher. Not going to tear your clothes off again. I'm not that desperate."

He was quiet for a moment and then said, "Fox mentioned you were seeing a few people, but he wouldn't tell me who."

"That's none of his business. Or yours."

"Oh . . ."

"Do you have a girl back in Belfast?" I asked.

"Too busy working."

"Well, I'm too busy studying," I said. The truth was, I tried dating once, earlier this year, but there was no magic. Huck poisoned my head for other people. And I hated him for that. "But I get lots of offers," I lied.

"You always know how to make a guy feel good about himself, banshee."

"I told you not to call me that."

"Did you, now? I'll try to remember it next time."

I gazed up at the small windows on either side of the wagon, but everything was spinning. I shut my eyes for a moment and said, "I forgive you for what you said out in the fields. Do you forgive me?"

The wagon creaked and shifted. Huck's silhouette passed over me and lay down somewhere near me. "Tell me tomorrow," he said. "After you're sober."

How was I supposed to take that? I opened my mouth to ask but couldn't figure out how to say it. So I didn't. I just flipped up my fur collar, rolled to my side, and curled shrimplike inside my coat. I was done. I'd said my piece and received nothing remotely satisfying in return. Time to figure out a way to stop caring. I was tough. I could do it. I didn't need Huck's stupidly pretty face in my life.

The traders' blankets smelled of dust and earth, and I wondered how far they'd traveled and what they'd seen. And I wondered where my father was sleeping that night. I guessed I'd find out tomorrow, when we'd meet up with him in Bucharest. Then this brief adventure would end. And no one would care that I'd drank too much and slept inside a wagon in a forest with a boy who'd broken my heart. Maybe not even me. So I pretended to casually, accidently, fortuitously flop over until we were facing each other. Until I felt his breath on my forehead. Until my knee jabbed into his leg.

"Ow," he complained a few inches from my face.

"Sorry," I mumbled. But I wasn't. And I didn't move away. Yet while a hazy, plum-brandy sleep pulled me under, I realized something interesting: neither did he. . . .

Unfortunately, that small, stolen joy didn't last, because at some point during the night I dreamed of meeting Valentin's legendary white wolf. Or was it Mr. Sarkany's Carpathian wolf dog? The creature was outside our wagon, circling and sniffing, and Dream Me crawled over the wagon floor and opened one of the tiny shuttered windows to reach out and offer my hand for him to sniff . . . until I became afraid that he might bite it off.

I awoke in a cold sweat, head aching from the brandy but painfully sober. I hated vivid dreams. My mother used to say that vivid dreams were your brain's way of sending you messages that you tried to ignore or had forgotten while you were awake. Was my dreaming brain trying to send me a warning? Perhaps so, because I had a terrible thought:

Mr. Sarkany and his wolf dog trailed us across Europe from Istanbul.

Were we fools to think that he wouldn't try to follow us into Romania?

JOURNAL OF RICHARD FOX
June 25, 1937
Bucureşti, Kingdom of România

Jean-Bernard has become addicted to the roasted eggplant ("aubergine," he insists on calling it) that is served on toast at the café across the street from our hotel. We spent half the afternoon there, drinking too much coffee and reading several books for information on the bone ring. I had the distinct feeling that someone was listening to our conversation—I couldn't say why really. Just a feeling. But we switched to French to be safe.

If Theodora were here, she'd team up with Jean-Bernard and poke fun at my poorly conjugated French verbs. I can hear her now in my head, an eight-year-old slip of a girl, practicing French alone in her room, pretending to have cosmopolitan conversations with teddy bears.

Wish she could spend more time with Jean-Bernard.

Wish I weren't such a coward.

PLUM BRANDY DID NOT TASTE GOOD COMING BACK up. Not the first time and *definitely* not the second. A few hours after we'd woken to the sounds of the traders' camp being torn down and packed up, this was all I could think about. I was well on my way to some kind of vomiting world record. And while the midmorning sun blinded the sandpaper surface of my dried-out eyes, Huck was kind enough to ensure I didn't tip head-first out of the canoe that was currently our transportation, holding me by the scruff of my coat while the rest of the passengers looked on in amusement.

I knew one thing: boats and hangovers did not mix.

We were crossing the Danube into Romania, packed like sardines with Valentin and Ana and a dozen other traders. Three other canoes paddled in front of us while the wagon, horses, and carts sailed on what Valentin called a ferry—and what *I* would call little more than a giant raft.

It was all completely unsafe and undeniably illegal, as we were crossing from one country to the next without going through a customs checkpoint. Valentin estimated that we were three or four miles from the Orient Express's steamboat landing, and though the sky was overcast and the river was the color of dingy pewter, when I squinted I could make out the Romanian port town of Giurgiu along the distant shore.

"Here," Huck said when I was fully back in the boat, handing me his handkerchief. "Maybe you should concentrate on looking at the horizon? Isn't that supposed to help with motion sickness?"

Probably not when you're hungover. "I'm never drinking again," I whispered. I'd already apologized to Valentin for my drunken speech at the campfire last night. I don't think I'd ever regretted anything so much. "Why are you not sick?" I asked Huck, miserable.

"Know my limits, don't I?"

"Bully for you," I said sourly.

He found this amusing. I didn't understand how he could remain so obnoxiously cheerful in a swaying boat. I'd never felt so awful in my life.

Thankfully, though, the Danube crossing was not a lengthy one. When our boats glided through rushes near the shore, I was feeling marginally less sick and eager to debark. We were in Romania! Finally! Shame that it looked much the same as Bulgaria here. I wasn't sure what I expected, but trees were trees were trees, and there wasn't much else to see. Still, we were so close to civilization, I could almost weep with joy.

There was little time to appreciate it, because even though we'd successfully made our illegal border crossing, now we had to load ourselves back into horse-pulled carts and journey on back roads for several more hours. To top it all off, it looked as though it might rain.

I tried not to think about it. I just huddled between Huck and sacks of horse feed and tried to keep my eyes closed, drowsing occasionally. And before I knew it, Huck was shaking me. "We're getting off here."

"Here" wasn't Bucharest, but instead a crossroads near a village commune called Călugăreni. The traders were gathering in a small field off the road in a well-worn area next to a river, with remnants of previous camps. Valentin informed us that the caravan would rest here and wait for two other traders to join them; in the meantime, he needed to conduct some additional business for his father, which would require him to travel to a local village, away from the city.

"Bucharest is six or seven hours by cart, but less than an hour by bus," he informed us. "You will be better off parting ways with us here and journeying the remainder of the way on your own."

He then helped us gather up our luggage and walked us across the road to a rural bus stop—a wooden sign basically. No bench. No nothing. Just the dust of the road and fields for days. Huck asked how much the fare would cost, and I was relieved to find out that not only was it cheap, but Valentin's wife was more than happy to help exchange a few of Huck's Turkish bills for Romanian lei, as several of the traders were used to doing business with different groups of people.

When Huck thanked Ana, she told Valentin something which he translated for us: "She says it is nothing. Now, you may have to wait here awhile, but the bus will come. It takes you straight into Bucharest. Get off in Old Town at the first stop over the bridge. Walk a few blocks north to the Grand Café on the corner of a busy cross street. Big awnings. It is the meeting place for Europeans. You will find people who speak English there. Someone there will tell you how to take a taxicab to your family."

"We're ever so grateful for everything you've done for us," I told him and Ana. "I wish we could pay you."

He waved a dismissive hand. "We do not know any strangers, only friends. Travel well. And if Ana and I ever find ourselves in New York, we will come stay with you."

She shook both my hands, and I thanked both her and Valentin in Romanian. And with that he doffed his hat, and the young couple bade us goodbye.

Well, then. We were on our own now. Huck glanced around at the lonely road and rolling hills. "Think you can wait for a bus? Are you still hungover? You need water."

"I'm fine," I assured him. Truth was, I had a splitting headache, but at least there was nothing left inside my stomach to heave up.

As luck would have it, we waited only a half hour for the bus, which was small, old, and carried three elderly women and one child. The driver looked at us suspiciously and counted out Huck's coins from his palm, taking enough for both our fares, and after we sat down near the front, the bus was on its way.

We were in my mother's country, headed to meet up with my father.

Life was strange.

Huck and I were quiet with each other on the bus. Now that we were alone again, the divide between us grew wider. Everything felt unsettled and confusing. We weren't friends. We weren't lovers. We weren't family. And thinking about yesterday's argument and last night's drunken humiliation only worsened my headache. So I didn't think much. And we didn't speak . . . much. We just sat together and stared out the window.

Better than fighting, I supposed.

Thankfully, the ride took a little under an hour and the bus made only two quick stops. I watched the landscape with growing interest as the city appeared in the distance and houses, then buildings began springing up on either side of the road. Slowly, cars and trucks filled the street, and we passed all the signs of civilization—petrol stations, streetlights, and parking lots. Beautiful old buildings. Outside an Orthodox church, I even spied a statue of the Capitoline Wolf, from Roman mythology, suckling Romulus and Remus, and it reminded me of Valentin's Dacian wolf stories. But before long we were slowing on a busy boulevard near a park, and when the door creaked open, we gathered our things and filed outside with the other passengers.

"Look, Huck," I said, craning my neck to take it all in.

"It's a proper city," he agreed.

"Pavement. Isn't it the most glorious thing you've ever seen?"

He laughed. "Bit better than rocky fields, yeah?" He held up a hand to shield his eyes and looked around. "Didn't know Bucharest was so big."

"My mother said it was once called Little Paris of the East." And it was easy to see why as we walked along the busy, tree-lined *stradă*. The city was pleasantly charming in an old-world European way, an interesting jumble of old and new. Horse-drawn taxis cantered alongside fast cars, and fedoraed businessmen tipped their hats at dark-haired peasants, carrying baskets of Moldova grapes on the ends of long poles that sat across their necks like oxen yokes.

Despite my lingering headache, the traveler in me wished to linger and sightsee. I got out my camera and snapped a couple of photographs until I noticed passersby giving me a once-over. I glanced down at myself and saw why they stared: stockings covered in runs and snags. Muddy shoes. Rumpled clothes. I looked like a hobo.

"Sleeping outside under the stars has its price," Huck said, eyes following mine. "It's rough, dangerous, and untidy. And you'll never cease to amaze at just how awful the human body can smell. No one writes that part down in travel books."

Yes, well, I never got the chance to sleep under the stars, as I was always shoved into hotels. I discreetly sniffed my clothes. They still smelled strongly of smoke from the traders' bonfire and possibly of brandy. God only knew what foulness was lurking in my armpits. "Let's get to the hotel before we begin to attract rats and insects." I said, tightly pulling down my beret to cover my scraggly hair. "Sound good?"

"Deal," Huck said.

We found a public water fountain, from which I drank copious amounts of water under Huck's direction that it would ease my headache—and it did, a little. Then, after strolling up a couple or ten blocks, we found the Grand Café . . . *approximately* where Valentin had said it would be, on a busy boulevard filled with bars, shops, and cinemas. Beneath a massive, striped awning, dozens of people lingered at tables, watching pedestrians while casually dining. But Huck didn't seem to care. He was too busy looking across the street, where a grand, domed Belle Époque Hotel stood on the corner, one that would not look out of place in Paris. Even the sign above the entrance was an art nouveau style similar to the Paris Métro signs.

Hotel Regina.

Regina. Queen. *Take her to that royal hotel* . . .

"Is that—"

Huck nodded. "That's where Fox stayed when he was in Bucharest this summer, trying to authenticate the bone ring for Mr. Rothwild."

"What's so special about this hotel?" I asked. "He must have known you'd remember, the way he said it in the letter, all coded and covert—'royal.'"

Huck gritted his teeth. "Uh, yeah. Fox told me a lurid story about something that happened at this hotel. I shouldn't repeat it." His eyes flicked to mine. "Don't look at me like that. It's not a secret. You just . . . don't want to know. There was no woman involved, if that's what you're thinking."

That's *exactly* what I was thinking. My father hadn't dated anyone since my mother died. Not anyone he cared to introduce to me anyway. I felt quite sure he wasn't a monk, but he kept all that private.

"Let's just get over there and find out if he's checked in yet. Then he can tell me his dirty secret himself." Or not. My father played his cards close to his vest. But I cared less about that than actually seeing my father. Now that my head was clearing, yesterday's worries about Father's safety shifted back to the forefront of my thoughts. Father. Vlad Dracula's war ring. The journal. The cipher I couldn't crack. The Dragon. Mr. Sarkany and his white wolf dog . . .

What if Mr. Sarkany had somehow trailed us here? I glanced around the busy street as if I'd find him leaning against a streetlamp.

We crossed the street and pushed through gilded doors under a row of flags that jutted from the building, currently being used as a perch by dozens of black birds. Inside, the lobby was grand and spacious beneath a dome of glass and iron. The clientele seemed to be a mix of European aristocrats and traveling businessmen, who were mostly heading in and out of a vaulted corridor that branched from the lobby; a sign pointing in that direction said there was a brewhouse and a cinema on the ground floor.

But no Father.

My nerves jangled anxiously as we headed toward the registration desk to the right. Two starched uniforms stood behind it, both dark-headed men in their twenties, and the taller of the two—ANDREI was engraved on his gold name tag—greeted us in English.

"Welcome to Hotel Regina. How may we serve you?"

"Good afternoon, Andrei," I said. "My name is Miss Theodora Fox, and this is my—"

"Brother," Huck said.

I shot him an ugly look that said *I'm going to murder you in your sleep.* He shot me one back that said *Just go with it.*

"Brother," I repeated. Whatever. "Anyway, we are supposed to meet my father here, and I was wondering if you could tell me if he's already checked in? He's an American by the name of Richard Fox. Very tall. Dark hair. Beard. Built like a grizzly bear?"

The man did a double take. "You are the Fox's daughter?"

"Yes? Is he here?"

Andrei snapped at his associate. "Look! It is the Fox's children."

"The Fox?" the other man murmured.

They both stared at us as if we were circus oddities. Then Andrei said, "My apologies. We have heard stories about you. The Fox is a great man. What a character! A favored and generous guest. Because of him I was able to buy a new refrigerator for my wife."

"Uh . . ." I glanced at Huck, questioning.

Sheepish, he gritted his teeth and avoided my eyes.

"We will never forget the Fox," the desk attendant said. "He is always welcome, and so are you. How is he? And Jean-Bernard? Are they here in the city now?"

"That's what I'm asking you," I said. "We're looking for my father."

His brow wrinkled. "He is not with you?"

"We were to meet him here," I said impatiently, feeling as if I were in a Marx Brothers film.

"Ah," he said, realizing—finally. He shook his head. "No. We have not seen him since he left in July. I am sorry."

My heart plummeted into my stomach. Not here yet. Well, he did say to wait until Friday. It was only Thursday. Maybe he'd show up later today or even tomorrow. But that would mean we needed to get a room—if for no other reason than to wash the bonfire out of my hair and change clothes. I could see Huck thinking along the same lines as he reached into his long gray coat and pulled out a few green bills. "Would you be able to exchange American dollars for Romanian lei?"

Where did he get American money? Had to have been from Father.

"Of course," Andrei said, and they talked exchange rates and room rates, and it seemed as if Huck had enough cash for two, maybe three nights, if we didn't eat. So Father had damn well better show up soon. Huck registered for one room despite my mumbled protests. "This is all the cash I have," he whispered. "You lost the traveler's checks—"

"They were stolen from me!" I whispered back.

"My job is to keep you safe. My money. One room. End of story," he said in a low voice. "If you want to punch me later, feel free."

I grumbled under my breath, but he just ignored me. As he was signing our names in the registration book, Andrei said, "I'm very happy Fox is returning. We last heard from him when he sent a letter and money."

"Money?" I asked.

"It was generous but unnecessary. I told him it would be fine. The mayor's wife doesn't even remember fainting. It is all forgotten.

Just an amusing story now of the wild American treasure hunter."

Mayor's wife?

The other desk attendant said something under his breath in Romanian that I couldn't quite catch, and they both chuckled.

"My father . . . is always the subject of great stories," I said, squinting at the attendants. Huck's back was turned to me now, so I asked Andrei, "How exactly did it happen? The incident with the mayor's wife?" and ignored Huck's groan.

The desk attendant was more than happy to tell me. "It was a Saturday night, and the hotel was busy. The film in the cinema was letting out, and the mayor and his wife were leaving a dinner in the ballroom, just there," he said, pointing to a stanchioned-off set of doors at the back of the lobby. "And as they were passing the staircase, the Fox stumbled around the turn in the stairs—you see it there? And that is when we all saw him. Not a stitch of clothes."

"He was wearing black socks," the other attendant reminded him in a heavy Romanian accent.

"Ah, yes," Andrei said, grinning. "Fox in socks. And drunk as a skunk."

"Oh God," I whispered.

"He was shouting like a maniac. No one could understand him, and he is such a large man, and so—how do you say?"

"Hairy," the other attendant provided.

I squeezed my eyes shut.

"Like a great big bear," Andrei said.

"Like a bear," I repeated. "Indeed."

"People were screaming and running from him," Andrei said, smiling as if he was remembering it fondly. "And then . . . the mayor and his wife were in his path, and he tripped over the last stair and knocked over the mayor's wife. She fell on the floor. That is when he got sick."

For the love of Pete . . .

The other attendant said, "The mayor's wife fainted but was otherwise unhurt. The mayor threatened legal action against the Fox—and the hotel."

"But it was all fine," Andrei said, waving his hands. "Because that is when we found out it was not just the whiskey, but also the *sirop de tuse*—cough suppressant? The medicine. He had mixed the two. It was potent. He was not himself."

"And the reason he was coming to the front desk was because he'd accidently locked Jean-Bernard in the en suite inside his room," the other attendant added. "We called a doctor and a locksmith."

"He had much regret when he sobered up the next day," Andrei said. "And because we smoothed everything over with the mayor—"

"And the police."

"And hotel management," Andrei said. "Well, that is why my wife has a new refrigerator."

"And why the city has a new copper statue of a goddess in Cișmigiu Gardens that is modeled on the mayor's wife."

I tried to make my smile match the desk attendants', smiles that conveyed we were all broad-minded enough to laugh at my father's foibles, ha ha, ho ho, isn't this a riot?

After a few more chuckles, other guests came to the desk, and the embarrassing story finally got buried. We left instructions with Andrei to let us know immediately when my father arrived—and I left further instructions requesting as many Romanian newspapers as they could find. Then we exited the lobby and took the elevator to the fifth floor.

"Sorry about all that. But I did warn you that you didn't want to know," Huck murmured, looking down at the floor of the elevator, arms crossed.

"Ugh. Why is my father such an embarrassment? High as a kite on cough suppressant and whiskey . . . He's lucky he's not dead."

"Bigger question is, how does he fall in a puddle of his own sick but everyone here still adores him?"

A conundrum for the ages. My poor mother would be humiliated if she were still alive. I could almost feel her rolling in her grave.

Huck sighed heavily, and we were lost in our own thoughts until we made it to our floor and unlocked the door to our hotel room.

Accommodations at Hotel Regina were perfectly fine: pristine white duvets, crown molding, fresh flowers on a desk, and a wingback chair for reading. A bit cramped for two people, though there were indeed two beds and a balcony to make it feel roomier. Better than the train compartment, at least.

I set down my satchel and tried to ignore the en suite bathroom, because all I could picture was Jean-Bernard locked inside while my lunatic of a father was running around in the nude downstairs. Jean-Bernard must have wanted to strangle him; he was the epitome of class and sophistication. Come to think of it, he was my father's opposite, and I had no idea how they'd been able to keep their friendship going without one of them ending up strangled or threatening a lawsuit.

I pulled open the room's terrace door and looked over a wrought-iron Juliet balcony. Sunshine peeked out of a raincloud and shone over the rain-slicked boulevard, where cars sped several floors beneath us. A thousand painted signs hung over the sidewalks, pointing the way to cinemas, restaurants, cheap hotels, and grand theaters—Bucharest's version of Broadway. I wondered if Father had taken the time to see any of it when he was here, or if he'd just spent all his time researching Vlad Dracula's ring and ruining the Fox family name.

I supposed I'd find out soon enough. After all, Father could show up any minute. Then he could explain everything to us, and we could tell him about Mr. Sarkany, and all of this mess would start to make sense.

But he didn't show up.

Not that night, while I sat up in one of the hotel beds, reading his journal. And not the next morning, while Huck and I took breakfast in the hotel's restaurant.

When the clock struck midnight on Friday night, I called down to the desk, to bother them for the umpteenth time, inquiring if he'd arrived. But he hadn't, and as I worried myself sick, Friday night turned into Saturday, and I'd finished every Romanian crossword puzzle I could get my hands on, newspapers stacking up on the floor by my bed, trying desperately to keep myself distracted. . . . That's when Huck said exactly the thing I already knew in my heart but didn't want to hear.

Father wasn't coming to meet us.

Something was very, *very* wrong.

JOURNAL OF RICHARD FOX
June 30, 1937
București, Kingdom of România

After I wasted several days in the archives, the only additional mentions of any kind of ring associated with Vlad the Impaler I uncovered were merely in passing and related to a militant organization called the Order of the Dragon. It was founded in the Kingdom of Hungary by the Holy Roman Emperor Sigismund twenty years before Vlad was born and was, in fact, the reason his father was given the sobriquet of "Dracul" ("the Dragon") and why the Impaler was called Vlad Dracula ("son of the Dragon").

This dragon society was open to only a select few aristocrats, church officials, and politicians. It was modeled after the Order of Saint George, whose legendary defeat of a dragon was used as the order's symbol. The order to which Dracul, the father, and Dracula, the son, both belonged had a purpose: to drive out the Turks from Eastern Europe and to protect the Catholic church from pagans.

Funny, that last part. Documents mention a special dragon ring being given in ceremony to Vlad's father upon joining this aristocratic society—a ring that was rumored to have occult powers. After Vlad's father died, the Impaler inherited the order membership.

Did he also inherit his father's occult dragon ring?

I COULDN'T SIT IDLY BY AND DO NOTHING. MY FATHER could be in danger. I mean, maybe he just couldn't get here in time, or maybe he was hiding out somewhere until the coast was clear. Or perhaps he was in jail—there was always that. I mean, what girl hasn't had to bail her father out of a foreign jail? Completely normal, our little family. Average in every way.

Thing was, my gut was telling me that it wasn't jail.

My gut was telling me that he was in trouble.

Early Saturday morning I did what I could. I sent a telegram to Jean-Bernard in Paris, and I sent one to Mr. Rothwild—at his city address in Budapest, which Father had jotted down in his journal. A long shot, but I thought maybe Father had contacted him recently with an update on the search for the ring.

By noon I hadn't heard anything back from Mr. Rothwild. Total silence. But an hour later I received a response from Paris—from Jean-Bernard's personal butler. It was not what I'd hoped for. Things were far worse than I'd imagined:

MADEMOISELLE THEODORA FOX= HOTEL REGINA= BUCUREȘTI, ROMÂNIA=

REGRET TO INFORM YOU THAT MSSR JEAN-BERNARD BISSET IS CRITICAL IN HOSPITAL STOP CONTRACTED UNKNOWN ILLNESS PERHAPS POISON SIX DAYS AGO STOP RECOVERY UNKNOWN STOP WHEN YOU FIND HIM PLEASE INFORM YOUR FATHER TO COME TO PARIS URGENTLY= MSSR DUJARDIN

Standing at the registration desk, I read and read again the tiny strips of type that had been pasted onto the telegram slip before Huck snatched the frail paper from my fingers to read it himself. "Poisoned? By what? Does he mean foul play?"

"Is poison ever *not* foul play?" I said, frantic.

"Could be accidental."

Sure. Like the rest of this wretched mess in which we were embroiled. Though I didn't know Jean-Bernard as more than a friend of the family and saw him only once in a blue moon, he always sent me pretty cards and gifts for my birthday and books for Christmas—every year, without fail. But it wasn't even that. It was that my father would be so terribly upset to hear this if he were here.

Then something struck me.

"Huck," I murmured. "The telegram says it happened six days ago. That's when you were in Tokat with Father."

"Six days ago would have been when we returned from the mountain," he said, following my line of reasoning. "Fox left me the next day. After the mystery meeting."

I scanned the telegram again. "Now I'm wondering if Father learned about Jean-Bernard being poisoned during that meeting. Maybe that's why he left you. Because he was worried that whoever came for Jean-Bernard would come for us."

Hazel eyes stared at me, blinking. Unsure.

"Look, this is what we know. Jean-Bernard traveled with Father in Romania this summer. He did research with Father. . . . He read books and advised. He's very knowledgeable about medieval European history. And Father's journal is filled with entries that mention Jean-Bernard helping him. If someone was following you in Tokat, who's to say someone didn't follow Jean-Bernard and Father when they were traveling through Romania last summer?"

"I wouldn't doubt anything anymore, to be honest."

"But let's say someone was following them. The only reason to do that would be to get their hands on the ring, right? Because they wanted it?"

"Or wanted to prevent someone else from finding it."

Oh. Huh. Right.

"Either way," Huck said, "why would someone poison Jean-Bernard?"

"Maybe Jean-Bernard knew something. Maybe someone was trying to prevent him from warning Father."

"About what?" Huck asked.

I didn't know. But people didn't just get poisoned out of the blue.

"Look," Huck said. "We don't know what Fox found out during his mystery meeting. But whatever it was, I can't believe he would send us into danger. He said for me to take you home if he didn't show up here. And he hasn't. So I think we need to find a Wagons-Lits office and find out how we can use the rest of our train ticket credit and book passage to a port. I have our ocean liner tickets for December. Surely we can exchange them for the next ship bound for home."

I squinted at him. "New York, you mean?"

That was my home. Not his. Not anymore.

He blinked rapidly and scrubbed the back of his neck. "Your

father told me to see you back to Foxwood. What happens after that, I don't know. But I'll not put you on a week-long journey across the ocean by yourself. I'll escort you home."

Home was the last place I wanted to go. It felt like giving up. Was I supposed to just get on an ocean liner while my Father was in God only knew what trouble?

"I wonder if this is why Father's letter to you said for us to avoid Paris. Do you think he knows about Jean-Bernard?"

"Do I look like a crystal ball?" Huck stared up at the domed ceiling and groaned in frustration. I knew what he was thinking—that this was all a big mess, and he didn't have any answers.

But *I* did.

They were right here in the red journal stuffed inside my handbag.

Father gave it to me for a reason. And if I wanted to uncover his secrets and find out where he could be right now, I needed to get serious about cracking his code.

"Give me one more day to study the journal," I told Huck. "Maybe I'll learn something that will help us. Or Father. Or Jean-Bernard. We have enough cash for another night in Bucharest, right? If I can't decipher the code, then we'll go home. What harm can it do? At least we're safe here."

"*Now*, sure," Huck said sarcastically. "In ten minutes, who even knows? And your father told me—"

"My father is MIA! He could be dead for all we know. He's abandoned us in the middle of Europe with dwindling resources and an instruction not to make our way to someone who is currently lying poisoned in a hospital bed—possibly as a result of a hunt for a cursed ring that is still out there unfound and the cause of all this chaos. Besides, Father may have given you an instruction, but he gave me this journal. And I say we stay here."

Huck sighed heavily. He said nothing for several heartbeats. Then he came at me like Frankenstein's monster, outstretched arms and feigned monstrous rage, pretending to strangle me. "You're stubborn—you know that, right?"

"Better than docile and compliant. Are you staying here with me, or are you going to shirk your 'me big man, me protect little woman' duty?" I said.

He sighed dramatically, as though the world were ending and all he could do was give in and let it happen. "All right. I suppose another day won't hurt. You know what they say. Nothing ventured, nothing strained."

"Gained."

"Are you sure?" he teased.

Honestly, I wasn't sure of anything anymore, because at that moment I was utterly relieved that he'd agreed to stay. Not because I couldn't have managed without him. I could have. I just . . . didn't want to. Not right now. Not with everything going on. Besides, we were just getting to a place in our newly reconciled relationship where we could put aside our differences and pretend they didn't exist. That was healthy, right?

After talking to Andrei about keeping the room one more night, we counted up the money we had left and headed across the street to the Grand Café, which looked like a good place to spend the afternoon working—better than our cramped hotel room, anyway. Scattered droplets fell from an overcast sky, so Huck found us a table under the café's big striped canopy that was well out of the rain. He flagged down a waiter, and our small table was soon filled with dark coffee, some sort of sweet cheese pastry, and open-faced sandwiches topped with an eggplant spread. And while Huck ate, I cracked my knuckles and got to work on solving my father's secret code.

I'd definitely decided that the particular code he'd used was a Vigenére cipher. That kind of cryptograph requires a Vigenére square, which is a grid of letters in neat rows and columns that looks a bit like an unsolved word-search puzzle. I'd made one on the Orient Express that night I stayed up trying to crack this code the first time, so I took it out now and opened Father's journal, flipping to each of the pages that had a code, dog-earing them for easy access.

Cracking a cipher like this wasn't a straightforward task. You could either spend hours (days, weeks, months) guessing the passphrase, or you could spend hours—*days, weeks, years*—trying to find patterns in the cipher and plugging code letters into the Vigenére square, hunting for the real letters. Either way, there were too many possibilities.

But since I'd already failed to guess the passphrase, I tried the pattern-searching method. I tried it through two plates of eggplant spread and three cups of coffee. I tried it while Huck read random journal entries out loud in my father's voice in an attempt to make me laugh. And I continued to try it while Huck leaned back in his chair, providing commentary on the pedestrians strolling past the café under umbrellas.

To make things easier, I focused on one block of cipher from the next-to-last journal entry:

> **I need to retrace my steps back to my summer trip in Romania. Must talk to:**
> XTTNMVGAFWVLWJQUIKLWLAUCJ.
> **One of these three has the true ring, I'm certain.**

If I could solve that, I could solve the rest. I was almost positive that Father had used a seven-letter passphrase. I could tell that much. Seven-letter words . . . There were, oh, I don't know—ten thousand possibilities? Twenty?

Hoping the word was something common, I madly scribbled lists of seven-letter words—a task with which Huck happily aided me—but none of them fit. And by late afternoon, when the drizzle turned to a steady rain, I was completely frustrated and out of ideas. My brain felt as if it were about to explode from overuse.

"I'll never crack it," I moaned to Huck, who had kicked a leg up onto an empty chair and now awoke with a start.

"What?" he said, groggy. "What time is it? It's night already?"

"It's just the rain clouds making it look dark." I checked my watch and gritted my teeth. "Oops. It's half past six." I hadn't meant to work that long.

He stretched and stared at the table. "Christ. We ate lunch here, and now it's time for dinner. I think we've outstayed our welcome."

Maybe he was right. It was time to give in and pack it all up. I blew out a long, frustrated breath and stared at the café table. In front of our empty coffee cups stood three origami animals Huck had created with folded café napkins and twisted paper straws. I smiled at his handiwork and asked, "Cat and dog?"

He pretended to be outraged. "That's you and me."

"Us?" I said, a little embarrassed. "What's on your head?"

"Pilot goggles," he said, crossing his arms over his chest. "Anyone could see that."

"Naturally," I said. "And that other napkin is me?"

"The pointy part is your crown, and the coffee stains are your big eyes, little empress."

I groaned. "Don't call me that. You sound like Father."

"Empress this, empress that," Huck mocked, reviving his Richard Fox impression. "So smart, so defiant, so beautiful . . .

most amazing girl in the whole wide world, blah, blah, blah."

My cheeks warmed. "He does not say that."

"It's *all* he says. I could never compare to his beloved Theodora, empress of his heart."

I started to tell him to shut the hell up, because (a) Father never talked that way about me, and (b) all I ever heard was praise about Huck. But lightning struck, both in the dark sky above and inside my head.

Seven letters. Empress.

Ignoring Huck, I copied down the same section of my father's code that I'd been focusing on, and using my Vigenére square, I found the row for *E* and followed it to the column for the first letter of the code, and then *M*, and on and on, writing each new letter beneath the cipher until I was finished. I set down my pencil as Huck looked over my shoulder.

XTTNMVGAFWVLWJQUIKLWLAUCJ
THEWIDOWTHEHERMITTHETWINS

We stared at the letters in silence. Then Huck read it aloud. "The widow, the hermit, the twins. Don't know what any of it means, but, banshee, I think you cracked it."

My heart raced. I felt the same thrill I used to feel when I was a child, cracking Father's silly cipher messages. And maybe I was feeling something else, too: a little ache of sentimentality because he had used my nickname as his passphrase. Maybe he'd used it only because it was convenient; just because you use your kid's birthday for your safe code doesn't mean you should win Parent of the Year.

But regardless, the code was cracked, and that was what mattered. It was all I could do not to jump on the café table with my arms in the air. But cracking a code was one thing. We still had to figure out what my father meant.

"Widows, hermits, and twins . . . ," Huck mumbled. "These are people he talked to this summer, and he thinks one of them has the real Vlad Dracula ring, yeah?"

"Seems so, yes."

"Well, who are they?"

I hadn't read every journal entry yet. But now that the adrenaline of victory was wearing off, I realized I might know who one of them was. In fact, I was quite sure of it. I'd seen it in passing when I was flipping through the journal the first night, on the train.

I flipped through pages until I found the right entry. "Look," I told Huck. "Father mentions her here. The widow is the first person Father interviewed this summer—the widow of the collector who first owned Rothwild's ring. The collector was Cezar Anca. He died the day after Rothwild purchased his bone ring. His wife's name is Natasha. Read," I told him, sliding the journal his way.

JOURNAL OF RICHARD FOX
June 27, 1937
București, Kingdom of România

In taxicab. Jean-Bernard and I just paid a visit to Natasha Anca, the widow of a wealthy collector in Bucharest, one Cezar Anca. Rothwild purchased his bone ring from Mr. Anca last month before the man died. Hence, widow.

She tolerated my shoddy Romanian accent for several minutes, until I discovered she spoke English just fine. She was tall and leggy and blonder than blond. Jean-Bernard complained that my eyes were on things they shouldn't be, but she was holding her sherry glass near the plunging neckline of her dress, and she kept tapping the glass with

one red fingernail, click-click-click, like some kind of cannibalistic insect, luring a mate so that she could behead him.

Anyway, it didn't matter, because when I asked her about the sale of Vlad Dracula's bone ring, she confirmed that Rothwild was an acquaintance of her late husband, Cezar, that she didn't know him well. All she knew was that Rothchild had been eyeing the ring for some time and that her husband had sold it to him in a moment of charity between friends. There was no documentation accompanying the ring—nothing historical that would authenticate it. That's what she said. I'm not sure I believe her, but I didn't have the patience to press her about it too far, because the room was filled with taxidermy that smelled of bad chemicals and hellfire, and my damn lungs were strained by a summer cold, so I couldn't stop coughing.

Regardless, the interview seemed to be going nowhere, around and around, so we left. The only interesting thing of note was a photograph I saw in the hallway as we were being shown the door by the maid. It was taken in 1929 at some kind of fundraiser for a political cause, according the caption. It was Rothwild with his arm around Natasha. Which made me wonder if she was keeping secrets.

"Huh. I suppose you're right," Huck said as his eyes flicked across my father's scrawled words. "Natasha is probably 'the widow' from Fox's cipher."

"She lives here in Bucharest," I said excitedly. "We could go talk to her. Maybe she's seen Father. Maybe she can point us in the right direction. Or, oh! Maybe Father is even there right now."

"Let's not get ahead of ourselves," Huck warned.

"Andrei can help us find her address, I'll bet."

I was talking too fast, and I fully expected Huck to tell me I was mad. But he didn't. He just stared at the journal entry, scratching his neck. And then his eyes met mine. "Well, then," he said. "We'd better go before it gets too late."

"Yes, let's," I said, happier than I should have been that he was willing to trust me and give this a chance.

"Let's hope she isn't really a praying mantis," he added with a smile that revealed the attractive gap between his teeth.

If she could point us to where my father might be, I honestly didn't care.

After paying the check on our hours-long meal, we dashed across the wet boulevard and flagged down Andrei at the desk. He was able to track down an address for the widow in minutes. By the time we'd hopped into a taxi and passed along the written address to the driver, it was well past seven o'clock and pouring down rain. An ominous start to our journey across the city and one that only worsened during the drive. Thunder and lightning cleared the streets of pedestrians and snarled the traffic. So badly, in fact, when we neared the *stradă* we needed to be on, we found it had been blocked by police, who were clearing away an automobile accident.

Our driver muttered something rapidly in a low voice that I couldn't quite catch over the noise of the rain beating down on the taxi. In Romanian, I asked him to repeat himself, but he was busy rolling down his window to shout at another car that was trying to turn around in the middle of the street.

"I think he's telling us we'll need to walk the rest of the way," Huck said. "The road's blocked."

"We'll be soaked," I said. If not from rain above, then from the water below that was flowing down both sides of the street like small rivers. I tucked my fur collar into my coat and did the same with the cuffs of my sleeves. "Oh, well. At least the rain's slowing a little. Can't be that far."

Huck paid the driver the taxi fee and a bit extra to wait for us. At least, I thought it was understood. But as soon as we were out of the cab, it turned in the middle of the road, backed up, and then sped away in the opposite direction—and no amount of shouting brought it back.

"We'll find another one," Huck shouted, flipping up his wool coat's wide collar and lapels to shield himself from the rain. "Come on."

We avoided the uniformed *poliției* and made our way down a hill, trying to match up the numbers on the handwritten address to the homes that sat along the road. But half were unmarked, and others were hard to see in the dark. Just when I was ready to throw in the towel, Huck made a funny noise. I looked up and saw what he saw.

An ambulance. Police. A crowd of black umbrellas.

They were all gathered around a three-story house covered in ivy; gold light shone from two windows on the top floor like a pair of malevolent eyes. They looked down on the driveway, watching a scene playing out, and as we quickly approached, we saw it too.

A coroner's van was parked there, lights flashing in the rain. And into the back, a bagged body was being loaded. Another body lay facedown on the wet pavement just outside the side entrance. From her uniform, she was a maid, and her head was bleeding so badly, even the rain couldn't wash it away. Two other servants stood under a portico, weeping.

"Please tell me that isn't Natasha Anca's home," I said as we gawked at the gruesome sight with the rest of the onlookers.

"That it is," a middle-aged man to my side said in a heavy accent. "I hope you were not friends."

"No," Huck said. "Not friends. We didn't know her."

"Very good." The man nodded approvingly. White hair stood out under the dark of an umbrella. His coat and suit looked well made and expensive. "I live two houses down," he told us. "And ever since she and her husband moved in five years ago, she's been a blight on polite society. Séances. Tarot card readings. Debauched parties and orgies . . ."

"Oh?" Huck said, sounding as scandalized as I felt. "She and her husband—"

"Not her husband. Just Natasha," he said. "Before he died, her husband had been . . . How do you say? Bedbound. Paralyzed. He hadn't left the upstairs room in two or three years. All the parties were downstairs. Natasha lived off his money and did as she pleased. She was a wicked woman. No one will be surprised that this has happened."

"What exactly *did* happen?" Huck asked.

"They say a hound from hell burst into the home and ripped out her throat before chasing down one of the maids, which I suppose is that poor girl," he lamented, gesturing toward the body on the ground. Bulbs flashed in the rain as the police took photographs.

I gave Huck a worried look. He returned it.

"A hound from hell?" I repeated.

The man shrugged. "A rabid stray, perhaps. The priest says hellhound"—he pointed to a black-attired Romanian Orthodox man of the cloth, who looked as if he might have come from the small church across the street—"and the servants who believe in superstitious folklore say it was Satan's beast, collecting a debt. Regardless, this is what happens when you court disgrace."

The police were blocking the bodies now. My gaze slid over the ivy-covered stone of the widow's home, up to the demonic windows that looked like eyes. Despite both the rain and the police attempting to disperse the crowd, no one was leaving.

The man tilted his head beneath the umbrella and studied us a little closer. "How do you know Natasha?"

"Aye, well, you see, we're looking for someone," Huck said diplomatically. "We were hoping she had some information about them."

I opened my mouth to add something to that, but no words came out. Because on the other side of the ivy-covered house, I spied movement. A man was taking refuge from the rain in a doorway. He watched the police while a white dog sat obediently at his feet. My pulse doubled.

"Time to leave," I said quickly, pulling Huck away from the neighbor. "Thank you for talking to us, but we must go. Now."

"Don't blame you, young lady," the man said, before stepping toward the curb to cross the street. "Get as far away from this as you can. Nothing good can come of it."

When we were out of earshot, Huck said, "Mind telling me why you're yanking on my arm like you're trying to outrun a demon?"

"We are! Look over there, in the doorway," I whispered.

Huck jerked his head toward the man and froze. Sarkany couldn't see us—at least I didn't think so—and I didn't want to take any chances that his dog might sniff us out. For once Huck and I were on the same page. He grabbed my hand, and I didn't have time to think too hard about the forgotten pleasure of his fingers around mine while we splashed through puddles, away from the police. Away from the bodies. Away from the devil and his white dog.

When we turned the corner, we couldn't see the coroner's van anymore, so we ducked under the overhang of a building to get out of the rain and caught our breath.

"Andrei warned me," Huck said, letting go of my hand.

"What do you mean?"

"When I went to the registration desk to have him look up the widow's address," Huck said in a daze. "Andrei warned me that there was a house in this neighborhood that has a dark reputation. I thought it was just a silly urban story."

Even our taxi driver had known. He hadn't been warning us about the traffic accident blocking the street. Now that I replayed his rapidly spoken words in my head—the ones I couldn't catch before—I was able to ferret out the taxi driver's meaning. *Casele diavolului*, he'd repeated in warning.

House of the devil.

JOURNAL OF RICHARD FOX
July 1, 1937
București, Kingdom of România

Jean-Bernard and I got mildly soused in a friendly pub with a young Romanian scholar named Liv, a boy not more than a couple years older than Huxley. Not only had Liv heard about Vlad Dracula's war ring, but he knew all sorts of stories about it. Most of them were half-baked (or maybe that was me after several glasses of pălincă), but the most interesting were stories about who owned the ring after Vlad.

According to Liv, the ring has been hidden dozens of times for hundreds of years, but it is always found. Gilles de Rais was the first to acquire it after Vlad. He was a noble French knight and a comrade-in-arms to Joan of Arc. Then he obtained the ring and killed a hundred children.

Then Elizabeth Báthory, the Blood Countess of Hungary, supposedly owned the ring. She's said to have murdered up to six hundred girls. (The court stopped counting officially at eighty.) The bone ring worn on her thumb was not able to be removed, so her entire thumb was cut off, ring and all, before she was imprisoned in a tower, where she remained until her death.

John Dee, infamous court magician to Queen Elizabeth, also got his hands on it. Dee's equally infamous assistant,

Edward Kelley, said the ring instructed him that the two men should share their property. And wives. But when he said the ring told him to kill, Dee drew the line and sold it, saying it was bedeviled.

And let's not forget Peter Niers, a German bandit who dabbled in the black arts. He confessed to killing five hundred people before he was executed—broken on the wheel.

Several politicians acquired it. And a pope. Oh, and the son of a Turkish sultan. Actually, it was rumored to have left Europe and crossed into the Ottoman Empire twice. The first time was a few months after Vlad Țepeș was beheaded; the Hungarian king Matthias Corvinus sent it to the Turks in exchange for Vlad's head. The second time, it was secreted away in a mosque for five years in the 1800s before they wanted nothing more to do with it and sent it back to Wallachia.

That's what I'm most interested in—that second time it returned to Europe.

Where did the Turks send it?

WE WALKED AROUND BUCHAREST FOR WHAT seemed like a lifetime to make sure Sarkany wasn't tailing us. Then it took a second lifetime to find another taxi that would take us back to Hotel Regina. By the time we got up to our room, it was almost eleven o'clock. Both of us looked and felt like drowned sewer rats and took turns in the bathroom, changing into dry clothes. My coat was probably ruined. I dried it off as well as I could and hung it up, hoping for the best.

Trying to clear my head of both the shock of the murder scene and of seeing Mr. Sarkany again, I stood in front of our balcony doors, peering out over the busy boulevard's bright lights. Across the street, rows of city rooftops were still wet with rain and shining in the moonlight. I shivered while my hair dried, wishing the hotel would turn on the heat, and then I tried to figure out what to do next.

No, we didn't find my father tonight. But at least we found out a few things. We learned that the widow, Natasha, dabbled in the occult. Which was interesting. And that my father's notes had mentioned a photograph hanging inside her house that showed her cozied up to Rothwild. That was doubly interesting. Were Natasha and Rothwild lovers? Was he aware of her extracurricular esoteric interests? Or was the picture my father saw merely a random photograph from a random event?

Maybe Natasha Anca was a dead end, both figuratively and literally.

Except Sarkany and his dog were there.

And Sarkany and his dog had killed her.

Why? I dug my father's journal out of my handbag and flipped through the pages, trying to spot something that would help me understand or point me toward something that could.

"Ugh. I can't stop thinking about all that blood," Huck said as he toweled off his hair. "A dog tore out that poor woman's throat."

"Seems so, yes," I said.

"Not just any dog. The white wolf dog. I told you that man was dangerous."

"You did."

"And I told you that wolf dog of his was a beast."

"Uh-huh."

"Then why do you have that damned journal in your hands? What more do you need to see to know that this is all a terrible, dangerous game? We can't play—we don't even know the rules! Only Fox did, and he's not here."

"No, he's not here!" I shouted back at him, suddenly angry and scared at the same time. "Don't you get it? Something is wrong, Huck. Really, terribly wrong. We need to find him. The widow couldn't help us, so we need to follow Father's path to the ring—just like he said in the journal."

"The same one that says one of the people he questioned last summer was a hermit? Have you lost your mind? I am *not* tracking down some hermit in the middle of nowhere." With a flick of his wrist, he threw the wet towel he'd been using on the floor. "That's a fool's journey, banshee, and I'm no fool."

"Well, maybe *I* am," I snapped. "Because my father is in trouble, and I'm not going to twiddle my thumbs in a stupid hotel room, hoping he'll come back. I'm going to find him."

"Oh, are you, now? You're going to ride out into the night like Grace O'Malley on horseback just to prove something? Do you know how stupid that is?"

"Don't really care." I lifted the leather journal. "Follow the ring, find my father. That is the official plan now. If you want to leave, fine. Leave. I'll find him by myself."

"With what money? We're nearly broke!"

"I'll sell something. Or send a cable to Father's accountant and ask him to wire me cash."

"Mr. Fitzgerald? *Pffi.* Good luck with that. When we were in Tokat, Fox mentioned he was somewhere in Canada, hiking up a mountain. You'll never reach him."

Not for the last time, I was incensed that Huck had been gone for an entire year and still managed to know more about my father's work than I did.

"It doesn't matter," I said, a little flustered but also too worked up to give in now. "I'll think of something. Whatever it takes. I'm going to find Father, and he's going to be fine, and maybe I'll even find Vlad's cursed ring, too."

"Ugh. You sound just like him. You know that? Stupidly stubborn."

"Whatever. Better to be stubborn than give up."

"Better to be dead, you mean? Did you not see the coroner

hauling away a bloody body?" he said, sounding nearly hysterical. And for a moment my heart clenched, because it struck me that the bloody murder scene we'd witnessed may not have looked all that different from the scene young Huck had been a part of when his parents died in that streetcar accident. I worried it stirred up traumatic memories for him—just for moment. Then his jaw turned steely, and I realized I was probably just being overly sensitive, because clearly he was fine.

That's what I got for caring.

I made a shooing gesture. "Go on, then, leave. I really don't care. Enjoy the Orient Express while I'm off doing what needs to be done. But know this, Huxley Gallagher," I said, pointing at his chest. "I'll never forgive you for deserting me again. Not as long as I live. So if you walk out now, I never want to see your damned eyes in front of my face!"

He swatted my finger away, scowling down at me. "Do you think that little of me? Do you?"

"I don't know what to think anymore. I thought I knew, but I've been lied to so many times, I just . . ." Unable to finish, I fought back a sudden swell of tears, angry at Huck. At my father. And at myself for caring about either one of them.

"Look at me, banshee," Huck said, bending down until his face was in front of mine. "You aren't the only person worried about Fox, you know. He may not be my father, but he did help raise me. If I were the one who'd disappeared, he'd come looking for me. So shut the hell up about it. I'm not deserting you in the middle of Romania. I'm supposed to be keeping you safe."

"Only because Richard Damn Fox told you to," I said. "Clearly you care more about him than you ever did about me—which I was too blind to see at the time. Thank the gods he caught us together, because it saved me from more heartbreak."

Something like fire caught behind his eyes. "C'mere to me," he said as he reached forward with both hands and firmly held my face. He spoke in a low, tense voice, nose almost touching mine. "You don't think I've suffered?"

"Not like I did."

"Is that right?"

"You left me!" I cried, angry and hurt and feeling as if he'd stripped away my armor.

"And it nearly killed me!"

"Good!" I shouted. "Because it *did* kill me."

His fingers trembled around my face. "Losing you shattered me into a thousand pieces. Ever since, I've walked around with this misery inside me, trying my damnedest to keep this tiny spark of hope alive that Fox would let me come back—that your heart hadn't grown cold. That you hadn't moved on to someone else and forgotten me. That all of it wasn't for naught, because if it was? Christ, banshee. I didn't know what I'd do. So there. Are you happy now? Are you happy to know that I wanted to die without you? Are you?"

Seismic waves vibrated inside me and shook silent tears from my eyes. They streamed down my cheeks before I could stop them or fully come to grips with what he'd said. I wanted to tell him that I hadn't moved on to someone else, that I couldn't, maybe not ever. That this battered, broken heart of mine wanted him still, even now.

But the words were trapped in my throat.

"Ah, hell and fire," he mumbled as his thumbs swept over my cheeks, wiping tears away as his own eyes became wet and glossy. "Please don't cry, banshee. You know I can't handle it when you cry. Then *I* want to cry, and it ruins my tough-guy reputation, and none of us want that, do we?"

"Maybe," I choked out, laughing a little, because if I laughed, then I wouldn't cry, and if I didn't cry, then I could regain some semblance of control over my wild emotions and attempt to figure out what all of this meant.

"I shouldn't have said any of that," Huck said in a softer voice, fingertips brushing hair away from my face. "It's not fair. Not right now when there are other things to work out. Sarkany and that damned dog. Your father . . ." He paused and said, "And maybe none of it matters. I don't even know if he'll let me come home yet."

"Of course he will," I said.

"He hasn't decided. And that could mean that when this is all over, I go back to Belfast. I don't even know when I'd see you again. If."

If? That was impossible. Father wouldn't do that.

Would he?

"He told me . . . ," Huck started, hesitating. "Fox said if he ever allowed me back home, it would be strictly as a member of the family. Not as his 'daughter's paramour.'"

"Oh," I said, both insulted and embarrassed. "I see."

I gently pushed Huck's hands away and wiped beneath my eyes with the side of my hand. He stepped into the bathroom and returned with a wad of toilet paper. I thanked him with a nod, blew my nose, and tried to gather my thoughts. Tried desperately to summon my armor back and stop shaking like a frightened Chihuahua caught in the rain.

"Banshee?"

I looked up at him. His face was a collection of sharp lines and deep hollows, and I couldn't decide if he was trying to tell me something or ask me a question.

"Never mind," he mumbled, shaking his head, and the mask slipped back on. Nothing was wrong at all. Nothing to see here. A quick tilt of his mouth that didn't quite make a smile. "Let's draw a line under this conversation for now," he suggested. "At least until we figure out what to do about Fox, yeah?"

Was that what I wanted? To leave this gaping emotional wound open and undressed when it likely needed stitches? Everything felt raw and confusing between us again, and that wasn't what I'd imagined it would feel like. Because I *had* imagined it, a thousand times in a thousand different ways—Huck telling me that what I felt for him wasn't one-sided or temporary. I fantasized about him showing up at Foxwood after piloting a plane over the Atlantic, telling me that he couldn't bear to stay away any longer. Or finding out that he'd gotten conked on the head and had amnesia this entire time, and that he'd woken up in a hospital whispering my name.

However I imagined it, though, I always pictured myself falling into his arms and him kissing the daylights out of me and both of us blissfully happy forever and ever more, amen. I didn't picture myself hurting and hollow. Or feeling bewildered. Or still unsure about where we stood. Wondering whether, if I freely opened myself up to all the wild feelings I used to feel for him, my father would snatch him away from me a second time.

"You're right," I told him, my voice still a little rough. "We need to focus on finding Father right now. That's what's important."

"Yes, that's what's important." He nodded firmly, hands thrust in his pockets, jingling loose change. "So then . . . just how do you propose we do that?"

HOW TO FIND MY FATHER IN ROMANIA. RIGHT. THAT.

To figure that out, I needed my brain. And to access my brain, I needed to stop thinking about everything Huck had just told me. So I shoved all my erratic emotions into a box, nailed the lid down, and buried it deep and dark. Then I focused on finding a solution to the problem of pinpointing Richard Damn Fox's whereabouts.

The only way I knew to accomplish this monumental task was to do what I'd already suggested to Huck and continue what we'd started. The widow, the hermit, and the twins . . . Retrace Father's summer trip through Romania to find Vlad Dracula's ring—and pray to God that was what *he* was currently doing.

The widow was a dead end. Next on Father's list was the hermit. I figured I'd look through the journal until I found a clue to the hermit's identity. The only entry I could recall offhand that even remotely suggested a hermit-type person was one in which Father mentioned visiting someone who lived in a colorful cottage outside

Bucharest. But I'd need to decipher the name, because if I remembered correctly, part of that entry was written in cipher.

Sitting against the headboard of my hotel bed, I began half-heartedly flipping through the journal's pages, but it was well past midnight and I already had a headache from working with the journal for hours this afternoon. Maybe also from all the crying, but I was trying not to think about that.

After a few minutes I found myself staring blankly at the pages, unable to even summon the will to read them. I suppose Huck saw this, because he quietly tugged the journal out of my hands, closed it, and said, "We'll do it tomorrow, yeah? We're cold and tired, and neither of us has slept well in . . . well, days, really."

"I *am* tired," I admitted.

"Let's just call it quits and try tomorrow. Things will seem easier in the morning."

He was right, and I knew it. So I packed away the journal, stopped thinking, and fell into my bed like a body into a grave. I wasn't sure how long I dozed, but I didn't stay asleep. I woke suddenly and harshly, blinking into darkness.

Someone was shaking my shoulders.

"Theo!" Huck whispered. His distinctive silhouette blocked the moonlight streaming in from the balcony doors. "For the love of the saints, wake up!"

I started to answer, mildly panicked, but he clamped a hand over my mouth.

All right. Now I was *absolutely* panicked.

"They found us," he whispered. "A porter just knocked on our door to warn me that two men in black robes are asking for our room number downstairs. They know we're here."

Images of the men who had broken into my hotel room in

Istanbul filled my head. I pried his fingers off my mouth and sat up. How had I not heard a knock on the door? And how had these men followed us? Was Sarkany here too?

"Get up, now!" Huck was in his underwear, struggling to get a leg into his trousers, hopping on one foot. "We need to leave. Hurry!"

Body on autopilot, I threw off the sheets and quickly dressed, uncaring about impropriety. We both tossed our possessions into our bags, struggling in the dark, and met at the door. Huck listened, ear against the wood, and then cautiously opened it to peer outside.

"Clear," he whispered, motioning for me to follow. I closed the door behind me, squinting into the hallway light. Huck headed toward the service stairwell with access to the roof—one that we'd seen porters slipping past during cigarette breaks. But when Huck tried the handle, it wouldn't budge.

Locked.

He uttered a string of profanities as we changed course and jogged toward the main corridor. We had two options: the guest stairwell or a single, small elevator behind an ornate metal door. I stood on tiptoes to peer through a diamond-shaped window into the black of an empty elevator shaft and moving cables. "The lift is coming up," I told Huck.

"Might be them. Can't chance it. Come on!"

We sprinted to the stairwell and raced down several flights, my short legs struggling to keep up with Huck's generous strides. Why oh why were we unlucky enough to be booked into a room on the highest floor? When we circled around the second-floor landing, Huck peered over the railing and stopped short. I slammed into his back. A shout from below echoed around the walls, and that's when I saw them: the two black-robed men from Istanbul.

And they saw us, too.

Huck shoved me back up the way we'd come. I raced up a flight of stairs, lurched through the third-floor door, and ran down the corridor. A finely dressed couple was headed toward their room, and I nearly bowled over the woman as I sailed past. Her partner said something nasty in Romanian to my back, but I didn't turn around. I just made a beeline toward the elevator and pressed both the *up* and *down* buttons repeatedly.

"C'mon, c'mon!" Huck whispered.

Our pursuers burst onto our floor right as the elevator *ding*ed.

Huck rattled the elevator handle until it opened to reveal a wide-eyed lift operator behind a scissor gate. No time for niceties. I pulled open the gate myself, and we stumbled onto the lift—an old, rickety box barely big enough for the three of us. While Huck closed the scissor gate, I shouted, "Lobby!" at the operator, a pasty-faced boy no older than me. Thankfully, he reacted quickly and threw the crank into the down position. The elevator groaned in protest. Then it began descending.

I fell against the elevator's wall, head sagging in relief.

"Is everything okay?" the elevator attendant asked in halting English.

"No," Huck said. "Bad men are chasing us. Can you let us out at the lobby and go find help?"

He agreed, though I wasn't sure he completely understood. And either he was new at the job or as nervous as we were, because when he pulled the lever to stop the lift, he missed lining up the elevator with the lobby floor by several inches. Huck didn't care. He yanked the scissor gate open and half shoved, half lifted me over the mismatched floors, then scrambled behind me into the lobby.

I frantically glanced around the large, domed space. Where was everybody? Our helpful friend Andrei was gone for the night, and in his stead was a boy I didn't know, bent over the registration desk with his head on an arm. The guard sitting on a stool by the hotel entrance was asleep too. The elevator attendant shouted at the boy behind the registration desk. He didn't move. For the love of Pete, was he drunk?

Or drugged.

My blood ran cold.

I didn't *think* the employees were dead.

But I wasn't sticking around to investigate.

"Hide!" Huck warned the elevator operator as he grabbed my hand. Then we both sprinted across the lobby together.

At first we headed for the entrance. But the idea of racing down the well-lit boulevard—where we could easily be spotted by the men chasing us—made me nervous. "This way!" I told Huck, and we turned into the nearby corridor that housed the hotel's amenities.

We jogged past a pair of late-night lovers locked in an embrace and a restaurant that was turning up chairs onto tables for the night. The only establishment that was still open was a brewhouse, and the sharp scent of beer and cigarette smoke wafted as a man stumbled out of its door. Men in tuxedoes were drinking and laughing at the bar, and someone was singing a folk song at the top of their lungs.

Behind us, a stampede of footfalls raced through the lobby. The robed men were catching up.

We picked up speed and raced past a gated cinema lobby with a single ticket window, a self-serve popcorn vending machine, and double doors leading into the theater—locked for the night. The only person here was a befuddled old man, sweeping up.

Huck tugged me forward, toward a door on the other side of the cinema. The knob turned, and he swung the door open.

For one terrible second I thought it was a broom closet. But no, it was a dim stairwell. The service stairwell—the one that was locked on our floor. We quickly ducked inside and found two choices before us: the first was a windowed door to our right that led down a dark corridor, perhaps to the hotel kitchen or laundry, but we'd never know, because it was locked.

That left the second choice: the stairwell.

"Up!" Huck said, and we took the dimly lit stairs two at a time, jogging around the landing. The floor numbers were crudely marked in paint on the concrete walls—2, 3, 4 . . . My calves burned, and I couldn't get enough breath into my lungs. I mentally cursed both gravity and my own lack of athleticism as I stumbled up flight after flight of stairs, too afraid to look back when I heard a door slam somewhere below us.

Huck raced up the final flight of stairs to the door at the top. He pushed it open, and we rushed out onto—

The hotel's roof.

Fresh air! Night air. *Cold* air. It needled my struggling lungs as I inhaled the chemical scent of pitch and smoke rising from chimneys.

We were six stories above midnight streets, and the rooftops of Bucharest stretched as far as I could see in the darkness. Cars streamed down the boulevard, and an ambulance's siren wailed in the distance. For the briefest of moments it all felt like freedom.

Until I realized there was no place left to run.

"Shut it!" Huck said. "Shut the rooftop door."

Next to my feet, a large cement block looked as if it was there to serve as a doorstop. "What if it locks?" I asked, frantic.

"I hope it damn well does!" He shouldered past me and slammed the metal door until it clicked into place, testing it for good measure.

Locked out. Them. And us.

Do not panic. Steel spine, chin high. You are not a coward.

I surveyed the roof. Cigarette butts, glass soda bottles, and a dead pigeon littered the area near the roof-access door. At the other end of the building sat the hotel's glass dome, shining light over the roof, but there was no viable path to get to it. The building was shaped like an L that cradled a courtyard in the back, and the only thing to do was to head there, so we stepped over broken tile and telephone wires, threading our way across the rooftop.

"Look!" I said when we got to the end. "There's a drop-down ladder. I think it leads to the hotel courtyard."

We glanced over the parapet. A secondary roof blocked our view of the ground; the ladder looked as if it stopped at a narrow ledge extending around the building, two floors down.

"We may be able to reach room windows from there," I said as a chilly night wind whipped my hair into my eyes. "Surely someone will let us inside." And if not, we could break a window. I was desperate, but when a wave of dizziness rolled over me, I was not entirely convinced that I didn't have a yet-unrealized fear of heights. I couldn't remember ever being this high up.

A noise sounded from across the rooftop. The roof-access door. Someone was pounding on it.

"Damn it all to hell!" Huck whispered.

"How did they find us here?" I asked, feeling mildly hysterical as another wave of dizziness hit me. "This is impossible!"

"They've tracked us somehow. Maybe that hellish wolf dog caught our scent at the murder scene in front of Natasha Anca's house."

"Through a taxicab? Miles and miles through a big city?"

"I don't know! Jesus and Mary, banshee . . ."

"Oh!" I said, holding out my hands. *"Oh!"*

"What? What?!"

I patted my coat pockets. "You're going to think I'm mad."

"Already do. Tell me!"

"That banknote . . ." I quickly pulled my handbag from the top of my satchel and thumbed through it as I talked. "Sarkany handed me an old Turkish banknote in the hotel lobby in Istanbul. Remember, I told you? He said I dropped it, but I didn't, and oh God—where did I put it? I went to my room, and you were there, and I got all discombobulated, and it's not here!"

Huck's eyes flicked toward my satchel. "Was that in the hotel room in Istanbul?"

"Uh, yes, but—"

Before I could protest, he snatched it from me, turned it upside down, and shook half the contents onto the roof. Deft fingers sorted through my silk underclothes and stockings. "Think, banshee. What did you do with it when—"

Huck stopped, midsentence, and pulled out a scrap of paper: the banknote! He unfolded the wrinkled paper, flipped it over, and held it up to the moonlight. And I knew immediately that my hunch was right:

A design had been inked onto the back.

Not a design. An ominous-looking occult sigil.

"I've seen this!" I whispered. "In the *Hammer of the Witches*."

"What the hell . . . ?" When Huck tilted the banknote, a spiderweb made of dusty light blossomed over the paper and shot across the roof toward the door.

We both yelped. Huck dropped the banknote.

Not an illusion. Very much real.

"What is this hellish wickedness?" Huck said, thoroughly alarmed.

"A spell," I said, astounded. "Some kind of tracking spell."

"This is . . ."

"Magic. Witchcraft. Spellwork." Right in front of our eyes! After everything esoteric I'd read, after all the research I'd done . . . Here was the proof that it existed. Maybe not tangible proof, but I knew what I saw.

"It's a trick of light—stage magic," Huck insisted.

I shook my head. "Sarkany isn't Harry Houdini. He's an occultist. And he's been tracking us since Istanbul. The train, and . . ." My wolf dream in the vardo wagon. Had Sarkany and his hound been outside, stalking us while we slept? A terrible chill went through me.

"Do you believe it?" I asked.

He blinked at me for several moments, eyes wild and panicked. Then he shook his head. "How do we stop it?"

I tried to recall what I'd read about spells like these, grappling with the excitement of discovery and the pounding on the rooftop door, which was sounding louder and louder. . . .

"Destroy it!" I said, hoping I was right.

From his coat pocket, Huck retrieved a box of matches printed with a black cat and gingerly picked up a corner of the banknote. "Here!" I said, taking the matches from him. I struck a match and held it to the paper. Flames devoured it. Huck waited until it was flaming too intensely to hold and dropped it onto the roof. In seconds it was nothing but ash and smoke that scattered across the rooftop.

Bang! Bang! Bang!

We swung toward the roof-access door.

Our pursuers weren't pounding anymore; they were trying to break down the damn door. No need to tell me twice. I bent down and rapidly shoveled all my things back into my satchel in three quick motions. Huck made a quick assessment and squatted on the edge of the roof to maneuver onto the ladder. "C'mon," he said, motioning. "Follow me. If you slip, I'm under you. Just don't look down."

Why do people always say that? As the battering on the roof-access door intensified, I quickly gathered up my skirt and knotted it between my legs to stop it from blowing. Then I twisted around until I was steady on the rickety roof ladder, and I descended.

Painted rust scraped my palms. The wind was fierce. Another bout of dizziness rolled over me, but I didn't look down—not until I heard Huck jump onto the narrow ledge. Then his hands were around my waist, and he helped me down the last few rungs.

"Nice trick," he said, smiling at my skirt. My garters were showing.

I tugged the knot loose and shook out the fabric. "Didn't want a pervert looking up it."

He opened his mouth to protest but was cut short by a loud crash from the roof. The men had busted open the roof-access door.

Without a word, Huck led and I followed along the ledge. When we heard noise above, we paused and hid in the shadows, flattened against the building, while silhouettes leaned over the parapet above. My pulse pounded in my temples. My chest rose and fell rapidly. Huck squeezed my hand. Or maybe I squeezed his; it was hard to be sure. But after several excruciating minutes, the silhouettes gave up and disappeared, and we were left alone with nothing but the sound of howling wind.

"We can't stay out here," I whispered, trying to see in the dark. If we kept going around the ledge, we might be able to reach a bank of windows. I pointed them out to Huck. He struggled to see them in the dark, so we switched places, and I got in front, carefully skirting along the ledge to the corner, then made the turn to the main part of the hotel.

Windows, and all of them were within reach. We tried four before one opened. "Hallway!" I whispered.

I chucked my satchel inside, and Huck boosted me up until I could climb through, then he followed suit. The hallway was quiet and empty. Two lonely housekeeping carts sat in a row. Maybe this wing wasn't currently in use. Huck looked around a corner before pausing in front of one of the rooms, ear pressed to the door, listening. He must have liked what he heard, because he wasted no time digging inside his inner coat pocket to pull out an old set of lockpicks wrapped in a scrap of leather. Then he squatted in front of the door. I kept watch while he worked, and within seconds the lock clicked, and we both stumbled into an unoccupied hotel room.

"Hurry," Huck whispered, locking the door behind us.

Metal rollaway bedframes with folded mattresses were lined up in two neat rows alongside wooden crates of new towels and blankets. The hotel was using this room for storage, it seemed.

We quickly pushed one of the larger crates against the door to block it—and stacked a second on top for good measure. Then we sat on the floor together, back-to-back. Huck watched the barricaded door, and I watched the window.

"You did see that on the banknote," Huck said in a low voice after several minutes had passed in strained silence. "Looked like a web made out of light? I wasn't imagining it, was I?"

"I saw it too," I said.

"You think Sarkany did that? He's some kind of sorcerer or warlock? Because now I'm thinking about what that man told us at the widow's house—that she dabbled in the occult. And her husband sold his ring to that Mr. Rothwild fellow who hired Fox. Who are these people, and are all of them practicing dark arts?"

"My *Batterman's Field Guide* says that Vlad Dracula's ring has power. And Father talked to people in Romania who claimed there were legends about other people who owned it over the years—mass murderers. Evil people."

"Let's just say, for argument's sake, that some of those stories about the ring are even partly true. What if it grants the wearer some sort of dark, murderous power? Could that be why all these bastards want it so badly—Sarkany and his goons? Maybe even Mr. Rothwild."

"What if they're competing occultists?" I said. "Rothwild and Sarkany."

"Maybe that's why Sarkany killed the widow—she was acquainted with Rothwild. Maybe they're in a race to find the ring."

And we were standing in the middle of their racing track with a journal that held secrets to help the winner get to their goal first.

Not a good place to be.

"Lazy birds," I murmured, reciting a crossword clue I'd missed yesterday morning, before the telegrams and the journal cipher and the murder scene . . . before Huck swiping away my tears and making me want him all over again.

"Lazy birds?" Huck repeated.

"Ten across," I said. "Sitting ducks."

"Aye, that's about right."

Both of us fell silent. For a long time I could feel Huck's heartbeat pounding through his spine. He felt solid and safe, a reassuring comfort. Yet even so, even with his back against mine, it still felt as if there were an invisible emotional wall between us. Everything we'd said. Everything we hadn't. Even with everything that had happened over the last few days, this emotional chaos molded itself into bricks and stacked up.

Losing you shattered me into a thousand pieces.

Did he truly mean that? Did he still feel the same way? I wanted to hear it from him again, to make sure that it wasn't a daydream or a mirage. I wanted to tell him that I was grateful he was here with me right now. That despite everything that had happened over the last year, I didn't want to lose him again, not for anything in the world. Even if it meant all we could be was friends. Or family. Or whatever my father decided was acceptable.

Could I, though? Just be friends?

Was it possible to stop loving someone and still be happy, settling for something less than it once was?

WE FELL ASLEEP IN THE STORAGE ROOM. NEITHER of us meant to, and when I woke, cheek sticking to the leather of my satchel and Huck's body heating my back, I was so discombobulated, it took me several panicked heartbeats to realize that (a) it was morning, (b) Huck had just woken up too, and (c) someone from housekeeping had found us.

The housekeeper tried to push open our barricaded door, calling out, "*Buna?*" repeatedly, and by the time she'd sent for the help of a porter, we'd unstacked the crate barrier. After an awkward conversation, Andrei showed up, and he was relieved to see us.

"My friends! We thought you were dead or kidnapped," he admitted. "Three workers were sedated by the men who chased you—Titus told me everything. He hid in the kitchen for hours."

Titus turned out to be the elevator operator. But he didn't know what had happened to the men in robes—only that they'd disappeared. I didn't like the sound of that. For all we knew, they could be lying in wait for us when we walked out of the hotel.

But we couldn't stay here forever either.

"This was not as exciting as your father's unfortunate incident with the mayor's wife in the lobby this summer," Andrei said. "But now I think that misfortune follows your family."

He had no idea.

"Brother, let me tell you what I think," Huck said to Andrei. "I think if Miss Fox and I make it out of Romania alive, you will have two new refrigerators."

Encouraged by this promise, Andrei was kind enough to have two guards escort us back to our room, where we washed our faces and changed clothes. After last night's fiasco and with the ever-dropping temperatures, I decided I was done with running around in skirts. I changed into wrinkled khaki trousers, thick socks, and a pair of short brown leather boots that I'd had the good sense to pack at the bottom of my satchel when we were escaping the train back in Bulgaria. Then we ate a breakfast of buttered bread, Telemea cheese, sausage, and coffee. Huck surveyed the street from the balcony while I broke out my Vigenére square and Father's journal. After a quick assessment, I was even more certain than I had been last night about where we should go next to find him.

JOURNAL OF RICHARD FOX
July 3, 1937
Snagov, Kingdom of România

Found a driver willing to take us to Transylvania. On the way, an hour north of Bucharest, stopped by a fourteenth-century monastery on a small islet in Lake Snagov. Long rumored to be the final resting place for Vlad Dracula's bones (minus the head), it was excavated five years ago by a colleague of Elena's,

Dinu Rosetti. He didn't find Vlad—only the bones of several horses. I hope to meet with him in Târgoviște, where he is excavating a caste, just to confirm that he didn't secret away any monastery treasures for himself, i.e., a ring of bone. In the meantime, I thought it wouldn't hurt to tour the monastery here. Glad I did, because I received a small windfall of information.

The monastery's caretaker told me about a woman who lives in the woods across the lake, Madmoazelă FXPXE. My poor excuse for Romanian is being tested on this trip—Elena would shake her head in shame if she heard me butchering her country's language—but I thought he called her a "hermit." Regardless, she was rumored to be in possession of a family heirloom: a medieval ring of bone. Call me crazy, but I wasn't passing up the chance that this wasn't a coincidence.

Update, 7PM:
Jean-Bernard and I found this woman's strange little house, which was isolated and accessible only by a dirt road. Seems the woman is less of a hermit and more of a folk herbalist, for which I have little patience. Let us just say that she and I did not get along. We spent five minutes talking on her front porch, and once she found out who I was working for, she told me that she didn't have any such ring, but if she did, she wouldn't let me see it because Rothwild is (and I'm translating here) "not fit to roll in pig shit." Seems Rothwild had tried to contact her about the ring long before he hired me, and she not only hated him, but she hated me for being associated with him.

Next time I'm keeping my mouth shut about Rothwild. But I'm also telephoning the bastard when we get to Târgovişte, because what is the point of me revisiting the same places he's already hit, looking for the ring? If he's not going to be up front with me about these kinds of details, Jean-Bernard and I will just leave Romania and head back down to Greece to enjoy our holiday in the sun.

"What's an herbalist?" Huck asked with no small amount of suspicion when I finished reading it aloud. "Please let it be someone who studies plants. I'm up to my eyeballs in occultists right now."

"Maybe she mixes up natural remedies for the villagers?"

"Where there's doubt, there's hope," Huck quipped.

"Where there's *life*," I corrected.

"There's more doubt than life right now, banshee."

He wasn't wrong. The ciphered word in Father's entry, FXPXE, I decoded to "Blaga."

Madame Blaga. I relayed this to Huck, then said, "Father mentioned that this Lake Snagov is an hour north of Bucharest. If I had to guess why she's on Father's list—widow, hermit, twins—I'd say he must have thought that this woman actually had a bone ring in her possession; she just wasn't willing to show it to him."

Maybe it was another forgery. Maybe it was the real ring.

And maybe, just *maybe*, Father was there right now, and in a couple of hours all of this would be over. I could tell him about Sarkany and the wolf dog and how we ran across a roof to escape goons who were after us . . . and after I told him everything, I'd punch him in the stomach for abandoning us.

"Well, you know what they say," Huck said as he peeked out the balcony, scanning the street. "Hope for the best; prepare for a raving hermit lady to chase us off her land. Let's find out if Andrei can locate the address of one Madame Blaga in Snagov. And figure out how we're getting out there with our limited funds."

It didn't take long for both of those things to get solved. Andrei was able to get an address and a taxi, and because he generously refused payment for our last night in the hotel, we had enough money to pay said taxi, which pulled around to a hidden side entrance in an alley to pick us up—just in case we were being followed by the robed men.

After explaining to the driver where we needed to go, Andrei shook our hands and waved goodbye. "You will tell the Fox I said hello when you find him?"

"I'll have him send you a check for the broken lock on the roof-access door," I called back as the cab began pulling away.

He gave me a thumbs-up sign, and then we were on our way.

I was a little sorry to say goodbye to Bucharest as I watched the city roll past my window and turn into farmland and rivers. A petrol station. A roadside memorial cross. A man walking two horned water buffalo on the side of the road. And then there was little more than the road itself, the occasional humble home, and great swathes of wooded land. Everywhere I looked, trees were bursting with gold and red leaves. It was idyllic, but that also meant there were fewer places to hide if someone was following us.

But no one was. In fact, I hadn't seen a car in miles. It was quiet out here. Very rural. Bandit-free. I realized I should probably have been more worried about the taxi driver getting lost than anyone attacking us. After a few wrong turns, the taxi finally found the right dirt lane leading into the right woods, and it wasn't long before we found what we were looking for.

Across from a wooden hill at the bend of a river sat a large cottage.

Its stone facade was covered in folk paintings. Bands of flowers and murals that looked as if they were straight out of a fairy tale: ravens, bears, wolves wearing clothes, a flying horse. It wasn't exactly enchanting, and maybe even verged on foreboding.

"This is the right address?" Huck said to the driver, who gestured loosely toward the cottage in confirmation. "Is it just me, or do you feel like Hansel and Gretel?"

"Whatever you do, don't get inside any ovens," I told him.

A striking middle-aged woman emerged from a wooden door, a long cigarillo clamped between two fingers. She limped across a front porch in a billowing white dress cinched at the waist by an embroidered black-and-red apron; a red kerchief was tied over silver-streaked hair.

The hermit.

And no sign of my father. Well, here's to hoping I had better luck with this woman than he had.

In Romanian, I quickly begged the driver to wait for us, just for a moment. And when he agreed, I exited the taxi with Huck and cautiously approached the woman.

"Good morning. We're looking for Madame Blaga," I said in Romanian, shielding my eyes with my hand to look up at her on the cottage porch.

The woman blew out a long plume of fragrant smoke and responded in richly accented English. "You have found her. But few ask for me with that name anymore. Most call me Mama Lovena."

Memories from the traders' bonfire rose like smoke inside my head. Valentin's story of a witch who lived in a cottage in the woods . . .

A creaky breath gusted from my mouth.

Huck sounded as if he were choking and tried to pass it off as a cough.

"You've heard of me, I can see." One corner of her mouth curled. "It's probably all true."

"Jaysus," Huck mumbled, tugging discreetly on my coat sleeve. "I knew 'herbalist' didn't sound right. She's a witch, banshee. We need to leave."

I laughed, nervous, hoping she hadn't heard that comment. And I wasn't going anywhere. Was it every day that one gets to meet a witch in a forest? I thought not. "I'm Theodora Fox," I called out. "And this is Huck Gallagher. We're sorry to show up on your doorstep unannounced."

"Many do." She beckoned us with her cigarillo to come closer and looked us over critically, gaze stopping on my silver coin pendant. "But few bearing the name of a Byzantine empress. Interesting souvenir you have there."

I touched the coin, surprised. "You know about her?"

"I know about a lot of things," the woman said through squinting eyes. "Just what do you seek from me, little empress?"

Little empress. That was what my parents called me. Hearing it now threw me off-balance and made my throat constrict.

"Yes, sorry . . . ," I said, a little rattled. "I think you spoke to my father a few months ago, in the summer? He was with another man, and they came here looking for a ring."

A smile grew. "You are the American treasure hunter's daughter."

"We were wondering if perhaps my father had come here again?"

"Oh, yes," she said. "Yesterday."

My heart went wild. "Yesterday? Are you sure?"

"Do you forget a bear growling at you? No, you do not. Richard Fox was here, but he left."

"Did he say where he was going? Was he with anyone? Was he okay?"

"So many questions, *tsk*," she said, more weary than irritated, before lifting her head to the taxi driver and telling him in rapid Romanian to wait. When he lifted a hand and nodded, she beckoned to me with her cigarillo again. "Come inside, little empress, and we can talk. I will tell you what I know."

Huck was still hesitant, so I elbowed him firmly in the ribs in an attempt to pluck up both his courage and mine. He muffled a groan. Then we followed the strange woman into the stranger house.

A narrow, dim hallway passed several doors—a kitchen, with drying bundles of herbs and roots that perfumed the air, and a bathroom with modern facilities. Photographs of well-dressed ladies lined the walls, and I remembered Valentin saying that Mama Lovena was rumored to have come from nobility. Seemed she was also educated: a framed degree blurred in my sight as I walked past, from a well-known Romanian medical university in Transylvania. She had medical training as a nurse.

An educated noblewoman, living here in a humble cottage.

The hall stretched the length of her home, and we ended up in the main living space, where natural daylight filtered in through a long pair of windows. It shone upon low bookshelves that ringed the four walls, overflowing with dusty books, and it illuminated a cluster of elaborate birdcages that hung from dark wooden rafters in the center of the room. The cages were old, a variety of shapes and sizes, but it wasn't until we walked beneath them that I noticed what was inside.

Crows.

A dozen or more—each black as the night, from beady eye, to beak, to claw. One shook its cage, and a dark feather fell out, gliding until it settled upon the woman's outstretched palm.

Mother of the forest, Valentin had said.

She knows the tongue of the beasts.

One of the caged crows squawked, and I jumped. A chill raced down my arms.

"Never mind their chatter, dear," the woman said. "My birds are only curious, as all creatures of intelligence should be. Are you curious, little empress?"

"I'm curious about where my father is," I said, trying to sound tougher than I felt.

"Yes, let me tell you what I know about Mr. Fox." She settled on a large velvet-upholstered armchair, its stuffing poking out in several places, and invited us to sit on a couch across from her, which we did. "He came to see me last summer with his pretty traveling partner, the French man."

"Jean-Bernard," I said, feeling hopeful.

She nodded. "And I didn't mind that your father was a rude American who demanded my time instead of asking. Nor did I mind that he insisted on looking at a ring that he was certain had been in my family for several decades. The problem was that he was sent here by my enemy, a Hungarian man by the name of Mr. Rothwild."

"He's the collector who hired my father to find the bone ring," I said.

"Collector?" She shook her head. "He is a wicked man."

"How so?" Huck asked carefully.

She looked at both of us, thoughtful, and then leaned back in her seat. "Don't suppose it hurts anyone to tell you. Do you know of the legend of the Solomonari?"

"They're wizards, aren't they?" I said, trying to recall whether I'd seen something about them in my *Batterman's Field Guide* or whether my mother had told me a folk story about them.

She nodded. "Travelers in the clouds, they were called by the Dacians. Said to be able to control the weather. They rode dragons in the sky. Well, our Mr. Rothwild fancies himself one of the Solomonari—at least, in an aspirational sense. You see, he's a devotee of a medieval Romanian organization with a checkered history. A secret society. The ring your father was hired to find is the centerpiece of some grand plan to revive the society, and Mr. Rothwild is a fanatic psychopath. He conspired with a woman to kill her husband in order to obtain what he thought was the genuine ring of Vlad Țepeș, and when he found himself holding a dud, he was furious."

Conspired to kill a man? She had to be talking about the widow Natasha Anca. Rothwild helped kill the widow's husband . . . and Sarkany killed the widow. That was an awful lot of murder for a "dud" of a ring—murders of which my father was smack in the middle. Of which *we* were in the middle . . .

I glanced at Huck; he was clearly thinking the same.

"Right now we're more concerned about where my father is," I said. "You mentioned he was here yesterday?"

She nodded. "He showed up here yesterday morning, looking like hell. Said he had to find the ring because he'd fallen into a dark rabbit hole—people were following him, and his family was not safe. It seems the Frenchman has been harmed."

"Poisoned," I confirmed.

"That is what Mr. Fox said, yes," she confirmed. "A shame, because the Frenchman at least had manners. No offense intended."

No offense taken. My father had the manners of a loudmouthed toddler covered in mud and jam who swore like a sailor on leave.

"Jean-Bernard was poisoned by Rothwild?" Huck said.

"That is what I took it to mean, though I'm unsure if Mr. Fox knows for certain," she said. "But I'll tell you what I told Mr. Fox—it doesn't matter if he finds the ring or not. Mr. Rothwild is not a man of his word. If he's willing to kill for the ring, he will not stop doing so. Especially if he gets his hands on the prize. How can I say this in English?" She paused, forehead wrinkling. "Do you know what a relic is?"

"An artifact?" Huck said.

"No, my boy, the earlier meaning. A relic is the body part of a holy person kept as a talisman. The ring your father seeks was made from human bone. It contains a sleeping power, and in the wrong hands, that power will wake up."

Goose bumps chased down my arms. "It's rumored to be cursed."

"Cursed? Perhaps," she said. "That is a broad term, and I don't think it was made as a punishment. I think it was made to bestow unnatural power or will upon its owner."

"This may be a silly question, but how do you know?" Huck said. "If you don't mind me asking, that is."

Lovena gave him a patient smile. "I know because my family owns the real ring."

I sat up straighter, head buzzing. "Is that so?"

She explained, "We have owned it for decades. A letter came with the ring when it was delivered to my mother, before the turn of the century. A priest from Turkey sent it to her, trusting that she would keep it hidden, because it could be dangerous in the wrong hands. When she died, I became its caretaker."

Father was right. The widow, the hermit, the twins . . . He knew one of them had it. But my God—he'd missed out on learning this during his summer trip here because he was rude to this woman? Could it really have been that simple?

"Ever since I was a child," Lovena said, "I could feel the power in that ring. I do not know what it does, exactly. However, since inheriting it, I have researched and learned that it was not crafted for Vlad Țepeș—Dracula—but his father, Vlad *Dracul*."

"The Dragon," I murmured.

She smiled. "Indeed. The elder Vlad was a pawn in a war between the Ottoman Empire and the King of Hungary, who was also the Holy Roman Emperor. And that emperor had a ring of bone made by someone with occult knowledge, a ring that would give Hungary the advantage in war. However, the elder Vlad never wore it. It was his son, the younger Vlad, who was depicted wearing it."

"In a woodcut of Vlad eating at a table before his impaled enemies," I said excitedly, thinking of the illustration in my *Batterman's Field Guide*.

"That's the one, yes," Lovena said, nodding approvingly. "And legend says that ring molded Vlad into an unstoppable warlord, a deathless killing machine—right up until he was beheaded in battle."

The woman paused, glanced from Huck's face to mine, and said to me, "That is only what I've read in my studies, but I have no reason to believe it's not true. You may be like your father and call me irrational; I do not care."

Irrational was the last thing I'd call her. She was calm and cool, if not a bit intimidating. She reminded me of my mother a little, in that way.

"I'm *not* my father," I told her.

"Perhaps not," she said, looking at me intently. Sizing me up. Measuring me. I held my chin higher.

"Hold on, now," Huck said, still trying to piece everything together. "Let me get this straight. You think your ring is real.

Rothwild believes that the ring he has is a fake. Yet Fox—that is, her father," he said, gesturing to me. "He left notes that suggested there were at least two other rings made to confuse anyone who might go looking for it. Someone has a third ring?"

"Yes, Mr. Fox explained that to me—that two reproductions were sent along with the real ring. I have no reason to doubt it, as I heard a rumor years ago that a similar ring of bone had been acquired by the owners of an antiques business, the Zissu brothers. They have a keen interest in arcane items such as this. Maybe their ring is a reproduction, or maybe they don't even have it anymore, but likely they know its history better than I."

Brothers. I wondered if my father had talked to them. Could they be the "twins" on his list?

"Their shop moves from city to city every year or so," Lovena said. "They are merchants who follow the estate sales, you see, and in that regard, they are a bit like your father, interested in obtaining unusual objects." She shrugged. "Last time I saw them, a few years ago, they were in Constanța, on the Black Sea."

That was all the way on the eastern side of the country. Miles and miles away. Days.

Huck warily eyed a crow cage above us and said, "How do you know your ring is the real one?"

"As I told you, I can sense that our ring has power. The markings on it are very old. But whether it is the ring Rothwild thinks he wants, I could not say. He is the expert on Vlad Dracula and the Holy Roman Emperor who founded a secret fraternal organization, one that Rothwild and his colleagues want to revive. One that gave Vlad's father his family name—the Order of the Dragon."

Adrenaline raced through me. My father had made several notes about this medieval order. "They were a militant group, created to stop the Ottoman government from invading and taking over Eastern Europe."

"A threat that doesn't exist today, as the Ottoman Empire fell nearly two decades ago. Rothwild's motives for reviving the order likely center on occult secrets to amass power. I don't know how many people are involved in this pet project of his, but they are experimenting with dark things that they do not understand."

That sounded . . . vaguely terrifying. Some part of my brain was intrigued and wanted to know more, but I tried to focus on why we came here.

"Did you give my father the ring?" I asked.

"And have him hand it over to Rothwild and his cultists? Never," Lovena said, shaking her head. "After Mr. Fox and the Frenchman left this summer, I gave it to my sister. As it was, I couldn't bear to have it in my house—its power was too loud. Enough to drive anyone mad. My sister isn't sensitive to these things, so it didn't bother her. She promised to keep it safe, though I'm worried now that I've made a mistake. . . ."

"Where is my father now?" I asked.

"Probably in Sighișoara," she said, pronouncing it like *Siggy-shora*. "That is north of here, in the Carpathians."

Something sparked inside my head. "That's the birthplace of Vlad Țepeș, isn't it? A medieval citadel."

She nodded. "Indeed it is, yes. My family home is also there, though not as famous as Vlad's perhaps, and so is my sister. She has married into Hungarian money and is a baroness—Lady Maria Kardos. That is what I told Mr. Fox, and that is where he seemed intent on going when he left my home."

A tightness inside me loosened. My father was alive, he was here yesterday, and we knew where he was going; all we had to do was catch up. I didn't know how far away this town was that she spoke of, but maybe Father was still there. . . .

Huck was relieved too. He gave my fingers a quick squeeze on the couch between us, and I squeezed back. Then a noise above caused us both to look up at the birdcages.

"Do you really talk to animals?" Huck asked.

"Do you believe such a thing is possible?" Lovena asked in a voice that was almost playful, teasing. Yet also challenging.

"I'm . . . not sure," Huck answered.

"Some call me a wisewoman, babă, mother of the forest . . . pagan. Some call me a crow witch," she said, lifting her chin to the cages above. "But I will tell you a secret. I am not special. Magic is in every natural thing. It waits in the grass, and it blossoms in flowers. It's concentrated inside metals, deep within the earth, and it's carried on the wind. Magic will speak to anyone who takes the time to listen."

"But animals?" Huck said. "I don't—"

"Animals, humans . . . we are all made of blood," she said, running a nail along a vein in her hand. "*That* is where magic is plentiful. When magic is plentiful, it is easy to hear, if you have sensitive ears and a willingness to listen." She leaned forward and squinted at Huck. "I am a good listener. Where I was born, in Transylvania—the land beyond the forest—is rich with magic. It makes the dead rise. And it gives the living power. Our blood is vibrant."

"Blood, eh?" he murmured, looking a little pallid. He tried to smile and said, "Truth be told, it's not my favorite thing in the world. Prefer it when it's on the inside."

"Blood is everything," she said. "Magic in the blood can be heard, which is where my talents lie. Some are deaf to its voice but are able to force results using old rituals. Wonderworkers, they were called. Occult magicians. They knew methods to take blood from a living thing and forge it into something new."

"Into a magical object," I said, intensely interested. "I've read about that in a few books. . . ."

"Theory is one thing," she said, "but in practice, this is hard to do, a rare talent. Maybe one in many thousand could even do it. Maybe one in a million. But likely it's how Vlad Dracula's bone ring was made—by bone and by blood."

Huck shuddered. "The dark arts."

"Depends on the intent. Like anything, it can be abused." Mama Lovena picked up a fallen feather and ran it through her fingers. "So, to answer your question . . . I am a good listener and a good conduit. But you don't need to fear me. My interests are always with the forest and the animals in it. People, I can take or leave."

Huck chuckled and nervously rubbed his palms along his trousers.

Lovena turned to me and held out her hand. Her fingers crooked. "Please. I am curious."

"You want to read my palm?"

"I want to listen to your blood." A small smile lifted her lips as she winked at me. "It is not as bad as it sounds. I am no vampire. Not yet, at least. When I die, who knows. Maybe my fool of a sister will fail to bury me properly, and I'll enjoy haunting her."

She was making jokes? I liked her more and more.

Ignoring Huck, who was squirming on the seat next to me, uncomfortable and anxious, I extended my hand for Lovena to inspect. She held the tips of my fingers, looking and listening. Then she leaned forward, squinting at the veins on the back of my hand, and made a purring noise. "Very interesting indeed. Who is your mother, little empress?"

A cool breeze from the open window rattled the cages above us, and after they stilled, an odd rustling noise swirled around the room. My pulse quickened. Was it the birds? I tried to spot the source of the noise but saw nothing.

"My mother has been dead for almost eight years," I told her.

"That matters not. You have old Transylvanian blood, do you not?" Lovena insisted. "Your mother's bloodline is from these lands—it's as clear to me as water from a stream."

I blinked. Had my father told her? Or had she investigated him after his first visit last summer? If it wasn't that, then maybe it was because I'd spoken a little Romanian to her and she'd just made an educated guess.

But I didn't think so. The way she looked at me made the hair on the back of my neck quiver and itch.

"Yes," I said quietly. "My mother was from Brașov. Her family goes back many generations, I think."

"Yes, I thought so. Old blood," she confirmed. "Do you speak with her?"

"My mother?"

"There are ways to speak to some of the dead. Ways to hear, ways to send messages between worlds," she said, glancing at her crows above us. "Or maybe, like the boy, you have doubts. Maybe you don't believe . . ."

An unsettling thrill shot through me along with an unexpected sense of desperation. "I believe," I insisted. "If there's a way to speak with my mother, a spell or a ritual, I want to know it—"

Lovena released my hand. "It's not a recipe I can write down for you."

"But—"

"Speaking with the dead involves more than your mere desire

to hear. I said there are ways to talk to some of the dead. Not all. *Some*. Some don't want to talk. Others are too far gone to hear, even for me and my crows." She gestured lightly to the cages above.

"But how would I know?" I asked. "Do I just talk to her? Does it need to be at her grave or where she died?"

She smiled. "So many questions. That is my fault. You came here to talk about your father, not your mother. Let us just stick to that, yes?"

Frustrated, I bit back a response and glanced at Huck, who couldn't keep his eyes from darting to the crows above us. All of this was making him nervous. He never had a strong stomach for the unexplainable. Or the dead. When I was at home in New York, I often went to my mother's grave to talk with her. It gave me comfort. Huck, on the other hand, refused to step foot in the graveyard.

But talking to my mother was one thing . . . The possibility of her answering was another. Perhaps I was too eager to believe what Lovena had said was possible. I wasn't sure, but it didn't matter. When I pushed her for more, she wouldn't budge. Subject closed. "Is there anything more you need to know about the ring or your father?" she said, as if she were ready for us to leave now.

"Could I ask you your advice about a symbol?" I said.

She gestured loosely. "You may."

"See, there's been this man trailing us by the name of Sarkany. . . . He's tangled up in this mess with the ring."

I proceeded to tell her a bare-bones account of how the man gave me the banknote in Istanbul and then appeared on the train, and how we saw him again outside the widow's house in Bucharest, hiding in the shadows with his wolf dog.

Lovena flinched. "What did you say?"

"Um, he has a one-eyed white dog?" I said. "He claims she's part Carpathian wolf—"

"She is," Lovena said sharply, hands suddenly shaking with rage. "Her name is Lupu, and she is *my* dog. She was lured into a trap and stolen from the woods outside my home a month ago."

"Christ alive," Huck mumbled. "The wolf is yours?"

"I tracked her blood for two miles down the road until I lost the trail and could not hear her anymore," the woman said, standing up from her chair. "I raised her from a pup. She'd been shot in the eye by a hunter, and I nursed her back to health. Lupu is special. She—" Lovena paused, hands on hips, eyes flicking as she considered something. "I thought Rothwild took her as revenge when I refused to give him the ring. Only someone with knowledge of spellwork could have hidden Lupu from me. But this Sarkany must have bewitched her to follow him. Who is this man? Is he a member of Rothwild's occult order?"

"We wondered if he was Rothwild's rival," I said. "Because it seems as if he's trying to get Vlad Dracula's ring too. We think he's been tracking us with magic on that banknote—the one I just told you about?"

Lovena lowered her eyes. "Tell me everything you know."

Huck and I talked over each other, threading together the story of when he first encountered Sarkany in Tokat. The banknote. The robed goons. And it was only when we told Lovena about the murder scene at Natasha Anca's home that she became livid. "He used my dog—*my* dog—to kill?" A string of curses in Romanian followed.

I didn't know what to say. Huck, either. We just sat there, feeling awkward while Lovena paced around the room, dragging one bad leg behind her, visibly upset.

"You may be right," she mumbled. "Perhaps this Sarkany is Rothwild's rival. But that makes both of them more dangerous, because men who compete for power often succumb to violence to reach their goal."

After a long silence she shuffled to a table filled with bottles, herbs, and small copper bowls. She picked out a small green pouch, opened it, and brought it to me, dropping its contents onto my palm.

A tiny bit of wood carved into a rudimentary female figure. It was about the size of a chess piece and smelled herbal. "Put this in your pocket and keep it close to you. Under your pillow when you sleep."

"What is it?" Huck asked, wide-eyed.

"A simple talisman anointed with comfrey root oil—for safe travel. A little goddess to guard the little empress, yes?" She gave me a soft smile and closed my fingers around the wooden talisman, patting my hand. "It seems your fates are now tied to mine. I do not know who this Sarkany is, but I will ask my crows. It may take some time, but I will see the truth. He cannot hide from me."

I did not doubt it.

It felt as if she was ready for us to leave, so I stood up and slipped the talisman into my coat pocket. "I'm sorry about your dog. We didn't know. I just want to find my father, that's all."

She looked me in the eye. "If you find him, little empress, please convince him to break from Rothwild. I said you shouldn't fear me, but you *should* fear those who would abuse blood magic and twist it—people who do not care about hurting people, animals, or the land to get what they want. These men who covet the ring? Sarkany, and whatever group he belongs to . . . Rothwild and his Order of the Dragon? They are all what I would call evil men."

That seemed a fair assessment.

She switched to Romanian and said in a low voice, "I fear that you are being pulled into their affairs by the hands of fate. Be wary. Do not allow bad men to take what doesn't belong to them."

"I don't understand," I whispered back.

"You will."

Hmph. Now she sounded like my father, doling out information as if it too much of it would rot my teeth. "Did you mean what you said earlier?" I asked in Romanian. "Can I really talk to my mother?"

A slow smile lifted her lips. "What do you think?"

Well, let's see. We were standing in the house of a self-proclaimed crow witch who was able to suss out my heritage by listening to my blood and gave me a magic talisman for protection. And the man following us was possibly mixed up in some sort of cult—or a rival cult, which could be worse. He was a dog thief, likely a sorcerer, and most definitely a murderer. So . . . what did I think? I thought we were up to our necks in all of this, and it would be nice if for once in my life someone told me the truth.

But Lovena was done dispensing esoteric secrets. Switching back to English, she quickly told us how to find her sister as she herded us back through the house and onto the porch. There was a train station in town, she told us, and our taxi was still waiting out front.

I didn't want to leave. She hadn't told me enough, and it felt as if we were walking out of a safe space and into the unknown. The witch's somber face told me I wasn't wrong. Maybe there was nothing more she could do.

After we thanked her, she watched us leaving and shouted out to us when Huck was opening the door to the cab.

"If the Frenchman's health does not improve, tell them to send me a telegram in care of the local Snagov post office. I will try to help. And if you see my dog again, you tell her to come home."

JOURNAL OF RICHARD FOX

July 6, 1937

Sibiu, Transylvania, Kingdom of România

Jean-Bernard and I made the mistake of hiring a car in Sibiu to take us to Sighişoara, and that's why we're currently sitting by the side of the road as the driver tries to repair a steaming engine. At least it's warm, and J.B. had the good sense to bring along a bottle of wine.

Since there's nothing to do but waste time, here is a partial list names I've pieced together from all my archival research in Sibiu and Bucharest—possible members of the Order of the Dragon by date:

Original Order, 1408:

Sigismund von Luxemburg, King of Hungary and Bohemia

Barbara von Cilli, Queen of Hungary and rumored alchemist

Albrecht Dürer, renaissance artist (dragons hidden in his work)

Vlad II ("Dracul") and Vlad III ("Dracula")

Stefan Lazarević, Prince of Serbia

Henry V, King of England

Pope Eugene IV

Revival of order, 1598:

Rudolf II, Holy Roman Emperor ("Golem of Prague")

Elizabeth I, Queen of England

John Dee, occult philosopher and royal adviser

Elizabeth Báthory, Blood Countess of Hungary

Possible second revival, current?

Unknown

OUR TAXI DROVE US AWAY FROM THE PAINTED cottage, down the lake's dirt road, and toward the village center. I spent the first part of the ride in a haze, trying to come to grips with everything Lovena had told us. Fighting the urge to return to her. I still had a million and one questions. About Rothwild and the Order of the Dragon. About talking to my mother. About the talisman she gave us and my so-called old blood. Should I be worried or upset or delighted?

Why wouldn't she tell me more?

Considering an ever-increasing range of possible answers to these questions made my chest buzz and my head spin. Which wasn't good. With everything going on right now, I needed my head to stay firmly stationary.

"Focused!" I murmured, snapping my fingers.

"What?" Huck asked.

"Twelve across, seven letters, 'head straight.' F-O-C-U-S-E-D."

"Banshee," he said. "You're the only person I know who does crossword puzzles in your head all day long."

"Must be my old blood," I said, feeling self-conscious and a little feverish at the same time.

"What does that even mean?" he whispered close to my ear, as if the taxi driver might hear and kick us out of the cab. "How did she know about your mother?"

"I don't know," I whispered back.

"All of this feels like one vast web of weirdness, and we've flown right into it like stupid insects," he lamented. "You trust her?"

I did. I couldn't explain why exactly. It was just a gut feeling, and my mother always said to pay attention to those. Oh, to talk to her again. Just the idea of it was . . . too much to hope for. Funny, but I think Mother would have liked Lovena. I held on to her coin around my neck, warming the metal with my fingers, and when Huck settled back in the seat next to me, I gave it a quick kiss.

Huck and I briefly talked about following our new lead to Lovena's sister in Sighișoara, but it wasn't much of a discussion. Of course we were going. It was the best clue to my father's whereabouts we'd had so far. Where else would we go?

Even so, we were both overwhelmed.

I was worried about my father. I was worried about Jean-Bernard.

I was worried for us.

It felt as if we were crossing over a threshold, going deeper into Romania, away from the Orient Express, away from Bucharest, and that once we committed to moving forward, there was no way back.

Our driver dropped us off at a tiny train platform near the village center, where we had to wake a snoozing ticket agent, who provided us with a printed train schedule. I asked the young man if he'd seen my father, giving him a name and physical description, but he just looked confused. "I only work three days a week," he told me in Romanian, shrugging his shoulders.

No matter. We were fairly certain where Father was headed. We just needed to catch up to him, and that was all there was to it.

The train that ran into the Carpathians was due to arrive in an hour. Huck and I waited on a desolate platform, studying railway tourist pamphlets about Transylvania while hungrily dismantling a fat cluster of purple grapes that we purchased from a friendly Romanian peddler. Despite both the taxi and the train tickets being cheap, we were now down to our last couple of lei. Another reason to find Father and fast: it was difficult to lead a daring rescue mission across a foreign country without proper funds.

When the train finally arrived, the Orient Express it was not. It looked as if it belonged in a Victorian museum, to be honest. No Pullman sleepers, no restaurant car . . . no anything but wooden seats, dirty windows, and facilities that were scarcely more than a hole cut into the floor. On a positive note, it was free of any shady cultist characters who'd been trailing us on this trip; maybe Lovena's pocket travel talisman was working.

Enduring a few curious stares from the smattering of passengers traveling with us, we chose an isolated seat and were promptly ignored. Then, with a puff of steam and a clacking rumble, the train departed and a five-hour trip into the mountains began.

After our tickets were punched by the conductor, Huck tugged down his flat cap to cover his eyes, slouched in the train seat, and promptly set out to take a nap. I couldn't understand how someone could sleep at a time like this.

"Hey, Huck?" I said softly.

"Mmm?" he answered, not moving his cap.

"I was thinking . . ."

"Uh-oh."

"If Rothwild is as dangerous as Mama Lovena claimed . . . If he really poisoned Jean-Bernard or put some kind of spell on him . . . Do you think Rothwild used that as a threat and that's why Father is chasing after the ring?"

"Maybe," Huck said in a sleepy, deep voice.

"Because if Father knew there would be people like Sarkany and the robed cultists following us from Istanbul, I can't believe he would just run off and feed us to the proverbial wolves."

"Or literal wolf dogs."

"By the way, what kind of person steals someone's dog?"

"The lowest kind, banshee," he mumbled from beneath his cap.

"Do you think Sarkany did it to intimidate Lovena into giving up the ring?"

"Don't know."

"I mean, what's the point of kidnapping if you don't ask for a ransom?" I considered this further and said, "Maybe all of these people are trying to intimidate everyone into giving up their rings until they find the real one. Rothwild hurt Jean-Bernard, which urged my father into action. Sarkany took Mama Lovena's dog and used it to kill someone else connected to the ring—"

"Yeah, but it sounds like the widow was part of this dragon society."

"Maybe she just dabbled in the esoteric. If she was part of the order, wouldn't Rothwild have had access to the first bone ring and known it was a reproduction before he . . . conspired with Natasha to kill her husband in order to get the ring?"

"Got me there, banshee. Don't know."

I sighed heavily, churning it all over in my head. "None of this explains why Father would abandon you in Tokat without so much as a word. Why not just tell you what was going on?"

"Maybe he wanted to keep us away from Rothwild. To draw fire while we got out of danger. Maybe he thought he was protecting us."

I snorted. "That worked out well, didn't it?"

"I never said Fox doesn't make mistakes. Maybe he was upset about Jean-Bernard. Maybe Rothwild threatened him to find the ring. Maybe he thought we could take care of ourselves."

Father knew damn well how I felt about Huck, so he must have known that seeing him again after all this time would be a shock. As callous as Richard Damn Fox could be, I didn't think he would carelessly just throw Huck and me together out of convenience.

Huck slung an arm over the back of our seat. Almost touching my shoulders but not quite. Close enough to cause a little tremor in my stomach. "Whatever the reason, I'm not sorry he did it. I mean, despite the constant terror, the dead bodies, and the witch saying that you've got old Romanian blood, some good things have come out of this . . . don't you think?"

"Yes," I admitted, checking to see if his hat was still covering his eyes. "I suppose there have been . . . um, some good things. It's hard to tell yet."

Fox said if he ever allowed me back home, it would be strictly as a member of the family.

"Give it time," he murmured. "You know what they say. Romania wasn't built in a day."

"I'm not even going to bother correcting that."

"That's half the fun, you know."

"I know," I murmured, smiling to myself.

Satisfied, he relaxed and made a noise that indicated he was done talking. I knew precisely when he fell asleep, because he began tipping sideways until his head rested on my shoulder and his cap fell into my lap. Good grief, he was heavy. And close. Draped on me like a heavy blanket. I should have pushed him away, but he smelled like shaving cream and the warmth of him was a comfort. So I just let him be and dug out the French crossword I still had in my handbag from the Orient Express.

The first half of our railway journey took us through boring, desolate country. It was overcast and a bit foggy, especially after we passed several potato fields. But the view changed drastically when we entered the Transylvanian region. Misty foothills rose up around the track. Pockets of quaint villages dotted the slopes between spiky firs. Here, there were fewer cars and more horse-pulled carts—even a shepherd and two fluffy dogs, herding slow-moving sheep into a valley.

But the farther into the mountains we went, the foggier and darker it got. Colder, too. Huck woke with a start as raindrops pattered against the window. He didn't apologize for falling asleep on me, and I discreetly rotated my shoulder to counter the effects of my arm going numb under his weight. It was as if we'd jumped back in time to when I was fifteen and using every possible excuse to touch his hand at the dinner table and he was sixteen and using every possible excuse to brush my arm as he passed by me in the hallway, and neither of us acknowledged any bit of it.

We still had a couple of hours to go. To get my mind off all that remembered touching and to pass the time, I suggested we read through tourist brochures Huck had picked up at the train station. One of them had a foldout map of Romania designed for tourists, with legends translated in several languages and whimsical Gothic drawings of medieval towers, castles, and pointy-toothed vampires.

Ignoring the schlock, I pointed out the Carpathian town where my mother was born, Brașov—east of where we were now—and it made my heart beat faster, wondering what she'd think if she knew I was finally traveling here, so close to her roots.

According to this map, we soon learned that everything worth seeing in Romania was either religious (painted Orthodox churches), medieval (villages in the Carpathians), or haunted—haunted monasteries, haunted homes, and even a haunted forest. "Outside Cluj. It's supposedly the place where Vlad was beheaded," Huck informed me, reading the English translation.

"I thought he was killed on a battlefield by the Turks?"

"According to the Romanian tourist board, he's been killed in multiple locations. In this particular one, on the spot where he was beheaded, there's a circle inside the woods where nothing grows. People who go into those woods disappear on the regular too."

"That sounds positively delightful. Let's be sure to stop there and take photographs."

He smiled, eyes merry. "I'll add it to our must-see list."

By the time we made it to our stop, the fog and drizzle had changed to fog and snow. Delicate flakes fluttered onto my coat as we stepped off the platform beneath a Gothic-script metal sign that swayed in the wind. It read:

SIGHIȘOARA

TRANSILVANIA

LOCUL NAȘTERII LUI VLAD ȚEPEȘ

Birthplace of Vlad Țepeș. If I remembered my history correctly, he didn't live here long, but the small town had clearly embraced him as their own. Apart from the sign, there wasn't much to see around the railway station. It was a bit desolate out here, with a smattering of weary cottages on one side of the tracks and a few newer buildings on the other. It was also cold. I dug a pair of thin leather gloves from my coat pockets and tugged them on as we left the station.

We zigzagged over a street along with a small pack of tourists from the train, avoiding horse-pulled carts and old black cars with overlarge skinny wheels while following signs to Old Town. The farther we walked, the more it felt as if we were stepping back in time.

Several hundred years back.

Perched on a mountainside terrace was a ringed Saxon citadel—one that looked as if it had sprung from the pages of a medieval fairy tale. And it was no abandoned ruin. There was a living, breathing village inside the old walls.

"Bram Stoker had it all wrong with the Transylvanian doom and gloom," Huck said, a little awe in voice. "This is enchanting, yeah?"

It really was, especially with the snow falling. "Keep an eye out for Father," I said.

"*You* keep an eye out. As your official protector, I'm looking for dangerous cultists and stolen wolf dogs."

"Fair enough," I said, rearranging my satchel and camera case across my torso as we both looked around.

We crossed a narrow bridge and passed through a stone fortifying wall dotted with turreted towers. Inside the citadel, crowds of people strolled hilly, cobbled lanes past medieval row houses painted in bright pastels: salmon, buttercup . . . sky blue. Geraniums decorated window boxes on gingerbread-roofed merchant houses.

It was dreamlike. Timeless.

Maybe *too* dreamlike and timeless: for one dizzying moment, passing by us in the crowds, I gaped at a group of serious-looking men dressed in medieval Saxon furs and chain mail. It felt as if I was losing my mind.

"What is happening?" I murmured, seeing other people dressed like illustrations from *The Canterbury Tales*.

"Middle Ages Festival," Huck said, head turning in all directions. "I just heard an English tour guide explaining that it draws twice as many tourists this time of year."

And almost as many Vlads. I couldn't stop staring at a group of scowling, raven-haired men with the Impaler's infamous thick mustache and jeweled crown—all of them smoking cigarettes and drinking frothy ale from metal mugs.

In addition to the Vlads, there were women dressed in furs, holding up carved wolf heads on sticks—wolf heads with serpent bodies, the symbol of the Dacians, which made me briefly think of Valentin's campfire stories.

Costumes. Wares. Food. White lights and banners strung between the medieval buildings. It was a feast for the eyes and ears. Unfortunately, we weren't here to celebrate.

We had a baroness to find: Lady Maria Kardos, Lovena's sister.

And hopefully my father.

"Lovena said their family home was up a hill in the center of town," I reminded Huck.

"More than one hill," he said, twisting to reach inside his rucksack. He pulled out one of the travel brochures that he'd picked up at the train station, and we tried get our bearings from a small map of the citadel. Fragile snowflakes dotted the folded paper, leaving wet spots as they melted.

"Looks like there's a public square up ahead," I said, pointing it out. "Maybe we can ask around there. Lovena said anyone could tell us where to find the baroness's house."

"Aye, aye, Captain," Huck said. "You lead the way."

As twilight turned into night, we headed into the town square, and I looked for a good place to stop and ask directions. There were several wine cellars and street cafés, but they were overflowing with knights and warriors and dark-haired maidens, huzzah! All of them costumed and mildly crocked.

"What's that?" I said, pointing to a mustard-yellow three-story home in the middle of the square. Snow was collecting on its slanting black roof and window baskets. A line of people extended from its front door, over which a wrought-iron dragon sign jutted.

"Why, I do believe that's dear old Papa Vlad's former home," Huck said. "Where a wee Vlad the Impaler was born."

A chill ran through me, and it wasn't because my nose was beginning to freeze. I pulled the lapel of my coat together at my neck and stood on tiptoes to get a better look at the painted canvas banner that hung from two of the building's windows. "'Drăculești Family Living Museum. Grand Opening,'" I translated for Huck. "They've turned his childhood home into a tourist trap."

"He must be rolling over in his grave," Huck said and added, "Wherever that is, because it damn sure wasn't under a massive pile of very heavy rocks in a cave outside Tokat."

"You know what they say. One man's pile of rocks is another man's treasure."

Huck laughed. "I've taught you well. Wait—where are you going?"

"To Vlad's house, of course. We'd be idiots to pass it by. That is the first place my father would visit here."

"Doubt we can afford the admission," Huck pointed out.

Right. That *was* a problem. We were virtually broke.

It wouldn't hurt to look a little closer, though, would it?

We snaked through the crowded square and slowed as we approached a line of people waiting to buy tickets from a small portable booth that had been set up outside the door. I lingered near the front of the line in hopes of asking the pink-cheeked ticket seller if possibly she'd seen my father. But at that moment the door was held open for several seconds to allow for a couple of tourists to step into what appeared to be a staged re-creation of a medieval home (roaring fireplace, wooden chairs). And in the middle of the room, I spotted an enormous figure. Big as a bear, dark hair. His back faced me, and he was leaning over a glass display case filled with small medieval weapons and tools.

My pulse sped like a downhill bicycle, picking up speed.

Without thought, I shouldered my way around the people waiting in line and burst through the entrance before the door could shut again, ignoring protests and heated Romanian cursing about my lack of manners.

Inside the house, it smelled of fireplace smoke and that peculiar scent that really old homes always have—generations of dust, must, and mold. For a moment my ears started ringing and my balance felt . . . off. A wave of dizziness struck me. Maybe my body was just briefly shocked, coming in from the cold to stifling heat. I shook it away and continued toward the display case.

"Father!" I called out.

He didn't budge. I caught up to him and touched his arm. He swung around, curious, and just like that, my billowing hope was burst.

A stranger stared back at me. Just a middle-aged Romanian man with a red nose and a gold cross around his neck.

"Pardon," I mumbled to the man, feeling the sting of my mistake. What was I thinking? That Father would just be casually browsing a museum without a care in the world while Huck and I were penniless and alone in a foreign country?

"Theo," Huck said, breathless. "What in God's name are you doing?"

"I thought . . ."

Ugh. I felt like a complete idiot. And another wave of dizziness hit me—not insignificant this time. I gripped Huck's arm for support.

"Whoa there!" he said. "What's wrong?"

Maybe my ears weren't ringing. Maybe it was a noise in the house. A high-pitched whine, and underneath it, strange cadenced noises. Like a dozen distant drums beating out overlapping rhythms. "Do you hear that?"

"Hear what?" Huck whispered, looking frantic.

"That music."

Maybe it was that group of costumed musicians out in the square, playing lutes. Maybe a group of drummers had joined them.

While I tried to pinpoint the source of the noise, something caught my eye. Something in the display case where the man who wasn't my father had been looking. Between a pair of medieval metal scissors and a glass stopper from a perfume bottle sat an odd little ring on a bed of red velvet. Ugly and crooked, it had been carved from what the nearby placard identified as ivory. Strange symbols were carved into the band—a band that looked a little different from the ring in my father's photographs.

"'Battle ring belonging to Vlad Țepeș,'" I translated aloud.

"Is that . . . ?" Huck started. Then his face appeared next to mine as he shifted closer to peer through the fingerprint-smeared glass.

The strange noise was so much louder now. It was making me nauseated.

"That can't be," Huck said. "That's not Lovena's ring, is it?"

"It's my family's ring," a stern male voice said over my shoulder in Romanian. "And I don't know who you are, but this exhibit is for paid ticket holders only. I'm afraid you must exit."

I stood up, fighting a wave of nausea, and turned around to find two large guards in black uniforms flanking a dark-haired, slender young man, perhaps a little older than Huck, standing in a stiffly pressed, expensive suit. Agitation flared in his deep-set eyes; he was not happy with our being here.

"My apologies. I thought I saw someone I knew. I'll leave," I told both him and the guards in Romanian, one hand up in surrender. I prayed I was being polite enough to placate him. I just wanted to leave, to get out of this musty house and away from this noise, pounding, drumming . . .

Thump-thump. Thump-thump-thump.

It was disorienting, this vexatious noise. It took me out of my body and made me feel . . . lost.

Focus, I told myself sternly, trying to pull myself together. A bone ring was here, after all. This was important.

Shaking away a wave of dizziness, I pointed to the display case. "Can you tell me one thing?" I asked the young man. "You said this is a family ring."

"It is," he said coolly.

"We just spoke with Lovena earlier today. . . ." I struggled to remember the surname my father had written in his journal. "Blaga? Lovena Blaga?"

"She is my aunt," he confirmed, shoulders stiffening.

"You're the baroness's son?"

He nodded.

I quickly translated this information to Huck.

"Do you speak English?" Huck asked the young man.

"A little," he answered.

"We came to speak to your mother," Huck said. "Lovena sent us."

That seemed to break through his icy demeanor. He considered Huck's words for several moments and then made a gesture to the guards. They backed away, but not all that far, and they were still watching us. But when they were out of earshot, he said in English, "I am David Kardos. You are . . . ?"

"Theodora Fox," I said. "And this is Huck Gallagher."

David nodded in acknowledgment and said, "My mother and Aunt Lovena aren't close."

"But this is her ring?" I asked.

"It was my grandmother's ring," David insisted. "Lovena shouldn't have been hiding it. It deserves to be seen by the people of this town. This is our history."

"We need to speak to your mother. Your aunt sent my father here to inquire about this ring. It's very important." I quickly described him, looking around to point to the man I'd mistaken for him.

"Oh, yes. The American treasure hunter. He was here yesterday. He talked to my mother and left."

"Why did he leave?" I asked, fighting another wave of nausea. "Is he coming back?"

"He asked to buy the ring," David said matter-of-factly. "My mother refused. It is part of the museum's collection now. He asked to inspect it, which she allowed, and then they argued, because he made insulting claims."

"What kinds of claims?" Huck asked.

"He claimed that the ring was not genuine. That it was a reproduction. Which it is not. It has been in my family for decades."

I hated to break it to him, but "decades" was nothing. Vlad

lived in this house more than four hundred years ago. If my father thought it was a reproduction, then likely it was. He was stupid about a lot of things, but dating artifacts wasn't one of them.

Then again, Lovena was convinced there was sleeping power in this particular ring. She was certain this one was authentic. Had she been wrong? Or was my father mistaken? Who was I supposed to believe?

Thump-thump. Thump-thump-thump.

My *God!* What was that infernal noise? Was I the only one hearing it?

David gestured loosely with one hand. "Mr. Fox was rude. He needed a bath. And he insulted my family, so my mother told him to leave. And now I am asking *you* to leave."

"Wait!" I said, trying to figure out what to do. I believed my father *thought* this ring wasn't real, but he also pooh-poohed the idea that my mother's death was due to that cursed crown she handled in India, of which I'd tried to convince him a hundred times. If she were still alive, she'd tell me to question—and document—everything. Just in case. So I set my satchel on the floor, opened it, and dug around for my camera bag. "May I snap a photograph?"

"Absolutely not!" the man said firmly. "No photography. This is a living museum. Did you not read the sign outside?"

I couldn't answer. My insides were trying to exit my body. And that noise . . . that damned noise! It was as though I were hearing everyone's heartbeats inside this room, all at the same time. If I concentrated, I could almost pick them each out. Huck's especially. How could that be?

Thump-thump. Thump-thump.

Was I hearing my own blood inside my temples?

When magic is plentiful, it is easy to hear.

I slowly stood up from my satchel and stared at the ring. Impossible. Or was it? I took a step toward it and put my hand on the case.

Thump-thump-thump-thump-thump.

Dear God. It was . . . alive.

Terrified, I jerked my hand away.

"Theo!" Huck said firmly. Confusion and concern churned behind his narrowed eyes.

"The noise, it's—" I started to explain.

But I never finished, because David was angry at me again. He raised a hand to summon the guards, so I quickly said in Romanian, "I'm sorry! We will leave the museum now. But I beg you, is there any way I can speak with your mother? Even for a moment? My father is missing. It's urgent that I find him. Bad people are after him. Please."

David hesitated, fidgeting with his cuff links. "Perhaps for a moment. But not now. She is giving a speech in a few minutes to officially open the festival, in front of the clock tower. Once it's over, you can return here and ask for me at the ticket booth. I will try to arrange a meeting, but I cannot promise. She is a busy woman. Please do not barge inside without a ticket this time."

"I understand," I said, switching back to English. "And thank you. We'll come back."

He nodded rigidly and said something to the guards, who hung back but were clearly there to escort us out of the house. As we left, the thumping noise grew fainter and fainter, until I stood out in the snow-wet square, wondering if I'd been imagining it.

I hadn't. I knew it as well as I knew my own mind.

I'd heard the ring.

"What happened back there?" Huck said when we were outside. "Are you okay?"

I shook my head, still reeling, and motioned for us to walk. We circled around the side of the mustard-colored house, trying to avoid a steady stream of people strolling past us down a narrow lane. *Steel spine, chin high. Do not fall apart. You are fine. Everything is fine.*

"Banshee," Huck insisted, finally pulling me to one side under an arch that connected the buildings on either side of the lane. "What's going on? Talk to me."

"You'll think I'm mad," I said, shaking my head.

"I will not. Talk to me. Are you sick?"

I held a hand to my stomach to steady my nerves. The nausea was passing. "Are you certain you didn't hear anything inside the house?"

"I heard people talking." He paused and gripped my shoulders, ducking his head to bring his face to my level, snagging my gaze with his. "What did you hear?"

I whimpered, and my body loosened under his hands. "I heard heartbeats. People's heartbeats. Everyone in that room. Huck," I said. "And that wasn't all. I thought . . . I *know* I heard the ring."

Emotions warred across his face. "Are you sure?"

In fractured sentences, I attempted to explain it, the nausea and the thumping. "I know how it sounds, don't I? I knew you wouldn't believe me."

I tried to push out of his grip, but he held on to me more firmly.

"Hey," he said, his face close to mine, warm breath blowing out in a billow of winter white. "I believe you."

"You do?"

He nodded. "If you say you heard it, then you heard it."

His acceptance meant more than I expected. Relief and gratitude poured through me. I wanted to hug him. I wanted to bury my face in his neck and feel his arms around me. For a moment there was something raw and desperate on his face, and I thought he wanted it too. And then a drunken man in a bad Vlad costume bumped into us and broke us apart, apologizing profusely in Romanian before stumbling away.

I looked at Huck, feeling suddenly shy and exposed.

He pulled off his cap, smoothed back his curls, and refitted the wool over his head, pulling the brim down tight. "Can you hear it now?"

I shook my head. "I could still hear it faintly right outside the house when we left, but it faded away."

"Okay," he said. "So, basically, what we're saying here is that based on what just happened, we think that ring inside there could be the real ring that your father is looking for."

I nodded.

"But Fox thought it was another fake, and he left."

"Seems that way."

"What do we do about it? I mean, we aren't here for the ring. We're here for Fox. But if Rothwild has threatened him into finding the ring . . ." He shook his head and considered it. "I think Fox needs to hear from you about what you heard. He needs to know. In a perfect world, we'd just walk in there and get the ring, find your father, and all of this would be over. But David and his family aren't going to hand over the ring to us, yeah? So we should probably just concentrate on finding Fox. That hasn't changed."

"Agreed," I said, warily looking back at the mustard-colored house. "Maybe the baroness can tell us more. Maybe Father gave her a hint as to where he's going."

"That's obvious, though, isn't it? If he thinks this ring was a fake, then he'll go to the next name on his little coded list of suspects."

"The twins," I murmured.

"Which could be the brothers Lovena mentioned? The traveling merchants—what did she say their name was? Zifu? Zizu?"

"Zissu," I said. "I haven't found any journal entries about any traveling merchants. There's that page that's been torn out, remember? Really hope it's not that. Maybe I missed something."

"We'll figure it out," he told me, rubbing my upper arm in reassurance, a simple gesture that he used to do without thought. Both of us seemed to realize this at the same time, and he withdrew his hand quickly. After a moment of awkwardness, he said, "Sure you're all right?"

I puffed up my lips and blew out a long breath, shaking my head. "I mean, I just heard a bunch of supernatural heartbeats, so, you know . . ."

"Wolves. Witches. Magic spells on banknotes. What's a few supernatural heartbeats?" he said, shrugging comically. "If a vampire in a cape jumped out of the alley, I would not be surprised at this point."

There were plenty of costumed vampires in capes shuffling in the crowd with all the historical Vlads, so that wasn't a stretch.

I turned everything over in my mind and looked back at the mustard-colored house. "You know, maybe we don't need David to set up a meeting with the baroness. He mentioned she was giving a speech at a clock tower. Maybe we can just catch her there. Do you still have the map of the town?"

"Don't think we need one. Going to take a wild guess that it's the big medieval tower with the clock at the top, there," Huck said, nodding his head down the short lane, where people were gathering in front of a small stage.

That would be it. "Perfect," I said. "Let's go see if we can find this baroness."

"How will we know who she is?" Huck said.

"We'll figure that out when we get there." Better than standing around in the snow.

We shuffled down the lane with several other people, ending up at the back of the crowd loitering in front of the empty stage. It was set up near the base of the clock tower, a stone building with needlelike spires that stabbed into the snowy night sky. A clock face adorned the top alongside a set of painted medieval figures that waited for the hour to strike and propel them into rotation. Glancing around, I was pretty certain it was the tallest structure in the fortress, and the only one that looked truly foreboding as it loomed over the cheery fairy-tale lanes.

And I wasn't the only one looking up. Everyone's attention was focused on the clock tower's observation gallery: a covered balcony that banded around all four sides. Several hundred years ago, the city guard probably patrolled that balcony, keeping a watch for foreign invaders.

Something moved up there. On a balustrade with large, open arches, a lone figure leaned into the tower's spotlights. A woman. Long, silver hair billowed in the snow-flecked wind. Her clothes were torn and bloody.

The watching crowd let out a collective gasp. Someone shouted out, "*Baroneasă!*"

Baroness.

"Lovena's sister," I told Huck. What was she doing up there? A palpable, contagious panic rolled through the crowd.

With an anguished sob, the baroness climbed onto the snow-dusted handrail, as if a gun was pointed at her back, but I couldn't see anyone else up there. What was she doing? She moved as if controlled by invisible puppet strings. As if her body wasn't her own. She flailed wildly—

And tumbled over the side of the clock tower.

A rag doll falling through the snow. Down, down . . .

Until her body crashed through the stage.

The crowd surged backward. For a moment chaos and mayhem ruled. Screaming. Shouting. At the base of the clock tower, dark figures rushed toward the broken stage.

Was she dead? Could anyone survive a fall like that?

In shock, I stood frozen, gaping at the clock tower, unable to process the violence I'd just witnessed. It felt surreal, like a nightmare from which I'd awake. Huck's firm hand gripped my arm and pulled me to the side to make room for someone who was trying to get their children away from the horrible scene.

"Was it her?" Huck shouted near my ear to be heard over the crowd. "It was the baroness? Lovena's sister?"

It had to have been. Even now I heard her family name, "Kardos," spoken in the buzzing chatter around us: *A shocking tragedy. Why would she do such a thing?* And then: *Her poor family.*

David.

His slender figure raced past us, pushing through the rubbernecking crowd with one of the guards who'd escorted us outside. A few others followed. There was more shouting and chaos. Uniformed police. Someone said she wasn't dead.

"Did you see her clothes?" Huck said, dark brows knitted into a slash above his eyes, forehead marred with worry lines. "She was covered in blood before she jumped."

My mind revived the ghastly scene, and a shiver raced down my back. I'd never seen anything like that before. The horror of it burrowed under my skin and made me feel shaky and unsafe.

And that's when everything fit together in my head.

"She didn't jump," I said.

"What do you mean?"

"She didn't do it of her own accord. She was pushed. Or coerced . . . like a puppet. She was trying to get away from something. Didn't you see her face? She was in agony."

"Bewitched," Huck said, making the sign of the cross.

Sirens wailed in the distance.

"A trail of blood is following us wherever we go!" Huck despaired.

It truly was. And this was no random act of violence. In an instant the shock of what we'd witnessed fell away.

Sarkany. He was behind this. Had to be. I didn't know how. I just *knew*. And from the look on Huck's face, he was thinking the same thing.

We both glanced around the crowd in a panic. No sign of him. No white wolf dog. And then it hit me like a bolt of lightning: everyone was out here gawking. All attention here. It was a distraction. A gruesome, horrific distraction . . .

"We're idiots," I said. "The ring!"

Huck understood immediately. In unison, we jogged up snow-slicked cobblestones, zigzagging through the crowd of onlookers. We ran until we came to the mustard-colored house, rounding the corner into the main square.

The line in front of the Drăculești Family Living Museum had broken up. The ticket-booth attendant was gone. A couple of people were scattering out of the front door, but I couldn't make out what was being said. When another person raced out of the exit, I didn't waste time; I just barged inside as I'd done before.

Glass crunched under my brown boots. Huck raced in behind me, wild eyes flicking across the room. He held up an arm as if he were prepared to take a swing at someone.

He needn't have bothered. The room was deserted—no Sarkany.

And no infernal thumping. No sound at all.

The display case we'd inspected earlier had been smashed open. Medieval tools were strewn. And the red velvet that cradled the dark family heirloom was now empty.

The bone ring had been stolen.

WE EXITED THE MUSTARD-COLORED HOUSE, RATTLED and confused. Not knowing what to do or where to go. Ambulances were arriving, along with more uniformed *poliție* reinforcements, their cars blocking many of the citadel's narrow streets as they cleared tourists and gawkers. I questioned a stranger, who said that someone who'd been near the stage confirmed that the baroness had, indeed, survived the fall, but her condition was unknown.

The tragedy at the clock tower had been a cruel distraction. I didn't know how, but I knew Sarkany was involved. He'd threatened the baroness, or drugged her, or compelled her with some kind of dark spellwork to jump. I believed that as much as I believed the earth was round.

Men who compete for power often succumb to violence to reach their goal.

Lovena. Had we brought this horror here to her family? Or were we just standing on the outside, unable to stop what was already in motion? With trembling fingers, I felt around my pocket for the witch's travel talisman. Still there. If it indeed had offered us protection, I felt horrible that it hadn't extended to Lovena's poor sister. "This is horrific," I told Huck. "What if Lovena's sister doesn't survive? Or what if she's paralyzed? Oh God, Huck."

"It's terrible," he agreed. "But this isn't our fault."

"Is it not?" I argued, feeling a sense of frenzy rising in my gut.

"No. I don't think so? Jaysus, banshee, I don't know!"

I exhaled and tried to breathe in slowly through my nostrils to calm myself. We'd witnessed something horrible. The bloody fall. The stolen ring. Chaos and confusion. I was still in a little shock. But I needed to get a grip on my emotions so that we could figure out what to do. While I was doing this, Huck realized something more immediately crucial. "They'll think we did this," he said, motioning toward the museum house. "They'll think we took the ring."

I glanced around, paranoid. "But it was already gone when we went inside. If Sarkany took it, someone had to have witnessed it."

"Aye, but people panic and get confused, banshee," he said. "We're outsiders here. Easy targets. We already had to be escorted out of the house, and David will be looking to blame someone. If nothing else, we'll be questioned by the police as suspects."

"Dammit," I mumbled, glancing around. My nerves were frayed. I still expected Sarkany to leap out of the shadows. But Huck was right. "We need to leave the town."

"Agreed," he said.

But where were we supposed to go? "Do we have enough money to take another train? We never got to talk with the baroness and find out where Father was going. . . ."

"We'll figure something out," he said, sounding surer than I felt.

"All I know is that we can't find Fox if we're behind bars, and there's nothing we can do for Lovena's sister. We've got to leave, banshee."

Part of me resisted, not wanting to feel like a criminal slipping away from the scene of the crime. But it wasn't *our* crime, and what good did it do us to stick around and volunteer ourselves up as patsies?

I nodded at Huck, breath white in the cold night air. "Let's go."

We made our way across the square. It seemed best not to exit the citadel the way we came in, due to all the police, so we walked in the opposite direction, past drunken revelers and shopkeepers who gossiped together in doorways and beneath the festive white lights strung over the streets. Once we'd serpentined our way to the citadel's walls and slipped out of an arched exit, I felt a little relieved.

And a little lost.

Huck spotted the river we'd crossed on our way from the train station. It wasn't until we picked our way down a snowy hill and found a bridge to cross into the newer part of town that we slowed our manic pace, and I forced myself to think about what to do next.

Snow fell harder. After counting what little money Huck had in his pockets, we were positive we didn't have enough for the train—or even a bus. Hotel? No. Meal? Everything here was closed anyway. The citadel was the heart of the town. This was borderland, something between civilization and countryside, and for the life of me, I didn't know where to go. Huck didn't either, if the permanent worry line in his forehead was any indication. But we kept walking. What else could we do?

Several minutes passed. We turned down a street and hiked alongside a paved stretch of highway that wound out of town. A few cars passed us, their headlights flashing in the dark. Huck stuck out his arm, attempting to hitch a ride, but no one stopped.

"These Sighişoarans are a tough bunch," Huck said. "Am I that ugly?"

"Maybe you should show some leg."

"If they hate my face, my hairy leg won't help. I promise you that."

"It's fine," I said. "We'll just freeze to death soon. No big deal."

Buildings were getting fewer and farther between along the road, and the snow wasn't letting up. We found a lone apartment building and considered trying to hole up in the stairwell but couldn't get past a barred gate. Had it been a lock, Huck could have picked it, but it looked like it could only be opened from the inside. I remembered my mother telling me that outside cities, Romanians lock up everything at night—farms, homes, barns. Night brought fear, fear brought superstition, and it was very, *very* dark in the outskirts of this Carpathian town.

"Looks like mountainous countryside out there," Huck said, shielding his eyes to see past the last lamppost near the highway. "We'll have to go back. At this point, I'd rather sleep in the clock tower. Maybe one of the churches or taverns will let us inside."

"Or maybe we could hot-wire a car," I suggested.

"Why, banshee, how dare you. I'm not a common criminal."

I huffed out a shivering laugh. "You hot-wired that car in France two years ago."

"French cars, sure," he joked cheerfully as he shivered, hands thrust into his coat pockets. "Romanian cars are a whole other bucket o' parts. Besides, you see any cars to hot-wire?"

Not in several minutes, I hadn't. However, I did see something else. Something much better. Bigger, too.

"What about that?" I asked, pointing to a metal building at the end of a short dirt road that branched off the highway. It looked like a small warehouse with a covered shed extending off the back. Less a shed and more a hangar, for beneath its metal roof was the silhouette of a small airplane. And on the side of the building, a lone yellow light shone on a painted pair of words: POŞTA ROMÂNĂ.

"That's a post office, yeah?" Huck said. "And their mail plane."

"Airplanes don't have locks, right?"

"You're suggesting I steal government property?"

"Better than stealing a crop duster from a poor farmer. Besides, it's not *really* stealing. It's borrowing."

"You sound just like bloody Fox," he informed me, and then mimicked Father in a deep, booming voice: "'Go on, pick the lock on that duke's summer home, Huxley—dumb bastard doesn't know Greeks from Romans, so we're almost doing him a favor, taking this priceless statue off his hands.'"

I snorted a laugh, and Huck flashed merry eyes at me. Maybe the cold weather was making us both a little loopy. Or maybe I was trying to get over the shock of seeing someone plunge several stories from a clock tower. Or maybe, just maybe, hearing heartbeats while under the spell of a four-hundred-year-old ring had damaged something in my brain.

Take your pick.

"Here's what I think," I said. "We should borrow the plane and fly it to . . ."

"To . . . ?"

"You know," I said, gesturing loosely. "Where my father went. To the twins. It's next on his list."

"We don't even know for certain that these Zissu brothers *are* your father's twins. Didn't Lovena say they traveled around? Last she knew, they were somewhere near the Black Sea. They could be anywhere now."

"There's got to be a clue in the journal. I just missed it," I insisted. "The hangar has light, so I can look it up there. When I find where they're at, we can just fly there, find my father, then bring the plane back. Zip-zip."

"Oh, *really*. That's what we'll do? That's your plan?" he said, sounding both perturbed and a little amused.

I shrugged one shoulder. "Unless you don't think you can fly a plane like that . . ."

"Pfft." He crossed his arms over his chest. "Not falling for that, am I?"

"Are you sure? That's what a coward would probably say."

"You forget, banshee. I have no male pride. Call me a coward. Call me soft. Bothers me not," he said, shaking his head slowly.

"All right, then. What do *you* propose we do? If what David told us was true, then Father left here yesterday, which makes him a day ahead of us. We need to keep moving to catch up with him. And besides, Sarkany could be back in the citadel along with the police, who you said would question us, so we can't go back there. And if we just sit here arguing, we'll likely die of frostbite."

"Yes, yes," he said. "Know all that, don't I? But we can't fly to *nowhere*."

"It's not *nowhere*. It's . . . somewhere in Romania," I said dramatically, fanning my hand out over the landscape.

Huck laughed. We both knew this was ridiculous.

"Let's just walk over to the hangar," I urged. "Maybe there's someone working inside the post office who can help us, or I can look at Father's journal. At the very least, it's shelter from the snow. One wall is better than none."

With this logic Huck finally agreed, so we made our way down the dirt road. The brick building had no windows, only a locked door. When we knocked, no one answered, so we headed around back to the hangar. Not much to see there: some locked tool cabinets, a locked back door that led into the building, and an air-to-ground wireless stand—also locked.

The airplane, however, was not. Huck walked the length of it, inspecting the fuel tank, popping open panels and checking cables and mechanical systems. "Fueled up. Probably used regularly. Not the best I've seen by a long shot. Needs service badly. But seems airworthy for a short trip. Probably."

"Marvelous!"

"No, *not* marvelous. I could lose my private pilot license back in the States—and completely ruin any chance of getting one in Belfast."

"If we sit around here and do nothing, I could lose my father," I countered.

"You act like I'm not concerned about that," Huck said, irritated. "We're both on the same side here."

Point taken. Before we could get into another fight, I hauled my satchel to a workbench and flipped on a small overhead light there. Then I rooted through my clothes and books until I found the journal, laid it out on the workbench, and began scanning through it. "Twins, twins," I mumbled, flipping through the thick pages.

"Maybe he doesn't call them twins. Try looking for brothers. Or merchants."

"Doing that already," I said in a singsong voice.

"Or maybe it's one of the coded words you haven't deciphered yet."

But it wasn't. And after going through every page, there was nothing about any merchant twins to whom Father had talked. No traveling merchants. No dealers in arcane items. No estate sales, no visit to the town of Constanța on the Black Sea.

Nothing but the torn page.

"Damn him!" I said, throwing the journal against the wall. It knocked a pushpin out of the corner of a map, and both the pin and the journal clattered to the floor. Candy wrappers and photographs spilled from the pages. I sighed at the mess I'd made—the mess my father had made, to get technical about it.

"I hate him," I said miserably.

Huck nodded. "I know. Me too, sometimes."

"Easy to love, hard to like. That's what Mother used to say about him."

"She must have liked him though."

"God only knows why." I blew out a hard breath and bent to pick up the journal and the rat's nest of scraps that had spilled from it. As I was shoving the photographs back into pages, my fingers stilled on a small ivory rectangle of heavy card stock. I didn't remember seeing this before. . . . I flipped it over and read the printed type on the front:

ZISSU BROTHERS
RARE JEWELRY AND ANTIQUES
ARCANE AND RELIGIOUS ICONOGRAPHY
BRAȘOV, ROMÂNIA

"Huck!" I said, shooting to my feet. "Look—look!"

"I'm looking. I'm looking." He took the card from me.

"It was here the whole time. They're in Brașov now. Or they were this summer, anyway, when Father was touring Romania."

"Does appear that way, doesn't it?" he murmured, inspecting the card as if he didn't trust it. "You never noticed this card before?"

"Have you seen the junk that's shoved in there?"

"Brașov . . . Why do I know that?"

"It's my mother's hometown. Remember? I showed you on the tourist map. With the vampire bat?" I flapped my arms and bared my teeth.

"That's right," he murmured. "Her parents aren't alive anymore, right? Do you think you still have any family there?"

"Cousins, probably. Not sure if they still live there, though. They don't know me." My Romanian grandmother died before I was born, and my Romanian grandfather died when I was a baby. I never knew them, and my mother was, like me, an only child.

"It was the same for me when I returned to Belfast," he said, almost as if speaking to himself. "Cousins I remembered were gone and other family I didn't know I had were there. Funny how a family can be solid one moment and then blow away with the wind."

Yes. Funny.

I nodded at the business card. "So what do you think?"

"About Brașov? Not much to go on. Lovena did say they traveled. What if they were in Brașov this summer when your father was traveling here, but . . ."

But they aren't now. He didn't have to say it. I was already thinking it myself. But the one thing I was hoping, the most important thing, was that at least my father thought they were in Brașov—it didn't matter if they were. It didn't even matter if the ring was there. After what had happened tonight, maybe I'd had enough of magic rings.

"What's this?" Huck said, leaning over the workbench to inspect a large piece of paper that I'd knocked sideways on the hangar's bulletin board during my moment of rage. "Regional map. Look—

these stars are the other rural post offices around Transylvania. And these here?" he said, pointing to sets of numbers written neatly on the map's wide bottom border. "Flight coordinates. Ten post offices, ten coordinates."

"So this plane normally flies to these other towns to deliver mail," I said.

"Indeed it does. And see this? Right here," he said, pointing to a star on the map. "That's right outside Brașov. This symbol means they keep lights burning on their runway. This airfield we're on is too small to bother with twenty-four-seven lights. Just a waste of electricity. But the Brașov airfield is bigger."

"So you could land there without problems?"

"*No*, not without problems. Look at the weather, banshee."

"The snow isn't sticking. The runway is clear. The plane isn't covered in ice."

"Not worried about icing so much, but visibility might be reduced if the storm picks up, or snow could block the intake. And who knows what it's like in Brașov. Maybe the storm hasn't made it there yet. Maybe it won't. Seems to be heading west, not east. But even if we're able to land, we'll have to deal with another postal employee who might be working there, and I don't speak Romanian, which makes lying rather difficult—"

"Or easy. I'll do the talking. Or we just make a run for it."

"We'll still need to hike from the airfield into town." He paused, scratching the back of his neck, and mumbled, "Maybe we could hitch a ride."

"Surely so," I said brightly, having no idea.

He wasn't listening to me anyway. He was too busy mumbling to himself, talking about the weather. Looking around the hangar. Making another pass around the plane again.

But after all his grousing, I knew he was seeing things my way when he took the map off the wall and handed it to me. "You're in charge of the coordinates. We may need to find an alternate place to land if Brașov isn't viable. Cluj, maybe. That's northwest from here, and it takes in planes at night, too."

"Aye, aye, Captain Huck."

"Sure you want to do this?" he asked seriously.

"Never been so sure," I said. "What's a grand adventure without a plane ride?"

"It's adventure, all right. And possibly a huge mistake. But you know what they say. When the going gets tough, the tough steal a mail plane."

"It's only stealing if we don't bring it back. And we will! Now, can we please leave this frozen hellscape? My nose is going to fall off."

He laughed. "If you think it's going to be any warmer in that cabin, you're in for the shock of your life."

JOURNAL OF RICHARD FOX

July 10, 1937

Târgşoru Vechi, Wallachia, Kingdom of România

Interesting discussion with an airdrome owner in what was once a medieval trading village called Târgşor, where a major road led from Bucharest in Wallachia to Braşov in Transylvania. I'd read about the ruins of a church here, one that was possibly built by Vlad's father—and where the Impaler may have sheltered after a battle with the Turks, eight months before he died.

Turns out I wasn't the first to discover this. The airdrome owner said a Hungarian gentleman by the name of Rothwild had been out here, looking for the site of the old church a month ago. He had a team of men dig up an acre of land. Why is Rothwild withholding all of this information from me? Is he paying me to run around Romania, working the same leads he's already investigated? How does that help him?

The airdrome owner told me one interesting thing. Rothwild was raving about politics, saying that change was happening in Europe. That Hungary and Romania needed to stand their ground or allow their land to be taken. And that he was going to ensure this didn't happen. Just a rant, I thought. But then the man said Rothwild told him that the Order of the Dragon protected these lands years ago and that Rothwild was searching for something that would help him resurrect the order.

Am I working for an unhinged man?

I'D RIDDEN ON MY SHARE OF AIRPLANES. MOSTLY PUDDLE jumpers, for short distances, and in Huck's little biplane, Trixie, over Hudson Valley.

But this aircraft was no Trixie, and we weren't flying over fields and rivers while the sun shone.

This was a ramshackle postal plane, and we were flying in a snowstorm, two thousand feet above the Carpathian Mountains.

"Stop clutching the instrument panel," Huck's voice said inside my headset. He sat next to me in the cramped cockpit, and though I had the volume turned up as loud as it would go, I was still having trouble hearing him over the insane racket of the single-engine plane. "Grab the coward strap up there, if you feel you must."

"I'm not a coward!" I said, clutching a leather strap above my window.

"No need to yell in my ear. Relax. We're fine."

Liar. None of this was fine. Snow drove against the windshield so hard, I couldn't see past the propeller on the nose of the plane—

which meant he couldn't see, either. When I dared to look out my window, I occasionally spied a single light in the mountains below, but mostly I just saw darkness. And the plane was rattling so hard, I was almost positive my tailbone was bruised.

Whose idea was this anyway, taking a stolen airplane up in a snowstorm?

Oh, right. It was mine.

"We're going to die," I said.

"I swear to all the saints," Huck complained, "if you say that *one more time*, I'm going to open that airdrop door in the back and shove you out."

My teeth chattered as I glanced over my shoulder at the belly of the plane and felt a twinge of guilt. Dirty canvas postal bags filled the narrow space. Pretty sure stealing mail was a worse crime than borrowing a plane.

"How far have we got now?" I asked.

"Twenty minutes, if this equipment is accurate. Let's add that to our list of prayers."

Several excruciating minutes passed in which my thoughts dwelled on the decrepit state of the airplane, how it was over a decade old and had been retrofitted with several improvements, half which didn't work, according to Huck. There wasn't even a working parachute onboard, which was the one thing that had truly given Huck pause before we took off. Why oh why hadn't I listened?

As I was thinking about all this, Huck suddenly changed the plane's direction and altitude.

"Um . . . what's happening?" I asked.

"Storm's too bad. I'll have to take a different route."

"Do we have enough fuel?"

"Couple hours' worth. Don't worry about that. I'm just going to circle back around and backtrack a bit. Try to fly around the storm so I don't have to fight the wind."

I hated all of this. In minutes, all our forward progress was lost as we flew back over Sighişoara, headed in the wrong direction. Just how far north was he going to fly in order to avoid the storm? Seconds ticked by, then minutes, and then we were entirely off track.

A sputtering sound rocked the cockpit. For a moment I thought it was coming from my headset, but when I pulled the padded rubber away from my ear, I heard something worse.

Silence.

The cabin was still shaking, but the unearthly sound of the engine had just . . . stopped.

No engine.

All the lights on the instrument panel faded.

It felt like being in Trixie the biplane when Huck was doing engine-stall tricks in the air. But this was no time for tricks, and Huck's face had gone still.

He was scared.

The airplane suddenly took a sharp dip downward.

"Shite!" Huck shouted, pulling the plane back up until we were stable again. Then he fiddled with the instrument panel, and I recognized what he was doing, the same thing he'd done when we'd first gotten inside this nightmare cockpit: he was trying to start the engine.

"C'mon, c'mon," he mumbled.

The engine didn't respond.

He smacked the instrument panel violently. "May the devil break you into a thousand pieces, you rusty metal fucker!"

"Huck . . . ," I said. And then: "*Huck!*" louder. "W-what is going on?"

"Engine failure. Probably the carburetor. I told you this was a terrible idea!"

And I knew we were going to die up here. I knew it, knew it, knew it!

"Okay, all right. It's all right . . . I'm going to try to land it," he said as he slowly forced the airplane downward. "Don't panic. We're gliding now. We can glide for miles. If I can just find a clearing or a road—a river even. Keep your eyes open for anything."

"I would if I could see!" I told him as my stomach dropped along with the nose of the plane.

"We'll have better visibility when we get lower. I just don't want to clip a mountain."

"Please don't."

"I'll try my best, banshee."

I blew out several huffed breaths, trying to calm myself, but it just made me light-headed.

But—oh! Huck was right: I could see things now. The dark mountains. And city lights. Couldn't be Brașov; we'd gone too far in the wrong direction. "Lights over there," I shouted.

"That's Cluj, I think. Best not try to land there. Too many people."

"Beggars can't be choosers!" I snapped.

"Beggars don't plow down a bunch of innocent people! We can't risk hurting anybody. We need to find a highway or a field outside of town."

"Where, then?" I said, squinting into the windshield. "All I see is mountains and forest outside the town. Which seems like a terrible place to die. If you're going to kill us—"

"I'm going to *save* us, banshee. See that? On my side."

I saw . . . a large black spot in the middle of a large forest—a circular clearing. Extremely large. I just couldn't tell if anything was built in that clearing.

"If that's Cluj, then these are those haunted woods. The Hoia Forest," he said, sounding *far* too excited for someone who was about to crash a plane. "Remember? The brochure we were reading on the train? One of the many places Vlad was beheaded? The brochure said it was near Cluj, and it had a big dead spot where nothing grew. This is that dead spot!"

"Yay?" I said.

"I think there's room to land."

"Wait!" I said. "Are you sure?"

"Fifty percent sure? Besides, it's too late now. Better there than in the trees." Huck took the plane lower. The sheer of wind as we descended was almost as loud as the engine had been before it died.

"My kingdom for a fucking parachute," Huck mumbled as he tilted the plane, guiding it over the treetops, lower, and lower, and lower. . . .

"Oh, Huck," I said. "I'm so very sorry."

"What's that? Must need to clean my ears, because that sounded like an apology. And Theodora Fox never apologizes."

"I mean it, Huck. I'm truly sorry."

"Why? You didn't kill the engine."

"But I may be killing us. We should've slept in the hangar as you suggested."

"It's done now. Don't think of it."

How could I not? I thought about that and about my father. Of the cursed bone ring calling to me back in Sighișoara. Of Lovena telling me I had old blood and of Valentin's stories about giant white wolf priests.

And I thought about Huck. His hands on my face in the hotel in

Bucharest . . . I left everything on the table, unfinished and unsaid. I should have talked to him. I should have told him how I felt. Now it was too late.

Still. If I was going to die with anyone, I was glad it was with him.

This was it. I braced for death. How truly ironic that we were going to die where the Impaler, Vlad Țepeș, was rumored to have been beheaded.

"Banshee?"

"Yes?"

"I'm going to try to land us best I can. But if I screw it all up and I die but you survive, I want you to know something." The entire plane was shuddering. Everything below was coming toward us far too fast. "I regret . . ."

The rest of his words were lost under the riotous sound of the plane.

Regret what? *Regret what?*

"What did you say?" I shouted.

"Hold on," he yelled back. "This is going to sting like Satan's whip!"

I squeezed my eyes shut and waited for death. Then I opened them again, because, dammit, I was not a coward!

Much!

Something banged against my side of the plane. Did a wing clip a tree branch? We tilted precariously to one side, and then—

We hit the ground with a terrible crash. All at once it was:

My head hitting the back of the seat.

A wave of earth and snow coming up over the propeller.

Glass shards flying.

The sound of *grating-ripping-screaming* metal.

Bumping, bumping, bumping . . .

And then: darkness. And the most awful silence.

Every muscle in my body had turned to stone. I couldn't move for several seconds. Couldn't even breathe. Snow gusted through my broken window and landed on the sleeve of my coat. Everything smelled like pine needles, engine oil, and *literal* scorched earth. Was I paralyzed? I moved one thing at a time, successfully testing fingers, arms, legs—*oof!* Sharp pain. I'd scraped the tops of my knees on the underside of the cockpit. But nothing serious.

"Banshee?" Huck's voice was broken, and that made me think he was, too. This jostled my foggy brain.

I ripped off my headset. "Huck?"

"Are ya hurt?" he asked.

"No. A little. Not much. Are you?"

"My back—"

Oh God!

"—feels like it got kicked by a horse, but I'm all right, I think."

Relief washed over me as he pulled off his headset and dropped it on the instrument panel.

He shook himself and said in a daze, "I never thought for one second that I could land this piece of junk, but, by God, I wrestled it down, didn't I? And we're alive, hoo-hoooo!" he whooped.

"Um, Huck?" I asked, sniffing the night air that was blowing in my window.

"Yes?"

"What's that smell?"

"Huh?"

"Is that diesel?"

He swore profusely and reached behind the cockpit seats to snatch up our bags. "Out! Out now!"

I brushed away broken glass and tried the handle. "My door is jammed!"

He kicked his own door—one, twice. It flew open with a bang, and a gust of wind rushed through the cockpit. He tossed our bags outside and practically ripped my arm off, dragging me across his seat as he exited. I couldn't even get a word out. His hands were around my waist, and I was half lifted, half jumping into the snow.

Snow! And ground, most solid! Who cared that it might be haunted ground where nothing grew? Not me, buddy! I could have dropped to my knees and kissed it—and I almost did exactly that by accident because my knees were wobbly as Jell-O. Huck yanked me back upright. We grabbed our bags as flames shot up over the plane.

"Now run!" Huck shouted.

He didn't need to tell me twice. I held my beret against my head as we dashed over the clearing. Light from the flaming airplane cast a disorienting, dancing shadow and made it difficult for my eyes to adjust to our surroundings, but I finally spotted the edge of the clearing . . . and the darkness of the forest beyond.

As we rushed into the trees, a thunderous explosion shook the ground and lit up the clearing, spewing up shards of metal that littered the ground behind us. I stumbled forward, racing as if the devil were behind me in the blazing inferno. Racing until my lungs and calves burned. Until Huck nearly tripped me, trying to gawk at the plane.

"Look!" he said, breathless, thrusting out an arm to slow me down.

I stopped to look. And to listen. The explosive fire was dying down. There were only muted pops and black smoke billowing as the blaze consumed the crumpled metal carcass.

We'd made it!

"*Oh God, oh God, oh God,*" I said between hard breaths, sprinting a few more steps just to be certain I was far enough away.

"Jesus, Mary, and Joseph," Huck said in a rough voice, clutching his rucksack against his heaving chest with one hand and using the other to hold himself up against the trunk of a tree.

"Are we safe?" I asked, still panicked. "Will it explode again?"

"It's fine, fine," he mumbled, catching his breath. "All the petrol . . . poof! No more fuel, no more explody."

"Hell's bells," I said. "That was . . . Oh God. Think I'm . . . going to have . . . a heart attack. That was . . . not good. Not good at all."

"Thought we were walking shish kebobs," he agreed, letting his head drop in relief.

That made two of us. We caught our breath and stared back at the wreckage in a daze. I patted my coat pocket. Lovena's talisman was still there. Maybe she'd saved us from death by flame. Or death by mangled bodies in a plane crash.

"What about the fire spreading?" I asked. I didn't want to be responsible for burning down an entire forest.

"The snow will keep it from spreading to the trees. It's too wet to burn. It's all right now," he assured me, flipping up his coat collar to shield his neck from the biting wind. "We're alive, and it's going to be all right now."

But it wasn't. Not exactly. Death by fire was quick. Now we were stuck in a dark forest, miles away from what we assumed was Cluj—a city far, far north of where we needed to be. On top of that, it was snowing, and there was no shelter in sight.

And it was cold. Very, *very* cold.

Right. Okay. "So . . . what now?" I asked as Huck slipped the straps of his rucksack over his shoulders. "How do we get out of here before we freeze to death? I'm worried this fire will draw wild animals."

"Nah. Just the opposite," he said, still a little breathless. "Animals run from forest fires."

"Coyotes are attracted to campfires."

"Europe doesn't have coyotes."

"But it has bears. . . ."

"Christ," he mumbled. "Like arguing with a mule, it is."

I frowned. "Mule? That's what you think of me?"

He shook both his hands and his head. "Now is not the time. I'm freezing my bollocks off. We need to concentrate on finding a way out of here, yeah?"

Okay, fine. "That's north," I informed him.

"Is it?" he asked, looking up at the moonlit sky for reassurance.

"Pretty sure. You looked at the forest on that map. Which way should we go?"

He glanced around. "That way."

"You sure? Are you just saying that? Because I seem to recall that time we got lost in Mexico City, and you wouldn't ask for directions but insisted you knew the way, and we ended up—"

"Bzzzt!" He mimicked zipping his lips together. "Not now, banshee. Just start walking."

"Since you know where we're going . . . ," I mumbled. "Lead the way."

Irritable and anxious, both of us headed off in the direction Huck insisted was right, farther into the forest, away from the clearing, our breath white in the darkness. We trudged through falling snow, tripping over underbrush and winding our way through the trees in silence. The farther we went, the more I worried. This didn't feel like the way out. Not that I was entirely sure where "out" was either. But it felt as if we were going *away* rather than *toward* civilization, and that made me nervous.

After a half hour or more of hiking through black woods with no foreseeable end, we came to an eerie grove of strange trees. Their curved trunks were shaped like fishhooks—as if some terrible storm bent them a hundred years ago and they'd just continued growing that way. I'd never seen anything like it. Along with the dead clearing, it was plain to see why people called this forest haunted. All I knew was that every woodland sound made my pulse race, and I was jumping at shadows.

When we spied moonlight on the other side of the strange, twisted grove of bent trees, I couldn't have been more relieved. Huck pointed out a small stream. "Let's follow that," he suggested.

I agreed. Better than roaming around aimlessly anyway.

Though the stream was narrow—we could cross it easily—its presence created a break in the tree canopy that allowed columns of pale light to filter into the dark woods. We hurried to the light like moths to flame.

"It's not cold enough to ice over yet, so that's something," Huck remarked on the flowing water before glancing upward. "I can't tell if the storm is passing or if the trees are just blocking out most of the snow."

"Perhaps this would be a good time to look at the map of the forest in the brochure you picked up. May be enough moonlight to read it."

He shook his head. "It wasn't a map so much as a vague blob with some symbols indicating ghosts and beheading locations, what have you."

"Are you joking? You said you were certain this was the way out!"

"Now, now. Temper, banshee."

"We're lost in a haunted forest, Huck!"

He held up a finger. "Not lost. Here's a stream. Bound to lead somewhere, yeah?"

I shoved his chest with both hands, and he stumbled backward in the snow. "Are you kidding me? You should have killed us in the plane crash while you had the chance. Because now I'm going to have to strangle you, and bears will eat your carcass!"

"I told you animals lust after my leg meats—" He shielded himself and laughed as I smacked his arm several times. "Hey, now! Control thyself, empress. We're not lost, I tell you. I know exactly where we are."

"So do I—lost! In a haunted forest."

"You love ghosts," he said, grabbing my gloved hand.

"I love warmth and not freezing to death too! I love not crashing planes in the middle of the wilderness."

"I told you I didn't want to steal it! You should be praising my name for landing that bajanxed hunk of metal! Now, stop trying to hit me, for the love of the saints." Exasperated, he grabbed my other hand too.

"What did you say when we were going down?"

"Pardon?"

"When we were crashing—"

"Landing," he corrected.

"You said 'I regret' . . . something. You regret what?"

"Nothing."

"Tell me!" I said, pulling against his grip.

"Just did," he insisted. "I *said*, I regret nothing."

"*Oh*," I said, a little breathless. I stopped trying to yank my hand away from his. "You mean . . . ?"

He looked down at me with snowflakes clinging to his lashes.

"You know what I mean. Everything. From the first time I kissed you until that night in your room. It's what I meant to tell you before. I do not think that what we did was sinful or a crime against God, no matter what Fox says."

"You don't?"

He shook his head, and in that moment I felt the invisible wall between us fall away with the snow. And there it was: our connection. It wasn't broken after all. It hadn't disappeared with the months we'd spent apart.

"I don't either," I said in a small voice. "I don't regret a thing."

His grip loosened, and his hands tentatively clasped mine. Such a simple thing, holding hands. Such a simple, miraculous thing. My heart pounded rapidly inside my chest.

Somewhere in the forest, a branch snapped. Might have been a squirrel or the weight of snow breaking a twig. But it was loud enough to invade the magical, perfect moment that I was feeling with Huck. And then something changed in my peripheral vision.

It was on our side of the stream and much bigger than a squirrel.

It was also moving.

"H-huck," I whispered.

"Yes?"

"What kind of haunted things are supposed to be in these woods? Ghosts?"

His head turned ever so slowly toward the approaching shape. It was moving with care.

Stalking us.

"That's no ghost," he whispered. "Ghosts don't growl."

No, but wolves did.

THE WOLF'S SHAGGY HEAD CAME INTO SIGHT INSIDE a shaft of moonlight. His body followed. His gray fur was filthy and patchy, and I could count his ribs. He was starved. Possibly sick. And as he prowled closer, two others appeared behind him, one tawny, the other white.

White. Not skinny or starved, this one. Not quite a wolf even.

And she had only one eye.

"Jaysus," Huck whispered, releasing one of my hands. "That's . . ."

Yes. Yes, it was. Lovena's stolen wolf dog.

The two animals with Lupu were clearly wild. Had she escaped Sarkany and joined a pack, or had Sarkany sent her here to attack us? How was that even possible? If Sarkany indeed had stolen the ring in the Sighișoara museum as we'd assumed, and Lupu was with him then? There was absolutely no way he could have made it here by car in the same short time it had taken us to fly here.

Impossible!

Logically, that meant she might have broken away from him

since the last time we'd seen her. Her collar with its strange symbols was missing too. Perhaps that was the spell holding her hostage.

Or maybe I was wrong on all accounts. All I really knew was that wild animals were closing in, predators bigger and stronger than me—ones with teeth that could rip skin and break bone—and there was nothing to protect us. No weapon. No shelter to run to or gate to close.

Nothing between them and our throats.

I'd never been so afraid in my entire life.

"Nice wolfies," Huck said softly. "If we had any meat to give ya, I promise we would share. But we, uh . . ."

We were the meat.

"Run across the stream on three," Huck whispered to me, more firmly grasping the hand he still held. "One, two—"

Three!

Racing away from the wolves, we crashed through the stream's icy water—Huck in one stride and me in two. Cold lashed around my ankles, but I scrambled up the snowy riverbank, hearing the wolves behind us.

Huck and I sprinted through the trees. Blindly. Instinctually. All I smelled were spruce needles and rotting leaves beneath the snow. All I heard was the steady lope of wild predators on our tail.

Branches whipped my face. Thorns snagged my coat. We couldn't outrun them. They were fanning out behind us, two flanking and one behind. I caught snatches of the tawny wolf weaving past trees on my right. Pointed ears. Tilted eyes. Fangs. He was closing in.

Desperate, I made one final push to outrun him. My boots pounded the snowy ground. My lungs were close to bursting. But right ahead of us there was light—silvery moonlight. Another clearing? The end of the forest?

Cliff!

I couldn't have stopped myself if I'd tried.

My foot slipped. I went airborne. Then my back hit solid earth.

Down a steep hill I went.

Tumbling. Rolling. Screaming.

Earth, snow, rocks . . .

No sense of up or down. I pitched sideways and caught a glimpse of Huck falling next to me. All I could do was scrabble the ground with flailing hands, trying to slow my fall, until I blessedly slid to a stop, slamming my hip against the trunk of a tree.

Pain shot through my bones. All my muscles seized, and if I couldn't force them to stop, I feared I'd die. I needed air in my lungs. I needed everything to stop hurting.

Come on, I told myself. Breathe, lungs, breathe. . . .

I heard something in the distance. And again, this time clearer:

"Banshee!"

My lungs spasmed. I coughed up dead leaves and gasped for breath—sweet relief! After a few painful inhalations, I managed to get my stinging palms flattened on the ground and pushed myself up. We'd landed in a sort of valley or gorge between two foothills. I couldn't tell how wide the gorge was, but there was another river here; I could hear it, flowing much more rapidly than the stream above.

"Huck!" I coughed out weakly.

I needed to move. My legs worked. Nothing felt broken, just a lot of scrapes and various pains that felt destined to become bumps and bruises. Still had my beret, amazingly, but not my satchel.

Pebbles tumbled past me. I squinted up the hill to the ridge above—*Dear God, I fell that far?*—and spied three wolfish shapes picking their way down. There was a strange, almost humanlike manner in the way they were descending. Valentin's wolf story flickered inside my head, and a fresh wave of panic washed over me.

"Huck!" I shouted, desperate.

"Banshee!"

"I'm over here!"

Branches snapped, and then I spotted him, stumbling toward me. "Where are ya, Theo? Talk to me!"

"Here!" I said, pushing to my feet with a groan.

"Thank God," he said, grasping my shoulders, touching my arms as if he didn't believe they weren't broken. "Are you all right?"

I nodded, metering out my breath.

"Found your satchel way over there," he said, holding it up and gesturing loosely. "Christ, banshee. Scared me to bits. I saw your life flashing before my eyes."

"We have bigger problems, up there," I told him, pointing to the descending shapes as he handed me my satchel. "They're following."

"Mother of God," he mumbled.

"We can't outrun them," I said, turning toward the river. It was *much* wider than the stream above. Impossible to cross on foot. We'd have to swim it, and even if we made it across, how long would we last tonight, roaming the mountains in freezing, wet clothes? My wet feet were already numb.

But I spotted something else in the distance. Something beside the river.

A building.

"There!" I told Huck, pointing. "Shelter!"

"Thank the saints—c'mon!" he said, grabbing my hand.

Stumbling through the snow, we barreled toward not just one but several rough-hewn wooden cabins that lined the riverbank. They were half-timbered with shaggy, thatched roofs and wooden shutters blocking all the windows. No smoke in their stone chimneys.

They looked chillingly dark and deserted.

"Hunting cabins?" Huck said between huffed, strained breaths and the sound of our feet racing across the snow-swept ground.

Possibly. But what I *did* know after a quick glance over my shoulder was that the wolves were still descending and nearing the base of the ridge; once they hit level ground, we'd have seconds before they were on us again. "If we can steal a plane, we can break into a house," I told him, and we raced faster toward the first cabin.

It was very small: four walls, a chimney, and a door. A single dirty window flanked the door, but it had been shuttered from the inside. We came to a sliding stop, and Huck banged on the door. "Hello? Is anyone there?"

Most definitely empty.

"Pick the lock, Huck!"

"What lock? You see a bleedin' keyhole?"

That was strange. I rammed against the door with my shoulder. It gave a little, but so did my arm. "Ow!"

"Move," Huck said.

He rammed the door with gritted teeth. Once. Twice. Three times.

On the fourth attempt, he bellowed out a battle cry and threw his weight hard against the door. Wood splintered, and the door flew inward.

I tossed a glance over my shoulder to see Lupu's white body alongside her new packmates, all of them bounding across the snow. She turned her head in our direction. In a flash, the three animals were speeding toward us, heads down, eyes reflecting moonlight off the river.

"Inside!" I shouted to Huck.

We lunged into darkness and slammed the door behind us.

"Help me hold it," Huck shouted.

As soon as I braced the door alongside him, wood rattled against my arm, and I yelped.

The wolves were trying to get through!

"Keep holding it," Huck said, struggling for breath. "No way they can bust the door down. It's as thick as my arm. Only reason we were able to get inside is because I broke a plank barring the door."

The heavy wood door shuddered again. I wasn't sure if Lupu and her new wolf pack agreed with Huck's assessment.

"Lupu!" I called out against the wooden door. "Go home. Go back to Lovena."

"Doubt she's going to pay attention to that," Huck muttered.

Well? That was what Lovena told me to tell the dog if we ever saw it again. Couldn't hurt, could it? I called out again in Romanian, just for good measure, as we used our combined weight to keep the door shut. My chest rose and fell as I counted seconds, bracing for the next attack. Ten seconds. Thirty. A minute.

Nothing. No attack. No sound of paws in the snow. Silence.

"Are they gone?" I whispered to Huck.

"No idea," he said. "But I'll tell you what; I'm not going back out there to find out, that's for damn sure."

That made two of us. I shifted my arm to shove a hand into my coat pocket and felt around until the tips of my fingers grazed Lovena's wooden talisman. Safe. Like us. *Thank you, thank you, thank you.*

Dust tickled my nose. The cabin smelled old and dirty. As I switched shoulders on the door, I kicked something with my foot. Toeing it, I realized it was Huck's broken plank. I felt around until I had it in hand. One end was splintered, but what remained of the board was still a good length. And when we shuffled it around between us, testing, we found that it was *just* long enough to slide back into both brackets and bar the door.

"We need something else to barricade it," Huck said, and after a moment he shoved a heavy table my way. I helped him pull it into place, wedging it against the door.

"That's better," he said in the dark. "Hopefully. Do you hear them out there?"

"I hear the river," I said. "How is Lupu here? How, Huck?"

"She couldn't have been with Sarkany. It's not possible for them to have made it here this fast."

"Unless she wasn't with him. Maybe she escaped. We never saw her in the citadel."

"We never even saw *him*," Huck pointed out.

A chill ran through me. If it wasn't Sarkany there, who was it? Rothwild? The robed cultists? How many people were after us?

"Maybe we're okay for now," Huck said after a few moments of silence.

"You think?"

"Yeah, I do."

I let out a little breath and tried to relax. "How okay are we? Okay enough to light a fire? It's too dark in here."

"Couldn't agree more. It's giving me the willies. I feel like Sarkany's going to jump out from behind us any second now. Oh, wait. Think I feel a lantern over here. Hold on." Metal rattled; liquid sloshed. "Sounds like there's fuel." It took him a couple of strikes before a golden flame danced between us. He stuck the match inside a hole in the base of an old hanging oil lamp and lit the wick.

Light blossomed inside the small room.

So much better.

My eyes adjusting, I quickly scanned the space around us. Dried herbs hung from the rafters in a net of dusty spiderwebs. The walls were lined with dusty shelves, and there was an old stone fireplace.

But it was hard to pay attention to any of that, what with the animal skulls covering the walls. Dozens and dozens of them. Rabbit, racoon, fox . . . any number of small woodland creatures. They hung like trophies, all bleached bone and dark, empty eye sockets. Each one had a tiny symbol carved into the forehead, mostly crude *X*'s.

Huck whistled softly as he held up the lantern to inspect the walls. "What the devil is all this?"

Some bizarre local custom? I didn't know, but it gave me chills.

My gaze jumped from the skulls to a shelf filled with rusted iron traps. Ugly ones, with rows of iron teeth built to snap the legs of animals that had the terrible luck to walk into them.

Huck saw them too. "Trapper's cabin."

"Umm," I said nervously, tapping Huck on the arm. "T-trapper."

In the far corner, tucked behind some dusty open shelving that served to divide a sleeping space from the rest of the room, a human skeleton lay on a narrow cot atop a darkly stained quilt. Trousers and a shirt hung over bare bones. A few bits of gray, petrified skin clung to its skull.

"Ah *Jaysus!*"

I gritted my teeth and stared at the monstrous sight.

"Oh, my dear holy God," Huck whispered, craning his neck to see beyond the shelving. "That's not a real body . . . is it?"

"A dead one," I confirmed. "Very, very, *very* dead."

Huck swore profusely and made the sign of the cross in the air several times in a row.

"It's just a skeleton," I assured him . . . and myself. "We've seen a million of them in museums. My mother used to dig them up."

"Ancient ones, banshee. Not fresh ones!"

"He's not fresh. No smell." Hesitantly, I shifted closer to inspect it. My heart thudded against my rib cage.

"Small relief, I suppose. An ugly bastard, isn't he?"

"He's, uh, remarkably preserved. I can't even guess how long he's been in here. A decade or more? Longer?"

"*Oh*," Huck said from several feet away. "Now it makes sense. That's why the door was barred from the inside—the trapper was inside. You think he passed on in his sleep? Why did he die in here?"

"See how his leg is twisted? Maybe he got stuck in one of his traps."

"Or he got attacked by something with big teeth," Huck said. "Hey, Theo?"

"Yeah?"

"Now I'm thinking about everything Valentin told us at the camp. . . . This man wasn't buried right."

"He wasn't buried at all, Huck."

"That's what's worrying me! What did Valentin call it, the vampire creature?"

"*Strigoi* or *mullo*," I said. "But I think that involves the body reanimating. Clearly this guy isn't going anywhere, unless he can figure out a way to keep his bones together."

"What about things like fetches? Wraiths? Ghosts?"

I glanced around the cabin, a little nervous. Maybe also a little interested. "Don't see any ghosts."

"Don't sound so disappointed! What about . . . ? I mean, the heartbeat sound when you were near the ring in Sighișoara, and all that stuff Lovena told you about your blood . . ."

"What about it? You think I can attract ghosts now?"

"No! I meant, can you hear any?"

Oh. I glanced around the cabin, listening. "I don't think so?"

He let out a long breath. "Thank the saints."

"Maybe I should take a photograph, just in case it shows up on film?"

"Please don't tempt fate. Something's not right in these woods. Maybe there's a reason it's rumored to be haunted. I swear to God, banshee. If we see the trapper's ghost, I'm giving up—what are you doing? You're seriously going to take photographs?"

I pulled my camera out from my satchel and checked the lens to make sure it hadn't broken during our tumble down the ridge. It seemed fine. While Huck complained, I snapped several quick photographs of the skeleton and animal skulls.

"Are you quite finished?" Huck said.

I capped the lens and stowed the camera. "You may thank me later if any apparitions show up on the film and I become famous."

"No. I'll be pissing my trousers in fear, as I'm close to doing now. First wolves. Now this . . ." He glanced at the door. "What do we do about it?"

"The wolves?"

"The *skeleton*! The fucking body on the bed, banshee!" he said, his Irish lilt rising an octave.

"It's not going anywhere, Huck."

"I can't stay in here with a dirty, dead hellion leering at me. Isn't it enough that we have to stare at all of these poor, dead creatures with spooky symbols carved into them? This is a bad place. A man died here. Right here!"

"Not sure what choice we have. If we open the door to get the skeleton outside, the wolves might tear out our throats."

"Death by wolf or death by fright? That's our choice?"

"Plus, it's never a good idea to disturb remains. Could stir up bad bacteria." Or bad juju. "Best to just hunker down here until morning and forget about it."

Huck set the lantern down on the table barricading the door. Then he paced the floorboards, staying well away from the cot. "Okay, okay. Let's think about this, shall we? We're alive. That's most important, yeah?"

"Would seem so, yes."

"And we have shelter," he said.

"Maybe warmth, too." There was a stack of dusty wood in the corner, covered in more spiderwebs.

"Warm is good," he said. "No food . . ."

"But we can surely make it through the night here," I said. "Better inside these walls than out. Let's just see if there's something we can use to cover Mr. Trapper over there, and you'll forget all about him in no time."

"You sound just like Fox."

"You keep saying that."

"You keep sounding like him!" he argued.

"I'll make you a deal, then. I'll stop when we get a fire going."

"You mean when *I* get a fire going with my manly hands."

"Terrific idea," I said sarcastically. "Wish I'd thought of it."

"If I survive this night, know that I may strangle you in the morning."

"With your manly hands?"

Grumbling to himself, Huck investigated the chimney flue and managed to get a fire started with the help of some dry kindling in a bucket. Meanwhile, I poked around the cabin and found a dusty newspaper by the bed.

"December 3, 1901," I read to Huck. "Do you think the trapper's been dead in here that long? Thirty-six years?"

"Don't know. Don't care. Not looking at him or his witchy animal skulls. Trying to preserve my sanity, aren't I?" He'd found a broom and was sweeping a clean spot for us in front of the hearth, to which he gestured now. "You're supposed to be impressed by this. Me big man, make big fire."

I laid sheets of the newspaper over the cot. "Me little woman, cover up skeleton so big man doesn't get scared."

"Hey, I'm already scared, so the joke's on you."

"If the ghost of Mr. Trapper decides to make an appearance, you can hide behind me."

He snorted and shook his head. "Remember that autumn in Hudson Valley when they did that haunted maze downtown? I think you were eleven? You were so scared of the vampire jumping out of the coffin, Fox had to carry you back outside."

"How could I forget? You laughed so hard, you slipped in that mud puddle when we were walking back to the car."

"*Oof!* Forgot about that. Must have blocked it out," Huck said, the corners of his mouth twisting up. "All I'm saying is how could a girl afraid of Mr. Kowalski dressed in a bad vampire costume grow up into a girl who delights in taking photographs of skeletons and ghosts?"

"When life gives you ghosts, make ghost lemonade?"

He shook his head, feigning disappointment. "Leave the proverbs to the experts, yeah? And get over here before you freeze to death and I'm trapped here with two bodies."

I shuffled across the room to join him, and we both sat in front of the stone fireplace, leaning back against our luggage. The fire was a little smoky, but it felt fantastic.

"Christ, banshee. You're shaking like a leaf," he said, huddling next to me. "Take off your boots. They'll dry faster closer to the flames."

I untied the laces with a groan. "Everything hurts."

"Me too." He waited for me to hand him my brown boots and set them closer to the fire. Now that we had light and heat, it was easier to see that we were both a little banged up from our downhill tumble.

"Your trousers are torn," I said, looking at his knee.

"And your face looks as if it lost a boxing match," he said, pushing my hair away from my face to inspect it. When he touched my swollen cheek, I winced. "Yep, that eye is going to be black tomorrow. Been there myself. Won't be pleasant."

Yes, I remembered too well. His eye was black when he came to my bedroom that final night at Foxhill last year. Maybe he was remembering it too, because he released me suddenly and stared at the fire, sniffling. Was he thinking about everything we'd said to each other in the woods before the wolves showed up? I was. And I was wondering how I could feel so close to him in that moment, yet so awkward now.

So awkward. So quiet. Too quiet.

"Maybe we can find a way to civilization now," I suggested, trying to thaw the chill between us.

"Yeah, good idea," Huck mumbled. He pulled out the train brochures and found the one that had a regional map of the nearby city of Cluj and our current location on the outskirts of the town, the haunted Hoia Forest. He was right: the map was made for tourists, but the dead clearing where Huck had landed the plane was marked, and so was the river outside this cabin—it looked to be a tributary of a larger river.

"If this is even remotely right," Huck said, "then Cluj can't be more than a couple hours' walk from here. Maybe we can rest here tonight and figure out how to cross the river tomorrow. It's going to be fine," he said, as if trying to talk himself into believing it. "We'll hike to Cluj in the morning and see what happens. Yeah. That's what we'll do. . . ."

What neither of us wanted to face was that while Cluj might be only a couple of hours away, it was several more to Brașov, where the Zissu brothers hopefully were—and my father.

Wind howled through myriad cracks in the old walls. As my thoughts turned in circles, my gaze roamed past the fire to the walls of animal skulls and the symbols carved into their foreheads. They made me think of the bone ring. How it had made me feel. The bizarre thumping noises. It was so all-consuming that I nearly forgot how the ring *looked* inside the glass case. An ugly ring. Human bone . . . I couldn't imagine what kind of person would sit down and carve some poor fellow's leg bone to make a ring. Perhaps that was why it bent to one side, all crooked—because there wasn't much bone to work with.

Huh.

Funny that it was an altogether different sort of bend on Rothwild's reproduction ring—the one I'd seen in the photographs stuffed inside Father's journal. If you're going to go to the trouble of reproducing a ring in order to confuse people from finding the real one, why not copy it exactly?

Maybe I was remembering it wrong. I sat up and tugged my father's journal out of my satchel, unwinding the leather strap to pull out the photographs.

"What are you doing?" Huck asked.

"Look at this," I said, handing him the photographs as I flipped to the final pages of the journal.

"I've seen them. Rothwild's fake ring."

I held up a finger. "Do you remember how the ring in Sighișoara looked?"

"Like the one in this photograph.'

"Exactly?"

He started to shrug, and then his brow tightened. "Now that you mention it . . ."

"It was different, wasn't it? It didn't have the same little crook in it like this one does."

"Maybe not. What's your point?"

"It's not an exact reproduction. Don't you think that's strange? Look here. This is the next-to-last journal entry, which has the cipher about the boyar's letter. Remember? This is what my father wrote about the rings—" I pointed at that section of the page:

> **Seems to me that there are three rings. Two fakes, one real.**
>
> **I can't be sure, but I think the actual ring was duplicated in Turkey. Two reproductions were sent back to Romania along with the real ring, and all were distributed to three historic families there for safekeeping. ("The power is in one" is what was written in the boyar's letter.)**

"See?" I said.

"No."

"Father thought two of them were fake because the boyar's letter said 'the power is in one.' But what if that doesn't mean that only one ring is real? What if it means there are three rings, and they only work when they are put together as one?"

"Not following."

"Here," I said, pointing to the photograph. "See how the ring bends at the top?"

"It's crooked."

"And remember the ring in the case?" I asked.

"Also crooked, just in a different way. Terrible jeweler, whoever made it. Someone should ask for a refund."

"What if it wasn't sloppy craftsmanship? Maybe it was carved that way on purpose because all three rings fit together to form a knot on top. Like a gimmal ring." I made circles with my thumbs and overlapped them to show him what I meant. "I've seen rings like this before, in the bazaar in Istanbul."

"The one you were accused of shoplifting?"

I grinned and touched my finger to my nose. "That's the one! In Turkey, they're called a wedding ring or a harem ring, and the story behind them was that if the wife took her ring off to cheat with another man, she'd have trouble reassembling it properly and would get caught, which is completely sexist and stupid, by the way."

"Very stupid," Huck agreed with a smile. "The wife could just leave the ring on."

"Right? Anyway, the Turkish puzzle rings have interlocking bands, but its English cousin, the gimmal ring, was meant to be taken apart—one ring for each of the betrothed to wear until they could be married."

"Separate rings . . . ," Huck murmured.

"That fit together," I said, twining my fingers together. "What if Vlad Dracula's ring wasn't one single band? What if it was three bands that fit together like a puzzle?"

He blinked at me. "That would mean Rothwild's ring is real."

"*And* Lovena's is real."

"And there's a third ring out there that fits with them. . . ."

"Is it possible?" I asked. "You tell me. You're good at this sort of thing. You're the one who can take apart a watch and fit it all back together."

His brow furrowed as he considered this. Then he rummaged inside his coat pocket and pulled out a battered pack of gum. After unwrapping three sticks, he twisted the foil wrappers into circles, molding them carefully with deft fingers. "This is how the one in Fox's photographs is shaped, yeah?"

"Yes," I said as he laid it on his knee. Then he quickly molded a second ring.

"This is sort of how the one in the museum looked," he said, and he gingerly slotted the foil bands together.

We both stared in amazement at his crudely engineered model.

"A third band would fit up inside these two," Huck said, pointing with the tip of his pinkie. "Where the space is between the kinks here on top."

It worked. It was possible.

"Three bands, one ring," I murmured, taking the foil model from his fingers. "Apart, their power is dormant. Remember? Lovena said she sensed a sleeping power in her ring."

"One that you heard in Sighișoara," he said.

I nodded. "Maybe that was just the tip of the iceberg, so to speak. All the stories about Vlad's insane bloodlust—all the impalements and dipping bread in blood—maybe when Vlad wore the three rings, he was . . ."

"An all-powerful killer who slaughtered tens of thousands?"

"The Impaler," I said, heart beating rapidly with excitement. "All the people that Father mentions in the journal who've owned the ring over the years—mass murderers. The three bands together must activate its power and cause bloodlust in the wearer. Father's research in the journal matches up with the description in my *Batterman's Field Guide*—it was a war ring, originally intended to make Vlad's father unstoppable on the battlefield in order to aid the Holy Roman Empire's efforts to win land over the Ottomans. Maybe when Vlad's ring made its way back to Turkey in the late 1800s, as Father says in the journal, that's when the Turkish sultan had it divided into three bands, each one sent separately to different families in Romania. Separated, the ring's power is diminished."

Huck took the foil bands back from me and held them up in front of the fire. "Christ alive, banshee. How come Fox never saw this?"

"Maybe I'm smarter than he is."

He huffed out a breath, amused, and crumpled the foil bands into a ball before tossing it into the fireplace. "Maybe you are. And Fox never heard the ring in Sighișoara like you did, or maybe he would have known it was real. Then we wouldn't be stuck in this horror cabin with literal wolves at our door."

I couldn't tell if he was teasing me. Maybe he'd only said he believed me back in Sighișoara just to placate me outside the Drăculești museum? I stole a look at his profile, light from the fire dancing over his face, while my head swam with bone rings and wolves. It was enough to make me question it all myself. Had I heard heartbeats in the museum, or was I just suffering from exhaustion? Were there actually three rings that fit together like a puzzle, or was I grasping at straws? Had my father made the decision to track down the ring alone to lead Rothwild away from us, or had he selfishly abandoned us like unwanted luggage, uncaring about anything but the prize of another treasure?

I understood at that moment why people said worry is burden, because all of this felt heavy enough to weigh me down. I didn't want to think about it anymore. Not where my father was. Not the rings. Not whether Huck and I felt the same way or if we'd be separated again. Any of it. I only wanted to get warm and stay that way. Basic survival. That was far easier to manage.

Mentally and physically exhausted, we used clothes from our luggage to construct a makeshift pallet on the floor in front of the fireplace, and we lay down in our coats side by side, trying to keep warm. After I closed my eyes, I felt Huck's fingers between us, feathering over mine, gently urging. Asking. I turned my palm upward, and he twined warm fingers with mine. We clasped hands in silence, and then he tugged me closer.

"C'mere to me," he murmured, gathering me against his chest, my head on his shoulder, the wool of his coat scratchy under my cheek. His arms wound around me, and he was warm and solid, and my God, he felt good! I was terrified he'd hear my heart thundering wildly—until I realized it was *his* heart I was hearing.

We clung to each other while the wind howled around the cabin, until a deep peacefulness spread through me. This was everything I needed, right here. This comfort. This tiny bit of joy. This light in the darkness that told me everything was going to be okay. *We* were going to be okay. Somehow.

But as I drifted off to sleep, a stray thought bubbled up to the surface.

Rothwild had one bone band. Did Sarkany have a second band, stolen from the Drăculești museum? And if there were, indeed, three bands of bone, and the final one was in the possession of the Zissu twins, that meant my father could be headed to them right now, unaware of all this.

I hoped to God we made it to him before anyone else did.

JOURNAL OF RICHARD FOX
July 15, 1937
Cluj-Napoca, Transylvania, Kingdom of România

Being here has Elena in my thoughts again. She said in some ways this was more of a home to her than Brașov, because of all the years she spent attending university here and then doing fieldwork for the ancient history department. If it weren't for that work, we may have never met.

Left the hotel earlier with the intention of going to visit Elena's old mentor, Dr. Toma Mitu, her college archaeology professor, while Jean-Bernard was sleeping in late. Mitu has been writing me for months, pestering me for a telephone call. Said he'd been doing research on a side project and found something important. Granted, every history professor I've met thinks their research is earth-shattering, and it almost never is. Anyway, when I got to the university, I just couldn't make myself go inside. Maybe I'm a coward. Maybe I just can't handle listening to an old man dig up memories about Elena that I'd rather stay buried. Hurts too much. Isn't that strange? All these years later, it still hurts as if she died yesterday. Grief is a rotten, stinking bastard of a thing.

When I got back to the hotel, I told J.B. that I was done with the whole damn chase for this ring. I wasn't even convinced it existed, to be honest. So we're leaving Romania today and heading down to Athens as we originally planned. Rothwild can keep his damn money. I'm out.

THE WOLF PACK NEVER RETURNED. NOT THAT WE KNEW of anyway. We both dozed off and on, taking turns adding logs to the fire when it died down . . . and returning to each other's arms. But once daylight shone through cracks in the walls, we separated without a word.

We'd survived the night. Now we had to get out of the forest.

Huck bravely volunteered to step outside and check around the area to ensure we were alone as I watched from the door. No ghosts or rabid animals—no traps either, which was good, because I was worried our friendly skeleton had booby-trapped the area. However, after we both went in different directions to take care of nature's call in private, what Huck *did* find was a rustic but passable bridge over the river, just past the cabins. So we gathered up our things and wasted no time using it.

Hiking through even a little snow isn't easy; hiking through snow-covered bramble and underbrush was harder. We trudged along for a couple of hours, shoes soaked and feet numb with cold, and spotted seven red deer, ten squirrels, and one unidentified furry animal that may have been a marten or a weasel, or simply a large rat.

Just after nine o'clock in the morning by Huck's wristwatch, we found a dirt road (no more brambles!) then a paved one—no more mud! And when we stepped around a sharp bend in the road, an entire city sprang to life as if by magic.

Cluj. Unofficial capital of the Transylvania region. Home to Romanian revolutionaries, a large Hungarian population, and Bohemian expats.

And what a city it was, one that teemed with history—baroque buildings, heroic statuary, and Gothic spires. Sunshine glinted off sloping roofs dusted in snow, and traffic along the streets was lazy. It wasn't as big or bustling as Bucharest, but it had an old-world charm that was appealing.

We hiked through a neighborhood lined with quaint shops and restaurants that were just opening for the day, and on a not-as-quaint side street, I spotted a dark storefront with dirty windows. Big red letters were painted on the glass: AMANET. Pawnshop, last hope of the downtrodden and destitute. We didn't have enough money to send a transatlantic cable to Foxwood to beg Father's butler to wire cash, nor even to send a simple telegram to Paris—not to mention that it felt crude to ask Jean-Bernard's man for money when his employer was on a hospital bed. No. We'd gotten ourselves into this situation and depleted our resources. Best to climb out on our own four feet.

So I did the only thing I knew I *could* do:

I pawned my precious Leica camera.

I clicked through half a dozen blank photos to finish up the roll of film inside, removed it, and relinquished the best present my father had ever given me, RIP. Maybe some local university student would buy it and take award-winning photographs.

"I'm so sorry, banshee," Huck said after we'd exited the shop with a handful of lei. "I know you loved that camera."

But what else could we do? Even if the pawnshop owner gave us a quarter of what that camera was worth, the man was saving our rumps. And we were lucky he traded with us at all, because we looked like the devil's own rejects, booted from the second circle of hell—Huck with his ripped clothes and me with my black eye. Because, *oh*, was it black. And bloodshot. I looked like a drunk racoon that had wandered out into the street and gotten clipped by a motorcycle.

Four down, seven letters: H-A-G-G-A-R-D.

No matter. We'd gained enough coin from the pawnshop to feel momentarily wealthy, and that was something.

After stopping at a tiny *farmacia* to buy aspirin for our aches and iodine for our cuts and scratches, we hiked several blocks to the central railway station, where we purchased bus tickets to Brașov—because the bus was cheaper and faster than the local train. Then we sent a telegram to Jean-Bernard's house, inquiring about his condition. We had only a few hours before our train departed, but maybe we'd hear something. Promising the telegram window agent we'd return later, we walked across the street and found a window table inside a cozy and very warm café, where we ate a late breakfast: giant bowls of *mămăligă*, a creamy polenta dish, with cheese and a butter-fried egg on top. It was heavenly. I licked the spoon when I was finished; Huck ran his finger around his bowl. And when the dishes were being cleared away and we still had time to waste, something struck me.

"Father came here this summer," I said. "It's in the journal. He said he'd planned to go drop in on my mother's old professor at the university, that the professor had something important to talk about, but Father changed his mind at the last minute. Maybe it's nothing, but that was the entry before the torn-out page."

"Huh," Huck said. "Did Fox give a hint about what was so important that this professor wanted to discuss?"

"Something the professor was researching? He teaches history and archaeology. Father wrote in the journal that they'd been corresponding by mail, but he's never mentioned that to me." Then again, he never told me anything, so that wasn't a big surprise. "Dr. Mitu—that's the name of the professor—was my mother's mentor. She practically worshipped him. Nice man. I haven't seen him since . . . well, since my mother died. He came to New York for her funeral."

"Could have been anything, I suppose," Huck said. "If this man studies archaeology, he may have uncovered a lead about some hidden treasure or tomb somewhere that could interest Fox. Might be as simple as that."

Perhaps. "Might be. Father apparently lost his nerve after making plans to visit him. Guess it dredged up old feelings for Mother."

"Fox hates feelings."

"Loathes them."

"Unless they're angry feelings. He quite enjoys grumbling and shouting."

"Like it's cake with buttercream frosting," I agreed, repeatedly tapping my nails on the table. "It's probably none of my business, whatever Dr. Mitu wanted to tell Father. Right? Nothing to do with Vlad's ring. I mean, we already have a good idea about where Father is now, so speaking with Dr. Mitu wouldn't give us any insight."

"Don't know," Huck said.

"Then again, there's the torn-out page in the journal. Could be to do with all of this mess. Might be something helpful to know. Can't be that far from here . . ."

"Banshee?"

"Yes?"

"Would you like to go talk to this Dr. Mitu?"

I smiled slowly, flashing him my teeth. "We *do* have a couple hours before our bus, and he is an old friend of my mother's—and when am I ever going to be able to say 'I dropped in because I was just in the neighborhood' again? Maybe never."

"Grab your stuff," he said, pretending to be put out. "Let's find a taxi."

The ride to the university in Old Town was a few short blocks down wet streets lined with snow-filled gutters. The campus, a pretty collection of classical buildings topped with sculpted marble friezes, was small but elegant, and after instructing the taxi driver to pull over so that I could ask a couple of students for directions to the archaeology department, we stopped alongside a golden-bricked building with arched windows.

After paying the taxi driver, we passed through a pair of elaborate ironwork streetlamps and entered wooden doors into the building's threshold. It was dim and nearly deserted inside. Perhaps classes had already ended for winter break? We finally spotted someone who pointed us up a wide staircase to the second floor, and we took a long corridor to the history department.

"So strange to think that my mother walked these halls," I murmured as we passed a line of old photographs from archaeological digs—all before my mother's time. "She finished two degrees here, you know. Field archaeology and ancient history. She met my father after she graduated."

"Seem to recall Fox saying that, yes," he said in a low voice.

It was intimidating, being here. Felt as if decades of studious and serious academics were judging us inside the old walls. Like we didn't belong. Perhaps this was one of the reasons my father had gotten cold feet. Then again, I couldn't imagine him being intimidated by much of anything.

We found a small wooden door with an opaque glass window upon which was painted in gold:

DEPARTAMENTUL ARHEOLOGIE

DIR: PROF. DR. TOMA MITU

Heart racing, I pushed open the door, and we stepped inside a musty-smelling reception area with a sad potted plant and a few more photographs on the wall. I recognized the person in the largest picture: an older man in a dark gray suit, brimmed hat, and metal-rimmed glasses. Dr. Mitu.

But it wasn't the professor at the reception desk. It was a dark-haired girl who didn't look as if she could have been that much older than me. She looked up from a pile of graded tests and a paper cup of steaming coffee.

"Yes?" she said, looking us over critically. She had the kind of look in her eye that a bank teller might have when trying to decide if the customer who'd just approached could be a bank robber and she was considering whether to punch the panic button beneath the desk.

"Pardon me," I said in Romanian. "We don't have an appointment, but we were hoping to speak to Dr. Mitu? I'm an old family friend. Or rather, my mother was. She was a student here almost twenty years ago, Elena Vaduva."

"Elena Vaduva?" The young woman's face brightened. "I know her. At least, I feel as if I do. I helped Dr. Mitu work on a project, and she . . . that is, it concerned her. She was well known in this department. Practically a legend. First woman at the university to earn an archaeology degree . . . Dr. Mitu brags about her after all these years. You are her daughter? Your father is the American adventurer?"

I nodded, excited that she knew about my mother. And my father? Wow. My mother really must have been Dr. Mitu's favorite pupil, all right. "Yes, that's me," I told her. "Miss Theodora Fox, and this is my, um . . ." I gestured toward Huck. I'd be damned before I introduced him as my brother again. Friend of the family? That didn't sound right either. Boy who broke my heart? Love of my life? Best friend?

"Huck Gallagher," he said simply when I took too long. Then he told the young woman, "I don't speak Romanian. Sorry."

"I speak English," the woman said, switching languages. "I am Liliana Florea, Dr. Mitu's graduate teaching assistant. Just Liliana is fine."

"You're a student?" I asked.

She nodded. "For five years. Like your mother was, I suppose," she said, fanning her hand above the desk. Then her smile faded, and her brow wrinkled. "I'm afraid I have bad news, however. Dr. Mitu isn't here. He's at a dig in Egypt, outside of Memphis. He left two weeks ago."

My heart fell. Not sure why, exactly. I suppose, unlike Father, I was hungry for connections with people who knew my mother—hungry for memories and stories, anything that kept her alive in my head.

"I'm disappointed to hear that," I told Liliana. "He'd contacted my father, Richard Fox? My father mentioned that Dr. Mitu was doing some research, and I believe he was coming to see him this past summer but . . . got sidetracked."

Liliana nodded, eyes bright with interest. "I know all about that. I helped Dr. Mitu—it was such an exciting project. He was so looking forward to seeing your father to share his discovery."

"Really?" I said. "Do you mind me asking . . . what discovery was this?"

"Your father didn't tell you? I'm quite certain it's of interest, especially to you, since you're part of the tree."

I glanced at Huck. He wasn't following either.

"Tree?"

"Family tree. Is that the right word in English? Dr. Mitu was researching Elena's genealogy—her family's lineage. He's been attempting to trace it through historical documents. They started working on it when she was a student here. You didn't know about his project?"

"Oh, right. That project," I said, pretending I knew all about it. "The professor made a recent discovery about my mother's family?"

She took a sip of hot coffee, holding the cup in both hands. "About the House of Drăculești."

All the hair on my arms stood up. Huck made a small noise. "Vlad the Impaler's house," I said, trying to sound casual.

"The very one," Liliana said brightly. "Dr. Mitu was going to send all the documents to your father, but he was excited to show him in person. You didn't know? Vlad the Impaler was Elena's ancestor."

A wave of dizziness rolled over me. My legs stiffened painfully. I felt as if someone could push me over with the tip of their finger and I'd topple sideways to the floor like a captured chess piece.

"Her ancestor," I repeated, licking dry lips. "You mean, in a general sense? As in Vlad Dracul was a kind of founding father of Romania?"

"No. I mean quite literally. Elena was tracing her family tree before she died, and Dr. Mitu was helping her. Over the years he forgot about it, until he came across a record of a wedding in 1487. It was for the marriage of Vlad's child from his first wife, Mary—illegitimate daughter of John Hunyadi, Prince of Transylvania. Your mother can trace her family back to Vlad's daughter."

I blinked at Liliana, unable to process this.

Huck said, "Hold on. You're saying Theo here is related to Vlad the Impaler?"

"Why, yes," the young woman said, leaning back in her chair with the coffee cup steaming under her chin. "I helped verify the documents for Dr. Mitu. You see, Vlad's second wife was a Hungarian noblewoman, a cousin to Matthias Corvinus, the famous Hungarian king who was born here in Cluj—his statue is just down the road," she said, gesturing with her head. "That line may have died out years ago, or there may be a descendant—the professor is still researching that. But what's forgotten is that Vlad had a previous wife, when he was younger. His first wife drowned. She was a Transylvanian noblewoman from a village near Brașov."

"My mother's hometown," I murmured.

"Exactly," Liliana said in an excited voice. "In Vlad's time, there was no united Romania. Transylvania and Wallachia were under separate rule. His first marriage would have likely been an attempt to keep things friendly between the two regions. But yes, the professor believes the research is sound. You are a daughter of Wallachia and Transylvania. Vlad's blood flows in yours."

"That is . . ." Shocking. Alarming.

"Unbelievable," Huck murmured.

The assistant didn't notice though. She just looked pleased with herself—proud, even. "You are excited, I can tell."

That was not the word I'd use. In fact, I couldn't use any words. I was speechless, and possibly on the verge of passing out.

Liliana cleared her throat. Her gaze flicked from Huck's paled face to mine. "I hope you're pleased by the news. I know it's a little shocking, what with Vlad's dark reputation. But much of that was probably exaggerated by his enemies. You should be proud. The entire history department has been fascinated by this research. If you publicized it, you would be the darling of all Romania."

I blinked at her several times, trying to paste a smile on my face. "Thank you for sharing this. It's a bit of a shock, but I'm certain . . ." I trailed off, not knowing what else to say. "I'm sorry, but we need to . . ." Need to what? I was losing my mind. Was this shock? I thought it must be.

"We need to catch a bus," Huck quickly said, rescuing me deftly before tipping his cap at Liliana. "Sorry to rush out of here. It was nice to meet you. Please tell the professor we stopped by when he returns from Egypt."

"Of course!" she said, flustered. "The pleasure has been mine."

I mumbled my thanks in a daze, but when Huck put a hand on my shoulder to lead me out of the office, I remembered something. "Sorry. One more thing," I said, turning back to Liliana. "You said there was possibly another descendant. From Vlad's second wife?"

"Yes," she said. "He's a Hungarian in his forties. Dr. Mitu has been in touch with him. Actually, the professor was doing some ancestral research for this man this past spring when he first stumbled across the record that connected your mother to Vlad. It was a complete surprise."

I stilled. "You wouldn't happen to remember this man's name?"

"Let me see . . . ," she said, biting her lip. "I believe the man's name was a Mr. Rothwild."

"Fuuuuuu . . . ," Huck drawled under his breath.

Goose bumps blossomed over my skin. I was not going to faint. I was, however, very close to vomiting.

Liliana either didn't notice or misinterpreted our shock. "Dr. Mitu has yet to *conclusively* find a link for him like yours. Regardless, I can say in all confidence that you are Vlad's scion."

"Lucky me," I whispered. "Lucky, lucky, lucky . . ."

I didn't finish. I just turned around and headed for the door, strode down the hallway, away from the office. *Steel spine, chin up. Steel spine, chin up* . . . I repeated it endlessly, but it wasn't working. I couldn't calm down. I just walked and walked, aimless and confused, until I heard Huck's boots slapping against the floor as he jogged to catch up.

"How do we get out of here?" I said, spinning in a circle. "I can't remember how we came in. . . . I need air."

Huck grabbed my arm and hurried me across the hall to a set of glass doors. Cold air rushed over my face as we stepped onto a narrow balcony that overlooked an empty collegiate courtyard. A cracked porcelain bowl filled with cigarette butts sat near my feet.

"Breathe," he said, one hand flattened on my back. "Slowly. Exhale, inhale . . . There you go. You're all right now."

I grasped the railing and breathed in brisk air until the shock passed. "I'm okay," I said when I came back to my senses, and then, trying to minimize my embarrassment, "We keep ending up on balconies, don't we? Good thing you're wearing more than a towel this time."

He made a surprised noise in the back of this throat and glanced at me from the sides of his eyes, both sheepish and amused. "Well, you know what they say. Clothes make the man."

I wanted to laugh, but the cold air caused my eyes to water. "Oh, Huck," I murmured.

"What in the devil is happening?" he said, leaning on the railing with me.

"I don't know. I don't know," I whispered, knuckling away tears before they could fall.

"Is this what Lovena meant by the 'hands of fate'? Because they can go to hell right now."

When a student walked through the hall behind us, Huck mumbled something about ears listening and pulled the balcony door shut. "Okay, let's think about this. Let's say all this is true about your bloodline. It would explain why this dragon order has been hounding us. Maybe they don't want the journal. Maybe they want *you*."

"Why?" I whispered.

"Rothwild is obsessed with Vlad. Your father said as much in the journal. And this woman just implied that the professor was doing work for Rothwild. Is it a stretch to think they may have told Rothwild about your connection to Vlad? Maybe that's why Rothwild hired Fox in the first place. To get to you. To play some kind of cat-and-mouse game."

"That makes no sense."

"Are you sure? Think about it, banshee. Fox says in the journal that he was constantly frustrated because every lead he chased had already been investigated by Rothwild."

I heard what he was saying, but I couldn't make all the puzzle pieces slot together. Rothwild wanted Vlad Dracula's ring, and I was positive there were three bands—that much I knew. And when Rothwild hired Father this summer, I was back home in New York, so he didn't hire him to get to me. I think he truly wanted Father to track down the ring components. Father took the job, failed to find the other two bands this summer, quit the job, and then a few months later found a new lead in Turkey and renewed his search. There was no way Rothwild could know I'd be along for this trip.

I wasn't even convinced Rothwild knew there were three bands. For all we knew, he was still under the impression that there was one real ring.

And yet he'd hired Dr. Mitu to research his ancestry?

This was maddening.

"Do you think Father knows about this genealogy research? The page in the journal that was torn out . . . Do you think he came by here after all, or telephoned Dr. Mitu? Did Father know and not tell me? He kept everything else from me—I didn't even know he was in Romania this summer until he dropped me off in Istanbul. That's when he told me he was hunting Vlad's ring, Huck. When he had one foot out the door of my hotel room and was ready to go to Tokat."

"That was wrong," Huck said. "That was very wrong."

"And if he knew this . . . this bombshell about my heritage and kept it from me?" I shook my head violently as anger heated my chest. "It's not even his to keep. It's *my* bloodline, not his. *My* connection to my mother, not his!"

"Whoa," Huck said, hands on my shoulders, turning me to face him. "You don't know that Fox knew about this. I can't believe he'd hide that from you—"

"Oh, I can," I murmured. "He doesn't respect me. He doesn't care. He would definitely hide a piece of vital information from me and then toss me to the lions—or, in this case, the dragons. We're surrounded by murder and mad occultists, Huck. Father has kept this from me and put us in danger, all in the same stroke."

"*If*," Huck insisted, forcing my gaze to connect with his. "*If* he even knew about your mother's bloodline, maybe in his own bumbling way he thought he was protecting you from all this chaos—I know! It's still not right. It's more than not right; it's downright foolish. He's a great man, banshee, but he's also a stubborn, shortsighted, occasionally stupid man."

"Couldn't agree more," I mumbled.

"He doesn't think. He's not a planner. He just flies by the seat of his pants and hopes he lands on his feet. Usually he does, and that's the maddening part of it. But I can't for one second believe that he would do something on purpose to endanger you. And I don't believe you think that either."

"Believe what you want," I said, and then winced. "Damn it all! My eye hurts like something is splitting the socket from the inside out."

I turned away from him, angrily stripping off my beret so that I could rub my head in a feeble attempt to make the pain recede. Huck tugged on my arm and turned me back around.

"Go on, then, let me look at it," he said, hand lifting my chin, first gently, then insistently when I didn't comply. "Quit being mulish and let me see. There. Was that so hard? Oooh, yes, that's a shiner, all right. The swelling's gone down since this morning, though, so that's good."

"Nothing's good," I complained, shoving my beret into my coat pocket.

"Mmm. Nothing at all?"

"Almost nothing."

A soft smile rose, quivered, then hid.

"What?" I said.

"Just thinking."

"About what?"

He shrugged lightly with one shoulder and turned my chin, inspecting my face. "The last time one of us was tending to the other's black eye."

His gaze flicked to mine and then skittered away, back to the surgeon-like examination he was conducting on the scratches near my temple.

"I remember," I said softly. "First and last time I ever threw a party at Foxwood when Father was out of town."

"Aye, nothing like a little stolen champagne and a house full of rowdy teenagers to turn a birthday into a brawl. Scrapping like junkyard dogs."

"James Kendrick got you good in the eye that night."

"Sheer luck. It was his elbow, not his fist. And I recall getting in a pretty good hook of my own."

"You broke his beautiful nose, Huck—or at least, that's what he shouted about a hundred times," I said, smiling. "Saw him in town a month or so after you left. His nose looked fine, in case you were wondering."

"A shame." His thumb feathered over my jaw, tracing a path, ever so lightly, as if he were studying roadways on a map. Tingles blossomed across my skin.

A warm wave of shivers cascaded over my chest and down my arms. I forgot about the chilly air and the balcony. Forgot about Vlad Dracula and the bombshell that had been dropped on me. Rothwild. My anger at Father. The pain of my black eye. All of it vanished as I gazed up at Huck's face.

Hazel eyes, golden as whiskey, stared back at me under a fan of dark lashes and heavy lids. "Banshee," he murmured in a deep, rich lilt. "Swear by all the saints, I really want to kiss you right now."

My heartbeat went erratic.

"Do you?" I whispered.

"You have *no idea*."

Oh, but I did.

"Like I've never wanted anything in all my life."

"Like you'll die without it?" I said, fisting his lapel in my trembling fingers.

His nose grazed mine. "We shouldn't."

"Probably not."

"Will only make things worse if we're separated again," he whispered as his hand cradled my cheek.

"Unbearably painful," I agreed.

"But . . . ," he murmured.

"But . . ."

His mouth hovered over mine, lingering. Hesitant. His hands held my face. I tugged on his lapel, pulling him closer. Closer.

Until his lips brushed mine. We were both trembling. Both breathing as if we'd been running from a pack of wolves. I shuddered violently, and his mouth came down on mine.

For a moment a stranger was kissing me. Someone wholly unfamiliar, unsure and clumsy. Someone who was nervous and made *me* nervous, and it was all wrong, and it wasn't supposed to be like this, and then—

We found each other.

There you are.

Rapture.

We kissed each other like we'd been apart for lifetimes, searching for each other. Soft lips, warm mouth, deeply. Nothing between us. My armor disappeared, and he dropped his weapons, and we were both defenseless and exposed, and all the agony of the last year just . . . fell away. He was Huck. The same and yet different, a stranger and yet still mine. All mine. The scent of him, the taste of his mouth, the feel of his hands running down my back, pulling me against him until I could feel the unmistakable warm length of him between us, my breasts pressed to his chest . . .

He still wanted me.

I still wanted him.

Nothing else mattered.

This was too good, and I'd waited too long for it. Us. Together. Our separation had chiseled away at my soul, and now I held him like he was the answer to life itself. Everything I wanted.

"Banshee?" he said against the side of my head.

"Yes?"

"It's still there, what's between us. It didn't break or die."

"Still there," I agreed.

"Strong and stubborn, this thing."

More than I dared to imagine.

But was it strong enough to survive the wrath of my father again? Or would we live to regret this?

Being enemies was easy.

Falling in love was harder.

IN THE TAXI RIDE FROM THE UNIVERSITY TO THE BUS station, Huck and I held hands hard enough to make my knuckles ache, but I didn't let go. His kisses clung to my stinging lips like a blissful dream that lazily lingers after sleep. In another place, under different circumstances, it would have been everything I wanted. But once we were back in the bustle of the city, thrust out of the taxi and into the cold, the tiresome burden of reality returned.

We sloshed through melting snow to cross a busy street and barely made it to our bus on time. The driver was closing the doors, and Huck banged on them until we were allowed on grudgingly. The only seats available were at the very back of the bus. They smelled sour, and springs in the seats threatened to poke through worn holes in the fabric, but at least we were able to sit together.

Huck lifted our luggage into a sagging net above our seats' dirty window while across the aisle, a wizened Romanian woman with a floral kerchief tied over white hair stared at us as if we were monkeys in a zoo. If I had any hopes of canoodling with Huck, they were quashed; nothing like the judgmental stare of a nosy grandmother to put a damper on runaway feelings.

Brașov was a five-hour trip through the Carpathians. After I settled against Huck's side, my mind returned to everything the professor's assistant had told us. Now that I'd gotten over the initial shock of it all, I was having trouble letting it sink in. *I am related to Vlad the Impaler.* One of the most vilified men in European history was my not-so-great-great-great-times-twenty-grandfather? I mean, sure, he lived well over four hundred years ago. But Lovena's words still hung inside my head. Old blood. Vlad's blood?

Is this why I could hear the ring in the museum?

I had a killer's blood running in my veins?

And Rothwild might also be Vlad's descendant from another wife?

Did Father know this? *Did he?*

Huck glanced at me with a concerned look on his face. I tried to keep calm, to erect a false front and forget about all of it. Yet barbs of worry continued to plague my thoughts and prick at my chest.

My family bloodline.

Vlad the Impaler.

His cursed ring of three bone bands.

Order of the Dragon.

Rothwild.

Sarkany.

Magical spells on banknotes.

Wooden talismans.

Dead bodies.

Witches.

Wolves.

Father.

In the middle of all this chainlike panicking, I suddenly remembered that we'd forgotten to return to the telegram window at the station to find out if Jean-Bernard's butler had replied. How selfish was that? I was busy getting handsy with Huck, and the poor man could be at death's door.

That realization was my breaking point. I couldn't think anymore. Couldn't worry. Couldn't panic. Couldn't try to make impossible puzzle pieces fit together. My brain had reached its limits. It compartmentalized everything I'd learned on this trip into lockboxes, posted an "out of order" sign, and refused to cooperate.

Eighteen across, "admit defeat." W-H-I-T-E-F-L-A-G.

The bus ride became easier after that. I fell into a dull daze, and Huck and I took turns staring at sweeping mountain vistas and napping on each other's shoulders for much of the trip. Halfway through, the nosy Romanian woman in the floral kerchief kindly woke us when the bus stopped at a station with public restrooms and a street vendor selling fried dough. We took advantage of both, stretching our cramped legs, and returned to the bus for the final leg of its journey.

To my mother's hometown. And the Zissu brothers.

And hopefully, to my wayward father.

The rest of it could all go to hell.

By the time we rolled into Brașov, the late-afternoon sun was falling behind snowy mountain peaks that surrounded the town like arms. The medieval town was a fairy-tale skyline of snow-dusted terra-cotta roofs, Gothic spires, and baroque buildings. I tried to imagine my mother living here and struggled. It was old-world, and she'd been so modern and revolutionary. Maybe that was why she had left: it was too small to hold her. Too sleepy and lost in time. When she spoke of it, I recalled, it was as if it were the setting of a fairy tale. Not entirely real.

But it was. Very real. Did I still have family here? I didn't even know where her old family home was, and that made me angry at my father for failing to share any of this with me—for *everything*. All of this was his fault, and I couldn't even yell at him for it. All I could do was shadowbox a stuffed dummy that looked like him in my mind.

Sleep deprived and road weary, Huck and I exited our bus at a terminal across from the central train station and stopped at a posted tourist board to get our bearings. It had a helpful map and information in English, German, Hungarian, and Romanian.

"Oh, look," Huck said, reading a factoid. "Local legend not only claims that the Pied Piper of Hamelin reemerged here after luring away children from Lower Saxony, but also that Vlad the Impaler's army captured a nearby castle for a year when he was quarreling with local merchants. Maybe that's where you get your temper from, banshee."

"Thanks for that. Lovely to be reminded that I'm descended from a monster who murdered thousands of people."

"Everyone's family has some bad nuts," Huck said.

"Oh, really? Do you have a famously cruel warlord in yours?"

"I had a great-uncle who shot his wife and died in prison. That's close, yeah?"

I snorted. "Exactly the same."

He knocked his shoulder against mine as if to say "it's not so bad," but we both knew that wasn't true. And after staring at the information board like lost puppies, both of us deep in our thoughts, he sighed heavily and said, "Well, I suppose we're here for a reason."

"Suppose we are," I said gloomily. "Or we're the biggest chumps in the world on a wild-goose chase."

"Take heart, banshee. Fortune favors the chump. We just have to be patient."

"Bear and four bears?"

"Think we're facing about ten bears at this point, sadly."

But only one I cared about, and that was my father. Now that we were here, standing in the middle of this fairy-tale town, I felt the thousand and one reasons I had to be angry at him fall to the wayside, and taking their place were the thousand and one reasons I had to worry about his current safety. I mean, sure, *I* wanted to kill him. I just didn't want anyone else to do it.

My relationship with my father had always been complicated. Guess a whirlwind trip through Romania hadn't changed that.

"We'll find him," Huck said softly, giving me a supportive smile.

I nodded, a little embarrassed that he'd read my thoughts so easily.

Huck looked around the snowy streets, rubbing his hands together rapidly to stave off the cold. "Where should we go? Sun will be setting soon."

"I think we need to figure out where the Zissu brothers' shop is and try to make it there before it closes. I have their business card, but it doesn't have an exact address. Maybe we can find it on a public map?"

"Or we could ask someone?" Huck suggested.

"Maybe there?" I pointed a gloved finger toward a charming-looking building across the street from our train station. A sign outside read: CENTRUL DE INFORMARE TURISTICĂ.

"Looks promising," he agreed. "Let's hurry."

After making our way across the wintry street, we were greeted enthusiastically by a cheerful man behind a tiny information window. He was initially confused by the Zissu business card and insisted it wasn't listed in the well-worn telephone book on his desk, turning it around so that we could see. No Zissu. No shop. How could that be? But after he made a trip to find someone else in the center, he returned and said, "My manager knows of one antiques shop that may go by this name. It is near an old coffeehouse on a street called Porta Schei. Not far from here."

That was something, I supposed. Feeling hopeful, we exited the welcome center and followed the man's directions to a destination a few blocks away in the old part of town, where narrow streets connected to a bustling, open *piața*, Council Square. There, tourists were snapping photographs of horse-pulled carts and a stately European fountain. We headed past them toward a grand, cross-topped cathedral that towered over one corner of the town square: the Black Church, the largest Gothic cathedral between Istanbul and Vienna. I remembered my mother telling me about it. It garnered its name after a seventeenth-century siege, when an enormous fire blackened its walls.

I craned my neck and stared up at the church in awe. Would have been better if my mother were here to share the moment. I slipped fingers inside my coat and curled them around my Byzantine coin necklace. *I made it here*, I told her inside my head, and it gave me a little peace in a day filled with tumult.

Beyond the imposing church, we found a narrow, one-way *stradă* where the crowds dwindled. Renaissance-style corniced buildings bordered the street for several blocks, their facades crumbling and cracking. In one of these, near a sad, dark coffeehouse, Huck spied an old shopfront. Hanging in a lone window was a glazed blue palm that I recognized immediately: a *hamsa* talisman, to ward away evil. The sign above the window plainly said:

ZISSU BROTHERS

RARE JEWELRY AND ANTIQUES

"Appears to be the place," I said as I peered through the window. "Looks empty. Maybe they're about to close." A little tremor skittered down the back of my neck, and I wasn't sure if it was excitement or apprehension.

Had Father come here? Inside, I could find everything I wanted, or it could be another dead end.

Steel spine, chin up.

Huck sniffled and rubbed his nose, looking a bit apprehensive himself. "Don't get your expectations too high," he told me. "Fox isn't going to miraculously be inside here."

"No worries there," I said, pushing open the shop's wooden door. "I've never once associated Richard Damn Fox with a miracle."

A bell above the door tinkled as we entered the small shop. Old floorboards creaked and groaned under our feet. Huck was right, of course: Father wasn't here. No one was. Were the owners even here? We made our way past walls lined with old oil paintings in elaborate frames. Low shelves and display cases held anything and everything—antique clocks, ivory brushes, candlesticks. Beautiful old globes. Even a golden harp in the corner. But as I took in the potpourri of antiques, I realized something: I couldn't "hear" anything. No heartbeats. No weird buzzing. No nausea. Nothing I'd felt in the Sighișoara museum around the bone band in the glass case. Did that mean that the third bone band wasn't here?

I couldn't decide if that was a good or a bad thing.

Honestly, after everything that had happened over the last

twenty-four hours, I wasn't entirely convinced I hadn't imagined some of it.

In my *Batterman's Field Guide*, Dr. Lydia Batterman wrote an entire foreword titled "Believing in the Unbelievable." She said that sometimes, when things are too hard to comprehend, the mind makes excuses for them. Tries to match them up with logical reasons even when they don't quite fit—that wasn't a ghost; it was the wind rustling the curtain. A trick of light. The house settling.

And at that moment my father's skeptical gene reared its head, and I tried to tell myself that I hadn't "heard" the bone band. I was only exhausted. It was the cold weather clogging up my ears. I'd eaten bad food. For that matter, maybe Dr. Mitu had been wrong about his research. My mother would have known she was related to Vlad Dracula.

Right?

Dust motes danced in a sloping column of afternoon light that slanted through the front window, casting the *hamsa* talisman onto the floor. My eyes flicked first to the shadow and then to the back wall of the shop toward a wooden counter. Standing behind it were two rail-thin elderly white-haired gentlemen wearing identical red bow ties. Identical heavy, broomlike mustaches covering their upper lips. Identical bushy brows and curious eyes twinkling behind round, tortoiseshell eyeglass frames.

Twins. Most definitely twins. The only way to tell them apart was that one wore a suit jacket and the other stood in his suspenders and white shirtsleeves, cuffs rolled up to his elbows as he held an old quill over a ledger.

"Good afternoon, gentlemen," I said in Romanian.

"Good afternoon," the man on the right said.

"Lovely day," his twin with the quill said.

"Do you speak English, perhaps?"

"But of course," the first man said, switching languages with ease. "You are American, yes?"

"American," I confirmed.

Huck removed his flat cap. "We're looking for Mr. Zissu?"

"You found him," they answered in chorus, both smiling.

"I'm Mihai," the man on the right said with a crisp cant of his head, "and this is my brother, Petar."

Petar gestured with the feather on his quill. "May we help you find something?"

"I certainly hope so," I said. "Miss Theodora Fox and Mr. Huxley Gallagher. We're looking for my father, Mr. Richard Fox. I'm hoping he may have come here to see you?"

Mihai said, "We know of him, *domnişoară*."

"American treasure hunter," Petar said. "It's possible our paths have crossed, though not directly. We travel frequently. Sometimes we are interested in the same objects. Sometimes we hear gossip about places he's been or things he's found. . . ."

The twins gave each other a look that I couldn't quite interpret.

"You haven't seen him today?" I asked. "Or yesterday?"

They blinked in unison. "No," Mihai said. "He has never set foot in our shop."

But the business card . . . and the cipher. He said plain as day in the journal that he needed to retrace his steps from this summer's trip to Romania. Had he intended to come here but never made it? Had I missed something?

My gut twisted as a heavy hopelessness settled over me. I was *so sure* he'd come here. Where else could he have gone? Had he given up on the ring and gone to Paris? Back to New York? Was he dead in a ditch? WAS HE? I shared a worried look with Huck.

"Do not be sad," Mihai said, giving me a kind smile. "We may still be able to help you. We've heard rumors about what Mr. Fox is seeking."

His brother leaned against the edge of the counter. "He isn't discreet. And neither is his employer."

I stilled. *Steady*, I told myself.

"Do not look so surprised," Petar said. "We know of Mr. Rothwild."

"You . . . do?"

"Though he has never set foot in our shops, either," he added, gesturing with his quill toward the walls.

"Can't enter what you can't find," Mihai said, and the brothers snickered together with dark delight.

I sneaked a glance at Huck's leery face. Oh, he was *definitely* regretting coming here. Should we be backing out of this shop? My gut was useless. I had no instincts about these strange brothers. I felt as if everything I'd learned in Father's journal was just torn into a thousand pieces and thrown into the air.

Petar smoothed out his thick mustache with two fingers, taming both his bushy hair and his smile. "But you found us, didn't you? Which was no surprise. We had a hunch you would."

"You . . . did?" I said, feeling as if the walls were closing in. Like I was the victim of some massive inside joke and the world was laughing at me.

"In a way," Mihai said, excitement dancing behind his eyes, "we've been waiting for *you* to find *us*."

A DISTRUSTFUL NOISE BURRED FROM HUCK'S THROAT. His hand gripped my elbow and tugged urgently. He wanted to leave, but I couldn't just walk out. Not now.

"You've been . . . waiting for me?" I finally managed to say. "I'm sorry. I don't understand."

"Your father searches for the bone ring, yes?" Mihai said. "He mistakenly thought his employer's ring was a reproduction and that we were in possession of something that was more authentic."

Silence filled the small shop. I didn't know how I should respond, whether I could trust them or whether to run far, far away. But they already seemed to know this much, and I needed information. Since when was I scared of two skinny old men? *Steel spine.*

"Yes?" I said, and then more firmly, "Yes. That's right. But if he thought you had what he was looking for, why didn't he come here?"

"It would have been a waste of time for him to visit us," Mihai explained. "We would not have given him our ring anyway."

Huck made a choking sound. "You . . . have one of the bone bands?"

"Oh, yes," Petar said. "We acquired it twenty years ago in an estate sale near Sibiu."

"A few have coming looking for it," Mihai said with a small smile. "Recently, they have mostly been associates of your father's employer."

"Do not worry. They cannot enter our shop. We're protected." Petar gestured behind me to the window, and for the first time I realized there was more than the *hamsa* talisman there: scrawled Hebrew and esoteric symbols of the kabbalah were painted around the window's glass.

Spells. Magical wards.

This was no antiques shop. And the twins were not simple merchants.

I had the sinking feeling that they were like Lovena. Witches. Wonderworkers. Magicians . . . or at the very least, knowledgeable about such things. My head swam with disjointed thoughts; goose bumps raced over my arms.

"Maybe that's why Mr. Rothwild hired your father," Petar said. "He and his people wrongly thought they could trick their way in here."

Mihai chuckled. "They cannot."

"His people . . . Rothwild's associates, you mean?" Huck asked.

"*Societas Draconistarum*," Mihai said, spreading his arms.

"The Order of the Dragon," I murmured.

"Indeed." Petar thrust the inky tip of his quill into a brass stand on the counter as he elaborated. "Order of the Dragon, founded in 1408 by the Holy Roman Emperor Sigismund as a secret society. Kings, popes, politicians, noblemen graced its membership. It is said that the order dissolved and disappeared from history because its highest-ranking members were secret occultists."

Mihai added, "It was Sigi's wife, Barbara of Cilli, who was said to be the original occultist. She was accused of alchemy, witchcraft, and immoral behavior by the courts. They called her the Black Queen, and she would have likely been burned at the stake had she not been taken by the plague. Some say her ghost still haunts the Yugoslavian city of Zagreb."

His twin leaned over his ledger. "Some also say she had a macabre ring made to aid the order in their fight against the Ottoman Empire. They needed a secret weapon to keep the Turks from advancing across the continent. The Turks were rich and powerful, and very smart. The Holy Roman Empire needed something big to push their borders back."

"And what is bigger than a dragon?" Mihai said, eyes shining with excitement. "But they would settle for the might of a dragon tethered inside a human body."

Hot and cold chills raced over my body. My mind flicked back to the traders' camp and Valentin's stories of the Dacian great white wolf: a man's soul inhabiting the body of a legendary beast.

But this was inverted. A mythical beast inside a human body.

Petar held up one finger. "However, in order to achieve this miraculous weapon of war, the Black Queen fashioned a ring from the femur bones of Turkish sorcerers. And she forged this ring in the blood of a Wallachian ruler named Vlad Dracul, whom we would know as the father of Vlad the Impaler. But the older Vlad would not wear it. He was a bit afraid of the Black Queen and feared the ring was cursed."

"Rightly so," Huck mumbled, still gripping my elbow.

"So he instead secretly gave it to his son," Petar said.

Mihai smiled devilishly. "A bit like a king asking his right-hand man to taste his soup in case it's poisoned. He wasn't a very good father."

"Let me show you." Mihai retreated to a tall, overflowing bookcase behind the counter. When he returned, it was with a clothbound book that I knew all too well.

"*Batterman's*," I said, heart racing wildly.

"You know it?" Mihai asked, cracking it open.

"I have a copy in my bag."

He looked pleased. "It is an excellent reference. We have contributed many photographs to the last edition. Dr. Lydia Batterman is a personal acquaintance."

Had I been wary and mildly frightened by these two odd brothers? No more. I was in their thrall now and shook away Huck's hand from my elbow to inspect their copy of my favorite field guide.

Dozens of pages in the book were marked with tiny pieces of blue paper. Mihai bent low, grunting, until he found the right marker and flipped to a page. "Here," he said, turning it around to give Huck and me a better view. He pointed at the middle of the page. "Perhaps you have seen this already."

Pfft. Perhaps it was the wrong time to brag that I'd committed entire sections of the book to memory. I glanced to the open page, expecting to see the familiar woodcut of Prince Dracula enjoying a quiet lunch in front of his impaled corpses. But Petar had the field guide open to a different section in the book, two hundred years after Vlad. His finger tapped above an engraving of an infamous French woman: Catherine Monvoisin.

"More widely known simply as La Voisin," Mihai said. "She was a fortune-teller, a sorceress, and a poisoner for hire who confessed to the ritual murder of a thousand infants in black masses. That was before she tried to poison Louis XIV and was burned at the stake for her crimes in 1680. But look closely at her carved ivory ring in this rare engraving."

He offered me a magnifying glass. I held it above the engraving and saw clearly:

Three bands woven together to form one ring.

I inhaled sharply, unable to keep my hand from shaking with exhilaration.

Puzzle ring! *I was right. I was right. I was right. . . .*

Trying to stay calm, I read the notation next to the engraving, which said that though witnesses in Louis XIV's court claimed the ring once belonged to the devil, modern archivists have suggested this was a mistranslation and that they meant "dragon," because a scaled creature graced the tops of the joined bands.

How about that? It was here, in *Batterman's*, all along.

The giddy joy of discovery zipped through me. I felt lightheaded.

When I looked up from the page, the twins were both smiling at me. Petar said, "I can see from your face that you were already aware your father's quest was misinformed. He should have been looking for three rings, not one."

I elbowed Huck discreetly, but he wasn't feeling the same triumphant buzz I was enjoying. All of this was too much for him. Any second he'd be making the sign of the cross.

"I never thought to look for the ring in other entries," I told the twins, gesturing toward the book. "I know my father didn't either. He . . . doesn't appreciate *Batterman's* as I do."

Petar nodded, sympathetic. "He is a skeptic. If he'd consulted us at the start of his quest, we would have told him no good could come of looking for Vlad's war ring, because Mr. Rothwild uses people until he doesn't need them any longer. They are disposable to him. And Mr. Fox will be disposable when Mr. Rothwild gets what he wants."

Disposable? That was the last thing I wanted to hear. A fresh shot of panic pinged down my spine . . . and then something struck me.

"But Rothwild doesn't have what he wants yet," I said. "Not if you still own one band of the ring."

"We're only caretakers," Petar insisted. "It's not ours to own."

"But you have it?" I pressed.

"We should be certain," his brother whispered, and the two men exchanged a look and nod before Petar turned toward me.

"May I see your hand?" he asked, urging me to come closer. Looking at me much the same way as Lovena had.

"Do you want to listen to my blood?" I asked.

His smile was slow and broad. "If you wouldn't mind."

"Careful," Huck whispered low under his breath.

He wasn't wrong to be cautious, of course, but I was curious. And if these men were our enemies, I couldn't see why they'd share all of this information with us so willingly. Just because they were . . . well, a little odd didn't say anything about their moral character. At least, that's what my gut was telling me.

I warily extended my arm over the counter toward Petar, who gingerly took hold of my hand with cool, dry fingers and inspected my palm over the tops of his tortoiseshell eyeglasses. He flipped my hand over and ran a slow finger down my veins.

The shop fell into silence . . . just for a moment. Then he released me and nodded firmly at his brother. "Yes."

"Yes?" Mihai said.

Both of them were pleased.

Did they know? Could Petar hear whatever Lovena had detected in my veins? *Old blood . . .*

And was it the same thing Dr. Mitu had discovered when researching my mother's bloodline?

"We told you Mr. Fox hadn't been to our shop," Mihai said, "but it may be of interest to you that we have heard his Hungarian employer arrived in town yesterday."

"Mr. Rothwild is here?" Huck said, a distrustful look on his face.

"He was seen last night," Mihai confirmed. "It's not the first time. He comes here every now and then, a dragon, returning to his lair."

"I thought his, uh, lair was in Hungary—in Budapest?" Huck said.

That was where Father first had a meeting with Rothwild, in his home in Hungary, across the northwestern border of Romania, past Cluj and the horrible Hoia Forest . . . at least a day's ride from here by train.

"Budapest is his home, yes," Mihai said. "But he has . . . a lair, of sorts—here, inside the mountain."

Huck and I both stared at the old men.

"Perhaps it's best to show them," Petar murmured to his brother.

Huck shot me an anxious glance as Mihai tottered back to his overflowing bookshelves and ran his finger across the spines of several oversize books, making a happy noise when he found what he sought: an old atlas, bound in vellum. With no small amount of effort, he hauled the large tome to the counter in arms that were as thin as spring branches.

"Let's see," he mumbled to himself, turning thick parchment pages that made crinkling noises. "Ah, here we are. Brașov, 1712. There are many castles in Romania, and several are concentrated in this region. This is the thirteenth-century citadel of Rasnov," he said, holding a large magnifying glass over a drawing of a fortress on the old map. He then moved it to a blank spot on the map. "A little farther away on the other side of the mountains is the future site of Peleş, the fairy-tale castle that would later be built for King Carol. And, of course, there is the famous Castle Bran . . . here."

"Said to have been captured briefly by Vlad Țepeș," Petar remarked.

"Yes," Huck said. "We read that on the information sign at the railway station."

"Three castles," Mihai said, tapping his finger on each location again. "But there is also a fourth castle—Barlog."

His magnifying glass moved to a mountain in the middle of the city . . . and a drawing of a black dragon.

"What is that?" I asked, bending over the atlas.

"The mountain standing here in the heart of our town is called Tâmpa," Petar said. "Heavily wooded. Beautiful views of Brașov. After ascending to the summit on a secret path, it is said you walk through the woods until you come to Castle Barlog, Lair of the Dragon."

"Rothwild owns a castle on a mountain in the middle of Brașov?" I said.

"He inherited it from his grandfather, a Hungarian nobleman who owned several pieces of property in the Southern Carpathians."

"You mean we can walk right into it like tourists?" Huck asked.

Mihai shook his head. "No. It is private property. And no one can just walk into it. The path up the mountain is hidden. The castle is hidden. This was the last public map printed with its location, more than two hundred years ago. And you can see, it wasn't even marked clearly on a map at that time."

"The town has forgotten it was even there," Petar said.

We all stared in silence at the map until Huck cleared his throat. "Do you think Fox, I mean . . . Mr. Fox. Do you think there's a chance he knew about this castle?"

"Anything's possible," Mihai said. "But I would hope not."

"Most who journey inside Castle Barlog don't come out," Petar warned. "And Mr. Fox doesn't have what Mr. Rothwild wants, so he is not useful to the Hungarian. Mr. Fox has nothing to bargain with."

"*If* Mr. Fox is even here," Mihai added. "We haven't heard anything."

And by that I wasn't entirely sure if they meant "heard" as in *gossip*, or "heard" as in *let me listen to your blood.* But it didn't matter, because Father *had* to be here in Brașov! I believed that more than ever now. He knew this shop existed: the business card was in the journal, and the twins were on his list. Maybe he was stuck somewhere. A broken-down car or train. Waiting for money to be wired. But—

But. If he *had* come to Brașov, and Rothwild was here . . . Would he go meet with the man? I thought about Jean-Bernard. And the widow's gory murder scene in Bucharest. And Lovena's sister jumping from the clock tower.

What would Rothwild do to my father?

My pulse went erratic, speeding up until I could feel it swishing inside my temples. How could I find Father before it was too late? Was Rothwild our only clue to his whereabouts? And what were we supposed to do, demand a meeting with a mad occultist and politely ask him where Father was? Pray that the man hadn't already poisoned, bewitched, or "disposed of" him? That seemed like a terrible idea. Like walking into an angry lion's den without a weapon.

Weapon. Huh.

Several puzzle pieces slotted together at once inside my head and formed into an idea.

Nineteen across, "negotiator's grease." L-E-V-E-R-A-G-E.

"My father doesn't have a bargaining chip," I said. "But *you* do. May I see it?"

The twins gave each other a questioning look. Petar nodded. Mihai then took out a cluster of keys and opened a display case next to the counter. The glass was old and dirty, the contents of the display case hard to see until I caught a glimpse—small boxes. Cigarette cases, perhaps, or miniature music boxes. Yet none of them were very pretty or ornamental. They all were made from the same dark metal.

He reached inside the bottom of the case and pulled out one of them, about the size and shape of a ring box. And now that it was out of the case, I could see the rust covering it.

An iron box.

Huck drew in a sharp breath.

When I glanced at him, he swallowed hard and said to me in a low voice, "The box we dug up in the cave in Tokat . . . It looked just like that."

Something between fear and excitement burgeoned inside my chest as I scrutinized symbols inscribed on the rusted metal box—symbols I couldn't identify. Where were these from? They weren't Egyptian hieroglyphs. Sumerian cuneiform? My mother would know. She loved ancient writing systems.

"Iron is a good insulator against magic," Mihai said as he used a fingernail to open a tiny latch on the box. Then, without ceremony, he cracked open the lid. And though I *should* have been, I was not prepared for what would happen when he did.

The room swam in my vision.

All the noise felt as if it were sucked out of the air, and in its place was a familiar drumming cadence.

Thump-thump. Thump-thump. Thump-thump . . .

I covered my ears on instinct, but of course it didn't help. I was going to be sick. I teetered on my feet, dizzy and unsteady, feeling as if the floor were swirling below me.

Huck's mouth moved, but I couldn't hear him. This was *so* much worse than the museum in Sighișoara—oh God! My head was going to crack open. Pain lashed around my black eye. I was going to faint. Or be sick. I was going . . . I was going to—

Mihai slammed the iron box shut. With a whooshing sound, the thumping stopped, and the shop rocked back into place. My balance returned. Or maybe it was Huck's hands gripping my shoulders.

"Theo!"

I nodded . . . and nodded. Swallowed hard. Licked dry lips. And then I put a hand on Huck's arm. "I'm okay."

"Are you sure?" Huck said.

"I'm okay," I repeated, and then whispered, "It was just like before."

"She hears," one of the twins was saying across the counter.

"She hears," the other confirmed.

When I looked their way, Mihai slid the iron box toward me. "House of Basarab. House of Drăculești. Daughter of Transylvania and Wallachia. Scion of the Dragon."

A dark thrill fluttered through me.

"Go on, child," Petar murmured. "Take it. The bone band is yours."

Mine. *Mine?* It felt like a mistake . . . and a temptation. Surreal.

"It never belonged to us," Petar said. "We were merely stewards.

Perhaps it will help your father. Perhaps it will not. Please make wise choices. It is a heavy burden."

Hesitant, I started to reach for it, but Huck held up a hand to block me.

"Hold on, now," he said. "Is this the only way to find Fox? This cursed thing? Banshee, think about this for a moment, yeah? You've always told me that you believed in your heart it was a cursed object that killed your poor mother. Are you so quick to follow in her footsteps? If the legends are all true, then this thing causes nothing but death and destruction—it's evil. It should be destroyed."

"You may try," Mihai said. "Others have. No one has been successful."

Petar nodded. "Indestructible. Much like the person who wears it. They say that lawmen had to cut off Elizabeth Báthory's finger to remove it. Once all three pieces of the ring are joined together, it becomes a part of the person wearing it. You can't remove it by force. I'm sure you know Vlad Dracula's fate. The only way to stop him was"—he made a slicing gesture across his throat—"beheading."

A gruesome way to authenticate the ring . . .

Was that what my father had meant in his journal?

"Besides," Mihai said, "you don't want to destroy the bone band. It could be your bargaining chip, if you needed one. A very dangerous bargaining chip."

Huck was probably right. But my father was out there somewhere, and the longer it took to find him . . . I couldn't just walk away from this. Not now. Now after everything I'd learned.

I put a hand on Huck's arm and pleaded with my eyes. *Trust me.*

Deep lines crossed his brow. He shook his head, unhappy, but he moved out of my way.

Hesitant, I reached out and touched the iron ring box. The

metal felt . . . warm. But it was blessedly quiet. Subdued by the strange box with its stranger markings. Like a sheath for a sharp blade.

"Tell me how to get into the castle," I said to the brothers in a low voice.

"It's rumored that Castle Barlog can only be accessed after nightfall," Mihai said. "And that there's one way inside through a single, hidden entrance, but it's locked during the day and known only to members of their order."

"Any clue as to where?"

Mihai shook his head, apologetic, and said, "I know the old road was blockaded years ago, but that is all."

"We can ask around, but it is a delicate task," Petar said. "Maybe you can stop by tomorrow and we'll know more."

For all I knew, my father could be dead by tomorrow.

I tried to press them for more information. The conversation went around in circles before ending in the same place. Eventually, they politely informed us that it was time to close the shop and encouraged me to take the iron ring box.

And that was it. Business concluded. The cursed bone band is yours. Good luck with your missing father. Don't let the door hit you on the way out.

Only, now I had more questions than I did before we stepped inside the curiosity shop. About my father's precise whereabouts and his safety. About Rothwild and his own ancestral connection to Vlad. Did he have the other two bone bands or did Sarkany also possess one? Were they rivals, or were they working together? How was I going to find an entrance to this hidden castle?

And my God! Was I really, *truly* a descendant of Vlad Dracula? And did that gift me with some kind of arcane claim to the bone ring's cursed power, or was it just a blip on a dusty family tree—an exotic piece of party conversation?

I juggled these questions around in my head like flaming torches; drop one, and the world would catch fire and burn down everything I loved.

"Remember one thing," Mihai warned in parting. "Do not take the ring out of the box. Not only is that box a good insulator, but it keeps the ring hidden. Once out? It's only a matter of time before someone with occult knowledge can find it. If Rothwild obtains all three bands of the bone ring, he will not hesitate to wear it. And once he wears it, he will be transformed, no longer himself."

He'd be the Dragon.

God help us all.

I COULD FEEL HUCK'S ANGER BREWING THE MINUTE THE shop door closed behind us. It was dark now; twilight had fallen while we were inside. He hurried me down the deserted street, past storefronts that had shuttered for the night, and when we were a safe distance away from the antiques shop, his eyes went straight to my satchel, where I'd stashed the iron box.

"What the hell are you thinking?"

"Excuse me?"

"You know what I'm talking about," he said, gesturing flippantly. "Accepting that bloody thing was a mistake."

"Why? You heard them. The box keeps the band hidden."

"You trust that? You trust *them*? My skin was crawling the entire time we were in that bedeviled shop!"

"That was probably just the magic wards," I assured him. "Did you see the inside of the window? It's one thing to read about spell-work like that in books, but to see it in action was—"

"Downright frightening? Made you want to piss your pants and run in the other direction?"

"Impressive?" I said, flashing him a toothy, sheepish smile.

"It's not funny."

"I didn't say it was. Why are you being an ass?"

"Because I'm scared out of my mind, banshee," he said as a cold wind whipped a wayward lock of curly hair across his creased brow. "I'm bloody terrified of that ring and the people who want it."

"You think I'm not?"

"We don't even know if Fox is here. What if he left the country? What if he went back to the hotel in Bucharest and is tearing his hair out, looking for us?"

"Then he should have showed up days ago, when he said he was going to! Or he never should've left you in Tokat in the first place! I'm not happy about any of this, Huck."

"Aren't you? Earlier today you were as scared as I was when the professor's assistant told you all that about your ancestry, but now it seems to have settled in your mind. Because I saw the way your eyes lit up when those brothers were shoving the ring box toward you, all *Daughter of Dracula* this and *Transylvanian Princess* that . . . You looked like someone just told you that you're the son of God!"

I frowned at him. "Did not!"

"You did," he said, nodding his head rapidly. "That ring is cursed, and it's got its claws in you. We shouldn't have accepted it. No good will come of it."

"What about Father, huh? The entire reason we've raced all over Eastern Europe for the last week?"

"And we're going to do what now, exactly? Hike miles across a mountain in the dark until a magical castle that's not on any map appears in the fog? Maybe we'll run into another wolf pack while we're at it? That is, if this Rothwild doesn't catch us first. Or Sarkany. Or the rest of these evil cultists. Hey! Maybe we'll freeze to death in the snow this time and the ghost of that trapper will hunt us down and carve *X*'s into our foreheads."

"You're being hysterical."

"Yes! I damn well am! Taking that ring was a stupid idea! How are we supposed to even bargain with it if we don't know where to go?"

"If you have another idea, please do share it. And be sure to shout it out on a public street, while you're at it. I love it when the entire world knows our business!"

A retort was on his tongue until he glanced over his shoulder at a lone elderly couple who clung to each other and stared at us with curious faces as they passed.

The fire in his eyes sputtered and went out.

He dropped his shoulders and made a frustrated whimpering noise. "I have no ideas, banshee. Zero. I'm just scared, is all. This is all so impossible."

"That's not true!"

"Is it not? Feels a little like it is. I can't help but think that we should have never left Bucharest."

"Oh, is that so?" I said, embittered. "After all this, you still think we should've just found a way to get to a port and caught an ocean liner back to the States? And maybe in a few weeks, Father would find his own way home. Or maybe we'd get a cable from the European police letting us know that they found his body somewhere in the Carpathians. Is that it?"

"You know it's not. It's just . . . Christ, Theo. I feel like we've failed, and I'm going to lose you all over again, and maybe lose Fox, too. And I just . . . don't know what to do."

The thing about fighting with someone you care about is that it's no fun when they don't fight back.

"I don't know what to do, either," I said. "But we've got to try something."

"Yeah, I know." He flipped up the wide collar of his peacoat and held it tight around his neck while a streetlamp flickered to life above us.

"Maybe before we decide anything, we should find someplace warm that has food, because I'm cold and starving, and I can't think straight."

"Now, that's an idea I can get behind," he said from behind his collar, bouncing on his heels to stay warm. "Think I saw a place on our way here to Creepy Brother Shopkeeper Lane."

I snorted a soft laugh. "All right. Food truce?"

"Food truce," he agreed with a soft smile. "C'mon, before we turn into ice sculptures."

We hurried down the lonely street and cut through an alley until we were back in the town square. It wasn't busy here exactly, but it wasn't deserted either. Looked to be a couple of restaurants open, but Huck pointed to a golden-windowed tavern on a corner.

Ducking beneath a painted wood sign—a raven with a snake in its claw—that jutted over the tavern's entrance, we opened a heavy timbered door and headed inside to blessed warmth.

The sharp scents of ale and garlic floated on a haze of cigarette smoke. The tavern looked as if it were built in the 1500s and apart from electricity and running water, nothing much had been changed. Under a low ceiling, wooden tables were packed with tourists and more than a few burly local men. Several of them looked up at us with dark, suspicious eyes that followed us to the bar. The barkeep, busy pouring ale into pint glasses, informed me when I inquired that there were empty tables upstairs in a loft that overlooked the main floor and to sit where we pleased. So we hiked up old wooden stairs that creaked and groaned with age, and after surveying the loft—only two other customers—we claimed a small corner table that sat between a roaring fireplace and a window with a view of the moonlit town square.

Within minutes a curvy girl with plaited brown hair greeted us. No older than me and wearing a traditional dress and apron, she chatted affably about the snow and my black eye and where were we from? Then she brought us water, chewy bread, and an intoxicatingly spiced paprika chicken stew with dumplings that tasted as good as it looked.

The fire warmed my back as we ate, and I gazed through the paned window at silhouettes of snow-covered chimneys and sharp gables that lined Brașov's historic rooftops. It was an idyllic view, even at night. I couldn't help but think of my mother and wondered if she'd ever eaten dinner here or at any of the charming restaurants below, with their terraces draped in white lights.

I wondered what she'd do if she were in my shoes right now.

She'd figure out a way to find Father. I knew that much. Elena Vaduva was not afraid of anything. Maybe because she was descended from the notorious warlord who once wore the band in the box by my feet? Who might have supped in this very tavern and dipped his bread in the blood of his enemies? The red of the paprikash chicken's oil-slicked broth pooled at the bottom of my bowl, and I lost my appetite for the last bite.

"I'm going to find the restroom," I told Huck, who reached under the table and squeezed my fingers like he used to do before our long separation. Any aggravation I'd been nursing since his outburst outside the Zissu brothers' shop vanished.

"When you come back, we'll make a plan," he told me, eyes shining in the firelight. "It's not the end of the world. I was wrong. Happens on occasion."

"What's the proverb for that? Never point out the mistakes of others with a dirty finger?"

"Just for the record, you can put your dirty fingers on me any ol' day, banshee."

I laughed softly. And as I stood up, I leaned over the table and stole a quick kiss while the other patrons weren't looking. His lips were warm and tasted of the dusky, red spice in our dinner. "I'll take that under consideration," I told him with a smile, and then I grabbed my satchel and trotted downstairs.

The tavern's public restroom was near the bar, and after waiting for a large man with beer-dazed eyes to emerge, I locked myself inside, took care of business, and then removed the iron ring box from my satchel. The metal was still warm, which gave me pause and quickly quashed any stupid ideas I may have entertained about opening it. Best to follow the brothers' advice and leave it be. I did, however, inspect the etched symbols on the outside of the box. They were unfamiliar and strange, worn by time—not easy to see in the bathroom's dim light over a dirty sink. If only I hadn't pawned my beloved Leica camera, I could snap photographs.

Ah well. I repacked the box safely into my satchel alongside my father's journal, splashed water on my face, and headed back up the tavern staircase, determined to figure out what to do about this mysterious Barlog Castle and Rothwild and finding Father.

But as I crested the creaking wooden stairs, I had a moment of panic. Our table was empty. No Huck. Yet his rucksack still sat behind a pulled-out chair.

I glanced around the loft. A lone elderly man was still drinking.

Had he gone downstairs to the restroom? Wouldn't I have seen him? I raced back down and surveyed the main floor. No tall Irish boy. No flat cap. No Huck.

When I was turning to jog back upstairs, our friendly waitress strode toward me with a pint of beer. "Hello, miss? Are you looking for your friend?"

"Yes!" I said, breathless, trying not to sound as panicked as I felt.

"He just left with two priests."

I stared at her, unable to make my voice work for a moment. "Two . . . priests?"

"They looked like the ones from the cathedral?" She gestured down her body. "Long black vestments. Your friend seemed to be quarreling with them. I do not interfere with bar fights. I'm sorry."

This was no bar fight! "Where did they take him? When? Which way did they go?"

She only shook her head at me. "It just happened. They just left a few minutes ago . . . out the back door," she said, gesturing across the crowded room.

Head reeling, I raced up the stairs, snatched up Huck's rucksack, and sailed back down, bumping into the waitress while I took the stairs two at a time.

"I hope everything is okay," she called out to my back.

No. No, it was not okay at all.

Sarkany's goons had taken Huck.

THE TAVERN OWNER OFFERED TO FETCH THE POLICE when I asked him if he'd seen the men taking Huck. He hadn't. And I declined his offer. My father would say not to get them involved, and really, what could they do? In the time it would take to summon someone, I could be at the twins' shop. Because that was exactly where I was going.

They knew magic. They could help. They *had* to. Or I would burn down this entire town to find Huck.

Racing out of the tavern's back door, I found nothing but garbage cans and slush. No sign of any people whatsoever. I pulled my beret down, shivering as I hurried around to the front of the building, past wrought iron streetlamps haloed in fog and into the town square. No sign of them here, either.

The Zissu brothers' shop wasn't far, and I remembered the way, past the glowering Black Church. I inhaled brisk night air, head bright and empty, chest constricted as I scanned the town square, looking for anyone who remotely resembled robed cultists or Huck.

I tried asking a lone elderly man if he'd seen any "priests" passing by, but he only turned in the opposite direction, unwilling to even acknowledge me. A pair of lovers embraced by the fountain as I passed, which only made me angry. That might have been Huck and me if he hadn't gone and gotten himself kidnapped, or whatever he'd gone and gotten himself.

Stupid boy. *My* boy. My responsibility to find him.

Clouds of white breath trailed behind me as I headed around the Black Church and made my way down the smaller street to the twins' shop. It struck me that if Sarkany's robed goons had taken Huck, then Sarkany might be nearby. Would he trail me? But why take Huck? Why not take me, too? Wasn't I the one with Vlad's blood in my veins? Wasn't it my father who'd taken this damned job? Why not me?

I juggled Huck's rucksack onto my shoulder and reached into my coat pocket. My fingers grasped Lovena's wooden talisman.

To keep me safe, she said.

Me. Not Huck.

I had it in my possession. I left him upstairs in the tavern. Lovena told me to sleep with it under my pillow. To keep it close.

She failed to tell me to keep Huck close as well.

No one seemed to be following me—no Sarkany or the wolf. Nobody at all. But I kept my eyes on the shadows just in case, and I ran as fast I could, down the dark *stradă*, legs and arms aching, tears stinging the corners of my eyes. I ran until I spied the old coffeehouse, and there! Warm light behind the window of the antiques shop.

I prayed they were still inside.

In a billow of white breath, I came to clumsy stop in front of the shop. The door was locked, and a hanging sign was turned to say *Închis*—Closed—so I pounded on the door. I spied a silhouette passing by the window, and then the door swung open, and I found myself staring at an unexpected sight.

"Hello, little empress," a rough female voice said around a puff of cigarillo smoke that rose up in tendrils around a red head kerchief.

"Lovena?"

"Yes, my girl. Don't look so surprised. What is this? Did you get into a fistfight?" Quick fingers lifted my chin to inspect my black eye in the light spilling out from the shop.

"What are you doing here?" I asked, stunned. "How . . . ?"

"How did I get here?" Her eyes crinkled as a dark smile lifted her lips. "I am a crow witch, little empress. I flew here alongside my winged familiars."

I blinked at her, mouth open, until she laughed huskily. "I was an hour from here, at a friend's house in Rupea. You think just because I live in the woods, I don't have an automobile? I am not a heathen."

"But . . ."

She made a dismissive gesture. "The brothers sent me a message that you were here, and I just arrived. We've been communicating since you visited me. I was in Sighișoara earlier today. My nephew said you spoke to him before my sister's incident."

"The baroness," I murmured. "I'm so sorry, Lovena. Is she—"

"Alive? Yes."

"She didn't jump," I said.

"I know. She was compelled by dark magic. I told her to keep the ring in the box. It was the one rule in the house when our mother was still alive. There was nothing more I could do in Sighișoara but sit around the hospital and squabble with family, so I left to give them space." She shrugged and then added, "I am also looking for my dog. My crows tell me she is close."

"I saw her in the Hoia Forest with two wolves," I said. "Near Cluj."

"With wolves? That is good," she murmured. "If she's gone wild, there's a chance she has broken that man's magical hold. I will find her again. Funny that I've anguished more over Lupu than my own blood."

"This is all our fault. If my father hadn't taken the job with Rothwild, then none of this would have happened. Your sister . . . and now Huck. They've taken Huck!"

"Hush, girl." Smooth hands gripped my face. Smoke curled around my hair. "My sister's fate is her own making. Now, what is this about the boy?"

I started to explain about the tavern, but behind us in the distance, a shout interrupted me. Lovena dropped her cigarillo on the street and squinted over my shoulder, peering down the deserted cobbled street. I swung around and saw it too.

A dark figure ambling toward us. Stumbling. Shuffling.

Huck!

I knew his tall frame as I knew my own hands. But something was horribly wrong. I dropped our luggage and raced toward him as he staggered into the light of the adjoining rowhouse.

His peacoat hung open. Blood dripped from small cuts on his forehead, down the bridge of his nose and over his brow. His eyes were glazed. He moved as if drugged, barely standing.

"Huck!" I cried out.

Lovena yanked me back as I reached for him. "No! He's bewitched. Can you not hear it, child?"

I stared in horror at his dazed face, and then I *did* hear something. Faintly. A strange buzzing, like a cicada trapped in a spiderweb.

What had they done to him?

Lovena began murmuring something low and wicked sounding in a language I didn't understand, but Huck stopped a few feet away. He stared in my direction, but his eyes didn't see. Something was on his chest—a piece of paper. It was pinned to him with an old-fashioned hatpin, several inches long, like a note tacked to a bulletin board.

His eyes fluttered shut, and he collapsed on the cobblestone.

I wriggled out of Lovena's grip and ran to him, dropping to my knees by his side. "Huck? Huck!" He was out cold. Or dead. Was he breathing?

"Move," Lovena said. She opened his eyelid with her thumb and inspected his eye. Bloodshot. Pupils as big as the moon. "He's alive."

Relief gusted out of me as footsteps approached at my back. I glanced around to see the Zissu brothers hurrying toward us from their shop door. "He's been tampered with," Mihai said.

"Dark, quick magic," his brother agreed.

"He smells of *iarba fiarelor*—white swallowwort," Lovena said, and then explained, "It's an ancient plant known to the Dacians. Very toxic. It may have been mixed with something else, but I know it's used in possession spells. It opens the mind to the spellcaster."

"Sarkany," I said.

Lovena's face darkened. "The devil who stole Lupu."

"His goons took Huck from the tavern—the server saw men in black robes. She called them priests. It's the same men we told you about, the ones who followed us from Istanbul."

"This is what was used on my sister," Lovena murmured.

Petar bent over Huck's face and pointed. "That, on his forehead. A magical compass. He was sent out like a homing pigeon. Looks as if that's some kind of message he was bewitched to deliver."

My fingers trembled over the hatpin. The top was decorated with a small metal dragon. I yanked it out of him and whimpered when his body jerked in response. When I pulled the paper away from the pin, it left a smudge of Huck's blood.

It was a folded note. I opened it and read words scrawled in smeared ink:

I have your father at the castle.

Take the path under the Black Church. It will be unlocked.

Bring the ring. Come alone.

A chaotic storm of emotions thundered inside my chest.

"Sarkany has my father," I whispered in shock, showing the note to Lovena, who shared it with the twins. "This is Rothwild's castle? Barlog? Is this the secret entrance you were telling me about?"

"It sounds like it, my child," Petar said, reading the note.

I looked up the two of them. "Why is Sarkany in Rothwild's castle?"

"Perhaps they aren't rivals, after all," Lovena said, checking Huck's pulse. "We need to rouse him. The toxic plant in his system is similar to deadly nightshade. Very dangerous and unpredictable."

"Oh God!" I said. "Can you do something?"

She frowned at him as if he were an arithmetic problem to be solved. "Yes," she said, nodding. "I think so. I will try."

Mihai glanced down the dark lane. "We need to get him hidden inside the shop before someone from the order comes. Come, ladies. Let us help."

We hoisted Huck's limp body, and the brothers dragged him out of the street, shouldering his weight between them as they guided him inside. They laid him on the floor and locked the door, peering out the window warily.

"We are safe now," Petar assured me. "The wards hold. They can't see us."

"But what if they saw us walk in here? If they were hiding somewhere and watching from afar?"

The twins looked at me, brows furrowed. They didn't answer.

Lovena disappeared into the back of the shop. When she returned, she carried a small, handled case.

Kneeling by Huck, Lovena opened the case to reveal dozens of small bottles and vials. "I can brew something to counter the poison."

"Is this plant the same thing that was used on Jean-Bernard?" I asked.

"Same that was used on my sister, so it's likely. Is the Frenchman still alive?"

"I don't know," I said, miserable.

She held up a firm hand. "One thing at a time. I will care for the boy. Trust me, yes?"

I did, but that didn't stop my hands from trembling. He looked so weak and frail. I took a handkerchief from my coat pocket and wiped the blood off his forehead. Those bastards. Did the goons do this, or was it Sarkany himself?

"He has my father," I murmured. "What if he's done something like this to him? I have to go find him."

"If this man is working with Rothwild, then you may face two capable magicians, and that is not to mention their acolytes," Lovena said.

"It could be a trap," Petar agreed.

Mihai said, "We are certain Rothwild is in town. We do not

know this Sarkany that you speak of, but perhaps he is part of the dragon order. Very dangerous."

"You cannot go there alone," Lovena said. "Let me help Huck, and we can talk about what to do next."

"How long will it take?"

She shook her head. "Minutes. Hours. If I cannot rouse him fully, we'll need to take him to the hospital."

While my father was being held prisoner by the Order of the Dragon? "I can't wait that long. My father could be dead."

"They will not kill him until he is useless," Mihai said. "You have a bargaining chip; they have a bargaining chip. They will keep him alive until they have what they want."

"The castle is a dangerous place for a young girl, even one with old blood," Petar added, giving me a sympathetic look.

I didn't want their sympathy. I wanted their help. "Is there anything you can do? Magic of some kind? Lovena, you gave me the talisman—will it protect me in the castle?"

"I'm afraid not," she said, shaking a viscous substance in a small bottle. "Not when harm is looking you in the face."

I looked at the brothers. "Is there nothing you can do?"

"Everything we know about the castle, we have shared," Mihai said. "There is little written about it. No paintings, no books. That note is the most we've heard of it in years."

"Under the Black Church," his brother murmured. "That is amazing. Very smart of them. Very smart indeed."

"There is the old folklore . . . the children's tale about the temple inside. Remember the rare book we sold?"

Mihai nodded quickly. "Yes, that's right. Local stories spoke of a temple deep inside Barlog, one that was there long before the castle was built. Parents would tell their children who didn't behave, the dragon in the mountain would carry them away to its den inside the castle, to the ancient temple where it slept. But these were medieval stories. People also said the Pied Piper would lure children away with a magic flute."

They were right: that didn't help.

"We will try to research it," Petar assured me. "Maybe there is something we've missed. It's best to consider everything before rushing in."

They looked at me like a pair of frightened rabbits, adjusting their glasses and occasionally glancing toward the window, and it struck me that this is what they were: timid creatures, hiding behind magical wards, staying out of sight. But I didn't have that luxury. I had too much to lose. My entire broken family. My tribe. Everyone I loved.

Huck moved his head and moaned.

"Huck!" I said. "Can you hear me? Huck?"

Crouching over him, I tried to wake him, but he was in a daze. Like a man who'd overindulged in drink, in and out of consciousness.

At least he was alive.

I squeezed my eyes closed and tried to "hear" him. The cicada noise I'd heard outside was gone. Was that a good thing? Was the magic that had puppeted him now spent? Or maybe I was too panicked to hear anymore. I ran my finger over the white scar on his cheek, feeling as if I were standing alone on a beach, letting waves of jumbled emotions surge and retreat.

"Go sit down," Lovena encouraged. "I will nurse the boy, and the twins will figure out what to do about the castle. Be patient."

Anger rose inside me. They were treating me as if I were a feeble and stupid child, as if my father had all the time in the world. Were we all not staring at Huck's listless, poisoned body? What state was my father in right now? Had I spent the last week running around Romania with dead bodies piling up, merely to sit back now and hope for the best while absolving myself with a *not my problem* attitude?

No, I had not.

Frustrated and anxious, I paced around the dusty shop while the twins argued and Lovena bent over her work, mixing her remedy. I had to trust that she could heal Huck. It was out of my control now. But my father wasn't, and I couldn't afford a wait-and-see approach with him, which was more than likely wait-and-dead.

If my mother were here, what would she do? Wait by Huck's side, praying?

My mother never waited for anything. And she wouldn't hesitate to go after Father, no matter the risk.

And Huck, what would he do if our places were reversed? Would he stay with me or go after Father? I know I'd want him to go. So I had to assume he'd want the same.

Family first.

No one was paying attention to me. Keeping quiet, I dug around my satchel and put Father's journal inside my coat and the iron ring box in my pocket. The door was only a few steps away. I unlocked it and reached up to silence the shop bell. Then I gave one last look at Huck and slipped out of the shop.

JOURNAL OF RICHARD FOX

July 27, 1937

Cape Sounion—Athens, Greece

On day six of our lazy tour of the beautiful Apollo Coast, Jean-Bernard and I docked his yacht at a stunning spot that overlooks the Temple of Poseidon. I could stay here for months and never tire of the blue water. Alas, I was forced to take a break from sunbathing and drove back into the city to meet with my old friend Constantine. He'd been doing a little sleuthing for me as a favor, and what he'd found was surprising.

Seems our dear friend Mr. Rothwild has a past he's been trying to keep buried. In 1929, he was going by his father's surname: Bartok. With the help of some wealthy friends, he raised enough money to fund a political run for a seat in the Hungarian parliament.

The reason Rothwild's political career never took off was because during a 1930 fundraising trip to Romania, the twenty-year-old son of a wealthy Romanian businessman suffered a fatal head wound during an argument with Rothwild that turned violent. The incident occurred at the home of one Natasha Anca. The photograph I saw in the widow's house makes more sense now. There were rumors that she tried to cover for Rothwild.

Regardless, Rothwild was charged with involuntary

manslaughter and publicly shamed (someone painted "killer" on his car during the trial, and a photograph of the graffiti was in the newspapers for weeks) but got off on a technicality. With his political career in shambles, he retreated to Hungary and began using his mother's surname to rid himself of his past.

If I had to guess, I'd say that's about the time he decided to resurrect the Order of the Dragon.

I HURRIED AWAY FROM THE ZISSUS' SHOP, DETERMINED to disappear before they realized I'd left. And if I stopped for even one second to think about what I was doing, I was afraid I'd be tempted to tuck tail and run back to safety.

Scattered lights glowed in a few lonely windows down the long block, but no one was out walking on the street. That was good. Made it easier to spot any signs of Sarkany and his men. Nothing so far, but I half expected him to ambush me from every dark doorway. Probably should have armed myself—with what, I didn't have a clue. If Huck were with me, he'd probably misquote some proverb about pens and swords, but thinking about that only made my heart hurt.

After I turned a couple of corners, the town square came into view, and I spotted my destination lording over the other buildings.

Black Church, *Biserica Neagră*.

The path is unlocked under the Black Church.

Right. So how would I find that? Under a flashing sign that spelled out "Secret Entrance"? I squinted at the front of the cathedral. Beyond a low iron gate, a single candle sputtered near the Gothic cathedral's massive wooden doors. A signal in the dark? Or merely something left behind by the stewards of the church? I didn't know, but there was no one in sight.

My heart hammered against my ribs. I inhaled cold night air and approached the iron gate surrounding the entrance. It was cracked open, as was one of the carved wooden doors. Just barely. Steeling myself, I slipped through the gate and entered the medieval basilica.

I quickly glanced around the vestibule to ensure no one was lying in wait. I seemed to be alone. It was dim, but another candle sat on the floor, leading me farther inside.

I cautiously made my way forward, my gaze sweeping over my surroundings. The church was Gothic outside, yet baroque inside, rebuilt after the massive fire that burned the building in the seventeenth century. It smelled of candle wax and old wood, especially in the cathedral's nave. Electric spotlights shone down the walls, enough to see fraying tapestries hanging above dark pews.

I crept down the main aisle under grand arches that soared to the ceiling, reaching above a mezzanine balcony. The white columns were rib bones, and I was striding into the belly of the whale, one with an altar crowned by massive organ pipes. Where a single candle burned on the floor.

My heart pounded as I approached the candle at the altar. A waist-high iron gate circled a baptismal font—one that looked like a giant metal cup. Scratches marred the floor; the font had been moved to one side. Beneath it were wooden grates where baptismal water would drain below the floor. And near these grates was an open trapdoor.

I peered over the baptismal gate and into the trapdoor.

A steep set of stairs led into darkness.

Under the Black Church.

This was definitely under . . . and definitely terrifying. Not a sound down there. Shadows were still. Was I alone, or was this a snare? If it was, I'd have to take that chance. It was too late to go back.

Muscles tense, I crept through the baptismal gate and descended dark steps.

Candlelight from the church spilled through the slated wooden grates above my head. I steadied myself on a handrail of rope that had been strung to a wooden wall and carefully padded down the steps. Down below the altar into a small, dark space. It was cold and dank, and it smelled of mildew. Nothing but wooden supports, cobwebs, and plumbing pipes.

I spied a small flashlight. I picked it up and switched it on. A broad column of light shone onto the dirt floor.

And down a long subterranean tunnel lined with bricks.

Swallowing my fear, I carefully made my way down the tunnel. Foul-smelling water dripped onto my arm. Something scuttled across the floor. Was this once used for medieval sewage? Maybe for dragging plague victims through the city. I quickened my pace and loped deeper down the dripping tunnel.

And deeper . . .

Was it endless?

A claustrophobic panic tightened my chest. I stumbled through puddles, feeling like Theseus trapped in the Minotaur's Labyrinth—unsure which was worse: the darkness ahead of or behind me. How much time had passed? Minutes? A half hour? Just when I feared I'd go mad, the tunnel canted upward. After a minute or so, my flashlight's beam found a metal gate.

Fresh air!

Rusted metal whined as I pushed through and lurched outside. Chest heaving, I breathed in night air. Where was I? The gate was built into the side of a hill. A heavily wooded mountain rose in front of me. Mist clung to tree branches.

A narrow railway track split the trees with two sets of tracks; upon one sat a compact inclined railcar.

An old funicular railway. The hidden path up the mountain.

But not one that languished in disuse: several sets of footprints tracked through the crunchy snow. It was impossible to tell how fresh they were, but I listened cautiously and heard no movement. Saw none, either, though this gave me little comfort.

Leery, I approached the lone funicular car and peered inside. It looked big enough to accommodate three or four passengers. The rear and front doors were missing, through which a forlorn wind whistled.

I climbed inside. A single lever protruded between two bench seats. I pulled it. A terrible grating noise shook the old car as the motor groaned. Then the car jerked into motion and began climbing the track.

Up the mountain.

Into darkness and mist.

Brașov's lights were a blanket of fallen stars, winking up at me from below. I clung to a cracked leather handle near one of the windows. A companion car descended from the top of the mountain on the adjoining track. The cars were connected: one went up, and the other went down. And when they passed each other, I shone my flashlight into the second ghost car, half expecting another rider to jump out at me.

But no. Empty.

Fog thickened around the car. I couldn't see the city anymore.

Nor the stars. Then the car slowed. It came to an uneasy stop, roughly clanking into place. I leapt out of the funicular onto snowy gravel.

My flashlight's beam bounced around snow-dusted evergreen trees. Forest. Dense, gray fog. A narrow path headed away from the funicular car and wound through the trees. I followed it.

The path was well worn and mostly uphill, whiplashing around trees and underbrush. The fog was thick. It was difficult to see past my own feet, and the woods were dark. Every sound amplified inside my head. Twigs snapping. Wings fluttering. An owl hooting. I felt exposed. Unprotected.

Unsafe.

I hiked up the foggy wooded path until the forest opened to a large moonlit clearing. And in the distance, just up a gently sloping path that curved around the clearing's right side, I spotted the silhouette of a large building.

Barlog.

The castle that didn't exist. Forgotten. Yet here it stood, black against the rocky mountaintop. A spiny giant with flying buttresses and needlelike spires that pierced the mist. No light shone from its stained-glass windows. No life, either. Derelict, it crouched and slumbered against the mountain's peak. Difficult to see where the castle ended and the craggy stone began.

My heart thudded inside my chest. A flurry of snowflakes swirled in a bitter wind. I shivered. Pulled my coat collar tight around my neck. And I approached the sleeping giant.

The castle's entrance yawned across a stone terrace. More footprints trampled the snow here. Were they coming or going? And how many? I couldn't tell.

I stopped in front of heavy wooden doors. Two menacing

dragon-head knockers stared back at me. I tried a rusting door handle. It snicked. I held my breath. Then I pulled the door open wide enough to peer inside with my flashlight.

My flashlight's glaring beam fanned over a ruined entrance hall. Rubble. Weeds. Snow. Broken windows. A grand staircase, broken and blocked by fallen debris.

Dark. Deserted. Forsaken.

A good place for bats to breed.

A good place to disappear . . .

If the entrance hall was the giant's head, a corridor tucked behind the broken staircase was its spine. And it was there that I spied the only sign of life in the dark castle: a lone pinpoint of light. Flickering.

Beckoning.

The trembling in my hands worsened as I crept through the castle door. Hard to focus when my flashlight shook. But I picked my way across snow-covered rubble. Under the ruined staircase and into the slumbering giant's spine. A dozen dark hallways crossed the great hall like arteries. Every step I made echoed around crumbling stone walls. But I pressed on, eyes fixed on the flickering light ahead.

The corridor ended on the other side of several old chairs that had been piled into a heap like broken kindling. There, an open archway was poorly guarded by a rusted gate. Half of it had collapsed into a pile of loose stones. I stepped around the old gate. Ducked through the open archway. That's where I found the source of the light I'd been tracking.

Candlelight in a cavern.

The castle was built in front of a small cave.

Inside the mountain—that's what the Zissu brothers had said.

Several candles were strewn about the floor of the cavern, melting into one another—layers of puddling wax built up from years of use. And in the center was a standing stone, bigger than me and roughly carved into a double-barred patriarchal cross. Old. Hundreds of years maybe.

But this space—the stone cross, the candles—was only an entrance. An antechamber. A dark cavern tunnel sat in flickering shadows on the back wall, leading deeper into the mountain.

I glanced over my shoulder, back into the castle's long corridor. Quiet. Still. Nowhere to go but forward. So I pressed on. Across the small candle-strewn cave. Into the rocky tunnel.

Stalagmites grew up from the floor like stone flowers, and it smelled of loam and fungus. I took three steps. Four. One more. The tunnel turned sharply left. Around the tight corner, pale fingers of light traced the rocky tunnel walls. And as I crept forward, I emerged inside a second cavern.

A massive one.

If the cave behind me was an antechamber, this was the ballroom, dimly lit by a dozen candles. But instead of twirling dancers in its center, there was a black lake.

I'd never seen anything like it: dark, still water . . . and a viscous black substance dripping from the ceiling above. A stone bridge crossed the dark pool, and on the far side—sitting upon an isolated rocky terrace at the back of the cavern—was a towering statue, carved into a massive chunk of stone.

A great winged beast. Dragon's lair.

Ancient temple. The stuff of local fairy tales to scare children.

Only, it was real.

A steady flame flared from the statue's mouth, casting its twisted shape in shadowed relief while illuminating the cavern ceiling above. The serpentlike body of the mythic monster was wrapped around a massive cross.

The Order of the Dragon's symbol.

To the left of the statue, a natural shaft in the cavern wall let in a diagonal column of pale moonlight. It shone over the black lake's oily surface, iridescent and still. A sludgy naphtha-like scent tainted the air.

I took a cautious step. No sign of people. No sounds. Only the drip of the black liquid into the dark lake. I fanned my flashlight to the rightmost wall of the cavern. There, cut into the rock, were three arched gates.

Not gates: prison cells. Three barred medieval dungeons.

My pulse rocketed. I raced to the first cell, footfalls echoing around the cavern walls, and peered into darkness. Empty. The bars were rusting badly, and the door to the cell was falling apart.

I tried the second cell. Rubble. A pile of skulls and a tangle of old bones. I couldn't tell if they were human or animal. I didn't want to know.

Last cell. I raced there and found more rubble. The back half was cloaked in darkness. But the bars on the gate were made from a different metal.

This dungeon door had been repaired.

"Hello?" I called out, shaking the door to test it. Locked.

A scrabbling noise made me jump. I gripped my flashlight harder, ready to fight or flee. There was something spread out on the floor. A coat? Someone was sleeping here.

A shadow moved. Then it stepped into moonlight, big and broad as a bear, only wearing khaki pants and rolled-up shirtsleeves.

Father.

24

RICHARD DAMN FOX.

Somehow he seemed bigger than he was the last time I'd seen him, weeks ago, when he'd abandoned me in the Pera Palace in Istanbul. Looked older, too. His overlong dark hair was streaked with a little more silver above his temples. And his big, bushy beard was grayer than I remembered. Was that possible? It matched the steely eyes that blinked at me now.

All this time. Everything I'd been through . . . Here he was now. It felt like a mirage. Like I'd wake up from this nightmare any second and I'd be back at the Pera Palace Hotel, wrapped up in fine linens and Turkish coffee wafting next to my bed.

"Daddy?" I said, my eyes welling with tears.

"Empress?" he answered in his deep, bottomless voice.

Images flooded my head. Of him teaching me how to write ciphers. How to ride a camel in the Egyptian desert. Him giving me a polished Corinthian helmet when I was eight and his big, happy laugh when it slipped down over my eyes. Him holding me in his lap and quieting my crying when Mother died, night after night after night . . .

My father. Easy to love, difficult to like. That's what Mother always said.

I just hadn't realized how *much* I loved him until that moment.

I couldn't hold on to the tears any longer. A feral sound escaped my mouth, and I broke down and sobbed.

"Hush now," he said, reaching through the bars to curl his big hand around the back of my neck. "Foxes don't cry. And you know I'll be a blubbering damn mess if you don't stop."

I huffed out a little laugh and gripped his wrist, pressing my cheek against it. He smelled familiar, like Turkish tobacco and boot polish. "I thought . . . I worried you were dead."

"Me? Never. I've told you a thousand times, the devil doesn't want me and Saint Peter's busy. You're stuck with me," he said, flashing me white teeth in the dark. But his mood sobered quickly, and he released my neck. "You aren't supposed to be here. You were to be on an ocean liner headed back home."

"And *you* were supposed to be in Bucharest! We waited and waited, and I heard all about your drunken misadventure with the major's wife, FYI—"

"Christ almighty," he muttered.

"And when you didn't show up, we telegrammed Jean-Bernard and found out he'd been poisoned—did you know that?"

He nodded. "I talked to him yesterday. Long-distance telephone call cost me a fortune. He's still in the hospital, but he's awake."

"Thank God," I whispered. "Well, anyway, like I said, we didn't know if he was going to live, and you didn't show, so I figured out your cipher—"

"Goddammit," he muttered.

"You told Huck to give me the journal!"

He groaned, but not unhappily. "How'd you get to be so damn smart? Not from my genes, I'll tell you that. Unless stubbornness counts."

"Yes, well. I imagine that doesn't hurt." As I wiped my cheeks, I saw his other arm tucked to his chest and bound in a dirty sling made from torn cloth. "You're injured."

"Not more than usual. Rothwild's bruisers jumped me at the train station last night."

"You've been locked up in here since last night?"

"We can talk about it later," he said with his usual stupid machismo. Nothing ever hurt, he never got sick, and there was always a way out of trouble.

God, I'd missed him.

"No more of that, now," he warned, eyes glossy. "Need to be quick and get out while we can. How did you get into the cavern?"

"Through the castle," I said.

He gave me a concerned look, squinting over high, ever-pink cheeks that topped his bushy beard. "You just walked in here? Where's Huck?"

"With Lovena at the Zissu brothers' shop."

"The witch?" He squinted at me, confused. "You found the Zissu brothers? Why is Huck there?"

"He got kidnapped and poisoned?"

"What?"

"Some kind of witchy herb—probably the same one Sarkany used on her sister and maybe Jean-Bernard. But Lovena says she can help him. She's already helped us. You can trust her."

He blinked at me with gray eyes and murmured, "Told that boy to protect you or I'd kill him."

"Well, he's getting a head start," I said dryly.

"What in God's name have the two of you been doing?"

I narrowed my eyes at him. "A lot of talking, I can tell you that much."

A guilty look crossed his face. But only for a moment. Richard Fox never admitted to anything. "Anything else I need to know?"

"I figured out the ring. You had it all wrong. All three rings are real. They're bands that fit together like a puzzle to make one ring. And I've got one of the bands. Look." I retrieved the iron ring box from my coat pocket. It wouldn't fit through the bars, but I could tell by my father's shocked expression that he knew exactly what it was.

"Where the devil did you get that? Was it those twins? How did you find them?" He shook his head. "You know what? Never mind. Put that damned ring away and just get me the hell out of here before that monster comes back."

I shoved the iron box back into my coat pocket. "Where is he now?"

"Don't know. Need to quit yapping and hurry. Find something to pry open the lock."

Right. The lock. I wished Huck were here to pick it. "Can't you break it open with one of those rocks over there?"

"Tried that. They just break up into pieces. Is that flashlight solid?"

It was metal and weighed a ton. "Pretty solid," I told him.

"Could work. Let me see it—I think it'll fit. So close . . ."

I stilled. "Do you hear something?"

"Just rats," he said after listening. "One tried to bite my hand earlier. Probably carrying the damn plague."

No, it wasn't rats. It was more like . . . music.

He wasn't interested. "We'll worry about it later. Here, empress. Try it through these two bars on the door over here. They're farther apart, I think."

I did my best to ignore the niggling sound while trying the bars he suggested. They were far enough apart. But it didn't matter. The moment I slipped the flashlight into his waiting fingers, the barred cell door creaked and swung inward.

"What the . . . ?"

"It's open!" I said, joy rushing through me. I pushed it further while he moved out of the way.

"That's impossible," he said, squinting at the door. "I've been beating on it for hours."

"Don't kick a gift horse."

He started to argue with me. But before he could get a word out, he dropped the flashlight and jerked me toward him, into the cell. As he backed up, he shouted over my head, "You stay away from my daughter, you sick bastard!"

I twisted out of his grip and swung around, heart racing. A bearded man in a black suit stepped into the candlelight. And as he did, the music grew louder.

THUMP-THUMP.

THUMP-THUMP.

The bone ring!

In two quick movements, he strode to the cell and grabbed the door to swing it shut. And as he turned a key, locking me in with Father, my eyes went straight to the man's hand: Two ivory bands were linked together on his forefinger. The only band that was missing was the one that fit in the middle.

The one inside my coat pocket.

THUMP-THUMP, THUMP-THUMP.

My vision swam. I gripped my father's arm to stay upright.

"Miss Fox," the man said with no emotion through the bars of the locked cell. "I see you received my message."

"Hello, Mr. Sarkany," I gritted out over the thumping noise.

"Sarkany?" my father growled. "This is George Rothwild."

THE BEARDED HUNGARIAN SMILED AT ME. NOT A CRUEL smile. Not a victorious one, either. It was a bit sad, as if I were some dumb, poor beast that had just discovered it had been fatally shot and would soon end up on the hunter's dinner plate.

Behind him, two dark figures emerged from the misty cavern mouth and stood like soldiers, awaiting a command: the robed men who'd been following us.

Hands shaking, I dazedly stared at the man through the bars. Sarkany . . . Rothwild. One and the same. It was Rothwild who'd given me the bewitched banknote in the hotel lobby. Rothwild who'd followed us onto the Orient Express. Who'd stolen Lovena's wolf dog. Who'd killed the widow and made the baroness jump. All Rothwild.

And Rothwild who wore two of the bone rings on his finger.

He'd known the entire time that he needed all three rings.

He just hadn't known where to find them. Not until Huck and I led him to Sighișoara. And here, to Brașov.

I could hear his heartbeat. The men in robes. My father's—I could hear them all. Yet it was different. Not the scattered thumping from the ring in the museum. Not the stronger thumps from the twins' ring. This was louder, slower—as if all their heartbeats were nearly in unison. A heartbeat with a murmur. A sickening, rhythmic *swish* between the thumps.

Blood music.

"Now, then," Rothwild said as if all of this were perfectly normal. "I believe you have something that belongs to me. Kindly hand it over if you don't want to perish in that dungeon cell with your father."

"Do *not* give it to him!" Father bellowed.

Rothwild pressed his face to the bars. My father's big arm shot around my waist and picked me off the ground. He carried me several steps back. Away from Rothwild and the barred door.

"Touch her, and I'll kill you," Father said, setting me down.

Rothwild's deep-set eyes gleamed. "With what? Your arm is quite broken. A wounded bear cannot protect its cub. Miss Fox, make this easy on yourself and hand me the ring."

"Don't you dare!" Father warned me.

Like I would? I wasn't a fool. It was the only thing we had for bargaining.

Rothwild squinted at me. "You were clever, burning the banknote in Bucharest. Did you have help? Is it the crow witch's work? A protective spell? Maybe a charm? I know you saw her."

"And *I* know you stole her dog."

He spread his arms out, shrugging. "I only wanted the bone ring band. I asked nicely. I was even willing to pay. If she'd given it to me, I would have let her be." He let his arms drop to his sides. "Alas, she didn't deserve Lupu. What kind of parent can't protect their own children?" His eyes flicked to my father's face. "Not a very good one."

Father spat a string of filthy curses.

Rothwild ignored him and continued speaking to me. "She'll get what's coming to her. Right now I'm more interested in what the Zissu brothers gave you."

"Oh?" I said, trying to match his casual tone. "And what's that?"

He glowered at me. "You want to play games? We will play. Lovena's warding magic is weak. It won't hold, not here. For the time being, however, why don't the two of you take some time to think over your predicament. I think you'll come to the only conclusion."

"Which is?" I said, fighting dizziness and the horrible sound of the bone ring's bands.

"I'm the only person with a key to that cell," he said, smiling darkly. "And while you're wasting my time, who will protect the Irish boy? Not your crow witch, and certainly not the Zissu brothers. I can tell you that."

No!

I shouted at Rothwild, but he was already striding away. The thumping noise grew weaker with every step he took. And after he'd exited through the cavern tunnel, leaving his two robed goons flanking either side of it, the bone ring's sound disappeared completely.

"Empress?" my father said, sounding concerned. "You all right?"

I pushed his hand away, angry and frustrated. Panicked. I didn't have the strength or patience to explain the sound of the ring bands to him. And what did that matter when we were both stuck behind bars?

"Did you hear what that man said?" I picked up the flashlight from where he'd dropped it. The lens was cracked. The beam flickered off and on before steadying. "He's already hurt Huck once."

"He's a tough lad. If Jean-Bernard can survive that poison, so can Huxley."

"I'm more worried that Rothwild is heading down the mountain right now to kill him," I said, looking for a way out with the flashlight. Ceiling? No holes or shafts. We were basically in a smaller cave with bars blocking its mouth. "I don't know if he can get to him in the twins' shop. Lovena is there, but . . . I don't know."

He wasn't listening. He was staring through the bars at Rothwild's robed goons guarding the exit tunnel. They wielded falx swords that curved wickedly like sickles. "Those two bastards . . . make getting out of here harder."

"Let's think about getting past these bars first," I said. We had the flashlight, but that would make noise. It would only draw the guards.

"It's impossible. I've been trying to escape since the bastard shoved me in here yesterday." He growled and made a fist. Tapped it against the bars. "Christ, Theodora. Why did you come here?"

"To rescue you!"

"I wanted you to stay out of this," he said, miserable. "I was trying to protect you."

"I wasn't the one who needed protecting." I gestured toward the sling around his injured arm.

"We need to come up with a plan. For when he comes back. Maybe destroy the bone band . . . Let me see it again."

I put a hand in my pocket and shook my head. "It can't be destroyed."

"What do you mean 'can't'?"

"Don't act so surprised that I've learned more about it than you have."

"Don't get smart with me, young lady."

"Too late," I said, matching his hard stare. "It can't be destroyed. The Zissu brothers told me. If you'd found them last summer, you'd know that, but apparently you gave up and went on summer holiday with Jean-Bernard to Greece. By the way, here," I said, retrieving the red journal from inside my coat. "You can have this back. I didn't lose it."

He begrudgingly accepted the journal and started to argue. But I guess he thought better of it and just clenched his jaw.

"What about that rubble pile?" I said, pointing the flashlight at the back of the cell. "Have you searched it for something to pick the lock?"

"Can you pick a lock?"

He knew I couldn't. I smacked the flashlight against my palm to shake the bulb into place then used it to search the rubble pile in the back of the cell while Father continued to sulk near the bars.

"You lied to me," I finally said.

His body tensed. I could see it in his shoulders, though he wouldn't turn around and look at me. "Parents don't tell lies. They only do whatever it takes to protect their children."

I'd heard that before. "Well, you did a lot of protecting, then. I went to the university in Cluj. Talked to Dr. Mitu's assistant."

"Theodora, I—"

"You *lied* to me," I insisted. "You kept it from me. How long have you known? Since summer? It was the page torn out in your journal, wasn't it? You said you didn't go see him, but you must have changed your mind the next day—or telephoned? Something."

"Researching family trees is just a hobby for Mitu. He could be wrong."

"Doesn't sound like he thinks he's wrong." When Father didn't reply, I pressed him. "Vlad the Impaler. I can't even wrap my head around it. Did Mother ever suspect? Is that why she'd asked Dr. Mitu to help her research her ancestry before she died?"

He didn't say anything for a long moment. Then he sniffled and spoke to the cell bars in a quiet voice. "Her father used to tell stories about their family. She didn't know what to believe. I don't either. I don't want to talk about this now."

Or ever. That was clear from his disgruntled tone. Quietly fuming, I moved a large rock at the back of the cell and some kind of white bug scurried away. Maybe I'd better leave this be. Did snakes live in caves? I wasn't sure I wanted to find out.

I stood up and dusted my hand on my khaki trousers. "I know about Huck, too. You lied to me about that," I said quietly.

"I did it for your own good."

"No. You did it for *you*. I love him, Daddy. And I think he loves me."

"Don't start with this," he begged, squeezing his eyes closed.

"You're not going to apologize? You knew how we felt about each other for weeks before that night. Months! This wasn't something that just popped up out of nowhere. You knew, and you lied to me. You took away the one thing that brought me happiness, and shattered my entire world. And you didn't even have the decency to tell me the truth."

"It's not that easy!" he shouted.

"It is! Just admit that you lied and tell me you're sorry. You were wrong."

"I did what I thought was best."

"Bullshit!"

He pointed a finger at me. "You're still my daughter, and I'm still your father, in case you've forgotten. Watch your mouth."

"Or what? You'll take something else away to punish me? There's nothing left to take. You've hurt both of us, me and Huck. You've hurt us, too," I said, gesturing between us.

He stared through the bars, his big body in shadows, firelight outlining his troubled profile. His throat bobbed. "I know that," he said.

That was probably the closest he'd come to saying "I'm sorry." I should have been satisfied, but I wasn't. I was just . . . disappointed.

"I want you to know something," I said. "If we get out of this alive, I'm not going back home to New York unless Huck comes with us."

His brow lowered. Jaw shifted.

"Theo, I beg you. Can we please talk about this some other time? When we're not behind bars in a madman's lair?" He shook his head as if to clear it. Exhaled heavily. Then, in a softer voice, he asked, "You sure you trust the herbalist woman? The boy's going to be okay?"

"If he's not, I'll blame you."

He snorted a cynical laugh. "Get in line."

"Stop acting like you don't care. I know you do!"

"None of this is turning out how I planned. You aren't supposed to be here. You were supposed to be safe in Istanbul. Huck and I were supposed to find the ring in Tokat, and it was supposed to be the right ring, and then I could have beat Rothwild at his own wicked game and taken it back home. The ring is your mother's ancestry, and it belongs to her. I just . . . wanted to find it for her," he said, leaning against the wall. He slid down it and sat on the rocky floor. Defeated.

All the times I'd resented my father and wanted to prove him wrong.

This was as close as I'd come.

Strangely enough, it was less satisfying than I'd imagined.

"If Mother were alive, she'd be more concerned about keeping all of us together as a family than a ring."

He sighed as if the entire mountain had settled onto his shoulders.

"I could have helped, you know," I said. "This summer. If I had, things may have turned out differently."

"Maybe."

"But you never let me help you. You just stick me in hotel rooms, and that's not fair to either one of us. I don't need your protection. I need your confidence. I need *you*."

"Empress . . ."

"Never mind," I mumbled. "Just forget it."

I hadn't even meant to get into this with him. I needed to concentrate on figuring out an escape plan. So I methodically checked the bars, looking for a chink. A flaw. Something loose. There had to be a way out. If I could just focus harder. If I could stop thinking about Huck's ashen face. Now that Father was questioning my trust in Lovena and the twins, it made me doubt myself. I'd abandoned Huck with strangers—and for what? To get locked up with my father? Who wasn't speaking to me now?

There was no use trying. The prison cell wasn't a puzzle that could be solved. All of this was a mistake. I was no better than Father. I'd failed.

Despondent, I gave up and sat down against the wall across from him. We sat together in silence. Both defeated.

Twenty-five across, "all-time low." R-O-C-K-B-O-T-T-O-M.

Minutes passed. An hour. It was hard to tell.

The flashlight finally burned out, leaving us in the dark. That made things so much worse, which I didn't think was possible. Light from the candles and the flame in the dragon statue's mouth did not extend into our cell. I thought of the white bug, scurrying under the rock pile, and phantom itching made my skin crawl.

I tried to get my mind off our situation. To formulate some kind of plan. What to do when Rothwild returned. How long could he keep us here? Would he take the ring band from me by force? And what then? Would he slaughter us? Impale us? Wouldn't that be rich?

I stared through the bars, watching the robed guards. They didn't talk. Not much. Anything they said was too low and too far away for me to hear. But when they both jerked around and raised their sickle-shaped swords at the opposite side of the cavern, I sat up straighter.

"Is he back?" Father whispered next to me in the dark.

He wasn't. But something was here. Moving. Invisible in the shadows. Stalking. I couldn't see it, but I could sense it. The guards left their post and tried to seek it out. Only for moment. Then they gave up, muttering to themselves. But I was worried now, because they looked spooked. Were there ghosts in here? All the misbehaving children who'd been whisked here in the local fairy tales?

But I didn't have time to worry much longer.

The sickening thumping noise returned.

"He's coming!" I whispered to Father.

"I don't hear anything," he whispered back.

"Trust me."

We scrambled to stand as a dark figure emerged from the cavern tunnel. My pulse ratcheted back into overdrive.

Striding toward the prison cell, Rothwild stopped in front of the bars and clapped his hands together. "Now, Miss Fox. What will it be? Ready to make a trade? The ring band for your freedom."

He held up something in one hand. I fought back a wave of dizziness and squinted in the dark to see it.

A key.

He wanted to bargain? Fine. We'd bargain.

I squeezed Father's hand. *Trust me*, I thought. *For once in your life, please trust me!*

Stepping toward the bars, I took the ring box out of my coat pocket. And I held it up like Rothwild held the key. Just out of reach. "This is what you want?"

"I knew you'd see reason."

"Won't fit through the bars," I told him. "Open the door, and we'll trade."

He shook his head. "Open the box and hand me the band through the bars."

"Theo!" Father warned behind me.

I flicked open the catch on the box and cracked open the lid.

THUMP. THUMP. THUMP.

It was awful. Terrible. Unbearable. My knees went weak. I was going to be sick if I touched the band sitting inside the box. I was going to be sick if I didn't.

Funny thing was, Rothwild wasn't. He looked unaffected. Greedy for the band, yes. He reached his hand through the bars, beckoning for my band.

But not affected.

He didn't hear what I heard.

He wasn't the Dragon.

I was.

A terrible warmth raced up my hand when I touched the band in the box. I picked it up and dropped the box. Slipped the bone band onto my pinkie.

For a brief moment, it dangled loosely around my finger. Too big. Grotesquely curved. Then it seemed to . . . shrink into place.

And everything changed.

Dark, delicious chills ran through me in waves.

I felt relief. I felt stronger. I felt . . .

Rapture.

"No!" Rothwild shouted. A madman. Enraged. Like a whip, he lunged at me through the bars. Reached for my throat. Wanted to choke me. I seized his arm, and for one fevered moment, we were wild animals. Grappling. Shouting. Arms everywhere. He was too strong. His other arm flew through the bars and clutched my throat.

Pain seared through me. Breath left me. He was going to break my neck.

THUMP-THUMP-swish. THUMP-THUMP-swish.

Flailing, my fingers flew to his rings. Slipped. Found purchase.

And twisted.

Behind me, a big fist extended and slammed down on Rothwild's arm. The madman howled and released my neck. I gasped for air as Father's arm wrapped around my chest and pulled.

I was yanked backward.

Still gripping Rothwild's finger. The knuckle gave. Skin tore. The finger held, but it didn't matter.

I fell back against my father with Rothwild's bloodied bands in my grip.

"*No-o-o-o!*" he bellowed, retracting his arms. He flung his ringless hand, shaking out the pain. Maybe I'd dislocated his finger.

I didn't care. While he struggled with a trembling hand to force his key into the lock—while his robed goons raced toward us—I tugged the too-snug band off my finger with no small effort and quickly slotted it into Rothwild's bands.

It was easy. Just like Huck's gum-wrapper demonstration. My band fit in the middle of the others. They clicked together like magnets and formed a circular dragon design on the top.

Vlad Dracula's war ring. Made from human bone and blood. Cursed. Powerful.

Mine.

I slipped the puzzle ring onto my pinkie, felt it tighten against my skin.

Part of me. Bone against bone.

My knees weakened. I swayed on my feet as my vison went red. Rothwild, the cavern . . . all of it filtered through a dark, crimson haze.

THUMP.

THUMP.

THUMP.

Steady. Strong. In unison. It was a pulse, not a heartbeat. The pulse of something big and old and mighty.

The Dragon.

It was awake.

It was inside me.

It was me.

I was the Dragon.

THE RING'S SEDUCTIVE POWER SNAKED INSIDE ME. Rushed through me like wine. Warming me on the inside and scattering my thoughts. Chaos surrounded me, but I was unconcerned.

I looked down at myself, certain I'd find scales and talons. Still me. The thing inside me was stretching. Unhappy to share my body. It was as if I'd captured a wild horse inside me, and it was bucking and scared. Unwilling to be tamed.

Vision red, I glanced up at my father's frightened face. I could hear his despair. His fear. His broken heart. But I didn't care. He was only a curiosity, and my interest was drawn to everything else around us. Because I could hear it all. The sound of rats and insects skittering in cracks. The wind howling through the shaft in the rock above the dark cavern pool. The drip of black liquid from stalactites.

Everything.

Including Rothwild. He raged against the bars, shaking them.

Face twisted into a hideous grimace. "I will kill both of you! Acolytes!" he shouted in Romanian to the men rushing up behind him, sickle swords drawn. "Cut them down!"

Their falx weapons couldn't reach us through the bars. Rothwild would be forced to open the gate. But it didn't matter one way or another to me.

I closed my eyes and listened. The dragon sharing my body whispered inside my head. It told me secrets I couldn't comprehend. Old secrets. Lost secrets. It talked to my very soul, a dark conversation, deep down in the pit of my being.

The dragon was bargaining with me. It wanted control, and I wanted to give it.

Just for a moment.

I opened my eyes and saw red. A strange, hot wind gathered in the prison cell. Swirling. Strengthening. Growing larger. It rustled my clothes and bent all the candle flames in the cavern.

Wind. Blinding light. What was this? Where did it come from? It was marvelous. It coursed through me, this eddying vortex.

And then it exploded.

The cell door burst open. Blew right off its hinges and knocked one of the acolytes flat to the ground. His sword clattered from his grip and he lay still, sprawled unnaturally. Flattened under the weight of the barred door.

But it was difficult to pity the man. Not when the entire cavern had been transformed.

Flames circled the bridge.

The lake was on fire.

Rothwild jumped back and shouted. Shock and shadows danced over his face. The growing fire was reflected in his eyes as his head turned in every direction. Amazed.

Flames shot across the hem on one of the acolytes' robes. With a terrible yawp, he raced away from his recumbent partner and disappeared into the tunnel.

Behind me, my father made a noise that was part shock, part pain. I glanced over my shoulder to see him limp a step. Had I hurt him? Possibly. Somewhere inside my head, I thought this should matter more.

None of it mattered. Not my father, nor the robed man on the ground. Not the one who'd escaped in the tunnel.

What mattered was that my path was no longer blocked.

What mattered was Rothwild.

My enemy.

My father's voice bellowed, but I shoved his reaching hand away and stepped out of the open cell. Freedom. I bent to sweep up the dead acolyte's fallen sword. It was heavy in my hand. A real weapon.

I looked up from the blade. Excitement and an odd sort of terror rippled over me as I trained my gaze on the bearded man in front of me and saw the fear in his eyes.

He moved to make a run for the tunnel, but I blocked his path. He was big, and I was small and nimble. I watched him calculate the odds and make the decision to head backward. Across the rocky bridge in the middle of the flaming lake.

"Theodora!" my father shouted behind me.

"Stay back!" I said. It sounded like my voice anyway. Distantly.

I didn't want to hurt him. Not really.

But I *did* want to hurt Rothwild. A dozen reasons why filled my muddled head as he stopped in front of the stone dragon statue that sat in the back of the cavern on the opposite side of the fiery lake. Then he turned around and faced me, holding his hands up.

"Theodora," he shouted as I stepped onto the rocky bridge and walked toward him. Flames jumped and flickered on either side of me, burning brightly on the lake's surface. "We are not enemies."

"Oh, but we *are*," I shouted back.

"I'm not surprised you succeeded in finding the other bands of the ring when your father failed. It is why I followed you instead of him. He is a monkey who's outlived his use, but you are . . . family."

I laughed. "Family?"

"We are connected. You are blood of my blood."

My father shouted something indecipherably foul at Rothwild from the other side of the bridge. He sounded so far away now. The dragon's heartbeat inside my head was far louder than his voice.

"I'm not your blood," I told Rothwild as I crossed the bridge, closer and closer. "You aren't Vlad's descendant. There's no link."

"One will be found," he said confidently as he closed in on me. "My mother told me it was there. Everyone in my family knows it."

"That's why you originally hired my father, wasn't it? Through Dr. Mitu?"

Rothwild set his back against the base of the dragon statue. "He is a useful idiot. You are not, and I'll admit, I respect that. It only proves to me that we share a bloodline. I am descended from Matthias Corvinus. You are descended from John Hunyadi. We both have old Transylvanian blood, back when these lands belonged to their rightful owners, the Hungarians."

"Believe what you'd like," I told him.

"It will be proven, I assure you. We are family, Theodora. We can share the ring. Share the power. I know so much more about the ring than you do—things no one else knows. I can teach you."

I laughed. "Can you?"

"Theodora!" my father called from a distance behind me, limping. "Don't do this!"

"Teach me what?" I asked Rothwild, ignoring my father's pleas.

"I can teach you that spell I used on the banknote. I can teach you how to control animals."

"Like you lost control over Lupu?"

"I can teach you to control people! They will obey your command."

Something inside me darkened. The memory of Huck's body on the floor of the Zissu brothers' shop floated through my head. It felt like weakness. I pushed it away.

"You killed the widow and her maid," I told Rothwild, stepping off the bridge. And onto the narrow terrace of cavern floor that held the dragon statue. "You tried to kill the baroness. You've threatened to kill Lovena and Huck. Give me one good reason to let you live."

"Come closer," he said, crooking a bleeding finger, one hand behind his back. "And I'll show you."

"Theodora!" my father bellowed.

When I turned my head to look at him, Rothwild swiveled around. He grabbed a fat lever at the base of the dragon statue and used all his weight to pull it downward. Gas hissed. The flame in the dragon's mouth flared and shot out toward me.

On instinct, I dropped to the cavern floor as flames spewed where my body once stood. Heat engulfed me. Pushing forward, I scrabbled beneath the gas flame on hands and knees. My vision blurred and swirled.

Red flame. Red rock.

Red Rothwild, racing toward me.

His face was gnarled and monstrous. Deep-set eyes wide with

determination. He lunged for the sickle sword. But he was still big, and I was still small and nimble. I rolled away as his body flew toward me. The statue's flame torched his back. He howled in pain and stumbled, tripping over uneven ground around the fiery lake.

His scream filled the cavern as he sailed forward.

Into the flames. Into the black, oily water.

Gone.

I lay on my back, chest heaving with labored breath. And I screamed in anger. I'd lost him. Denied my revenge. I twisted around and pushed to my feet, hand wrapped around the sickle sword. For a feral moment, I considered jumping into the lake after him so that I could cut him down.

Then I spied another target. It limped across the bridge toward me. Weak. Injured. And the cause of so much anger.

He would do.

Vision red, I ducked under the statue's hissing flame and crawled back onto the bridge. When I emerged, I held the sword in both hands and fixed my gaze on the bear of a man facing me. He'd wronged me in countless ways. Lied to me. Embarrassed me. Sheltered me. Was ashamed of me.

Took Huck away from me.

He wasn't my father anymore. He was prey.

But as I took a step forward, my vision blurred again. The cavern swirled and ebbed with thick smoke that billowed from the flaming lake. I closed my eyes to make the dizziness go away. And when I opened them again, there was something standing between me and my prey.

Hazy figures stepped from the smoke covering the bridge. All raven-haired and dark eyes. Pale, regal faces. Faces that spanned centuries in dress and style. Generations. They all looked eerily familiar.

House of Drăculești.

Radus and Mirceas. Ioanas and Cristinas. Michael the Brave.

Vlad Dracul, the first Dragon. And Vlad Dracula, with his big mustache and dark circles below his eyes. The Impaler himself. Monster. Hero.

Family.

But from behind him, a tall woman shifted into view. Black hair, kind eyes, regal shoulders. She drifted to the front of the hazy figures, a dark angel without wings, fierce as a Valkyrie on the battlefield. Impossibly beautiful and ethereal.

"Mother!" I cried.

"Darling girl," she said in rich Romanian.

I wanted to run into her arms, but I couldn't move. My body was rooted to the cavern floor.

"My little empress," she said. "You're stronger than any dragon. And you know what you need to do. Your spine is steel, your chin is high, and your heart is open. Make me proud."

"Mother," I pleaded, but she only shook her head and turned away from me. One by one, the hazy figures behind her faded. She wavered in the smoke, smiling over her shoulder at me, and then disappeared.

"No!" I sobbed. My feet became unstuck, and I stumbled forward toward where she'd been, but there was nothing but smoke and fire. Nothing but my bear of a father limping toward me in the middle of the bridge.

You know what you need to do.

I did.

The Zissu brothers had told me. The ring showed no mercy.

Once all three bands were fit together and worn, it became part of the wearer. I tested it now: it couldn't be pulled off. It couldn't be destroyed. The dragon would not let go so easily.

It wanted blood. So I gave it.

Kneeling on the bridge, I set my hand on the rocky floor. I raised the sickle sword with a trembling hand, exhaled, and lopped off my pinkie.

And the bone ring.

I felt no pain. Not right away. There was only the blood spilling from my maimed hand. The surreal sight of my finger lying on the rocky floor. And the terrible loss of what had been inside me.

The dragon was gone.

My red vision faded away. I stood on shaky legs and kicked my finger into the flaming lake

I dropped the sword as the pain came—terrible and fierce and unrelenting. Like an injured animal, I drew my hand to my breast and pressed it against my coat to stanch the bleeding. I was suddenly, shockingly aware of my surroundings and no longer brave but terrified. No longer in a daze, either, because now I saw my bedraggled father across the bridge. A horror-stricken look had contorted his face.

"Theodora!"

I started to race toward him, but an explosion rocked the cavern. I swung around to see the head of the dragon statue falling to floor and the entire cavern suddenly illuminated in a blinding flash.

Flames from the lake spread to the dripping cavern ceiling and flickered down cracks in the wall.

The entire cavern was on fire.

"Father!" I cried, backing up. Nowhere to go. Flames everywhere. The bridge was covered in smoke. I couldn't see him anymore. I couldn't even see the bridge.

"Theodora!" His shout echoed around the cavern. So far away. Where?

"I'm stuck!" I called back in despair. "There's no way out."

Out of the plumes of black smoke, a white shape emerged. Two pointy ears, shaggy fur, one eye. More wolf than dog.

Lupu!

She looked at me, turned, and disappeared back into the smoke. Showing me the way out.

Walls of flame rose on either side of the bridge. Fire rained from the dripping ceiling. But the stone surface of the bridge itself was clear. Making myself small, injured hand clutched to my chest, I ducked and raced across the stone, jumping over lines of fire that seeped into cracks.

I coughed and stumbled. Between the smoke stinging my eyes and the blinding flames, I realized with terror that I'd lost my bearings again. I couldn't see. Not Lupu. Not the edge of the bridge or the other side of the lake. I was surrounded by smoke and fire.

In a disoriented, panicked moment, I stopped running, teetering on the stone, bleeding everywhere—unsure if I was about to run over the edge into the water.

Suddenly, a long arm shot out from the black smoke. Father grabbed the front of my coat and jerked me forward, into the toxic smoke . . . and then through it. He pulled me along until I stumbled off the bridge.

My lungs seized and spasmed in turns as I struggled to draw in a clean breath. And then I was floating. Lifted. Carried like a child in one tree-trunk-sized arm.

"I'm sorry," he said. "I'm so sorry."

He repeated it over and over, limping through the cavern's tunnel, carrying me away from the fire and smoke. Away from death.

Away from the terrible power of Vlad Dracula's ring. Away from it all, toward safety.

Richard Damn Fox.

Decorated American war veteran.

Brash explorer and adventurer. Wealthy antiquities collector.

Never met a risk he wouldn't take or a challenge he couldn't resist.

Forgiven.

GARA DE NORD WAS A PROPER RAILWAY STATION. Not only was Bucharest's terminus an interesting piece of nineteenth-century Romanian architecture on the outside—with massive columns and a winged golden eagle stretching over its facade—but inside, its main concourse stretched beneath skylights and an arched roof that kept out undesirable weather. Which was good, because it was snowing ferociously, and we had tickets for the Orient Express.

Night train to Paris. Departing at nine o'clock.

Me, Father, and Huck.

Our severed little family back together. At least for the moment.

After Father and I came down the mountain, things were . . . chaotic. There was my hand. Father's arm. And Huck, who'd been revived after Rothwild's poison but not fully recovered. How we got to the hospital was a blur; Lovena helped, and she and Father yelled at each other a lot. Did you know a finger could be reattached if you saved it? I wish I had. Now my left hand had three fingers, a thumb, and twenty-three stitches. I also had Father's blood inside me, because I'd lost a bit too much. If you're going to hack a cursed ring off your own hand, I'd advise doing it closer to a medical facility.

But hey, maybe that was just the morphine talking. I'd get another syrette injection once we boarded our train, then another tomorrow—pain-free until Paris, at which point Father said I'd get to tough things out. Lucky me.

Though Lovena sat with us in the hospital after that horrible night, the elusive Zissu brothers had vanished. Gone. Sayonara. Adios. When we returned to the shop to collect our things, we found our luggage but nothing else. Shelves were cleared. Antiques gone. No sign of them or their curiosities. Just a business card on the counter with no address and a scrawled note on the back that said: "*Noroc bun.*" Good luck.

"Their shop moves from place to place. I'll find them again one day," Lovena said with a shrug, as if it was perfectly normal for the brothers to disappear overnight.

To be fair, this was probably the least mysterious thing that had happened on our trip, so I didn't question it.

Lovena offered to drive us to Bucharest, but her car was small. Besides, she was still looking for Lupu. The wolf dog hadn't returned to her, which made me wonder if I'd seen a mirage in the cavern. Or maybe the creature was descended from the old Dacian wolves who looked after the people here.

A lot of unexplainable things happened that night. It was probably for the best that the cavern didn't show up on any maps. Maybe one day the Black Church would close off their underground tunnel and Castle Barlog would fall to ruins completely and never be seen again. Just a local fairy tale.

Wouldn't be the worst thing.

We said our farewells to Lovena and promised to keep in touch. She slipped something into my pocket when she hugged me.

"What is this?" I asked, peeking inside to find a tiny black feather pressed between a folded sheet of waxed paper.

She shook her head discreetly, eyes flicking to my father. "Just a little something from my crows to help guide you. Safe travels, little empress. Don't forget your homeland. Wherever you go, you can always return."

Now that Rothwild was gone, this prospect was more appealing. When I told her this, she just shrugged and said, "Anything can happen here. That's what makes it interesting."

With that, I couldn't argue.

After leaving Lovena, we spent one day traveling from Brașov, and most of the next having our clothes laundered while we waited for money to be wired from the States. I had to break it to Father about my tutor stealing our traveler's checks back in Istanbul. He was . . . less than happy. But less mad than he should've been. Nearly dying in a fiery cavern changes your perspective.

Right now Father had disappeared somewhere inside the Bucharest railway station. He was on an errand to send one last telegram while I dealt with the baggage porter. As I finished, I spotted Huck strolling toward me on the platform, flat cap pulled down over the scabbed-up occult symbol that had been carved into his forehead the night of his poisoning. We hadn't spent any time alone together since . . . well, since he was kidnapped from the tavern in Brașov. What with everything going on and all of us being injured and sick and traumatized. Surviving. A lot of somber faces between the lot of us over the past couple of days, so it was good to see him smiling now.

Really good.

"Jackpot, banshee," he said as he approached, holding up a small stack of newsprint pages. "A very friendly railway worker let me rip up two weeks' worth of old newspapers that were headed for the trash bin. Here."

Romanian crosswords, each neatly torn and folded into rectangles, just how I liked them. "Thank you," I said, smiling back at him. "These will last me till Paris."

"Or at least until we hit Vienna. That's when we'll get the French newspapers. Speaking of, is that our train, there?" Huck asked, nodding toward a line of blue Pullman cars. When I confirmed it was, he said, "I hope the restaurant car is stocked, because I smell bread somewhere, and it's making me hungry."

"Feeling less queasy?"

"My nose thinks so, but to be perfectly honest, I'm still a touch weak and rickety," he said, one hand pressed to his stomach. "Who knew poison was such a powerful appetite suppressant?"

"Minor annoyance versus the alternative. You could be dead."

"Takes more than a couple of brutes in robes and a psychopathic occultist to bring this lad down."

"Never doubted it," I said.

"That makes one of us, because I was sure I'd be meeting my Maker, banshee. I never want to see another wicked sorcerer as long as I live," he said, scratching the marks on his forehead briefly before tugging the brim of his cap down.

A couple of harried travelers strode by us, talking to a conductor in a blue uniform with a clipboard. When they'd passed, Huck asked me in a softer voice, "I've not had the chance to ask you . . . What was it like to put on the ring? Did you . . . ? I mean, was it like when we saw the bone band in Sighișoara? Or worse? It was worse, wasn't it? Fox said you were not yourself."

I could still hear the sound of the ring's magic. The altered vision. The feel of the dragon inside me and the rush of power. The dark pleasure of it. It was like a bad dream, one that haunted the corners of your mind for days and days. . . .

But mostly I thought of my mother's face. And as I stood next to Huck, stuffing his folded crossword puzzle pages into my coat pocket, I felt Lovena's crow feather, and the hope it gave me pushed away the nightmarish memories.

"It was probably a bit like what you went through when you were poisoned," I told him. "Being manipulated by dark forces is not the best way to spend a trip overseas. Let's never do that again."

"Aye, I'll raise a glass to that. We've learned a lot on this trip, the two of us," he said, squinting one eye at me. "Firstly, don't get kidnapped by occultists trying to take over the world through mayhem and murder."

"It's just good common sense," I agreed.

"Second, not all witches are bad."

"Probably most aren't. Women are always demonized."

"Very true," he agreed. "And then, of course, there's the third thing we learned."

"What's that?"

"When you care about someone, you should tell them while you are alone and have plenty of opportunities to put your hands all over each other. Not after the two of you have rescued her father and *especially* when that father has already kicked you out of the house for putting your hands on his daughter, so now he's watching you like a hawk, and you don't know if you'll ever get the chance to even so much as enjoy a chaste kiss."

"Is that so?"

"Brutal lesson to learn."

"Not too late, you know. For that last part."

"Is it not?" he said, sounding hopeful.

"Unless you're too . . . rickety."

"For that? I'd have to be dead, banshee." He warily glanced behind us, and when he turned back around, I stood on my tiptoes and kissed him.

Just a chaste one. At least, it started that way. Then he curled a warm hand around the back of my neck and pulled me closer. And *that* kiss was achingly, dizzyingly thorough. Much too long for a public train platform. We both realized that at the same time when the train whistle blew.

"Probably should"—he cleared his throat and glanced around—"finish that later."

I nodded quickly. Later sounded good. Yet it was hard to make plans when you didn't know where you'd be in a week. Because we were going to Paris now, to stay with Jean-Bernard and recuperate. After that it was anyone's guess. Back to New York? Drop Huck off in Ireland? Father hadn't decided, and I hadn't reminded him of the threat I'd made when we were locked up in that horrible cavern. No need. He hadn't forgotten. I could tell by the way he avoided my eyes.

Speak of the devil . . .

Behind Huck, I caught sight of my father limping down the platform. His broken arm had been set in a cast in the hospital. It hung against his chest now inside a black sling, and the pain of it along with his sore, hobbled knee made him grumpy. He'd be fun on the train, I could already tell.

And unfortunately for everyone unlucky enough to be assigned to our sleeper car, Father had acquired a Turkish meerschaum pipe when he and Huck were in Tokat—a carved, curving monstrosity that he now cupped in one hand, trailing sweet smoke over the platform when he gestured.

"There you both are. Everyone ready?" he asked in his big, booming voice. "Tickets. Money. Luggage. Anything else?"

"Think that's it," I said.

He glanced down at me and made a face. "Good Lord, Theodora. That black eye is awful-looking in this light. You look like a strung-out panda bear who stuck its hand into a wood chipper."

"Better than looking like a bear who fell out of a tree and broke its arm trying to get to a beehive," I said.

Father snorted to himself, looking down at me with merry eyes, and then leaned his cast toward me. "Under my arm. Take it."

I tugged out a slim book. Not a book. A blank journal. Black leather stamped with Romania's coat of arms. I juggled it on my bandaged hand so that I could poke inside to be sure. "What's this for?"

"Got it in the gift shop. Every traveler needs a journal. If you don't write down what you've seen, you'll never remember it." He gestured loosely with his pipe. "Or you'll need a rescue and no one will come, because they haven't cracked your secret code."

I smiled up at him, a little wary. Heart racing a little too fast. Maybe that was just the painkilling drug. "Travel journal," I said.

"That's right," he said. He glanced at Huck. "Don't look at me like a wounded puppy. I didn't get you one because you hate writing. Like pulling teeth to get you to leave a goddamn note on the refrigerator."

Huck shrugged. "I'm better at talking than writing. Then people can get the full breadth of my charm and dazzling good looks," he said, gesturing around his face. "All this is wasted on paper."

Father rolled his eyes, but not unkindly. It was nice to see them joking together. Maybe too nice. I didn't want to get my hopes up only to have them crushed again.

"Father?" I asked.

"Yes, empress."

"You said this was a travel journal. Where are we going?"

He shrugged and rotated his shoulder under the sling. "Well, I figured we'd stay a few weeks in Paris with Jean-Bernard. Sleep. Eat. Wean you off the morphine."

Huck chuckled.

"For the love of Pete," I mumbled.

"And while we're doing that," Father said, "I can figure out how I'm going to replace a crashed mail plane."

Huck held up a finger. "Did I steal a plane? Yes. But did I crash it? No. I landed it. That was a bloody beautiful piece of piloting I did there with that hunk of junk. And think of this—I probably did those people a favor, I did. The postal worker who normally flies that plane might've died."

"You're a hero," Father said, one dark brow raised. "That's what you're saying."

Huck shrugged his shoulders high. "That's what I'm saying."

"Never mind the fact that you stole the plane to begin with."

"We-e-ell," Huck drawled. "You know what they say. Petty thieves steal small things. I stole a *plane*." He waggled his brows and then added, "For the record, it was her idea."

"Heathens, both of you," Father said affectionately.

I tapped my father's shoulder with the spine of the black journal. "What about afterward?"

His eyes scrunched as he looked down at me. "After what?"

"After Paris," I said. "What happens after Paris?"

He puffed on his pipe and looked at the railway attendants

loading luggage into the baggage car. "Been thinking on that . . . I've heard some rumors about the Summer Isles, off the coast of Scotland. One of them has a strange little village that's been occupied since the Middle Ages, and some interesting pagan legends about a burial site."

"Sounds remarkably like a treasure hunt," I said.

"Sounds remarkably like another grave dig," Huck said. "Like Tokat."

"*Pshaw,*" Father said, hiding a smile. "That was just a small miscalculation."

"And this would be . . . ?"

"Just a research trip."

"Oh," Huck said. "Is that all?"

"Who knows. We'll have to see how we feel after Paris."

We. Huck and I shared a hopeful glance.

Spicy smoke floated past my father's head as he squinted down at Huck over pink cheeks. "It's just that I don't feel like going back to New York yet. I think we should stay in Europe a little while longer."

"All three of us," I insisted, wanting to make sure.

Father nodded once. Quickly. And then, as if we were merely discussing what to eat for breakfast, he added, "Christmas in Paris is nice. Elena always liked it there, and God knows Jean-Bernard has plenty of room. What do you both think? Play it by ear?"

My heart thudded wildly. I stole a look at Huck, and his eyes were glossy.

"Sounds like a workable plan to me," I said. "What do you think, Huck?"

He nodded vigorously, and a warm joy spread through my chest.

No, Father hadn't said Huck could come home to New York,

but he hadn't ruled it out, either. Considering where he'd stood on this matter a few weeks ago, and taking into account how stupidly stubborn he was, I'd say this was outstanding progress.

A shrill train whistle blew. We were the last passengers left.

Father clapped a hand on Huck's shoulder and turned toward the blue cars lining the track. "All right, then, that's settled. Let's board before they get a good look at us and leave this motley crew of reprobates behind."

And what a crew we were.

House of Drăculeşti, Fox, and Gallagher: the maimed, the hobbled, and the rickety. We were motley, all right. A band of survivors.

I mean, sure, our bedraggled trio may have been small and stubborn as mules. At times it was even heartsick and scattered across the globe.

But none of that mattered, because when we crossed the railway platform and boarded the last train to Paris, we were something more important than all of that. Something bigger.

We were together.

Acknowledgments

When I began developing the idea for this book, it was set in China and Siberia, and monsters were involved. It would have been a very different story—perhaps one that few wanted to read. Because of that, I can't tell you how much I appreciate my extraordinarily thoughtful and creative editor, Nicole Ellul, for spotting the seed of something good in that early vision and steering it toward the place it finally landed. Still erecting that monument to you. Maybe even a temple.

This is, of course, a work of fantasy fiction, and I took a few liberties with the ancestral line of Vlad Dracula; those who go looking for a cursed ring owned by the famous *voivode* will be sorely disappointed to discover that it exists only inside these pages. Regardless, I tried to build Theo and Huck's fictional world on the framework of fact, and I hope my interest and respect for the history of this region comes through in the story. Many thanks to Denisa Petrescu and Maria Tekin for answering questions about Romanian and Turkish history. Any mistakes are mine.

This book wouldn't exist without the continued support and guidance of many talented, bookish people. Thank you to my longtime agent provocateur, Laura Bradford, without whom I'd be lost, and to Taryn Fagerness. Also to Billelis, for the absolutely stunning cover art. And thank you to the fabulous folks at Simon & Schuster who've worked hard to make me look good, including Mara Anastas, Liesa Abrams, Jennifer Ung, Rebecca Vitkus, Heather Palisi, and everyone on the extended Simon Pulse team.

Awkwardly long bear hugs to my personal support team: Karen, Ron, Gregg, Heidi, Hank (if you only knew how many times I typed "Hank" in this book instead of "Huck," not to mention "Hunk"), Little Shield-Maiden, Brian, Patsy, Don, Gina the Hacker, Shane, and Seph.

But mostly, and I really do mean this, thank *you* for reading.